Acclaim for David Carkeet's
THE FULL CATASTROPHE

"Carkeet's premise is fresh, his characters utterly winning, and his comic observations full of affection for those caught up in the complex confusions of love."

—*Publishers Weekly*

"Laugh-out-loud scenes and witty dialogue abound. . . . Carkeet's novel is a wonderful amalgam of the lunatic and the serious, like life itself."

—*Rocky Mountain News*

"While THE FULL CATASTROPHE is clever, deft, and appealingly funny, its most notable accomplishment lies in making its simple message—that we should all listen more carefully—meaningful again."

—*The Philadelphia Inquirer*

"Carkeet seems to make a habit of producing remarkable volumes. . . . THE FULL CATASTROPHE is the funniest book I've read in five and a half years."

—*The Los Angeles Times Book Review*

(more . . .)

"The generous dialogue makes your heart sing and weep at the same time: Carkeet captures with precision and humor the daily conversations that can raise anger to a fever pitch between well-intentioned people who love each other. Carkeet is a writer who loves his characters, and this makes me love the novel in which he creates them."

—Deborah Tannen,
Professor of Linguistics,
Georgetown University, and author
of *You Just Don't Understand:*
Men and Women in Conversation

"With *THE FULL CATASTROPHE*, David Carkeet has pulled off a feat of literary magic. A deftly crafted story featuring a cast of deliciously quirky, endearing characters straight out of the American heartland. A trove of insights about the way we live and love and bump our heads trying, sweetened by some of the funniest writing since Mark Twain."

—Jonathan Kellerman

"A sly comedy of marital manners with fully realized characters and believable dialogue . . . a wonderfully engaging social commentary about the sheer mystery of the state of matrimony and love—and the power of speech."

—*The Washington Times*

Also by David Carkeet

Double Negative
The Greatest Slump of All Time
I Been There Before

For Younger Readers
The Silent Treatment

The
FULL
CATASTROPHE

DAVID CARKEET

WSP

WASHINGTON SQUARE PRESS
PUBLISHED BY POCKET BOOKS

New York   London   Toronto   Sydney   Tokyo   Singapore

For Barbara

This book is a work of fiction. Names, characters, places and incidents are either the product of the author's imagination or are used fictitiously. Any resemblance to actual events or locales or persons, living or dead, is entirely coincidental.

A Washington Square Press Publication of
POCKET BOOKS, a division of Simon & Schuster
1230 Avenue of the Americas, New York, NY 10020

Carkeet, David.
    The full catastrophe/by David Carkeet.
        p.   cm.
    Reprint. Originally published: New York : Linden Press, 1990.
    ISBN 0-671-73245-5
    I. Title.
PS3553.A688F85   1991
813′.54—dc20   90-25731
                                                                        CIP

First Washington Square Press trade paperback printing May 1991

10   9   8   7   6   5   4   3   2   1

BOSS: Are you married?
ZORBA: Am I not a man?
        And is not a man stupid?
        I'm a man, so I'm married.
        Wife, children, house—everything.
        The full catastrophe.

—Zorba the Greek

The
FULL
CATASTROPHE

One

The St. Louis Arch loomed into view through Jeremy Cook's bug-spattered windshield. He crossed the Mississippi like many a pioneer before him, squinting against the sun, his stomach lurching with fear of an uncertain future.

Cook was in transition. He *hated* to be in transition. He liked things to stay the same. He wanted tomorrow to be like yesterday. He wanted to know that where he was going was where he had been.

WHERE HE HAD BEEN: the Wabash Institute, a linguistics think tank attached to a daycare center, where for six years he had happily crawled around on the floor and watched young children learn to talk. His specialty had been toddlers in the one-to-three range, whose world he entered as easily as if he had never left it. Sometimes, at the end of a long day, he would go home actually confused about his own age, yielding sidewalk space to the rather threatening third-graders in his neighborhood.

The Wabash Institute, stuck in the outback of southern Indiana, had suited Cook in all ways. His colleagues had thought well of him and he had bathed warmly in their appreciation. Among the staff of seven linguists he had found only one good male friend, but that was all he needed, and he had found other friends among the divorced mothers who used Wabash for daycare and the occasional female graduate students and postdocs who stopped by Wabash for a spell of linguistic fieldwork and a bit of bed and breakfast down the road at Cook's place.

These many led, in time, to one special one: Paula, a summer intern who stuck around for eight months longer than she had planned, thanks to Cook, moving in with him while she finished writing her Ph.D. dissertation. But when she went to M.I.T. to defend it, she never came back. This made Cook feel like some branch office of a graduate fellowship program. His one great fear the whole time she had lived with him was that she would think he was not smart enough for her, despite his two books, his many articles, and his sharp comments on her dissertation chapters as she wrote them. Apparently he had somehow botched it, because the day she left she said to him, "Which would you rather be— clever or warm?" Being a man of careful language, he had objected to the question and thoroughly trounced it.

He had had a year all by himself to savor his victory. He heard from her just once in that time, by postcard, sent from the excitingly named town of Jones, Oklahoma, about six months after she had left him. He hadn't been able to figure out much about her life from the card. All she had written was "Well?"

The Wabash Institute followed the example of his love life and went to smash. Its demise came in the common way: the money ran out. As it became clear that this was happening, most of the linguists planned for the future and found jobs on college faculties or at other outposts of linguistics. But not Cook. He refused to believe Wabash could come to an end and, much to his colleagues' concern, took no action.

"It's because you're all alone, Jeremy," Wabash's mean secretary had told him, treating him to this summation at the final spring picnic before Wabash broke up. "You don't have anyone to help you make decisions. When you're sick there's no one to take care of you. When you have a bad day there's no one to talk it over with. There's no one to help you plan your life. You're all alone. You're all by yourself."

Cook had found this moment somewhat humbling. Uncharacteristically, he had said nothing to her. But, characteristically, he had brooded over it. At the picnic everyone was paired up except for him. Husbands and wives—they drove him nuts. They were so damned connected, with their linked fingers and blurry-edged egos. Watching them in action, he felt more than ever like a *mere friend*. He sensed that at the end of the picnic he could say farewell to everyone there and drop dead the next day, and no one would give him any thought at all.

WHERE HE WAS GOING: to the Pillow Agency in St. Louis for an interview, maybe even a job. One good thing had happened at the picnic—a colleague told him of an opening at this agency for a linguist. Cook had written and obtained an interview, which was scheduled for four-thirty this afternoon.

Cook knew little about the Pillow Agency. He knew it was well funded from the estate of a St. Louis businessman who had made a fortune in rat poison, or something like that. He also knew that its focus was language and society, but from odd perspectives. He remembered hearing a lecture at a Linguistic Society of America convention in San Francisco by a representative of the Pillow Agency—a wizened fellow whose grim subject was language death. The lecturer told one depressing tale after another of last speakers of languages like Cornish and Dalmatian going to the grave and selfishly dragging with them whole branches of family trees. He dwelt somewhat morbidly, Cook recalled, on their deathbed snorts and croaks—the last feeble vibrations of these choking tongues.

If this study was typical of the work that went on there, at this point in his life Cook felt that the Pillow Agency and he were made for each other.

He exited Interstate 70 into the bowels of downtown. The city seemed crazed with noise and motion. Either a parade was imminent or Indiana had completely ruralized him. He located his building and worked his way from there to a nearby parking garage. As he hurried to the garage elevator he found himself all aquiver, shivering from the cold (it was a mild day, but the garage held a chill), flinching from the screeches and honks that echoed off the concrete, and quaking from job-interview nervousness. Out on the street, a demented pigeon flew straight at his face and made him duck before it veered upward. St. Louis knew he was coming and was ambushing him with everything it had.

But he set his jaw, mustered his resolve, and discovered, upon his prompt arrival on the twelfth floor of the Hastings Building, that the Pillow Agency was closed for the day. Not a soul was in sight.

Cook wandered the halls and knocked on doors. He took the letter scheduling his appointment from his suit coat pocket and reread it. He looked at his watch (already set back for Central Time), checked it against the hall clock, examined his wallet calendar—in short, brought every paltry arithmetical fact to bear on the problem, more to dodge than to reach its obvious solution: the Pillow bastards thought so little of him that they had forgotten about the appointment.

Two

Just to be sure, just to make certain, just to be one hundred percent clear on the subject, Cook took the elevator back to the ground floor of the Hastings Building and reread the directory. The Pillow Agency occupied offices 1201 through 1209. Had he checked all of those? Maybe not, he told himself—although he had and knew it. He headed back to the elevator, glancing at the security guard at the front desk and wildly coveting his job.

"Steady, boy," Cook told himself as he boarded the elevator. When it stopped he bolted out with determination.

The change that had occurred in his brief absence took his breath away. Doors that were formerly sealed shut now stood open. Attractive women passed in and out of them, glancing back meaningfully at him. Music—Rachmaninoff, wasn't it?—wafted down the hall to him, seemingly borne by currents of perfume. The atmosphere was vibrant and industrious, with an undercurrent of lush sexuality. The Pillow Agency must have been on a break a few minutes earlier. Some break! He admired that kind of ability to swing into and out of action. Oh, he would fit right in here.

Fool that he was, the notion WRONG FLOOR! as an explanatory principle came to him late in the game, after he was already inside one of the offices—room 1101, to be exact. When the idea struck him he reddened and backed out quickly, after only about eight people had the chance to look up from their desks and wonder who he was and why he was so unemployed.

The elevator that had tricked him was gone. As he waited for another to take him to the twelfth floor, he wondered just how long this particular funhouse barrel-ride would last. He had been on many before—extended stretches of closely observed idiocies punctuated by near-criminal faux pas. It was the loner's nightmare.

"Easy, boy. Easy," he said aloud to himself—and, it turned out, to the woman behind his right shoulder, who had cruelly materialized from thin air. He grew suddenly angry, not with himself but with the linguistic law that licensed speakers to address themselves, but then revoked the privilege when others were present, even though these others committed self-speech, too. He tried to think of a way to mitigate his error, but what could he do? Tell the woman he was practicing talking to his dog?

An elevator arrived. Cook got in. The woman did not—spooked, no doubt. He managed to ride the one-floor distance alone without major incident. He exited and went to the right, back to the hall with rooms 1201 through 1209—still locked, each office as inaccessible as a dune-covered pyramid. At room 1209 he kept going, making two turns until he found himself entering an opulent waiting room near the elevators. He had come full circle.

Behind a counter sat a middle-aged woman dressed in a gray business suit and wearing round, rimless glasses. A large sign over the counter read THE BUSINESS PEOPLE.

"I'm looking for the Pillow Agency," said Cook. "Are you connected with them at all?"

The woman looked at him without expression. She had been doing nothing behind the counter, and she continued to do nothing. Her glasses reflected pure white light in his face.

"They don't seem to be here," Cook went on.

"'They'?" She gave the word a wavering, befuddled tone.

"The Pillow people. Could they have left any kind of message for me?"

The woman let out a laugh, but without any change of expression. "I don't know who you are."

"Jeremy Cook."

"No message," she said without checking anywhere. She said it so quickly that it partly overlapped his name.

Cook sighed and looked somewhat pointlessly around the empty waiting room. "Could you take a message from me for them?" he asked.

"I *could.*"

"*Would* you?" Cook was so frustrated by the woman's style that it took him a moment to see that she had a pen and pad ready for his dictation. This gave him a rush of mike-fright, and he had to collect his thoughts.

"Um, 'To Mr. Pillow. From Jeremy Cook.' Um, um, 'Sorry I missed you.' No, wait, um, 'Sorry I missed you . . .' Wait. Wait."

The woman slowly raised her eyes from the pad to Cook, as if to say, "In the world of business, when men dictate, they *dictate.*"

"Um, okay, 'To Mr. Pillow. From Jeremy Cook. Sorry I missed you. It's four-thirty p.m., Friday.'"

"It's four forty-five," the woman said sharply.

"I know, but I was here promptly at four-thirty. That's the whole point, you see."

"You want me to backdate the memo?"

Cook couldn't tell from her tone if this was a stroke of genius or a suicidal plan. But he said, "Yes. That's it. Back-date it. Write 'four-thirty.'"

She did so. "Anything else?"

"Um, 'Will return . . .' Are they open Saturday?"

"They are not."

"Okay. 'Will return Monday morning.' No, no—make it 'Monday a.m.' That sounds better, doesn't it? 'Monday a.m.'?"

The woman ignored his question and folded the note.

Cook's eye fell on a stack of mail at the edge of the counter. On top of it was the latest issue of *Linguistic Inquiry*. He smiled—the journal was like an old friend in hostile territory, especially this quarter's issue, because it would contain the results of the latest round of grant proposals to the Kartoffel Foundation. He was interested not for himself but for Paula, whose recent application he had supported, without her knowledge, with a warm letter of recommendation.

"May I look at this?" he asked, reaching for it.

"Mr. Pillow's mail? You're asking for permission to look at Mr. Pillow's mail?"

"I meant the journal," Cook said, lifting it from the stack and opening it to the back page.

"It came in the mail," the woman said. "It is part of the mail. It *is* mail."

"Just a peek," he said, and Paula's name leaped out at him—a winner. He grinned. Then he turned the journal over in his habitual way and idly checked the table of contents on the back cover. He let out a sharp yelp. The woman stared across the counter at him. "Look what they've done to me," Cook said, pleading for sympathy. "Look." He showed her the table of contents. He jabbed a finger at the title of the lead article: "Why Jeremy Cook's Theory of Kickapoo Adverbs Is Preposterous." But all he got from the woman was another flash of light from her eyeglasses. She went on with her business, attaching a piece of tape to the note she had written and carrying it around the counter and out of the waiting room.

Cook sighed and opened the journal to the article. A quick skim showed that it fulfilled the promise of its ugly title. The author was one F. F. Sweet—a name Cook didn't recognize. It stood alone, without the customary institutional affiliation. (Denounced by a layman! Cook thought bitterly.) But one so informed about Kickapoo *had* to be an academic. He was probably an unemployed one. (Can't land a job, Cook thought. Too much of a bastard!) F. F. Sweet's only identification was "Washington, D.C." (Good. Populous, strategically important. Likely to take a direct hit when the time came. Maybe soon! Cook hoped shortsightedly.)

Cook knew that the healthy response would have been to take pen in hand and show how this attack on his work was wrong—after reading it, of course. But there was a flaw in the plan: the article would make no sense to him. He had published his Kickapoo adverb theory some seven years earlier, while still in graduate school. Once he had conquered the subject he promptly forgot all about it.

But F. F. Sweet, it was clear, was Mr. Kickapoo Adverb himself. F. F. Sweet had a stranglehold on Kickapoo adverbs. F. F. Sweet spent holidays roaming rural roads and deer trails of the upper Midwest in search of garrulous Kickapoos squatting around their campfires, talking about time, place, manner, degree.

"This round goes to you, F. F. Sweet," Cook said aloud. Then he added a line from an old movie he'd seen late one night on TV, drunk. "Under other circumstances, I might have called you 'friend.'" This was so outrageously false that it made him laugh and contributed to his next act.

He took the journal out into the hallway and pressed the elevator button. When the elevator doors opened he looked down at the floor. *"Good,"* he said. The space was just the right size. He bent down and wedged the bottom of the journal into the crack between the elevator and the hall floor. It stood tall there. He lifted his foot, and with one swift stomp he shot the journal through the crack, sending it careening into the elevator shaft like a damned soul hurled into hell.

Cook returned to his car and studied his street map of St. Louis. Then he drove out of the parking garage and headed for I-70 again. But he would not go east—where he had been—but west, to a motel near the airport, where according to the P.S. in their letter the Pillow bastards had reserved a room for him.

On the highway he calmed down and calculated how long he could live on his savings. It was impossible to spend money in southern Indiana, and as a result he had increased his net worth just like someone who knew what he was doing. His money was presently sitting in an account where a dinky return was offset by the fact that he never had to think about it. He had few expenses, drove an old car (a 1972 Honda Coupe), and traveled little (where was there to go?), and if he gave it a little fix-up, he could live rent-free in a summer cottage in northern Wisconsin owned by his sister in Chicago. He would set out for it the next morning. He had always wanted to live alone in a cottage for a while, just to see what kind of work he could do in complete isolation. He had a title for his first project, and a helluva title it was, too: "Kickapoo Adverbs: Response to F. F. Sweet." All he needed was six months free and clear to relearn everything he had forgotten about the stinking subject.

A thought struck him—hard. The Pillow bastards' mysterious absence might not have been so mysterious. Maybe they saw the F. F. Sweet article and decided to scrap the interview. Who wanted to interview a loser? He imagined a gang of them hurrying away from the office, sneaking out of the building to avoid him, maybe even passing him on the sidewalk and wondering to each other if that was the preposterous job candidate and giggling as they ducked into a bar.

With this image snuffing the last ember of his self-esteem, Cook took the airport exit, crossed the highway, and drove to the Centurion Inn.

The first thing to catch his eye in the lobby was a tall, thin, sad-faced man standing near the windows that looked out to the swimming pool. He had whirled around when Cook entered, and now advanced toward him, his eyebrows raised so high they sent wrinkles up his bald head to its very crown.

"Jeremy Cook?" he asked. "Jeremy Cook?"

"Yes?" Cook watched him approach. He wore a gray suit

of overwhelming dullness. As if to make up for it, a gaily colored beach towel was wedged under one arm.

"Oh! Thank goodness!" the man said. "I'm Roy Pillow." He thrust out his hand.

With profoundly mixed feelings, Cook took his hand. "I missed you at your office."

Pillow frowned. This erased the wrinkles in the top half of his head and concentrated them just above his eyes. "My office?"

"I've just come from there. I left a note for you."

"Why?"

"So that you would know I'd been there," Cook said with a little laugh of impatience.

"Why didn't you assume you would simply tell me, as you have just done?"

"Because I didn't know I would *see* you."

"Of course you did."

"What?" Cook said, a little too loudly. He glanced to the front desk, where the clerk was watching them with undisguised interest.

"I arranged a meeting here," said Pillow, casting his eyes around the lobby.

"If you did, you didn't arrange it with me, and I'm the one who counts."

Pillow smiled quizzically. "But I *did*. In my letter."

Cook immediately produced the letter from his pocket. Pillow took it and read it, gently rocking back and forth from the waist up, as if pleasantly smitten by his own prose. He handed it back to Cook and said, "It's there in black and white."

"Are you kidding?" Cook was getting loud again, and he had to throttle down. "Listen. I'll read it. 'Dear Dr. Cook: Thank you for sending your dossier. I shall be delighted to meet you at four-thirty on Friday, June first. Please advise if this time is problematical. Sincerely, Roy Pillow, Director. P.S.: I have booked a room for you at the Centurion Inn on Williams Road, directly across from the airport.'" He looked up at Pillow, who of all things was beaming. "There is absolutely no basis for your interpretation of this letter," Cook said sharply.

Pillow flinched and his smile disappeared. "Oh come now," he said. "You're not going to maintain—"

"If you wanted me to meet you here at four-thirty, you should have said so."

Pillow shook his head. He seemed genuinely puzzled. "Why do you insist on pursuing this?"

"Because you're *wrong,* that's why. And you won't admit it."

"Would it help if I admitted it?" Before Cook could answer, Pillow looked at his watch and said, "Actually, I'm afraid we'll have to table the subject. Is that all right with you?"

Pillow sounded so conciliatory that Cook felt all alone with his anger. "Sure," he said. "Hell, I'm willing to drop it."

"No, no. That wouldn't be right. It's just that I have a plane to catch"—Pillow paused, then quickly went on—"which is obviously why I booked you a room here in the first place, so far away from the office. Don't you see?"

"That doesn't prove a thing," said Cook, suspicious again.

"I didn't mean it to prove anything. I was just telling you that I have a plane to catch."

"No you weren't. You were sneaking in a final bit of support for what you think your letter says, even though it doesn't support it at all and even though we agreed to drop the subject."

Pillow put his hands out before him in the air, palms down. He looked like Jesus calming the waters. Cook focused his irritation on Pillow's stupid beach towel, still firmly wedged under his arm.

"Let's get you settled," said Pillow.

"Fine," said Cook. He turned to the clerk, who managed to greet them with formulaic friendliness, despite the fact

that he must have considered both of them chuckleheads. Cook gave him his name. As the clerk typed it into the computer, Cook suddenly wondered about Pillow. Was he acting this way because he had seen that bit of nastiness by F. F. Sweet, or was he just permanently weird?

"I show no reservation under 'Cook,'" the clerk said.

Pillow said, "Oh come now."

"I'll check again." The clerk cleared the screen, retyped Cook's name, and shook his head slowly.

"Try 'Pillow' then. Mrs. Pillow made the reservation, and she may have used our name."

The clerk tried it. "No sir. Nothing under that name."

"Oh come now," said Pillow. "There must be some mistake."

This was true, thought Cook. "Do you have any vacancies?" he asked the clerk.

"Yes sir."

"Fine." Cook turned to Pillow. "No problem."

Pillow was frowning. "I don't understand what can have happened." He continued to brood and mutter while Cook registered. Cook got his room key, picked up his suitcase, and asked Pillow where he was going.

"Why, to your room. I intend to interview you."

"I meant your flight," Cook said. "You mentioned an airplane flight."

"Oh. That. Seattle." Pillow's delivery was sharp. It was as if he were flying to Seattle to face charges of some kind. The subject was closed.

The two men went out into the central courtyard and began to circle around to Cook's room, which was on the far side. Cook saw Pillow cast his eyes longingly at the pool. In light of Pillow's beach towel, Cook suddenly felt obliged, as host in this context, to offer Pillow a swim, and he did.

"No time now," Pillow said curtly.

Cook decided that the only way they would have a normal conversation would be if he acted as if he were interested in the job, though he no longer was.

"I once heard a paper given by someone at the Pillow Agency," Cook said. "It was on language death. It was—"

"Yes, yes," said Pillow.

"Is he still with you? It was quite an interesting paper."

"No," said Pillow. "He pursued his subject to its logical end."

"Oh."

Evidently fearing that Cook hadn't understood, Pillow said, rather loudly, "He's *dead.*"

"Yes, I see," Cook said quickly. "I'm sorry to hear that." He stopped at the door of his room and took the key from his pocket. "Here we are."

"He was a troublemaker," said Pillow. "I made a mistake when I hired him. Since then I have had to be ve-ry, ve-ry careful."

Cook nodded as he opened the door. His thought: "This guy is a nut for power." Then he revised it: "This guy is a nut."

Pillow walked in after Cook and sat down at the tiny table in front of the heavily draped window. "I don't mean to rush you," he said, rushing him.

"It's all right," said Cook, taking the other chair. "Let's get started."

Pillow folded his hands on the table and seemed to study them. Then he spoke: "In the life of the mind, criticism plays a vital role; feedback, be it positive or negative, should be *en*couraged, not *dis*couraged."

This threadbare truism, delivered in a form befitting it (one subjunctive, one passive, one tediously stress-marked antithesis), had an instant sedative effect on Cook, and he felt himself slipping fluidly out of his chair like a narcoleptic.

"How does a man climb a mountain?" Pillow asked, rousing Cook to semiconsciousness. Pillow kept his eyes on his hands. He made them rise, still folded, a few inches above the table. "He ascends and establishes a camp and stays the night. From there he ascends to another camp. Then to another. And another." Pillow signified these ascents with equidistant elevations of his folded hands. They had reached eye level now, and Cook had to sit up in his chair to see Pillow's face over them. "He is doing fine, our climber," Pillow continued. "He is making good progress up the mountain. And then? A wise old mountain dweller comes to him and says, 'You cannot climb the mountain this way. It is too dangerous. You must go a different way.'"

Cook found himself sadly disappointed by this news. He had gotten behind that mountain climber and was tickled by his progress.

"At first the climber disbelieves the old man."

Yeah, thought Cook. Press on.

"He challenges the old man."

Yeah. That's the ticket. Throw the old fart off the mountain.

"He even sets out the next morning in defiance of the old man's warning."

Cook wondered what happened to the old man. Did he spend the night? Was there room in the tent for him? Was there enough tea and chocolate bars and stuff like that for him?

"But soon the climber sees that the old man spoke the truth. The route is fraught with . . . with danger."

Cook sensed an illusion-threatening lack of actual mountaineering experience on the part of the narrator.

"Back he must go." Pillow's folded hands dropped a notch.

Maybe the old guy was waiting back at camp for him. Maybe he cooked the climber a nice hot lunch, just to show there were no hard feelings. Cook hoped so.

"Back. Back. Back." Pillow's folded hands descended until they lay at rest on the table. "But was the journey a waste?"

You tell me, sport.

"I say no. For the climb *had* to be attempted at that very spot. No other ascent could have been tried first. The climber *had* to fail."

Pillow smiled wanly and turned to Cook's window, even though the drapes were drawn tight. Cook wondered if the interview was over now.

"Let's say that our dramatis personae are scholars," said Pillow, turning back to Cook and looking him in the eye. "The young climber was brave, but he was wrong. The old man had to point this out. In this particular area—on this *turf*, you might say—the old man was the expert, and the climber was in need of correction."

Cook felt his stomach and intestines switch places. He imagined himself, young and impetuous, standing at his final mountain camp, gazing upward and contemplating his final assault. But look there! Look there! It's F. F. Sweet, bustling toward him across the frozen waste, his rucksack stuffed with Kickapoo counterexamples and a shit-eating grin on his face.

"Why don't you just come right out and say it?" Cook snapped.

"Very well," said Pillow. "If you wish." He took his beach towel from the bed, where he had set it, and began to unroll it on the table. He did it rather neatly, beginning a new roll at the end where he clutched the towel. Cook watched, fascinated, and waited for Pillow's swimming suit and jockstrap to plop out before him—props in some new allegory, perhaps. There came the swimming suit and—no jockstrap? Didn't he wear one? From inside the swimming suit Pillow took some printed sheets of flimsy onionskin. Pillow looked up at Cook. "How is your Icelandic?" he asked.

Cook had looked at the language maybe once in his life. "Rusty," he said, wondering deeply what was going on.

"Here. Try this."

Pillow held out the sheets. Cook took them and searched for his own name in the impenetrable text, under the assumption that his Kickapoo adverb theory was being denounced from all corners of the globe.

"Strong language, eh?" said Pillow.

"I'm having some trouble," Cook said, and at that moment he spied the name "Pillow."

"Oh? It must be the dialect. But you get the essence."

"Not really," Cook said. "You'll have to help me."

Pillow smiled. "I know you're just being modest, but I'll play along. You're quite a character. What we have here is a rebuttal of the very paper you mentioned earlier, the one on language death delivered by my former employee. He had it published shortly after he delivered it. Among the languages he listed as dead was the Icelandic dialect of Schnorrfark. This article takes issue with that claim, and rather convincingly—it is written *in* Schnorrfark by a living, viable speaker of it. There's a whole townful of them, and I assure you that the Pillow Agency is not welcome there."

Cook laughed heartily. Pillow seemed surprised at this, but then he joined in, his face and bald head instantly reddening.

"Now you know the worst about us," Pillow said, still laughing. Then he became serious. It was a sudden plunge. "To tell you the truth, my feeling is that to be challenged in print is actually a distinction. Even if one is shown to be wrong, at least one has said something worth addressing."

"Exactly," said Cook. Evidently Pillow didn't have a clue about Cook's own recent experience in that line. "As a matter of fact—"

"Now that I've done my duty, so to speak, let me say that I was delighted to receive your application."

"Really?"

"I've followed your work closely over the years, Jeremy. I must confess I barely knew the field of linguistics existed until I read *The Woof of Words*. Your book led me to others, but I'm still a newcomer. I just coordinate things for my people out in the field. I'm rather a linguistic ignoramus, to tell the truth. Please don't expect me to know anything. Please don't."

"I promise I won't," Cook said in a voice so friendly he wished he heard himself use it more often.

"As I said, your book led me to others, and in a sense it led to the Pillow Agency. You aren't exactly a Founding Father, but I think of you as the John Locke behind the Founding Fathers."

"My, my."

"You can imagine my delight when you wrote to us. Now, whatever you were paid at the Wabash Institute, I'm willing to better it by twenty-five thousand."

"Dollars?"

"Yes."

Cook was pleased, even though he had no idea what this would total. He had always had a problem remembering his salary, what with the way it changed every year.

"Well?" said Pillow. "I'm eager to get this settled."

A sudden cautionary impulse made Cook say, "May I sleep on it?"

A wave of disappointment crossed Pillow's face. He was flustered, but he fought it and rallied. "Of course. Sleep. Sleep three nights, right here." Pillow patted the bed like a jolly innkeeper. "I'll pick up the tab for the room. If your answer is yes, come to work Monday morning. I don't have to tell you where the office is." Pillow chuckled somewhat normally. "If the answer is no, stay away. I will construe your absence as a polite decline of the offer, and no hard feelings. How does that sound?"

"It sounds fine. I don't really know much about your agency. Do you have any sort of—"

"I'll have something sent here for you to read." Pillow looked at his watch and stood up. "I really must run now."

"You know," Cook said, rising with him, "in the spirit of confession, I should tell you about an article that just appeared about *my* work."

"Oh?" Pillow said. "How nice."

"Well . . . If what you said is true, yes, maybe it *is* nice." Cook told all, surprised at how much relief he got from it. Almost all, anyway. He didn't mention what he had done with Pillow's copy of the journal.

"*Linguistic Inquiry,* you say?" Pillow asked. He was a little less amused than Cook had hoped.

"Yes! That's what's such a killer about it—one of the top journals in the field."

"Mmm," said Pillow.

"Your Icelandic thing is peanuts compared to where *I* got blasted. Hell, you got off easy. Who cares what comes out of a culture that has only four or five surnames to pass around, right?" Cook laughed raucously.

"Yes, yes," Pillow said. He seemed distracted as he slowly headed for the door. "A long article, you say?"

"Oh! Endless!"

"Mmm." Pillow opened the door, then half turned toward Cook. Without looking at him, he said, "I've already offered you the job. I can't very well withdraw the offer. Good Lord—*Linguistic Inquiry.* It's a nightmare." He pressed his lips together and inhaled sharply through his nose. "I'm stuck. That's all there is to it—stuck."

Pillow didn't shake Cook's hand. He simply turned away and left. He crossed the courtyard, muttering and shaking his head.

Cook stood in the doorway, frozen, holding himself in check, deliberately pausing at the threshold of remorse and despair. Then he plunged headlong into the abyss.

Three

At the bottom of the deep end of the Centurion Inn swimming pool, Jeremy Cook hated his life. It was Sunday afternoon. He had resisted this feeling for two days, but it finally defeated him at an unexpected moment—after a deep dive out of the hot Missouri sunshine into the shock of cool water, performed with a run and a bounce and a splash that trumpeted joie de vivre. The sudden silence, the pressing weight of water, the hostility of the enveloping medium—these combined to cave him in, depressing him so much that it seemed unlikely that his body could rise to the surface. But it did, and he dragged himself sadly out of the pool.

Motels are venues of negative feelings. Thus it had been a mistake the night before for him to pause and reflect on how lonely he was after just one day away from his old milieu, and what this meant for his alternative career plan of splendid isolation in northern Wisconsin. It had also been a mistake that morning to check—again—in the motel office for the package of promised literature from the Pillow Agency ("Nothing yet, sir"), and to ask if anyone had indicated they would be paying for his room ("We were rather hoping you would do that, sir").

And it had been a mistake to look at the women staying at

the motel, not because the pretty ones worked him into a lather (he had long ago resigned himself to that futile exercise), but because they all reminded him of Paula. More than that, he thought they *were* Paula. Women who bore only the faintest resemblance to her fooled him into thinking she was *here,* in this hateful new environment.

And it was a mistake now, after his episode of aquatic depression, to lie on the poolside lounge chair, squinting against the bright, hot sky, and think about how "strange and difficult" he was—Paula's characterization of him during their worst fight. She had enumerated his problems for him. Although he saw social isolation as a kind of failure, he was alone almost all the time. He liked to talk about arcane subjects but was irritated and threatened when others did so. He took contradiction personally yet never intended *his* contradictions of others to be taken that way. Strange and difficult.

Jets droned in and out of the airport across I-70, which competed for supremacy in this asphalted hell with its own din. Cook groaned and rose from his chair. He gathered his newspaper, swaying a bit with dizziness. As he walked to his room, a plane came in low enough to strafe him. Its aluminum underbelly matched the strange metallic taste in his mouth.

His room was an igloo. He had turned up the air conditioner before going out to the pool, but he hadn't expected such a zealous performance. He shivered and went to the controls. A lid covered them. Gentle pressure on one side had easily opened it earlier but failed to work now. He pressed the lid several times, on every side, on every square inch. He pounded it with his fist. He threw his towel at it. Last of all—though least effective—he made an obscene gesture at it by grabbing his genitals in a look-what-I-got fashion.

He turned and lay facedown on the bed in his wet swimming suit, freezing but overcome with fatigue. He decided he was sick—or "ill," as some people said. Why did they say that? With that angry question, he drifted off.

He slept. He shivered. He moaned. In two hours he awoke twenty times, always with the same thought: got to get to those controls. The same thought every time, with the same image of the lid yielding easily to him and his hand reaching in and turning the thermostat dial. At some point he managed to crawl under the covers. Then he slept soundly, disturbed only once when the maid came in with the truly foolish hope of cleaning his room. He sat up wildly in bed and spoke to her, mainly in vowels, from deep within his fever delirium. There had been a meeting of minds, for she had backed out quickly and not returned.

When he awoke again, night had fallen. His room was dark. The air conditioner pumped away as if powered by its own direct pipeline to Saudi Arabia. He groped for the light switch by the bed, then bent close over his watch and squinted at it. Two-fifteen.

Excellent! He flopped back on the bed. A *perfect* time to be wide-awake. Wasn't this the "shank of the night" that Bing Crosby had sung about? No?

He got up and went to the window.

Missouri slept.

He was utterly alone.

Roy Pillow hid whatever he felt when Cook appeared at his office door Monday morning. Pillow's bald head was free of wrinkles, as was his forehead. He rose from behind his desk. In the small office he seemed even taller than Cook remembered him.

"You owe me one hundred and sixty-two dollars and thirty-eight cents," Cook said.

The wrinkles appeared as if Cook had plastered them there with a shot from a pistol. "Pardon?" said Pillow.

"My room bill. I've got the receipt right here." Cook took it from his coat pocket and waved it in the air dramatically.

Pillow stared at him a moment. Then he gestured to a chair across from his desk. "Sit down."

"No. I don't plan to stay."

"How's that?" said Pillow. There went the head, cocked to one side. Pretty soon he would say "Oh come now."

"Just write me a check and I'll be on my way," said Cook.

"But we agreed that if you came here today, you would become one of the staff."

"I'm here, yes, but for a different reason."

"But that's impossible."

"What?"

"Our agreement was—"

"Our agreement was that you would pay for the god-damned room. And that you would send me some literature about this place."

"Sit down," Pillow said in a fresh way, as if starting all over.

"No. Just write me the check."

"I assure you that I made arrangements for both of those things to be taken care of."

Cook laughed. "You and your arrangements. Now that I think of it, give me cash. No check. Cash."

"Are you telling me you had to pay for the room yourself?"

"What do you think?"

"Why didn't you tell the clerk that *I* would pay?"

"I did!" This was a lie. Cook had asked the clerk about it, but he hadn't actually told him what to do.

"You instructed him that the Pillow Agency was to be billed?"

Cook couldn't keep the lie alive. "I assumed *you* would do that. Besides, what about the literature you promised me?"

"That's a separate matter entirely." Pillow said this with a strong rebuke in his voice, as if Cook had made an unfair move.

"But what about it? You're not going to say I should have taken the initiative there, are you?"

If Pillow was tempted by this, he hid it well. "Of course not. I'm distressed to hear you didn't receive anything. I must take it up with my staff."

Cook laughed. It was his helpless, impatient laugh. He recognized it from his first talk with Pillow. This talk was just like that one. Only the words were different.

"Okay," said Cook. "Okay. You're doing real well. Point one: the bill for the room—my fault. Point two: the literature—your staff's fault. But there's point three: your reaction when I told you about the article that criticized my work. Think how that made me feel!"

By God, thought Cook. He'd hit home. Pillow was silent. He turned and looked out the window. Cook watched him from the chair across the desk, which he had taken without really planning to. Pillow seemed to be chewing furiously on the inside of his lower lip.

Pillow's phone rang. He grabbed the receiver, lifted it an inch, and immediately let it drop back into its cradle. The phone rang again, and Pillow looked at it as if surprised. This time he simply let it go on ringing. He said to Cook, "I would like you to meet the rest of the staff."

Cook shouted over the ringing, "What do you mean? In lieu of payment?"

Pillow seemed to study this idea. "That makes no sense."

"Exactly. One sixty-two thirty-eight makes sense."

Pillow nodded. "I can see you're in need of a gesture of good faith."

"Yes," said Cook. The phone was driving him crazy. "That's one way to put it."

Pillow stood up. "Come. Let's meet the rest of the staff."

It was really quite remarkable, Cook thought, how Pillow could state the prelude to an act without delivering on the act itself. The phone stopped ringing, and in the sudden calm Cook found himself, for lack of a better plan, rising and following Pillow out the door to the adjacent office, room 1202. Pillow knocked on the door, then tried the knob. It was locked. He repeated the same actions for rooms 1203 through 1209. Nodding as if this was exactly what he had expected, Pillow led Cook back up the hall. A young man emerged from the doorway leading to the elevators. He wore a dark suit and was highly groomed.

"Ah," said Pillow. "We're in luck. James Talbot, meet Jeremy Cook."

Cook shook hands with the man, wincing under his grip. Talbot, having displayed himself, gave Cook a departing smile and hurried on down the hall.

"And here's Matthew," said Pillow, for another one had appeared. "Matthew Benton, say hello to Jeremy Cook."

Benton was strikingly good-looking, and, like Talbot, was dressed for power. He boomed, "How do you do," but Cook beat him to the strong grip and evened the score. Benton then moved hastily on. Everyone seemed to be pressed by some sort of deadline.

"What are those two working on?"

"Mmm?" said Pillow.

"What are they working on? What kind of project?"

"I'm not sure right now."

Cook was impressed. He liked administrators who gave free rein. "You haven't assigned them something?"

"No."

"Don't they at least report to you?"

"Why would they do that?"

"Because you're the boss!" Freedom was one thing, he thought. Anarchy was another.

Pillow laughed. "I get you now. You think those two work for me. No no no. They're lawyers. They have offices up here."

Cook stared hard at Pillow. "You tricked me. You used those guys to impress me because they're so normal." Unlike you, he thought.

Pillow's face, showing a flexibility Cook hadn't suspected, raced into a mournful expression. "You certainly have a suspicious mind, Jeremy," he said.

Cook felt another helpless laugh coming, but he sent it away angrily.

"We've had a nice little walk," said Pillow. "Let's return to my office."

Cook followed, amazed at Pillow, amazed at himself. If Pillow walked out his twelfth-floor window, Cook would probably follow, asking for clarification all the way down.

"Jeremy," said Pillow as the two of them sat down, "how much do you know about the Pillow Agency?"

"Well, on Friday I told you I knew very little. Since then I've read nothing about it, learned nothing about it, and met two guys who have nothing to do with it."

"Mmm," Pillow mmmed. "I'd like to give you three choices." He took some manila folders out of a wooden file box on his desk and looked at the tabs on them. He shuffled them around a bit and said, "The Wingbermuehles, the Oberniederlanders, and the Wilsons. Take your pick." He looked at Cook.

"What are they? Antique airplanes?"

Pillow seemed confused by this. "Take your pick."

"All right. What the hell, eh? I'll take the Wilsons. You bet. Give me the Wilsons every time. They're for me."

"Mmm." Pillow returned two of the files to the box and opened the one before him. "A good choice. A charming pair, I'm sure."

"You know them?"

"Not personally, no."

"But you know *of* them. You have a file on them."

Pillow looked sharply at Cook. "This is not for your eyes."

"I didn't say it was. I . . . What would I *do* with the Wilsons?"

"*The Pillow Manual* will be your guide," said Pillow as he failed to produce one. Cook told himself not to leave the building without a copy of that manual, even if it meant taking hostages.

Pillow copied down some information that was in the folder. Then he closed the folder and set it to one side of his desk. He opened the top drawer, took out something like a large receipt book, and bent over and began to write in it. Cook bided his time.

Without lifting his head, Pillow said, "Brothers or sisters?"

"Pardon?" said Cook, even though he had heard him.

"Do you have any brothers or sisters?"

Cook looked at Pillow's bald dome for clues. "I have an older sister in Chicago." With a cottage in Wisconsin, he thought.

"Mmm." Pillow set his pen down and slowly sat up straight in his chair. He drummed his fingers on his desk for a moment. "Jeremy, let me ask you something. Why does a marriage break down? Why does it crack up?"

Cook squirmed. He had never in his life given this question a single moment of thought. "For lots of reasons, I suppose."

"For *one* reason." Pillow blinked slowly, heavily. With stony reverence, he said, "Communication."

"I take it you're single?" Cook said.

"Not at all! *Hap*pily married. Going on six months now."

"First marriage?" said Cook, surprised. Pillow appeared to be in his fifties.

Pillow became animated. "In a sense, yes. I'm glad you put it that way. I'll think of it in those terms myself from now on." He leaned forward on his elbows and said earnestly, "You see, Jeremy, I believe in love. It's a new belief for me, and it's taken the Pillow Agency in a surprising new direction. The Pillow Agency serves marriages. Our specialty is the linguistically troubled marriage. That's where our linguists roll up their sleeves and go to work. They *occupy* the marriage. The Wilsons are linguistically troubled. You, Jeremy, will *occupy* their marriage. You will *bivouac,* so to speak, on their figurative *marital battlefield.*"

"Jesus Christ!" said Cook. "I'd rather captain an Iranian speedboat."

Pillow said, "It will indeed be a challenge. Now for the details. Where are your earthly goods?"

"In Indiana. In storage. I didn't want to move them until I knew—"

"Fine, fine. Leave them there. You'll be staying with the Wilsons."

"You mean I'm supposed to sleep there?"

"Yes. Don't worry. They'll provide you with a comfortable bed. It's all in the contract."

"It's not the bed I'm worried about. It's the whole idea. How long will I be there?"

"As long as you are needed."

"What will I *do?*"

"*The Pillow Manual* will be your guide."

"Ah. Silly of me to have forgotten that."

"You'll do fine, Jeremy. You're eminently qualified."

"I am? My doctoral dissertation was on Miwok syntax. Since then I've been studying two-year-old Hoosiers."

"Exactly. I'm hiring your mind—what you *can* do, not what you've done. Now here are two checks for you. One is for your room bill. The other is for three thousand dollars—a small advance on your salary until we've gotten the paperwork on you completed." Pillow stood up.

Cook saw the cottage in Wisconsin. It was quaint, but it was cold. A moose stuck his head in the window. Amazing! But the moose looked stupid. As for Cook himself, in this vision he sat alone at a bare wooden table, unshaven, maybe even drunk. He was trying to speak to the moose, but words failed him: he had spoken to no one in months and his language was gone.

Cook rose to his feet and took the two checks.

"And here is the address of the Wilsons," Pillow said. He suddenly beamed at Cook. "What did the rich man say in that old TV show? 'Our next millionaire, Mike'?" Pillow chuckled. It was not a pretty sight. "If a happy marriage is money in the bank, then I say to you, 'Our next millionaire, Jeremy.'"

Cook spent the rest of the day in a tiny conference room on the twelfth floor, studying *The Pillow Manual* and filling out a long questionnaire Pillow claimed to need for his files. Pillow had escorted him to the room with crazed delight in his new employee, slapping Cook on the back and steering him around corners by the elbow. Cook had many questions about the agency, and Pillow answered some of them, but once Cook was in the conference room Pillow seemed in a hurry to get back to his other business, whatever it might be. As he left Cook, he jabbed his finger at the thick volume under Cook's arm and said, *"The Pillow Manual* will be your guide."

Pillow had intimated that he and Cook would eat lunch together around noon, but when Cook walked down to his office he found the door locked. Cook left a convivial note on the door that read, "Roy, I'm in 1242. Lunch?" Of course, Pillow *knew* Cook was in 1242—he had taken him there—but that made Cook's note all the more convivial, according to the principle that required a zero-information flow for conviviality. At two o'clock, irritated and starving, Cook gave up on Pillow and wandered downstairs and outside to a place with Spartan offerings—two types of chili, one kind of soda, and sit down and shut up and eat it. Cook never really fussed over food himself—he rated it for pleasure with gassing up his car—so he didn't mind the place much. Then it was back to *The Pillow Manual.*

Shortly before five o'clock, Cook had a visitor. It was the stern woman who had taken his dictation on Friday. Instead of a business suit she wore a white smock, and instead of a pen in her hand she carried a syringe with a long needle. Cook's eyes widened.

"Blood," she said succinctly. "Roll up your sleeve."

"What for?" said Cook, but to his amazement he complied.

She pawed at his arm and, to put him at ease, said, "Let's see if I can get it right this time." It hurt, but she managed to avoid hitting a nerve and crippling him for life. Cook had a dozen questions, but her manner commanded silence. She was gone, and so were several milliliters that used to be part of him, and he didn't know why.

He took a tissue from his pocket and wedged it against the puncture wound, holding it in place by flexing his arm. Working clumsily but hurriedly—for all he knew, the woman might return and wrest a stool sample from him— he packed up and set out for his assignment.

According to Pillow, the Wilsons were expecting him for dinner. They lived about a half mile west of the city limits, in a good-looking neighborhood of old brick houses—turn-of-the-century, Cook guessed. He located the house but drove by it without stopping. He cruised the neighborhood, telling himself he was researching the Wilsons' environment instead of stalling. The area was thick with oaks and syca-mores, almost overpopulated by them. The streets horse-shoed around confusingly, and Cook got lost twice. When he tracked down the Wilsons' house for the third time he was actually glad to do so, and riding on that feeling, he pulled to a stop in front of it. He got out and took his suit-case and briefcase from the car.

As he walked up the sidewalk to the front door, he felt like many things: an unwelcome relative, an IRS auditor, a schizophrenic tuck-pointer back to patch up a sloppy job, a fraud, and a pervert.

He pushed the doorbell. He figured he had about seven seconds to begin to feel like what his manual told him he was: a Pillow agent.

Four

"**H**oney, the linguist is here."

"Ooh."

Cook, standing out on the porch, was encouraged by these noises from within. Although the front door was closed, the man's voice announcing his arrival had carried to him easily from deep inside the house, as if borne by hearty optimism. The woman's reply, which reached Cook not through the door but by an open bay window on the second floor, was also good. "Ooh" meant urgency, but without annoyance.

This was all fine. It would be even better when someone showed up to open the door. Cook kept anticipating the click of the latch, the swing of the door, face greeting face. As the normal range of time for this lapsed, the warmth in the initial signals from the house gradually cooled. Cook lifted his finger to the doorbell again and hesitated, wanting to avoid the extremes of pushiness and passivity—the classic social dilemma. He counted to five and pressed it again.

"*Honey!*"

The husband's voice was louder, but it was still coming from some distance. The wife did not respond this time.

"*Honey!*"

No answer.

Through the upstairs window Cook heard the phone ring. This was a bad sign. The household's attention was already divided. He would fall into further neglect. Then he heard a repeated *ding,* as from an oven timer. He felt as if he were in the midst of Poe's "The Bells."

Two little yelps behind him made him turn around. In a small wooded park across the street, a boy was playing catch with himself. He was throwing a baseball high into the branches of the trees, presumably as a personal challenge, for he had to react as the branches deflected it. But this meant that twigs also dropped on him, and he yelped when they did. Cook watched and thought it was a strange thing to do. But it was also the kind of thing he might have done at that age—around ten, he guessed.

Cook turned back to the house. The porch extended about one third of the way across the front, ending just short of a wide window. By standing on the side wall of the porch and leaning far over, he was just able to snatch a peek inside. No one was in sight. He went back to the door, sighed, and, just to stay in touch, rang the doorbell again. No response —not even the *"Honey!"* he had grown to expect and draw encouragement from. He opened the screen door and tried knocking on the oak door, figuring the bell didn't work—a somewhat desperate theory, given that he could hear it every time from the front porch. His knocks felt puny on the thick wood, as if it absorbed them and dispersed them to all its cells.

He remembered a sentence from *The Pillow Manual:* "It is hard to get inside a marriage." He had assumed a figurative meaning to it. Perhaps he had been wrong.

Cook turned around and saw that the boy from the park was now on the sidewalk directly in front of the house. He apparently didn't see Cook on the porch. He wound up and thwacked the ball off the short run of steps midway up the walk that led to the house. Cook blinked, a little disoriented to learn that this boy, an object of his idle notice just a moment earlier, was about to become part of his life. Why hadn't Pillow told him that children would be in the picture?

"Hi!" Cook called out. "Do you live here?"

The boy was about to throw again, and he halted in mid-windup. "Yeah," he said.

"I'm kind of stuck. Your mom and dad are expecting me, but they don't answer the door."

The boy got a faraway look in his eyes and leaned his head to one side. "Someone's taking a shower."

Cook frowned. "What?"

"I can hear it." The boy pointed to the ivy between the sidewalk and the street.

Cook decided that if he left the front door and came back to it his luck might change. He walked down to where the boy stood. In the midst of the ivy was a small round grate.

"Hear it?"

Cook heard it—the trickle of water deep down in the sewer line from the house.

"It's got to be the shower because it's a steady sound," the boy said. "If it was real short it would be the toilet. That's definitely the shower." He spoke with conviction.

"Very impressive," said Cook. "Can you tell from the sound of the water who's in the shower?"

The boy hesitated, saw he was being teased, and suddenly grinned. "Yeah. It's my mom."

"Really? How on earth—"

"My dad's watching the Cardinals on TV."

"Ah. You got me."

The boy's grin grew, then suddenly disappeared when the flow of water stopped. "She's done," he said. "She's throwing the curtain open. Her body's all wet. She's reaching for the towel. She's drying herself."

Cook, who was always easily aroused, felt an erotic surge. He was uncomfortable with its origin and tried to clear his head. He looked up at the house—three stories of red brick rising like a huge hand forbidding entrance.

"Can you help me?" Cook asked. "My name is Jeremy."

"That doesn't sound like a man's name."

Cook smiled at the boy's bluntness. "What are you say-ing—it sounds like a woman's name?"

"No. Like a boy's name."

"Oh. Yeah, maybe. What's your name?"

"Robert."

"Now, *that* sounds like a man's name," said Cook.

"People call me Robbie."

"Oh. That's better. You know what? People don't call me Jeremy."

"What do they call you?"

"Robert."

The boy gave him a long look. Then he said, "Get out of town."

Cook laughed. "Do you think you could go tell your folks I'm here?"

"The front door's locked," said Robbie. "I have to go around back."

Cook thanked him and said he would wait out in front. As he walked up the sidewalk he watched Robbie run around the corner of the house. An odd kid, he thought. Such careful speech, such a sober face. A ten-year-old straight man. But he seemed to have a sense of humor, too.

In a short while Cook heard footsteps. Then the wooden door swung open. It was a wide door, and its opening seemed grand and baronial—an effect that was immediately destroyed when the man of the house cried out, "What a mix-up!" and threw open the screen door so violently that Cook had to jump back from it. "Come in. Come in."

Cook thanked him, picked up his suitcase and briefcase, and stepped into the entryway.

"I'm Dan Wilson," the man said, extending his hand. He was slightly shorter than Cook and athletic-looking, with a clean-shaven, broad, wide-open face. He seemed innocent, guileless.

Cook introduced himself and set his luggage down on the hardwood floor.

"Beth and I knew you were coming," Dan said, looking

around as if hoping she was there to support this claim, "and we got all ready for you, but then we bungled it."

"That's all right," said Cook. "It gave me a chance to meet your son."

"What fools you must think we are."

"Not at all."

"Can't even answer the door."

"No, no. Not at all."

"I thought Beth got it, you see, and I was waiting for her to bring you in. Then the phone rang, and... Things just got mixed up." Cook hoped they would get off this subject sometime soon. Dan's eye fell on Robbie, who had come into the entryway, and he transferred his animation from Cook to his son. "Mr. Cook is the man we told you about, Robbie. He's a linguist—someone who studies languages. He's here to study how people in St. Louis talk. He'll be staying with us a few days. Can you go get Mommy?"

Robbie gave Cook a sizing up, then said, "Sure." He dashed up the stairs.

"I hate to lie to him," Dan said to Cook, "but what can you do?"

Cook shrugged. "Sometimes you have to lie."

A wild grin took possession of Dan. Just as quickly, it disappeared, and his face relaxed into its normal, merely alert look. It was an intelligent look, Cook thought—almost too intelligent, as if Dan were starving for more than everyday life provided.

There followed an awkward silence. Dan had suddenly gone mute, sending Cook on a search for a thought to give words to. He asked Dan if he had any other children. Dan said no and seemed to want to say more, but he didn't. Another silence fell. Cook heard TV noises from the rear of the house, beyond a swinging door, and he said, "I don't want to take you away from your game."

"Bah! It's nothing." Dan looked up the stairs. "Honey!" he yelled, his face full of hope. "Honey!" Still looking up the stairs, he said, "I can't imagine what's keeping her." Dan seemed to lack a license to fly solo. Evidently nothing more would happen until Beth was on the scene.

Dan suddenly froze, listening, his eyes fixed on the swinging door. "Damn it," he said. "Game's in Chicago. Bottom of the inning. Cheers are a bad sign." He gave his head a jerk toward the door. "You sure?"

"About what?"

"That you don't mind if I go back to the game?"

"Of course! The whole point is that you should go on with what you normally do. That's how I understand this. Is that how you understand it?"

Before Cook finished speaking, Dan was gone, a final brush of the swinging door the only evidence he had been there. In a second or two Cook could hear him interacting with the TV.

Cook felt abandoned again. He had made it inside, but he was no better off. He looked around the entryway, which struck him as ridiculously large. It made him wish he had a basketball to dribble around. To his right was an upright piano with "Golliwogg's Cake-Walk" on the music stand—a title that always filled him with vague panic when he heard it pronounced on the radio. The living room was to his left. Ahead and to his right, stairs climbed a short distance to a landing with two large stained-glass windows. From there the stairs doubled back in the opposite direction and climbed beyond his view to the second floor. Ahead to his left was the swinging door Dan had just used. Between the door and the stairs was a wall with a mirror, in which Cook's reflection stared forlornly back at him. He wanted to lean back and cry out, "Is there no place for me here?"

All was silent. Cook could tiptoe out and be but a dim memory to them, not even a ship in the night but more like a piece of driftwood. He suddenly heard a monstrous wail from Dan. Then "No no no! No no no no!" Cook wondered if he was still watching the game or if he had switched to a documentary about torture. Another cry followed, and then a shout, apparently to Cook: "Why don't you join me? I meant for you to join me."

Before Cook could answer, Beth came down the stairs. It was a dramatic descent, more for the pent-up energy Cook brought to it than for any other reason. She was nice-looking, but in a comfortable, everyday sort of way. She wore a white sweatshirt and jeans. Like her husband, she had a wide-open, welcoming face. Her hair was a rich black. It was not long and flowing. Nor was it crazy with tarantula-leg curls. Nor was it severely short, to suggest she was neurotic or took drugs Cook had never heard of. Any of these styles and he would have been afraid of her. Her hair was simple—of medium length and straight, with a slight curl forward at the ears. Nothing special. Nothing scary.

"I'm Beth," she said, extending her hand. She added with a laugh, "And I'm very nervous."

"I'm Jeremy Cook, and I was too, but I'm not so much anymore." Easy to be with—that summed her up. Cook had never had such an instant feeling of comfort with anyone.

"Have you met Dan?"

"Yes. He's watching the game." Cook quickly added, "I urged him to."

"You say that as if I was going to go yell at him for it."

Cook was about to deny this, but then he laughed and said, "You're right. You read my thought."

"Isn't that what *you're* supposed to do? Read *our* thoughts?"

"I suppose it is," said Cook, laughing again and wishing she would join him with a laugh of her own—just a little one, anyway. But she simply stood there. Maybe *not* so easy to be with, he thought.

Her eye fell on his luggage. "Let's get you settled."

Robbie, whose footsteps Cook heard coming down the stairs, appeared on the landing and said, "I'll take him up, Mom."

Beth turned to her son, but then she sniffed the air and said to Cook, "Do you smell something burning?" Before Cook could answer—he was going to say yes, now that she mentioned it he *did* smell it—she dashed through the swinging door.

"Cookies," said Robbie from the landing. "Too bad. Want me to show you your room?"

"Sure." Cook picked up his bags. But some interesting sounds from the kitchen halted him. "Hang on a second," he said, and he set his bags down and took a few steps toward the door.

Robbie sensed right away what he was up to. "You gonna listen in on Mom and Dad?" His eyes widened.

"I wouldn't call it...I wouldn't..." Cook gave up. "Yes." He reached the swinging door and opened it a crack, not enough to see anything—just enough to hear clearly. Some metallic slamming noises made him close it quickly. He glanced back at Robbie, who was tiptoeing to him with dramatic stealth. Cook was about to give it up, but then he heard voices and cracked the door open again. He strained to hear over Robbie's noisy breathing right behind him.

"...believe this. Didn't you hear the timer?" Beth made an exasperated sound.

"Yeah. I turned it off but I forgot to take them out." Dan laughed. "Jesus, this is classic. He's gonna think we're idiots."

"Why? For burning cookies?"

"No. For arguing already, when he just got here."

"I'm not arguing. I'm just mad the cookies burned. This top batch is shot. Didn't you smell them?"

"Not really. I was in the sun-room. The Cards lost."

"How come you turned the timer off and didn't take them out? That's what I don't get."

"Well—"

"And why did you just leave him in there?"

Dan laughed. "Be sure to let me know when this becomes

an argument. I want to be ready. Now, first, he *told* me it was okay to watch the game. We're just supposed to do our thing. Second, knock it off or he's gonna think I'm henpecked."

"Henpecked? You just step out of 'Dagwood'?"

"Okay. Pussywhipped."

"Ugh. My favorite word."

"You know what happened?" Dan sounded spontaneously cheered, heartened. "I just figured it out. I forgot the cookies because the phone was ringing. Oh, shit." The cheer was gone. "Your mother's on the phone."

"Right now? I didn't hear it ring."

"You must have been in the shower."

Beth made another exasperated noise. "I got out of the shower *ten minutes ago*. God." Cook heard footsteps, then Beth on the phone apologizing and saying she would call back later. Then the sound of the phone being hung up. Then the rattle of a cookie sheet again.

"Where are you going?" To Cook's surprise, Beth's voice was almost free of anger. He wondered if her anger didn't sound like anger (that would make observation tough, he thought), or if she simply wasn't angry.

"Where do you *think* I'm going?" Dan's voice came from much nearer than before—from just the other side of the swinging door. Cook hadn't heard him approach, and he had to fight the impulse to back off. He was exerting some pressure on the door to keep it open, and a sudden swing in his direction would give him away. Robbie, not troubled by this consideration, reacted purely to the proximity of his father's voice and backpedaled away from Cook up the stairs to the landing, where he threw himself down on his belly like Audie Murphy in *To Hell and Back*.

"Shouldn't I be with him?" Dan said.

"Robbie took him up," said Beth. "Don't worry about him. What did my mother say?"

"Oh, the usual stuff. We didn't talk long."

"You mean she just *waited* all that time?"

"Maybe I should go up and help him get settled. I want to show him I can be sociable."

By degrees, Cook was babying the door back into its at-rest position. A few more sentences and it would be there.

Beth said, "I can't imagine her sitting there and . . . I don't know what's worse—that she had to wait all that time or that she could hear everything going on. You think she heard him come?"

"No. No way. What's he doing? Unpacking?"

"Probably. What do you think of him?"

"Seems okay," said Dan. "What do you think?"

"I don't know."

"Think he's good-looking?"

"What's that got to do with anything?"

"Just tell me. I'm curious."

"Yeah," Beth said, but in a high nasal tone that vaguely qualified it. "He's kind of cute."

Cook found himself staring in the large wall mirror, right beside him, to see if this was true.

"These'll be okay for the bake sale, don't you think? Are you *sure* she didn't hear him?"

"*Yes,*" said Dan. "Yes to everything. Relax, will you? She couldn't have heard anything, except for the ball game. No real excitement there—your dad was probably watching it, too."

"Why don't you ever have him over to watch it with you?"

"Your dad? Nah."

"You both enjoy it. You could watch it together."

"Nah."

"Why not?"

"It wouldn't be the same."

"What do you mean?"

"With him here I'd *have* to watch it."

"But you *love* watching it. What do you mean, *have* to?"

"I like being able to turn it off if I want to."

"But you *never* turn it off."

"But I like being able to if I want to."

"It seems like it'd be a painless way to be with him."

"Nah."

"Try it once. When do they play again? I'll make a dip."

"Clam dip?"

"Whatever you want."

"Nah. What would your mother do?"

"I don't know. Play with Robbie."

"Really? Geez—a breakthrough!"

"I wonder if she just sat there the whole time or shouted into the phone or what."

"I don't know. I guess the TV drowned her out. . . . You know, now that you mention it, I did hear something. I kept looking out the window. I thought it was a bird."

Beth laughed. It was a deep laugh, rich with honest pleasure. "You're im*pos*sible."

Cook's door problem was solved. Indeed, considering the leisurely mode into which Dan and Beth had lapsed, Cook felt he could remove the door, take it out to some shop for refinishing, and return and reinstall it without anyone noticing. In all his years of eavesdropping, both professionally and otherwise, he had rarely heard conversation as fluid as this. He hadn't expected anything of the kind, considering his reason for being here. This didn't sound at all like a marriage in trouble. It made him wonder if he had misread the address and come to the wrong house.

Cook moved away from the door. Meanwhile, for some reason Robbie began to slither on his belly from the landing down the carpeted stairs. Cook grabbed his luggage and was about to suggest to Robbie that they go up to his room, when the kitchen door swung open and Dan burst through it.

"Whoa," Dan said when he saw Cook. He pronounced it like "woe," only with an extreme intonation drop. "Still stuck on dead center, eh?" Dan blinked rapidly. He seemed a little flustered. Cook guessed that he was replaying his conversation with Beth, examining it for regrettable sentences. "Come on. Let's see if we can make it to your bedroom. Here. Give me that suitcase."

Cook obliged. "How are the cookies?" he asked.

Dan shook his head sadly. "Beth tries to involve me in the cooking. She tries like hell. And *I* try. But look at me. Look at me." He set Cook's suitcase down and held his hands out. Cook expected to see flippers instead of the normal-looking, rather strong hands Dan presented to him.

"I'm not much of a chef myself," said Cook.

Beth called from the kitchen, "Honey, did you start the coals?"

"Ye-es, I did," Dan called back melodiously—but his face was a clinker. To Cook he said, quickly, as if under fire, "Listen. You go on up. Robbie can show you your room, okay? He's quite capable, as you can see." They both looked at him. He had frozen in his prone position on the stairs when his father had entered, as if no one would see him if he didn't move. Cook smiled. Dan laughed with a restrained wildness. "I'm gonna have to go out the front and sneak around back and get the coals started. You got a match? No? A nonsmoker, hunh? Me too. Shit. Never mind. I think there're some in back, unless they got rained on. If they did, I'm a goner. So. Okay? Okay. Good luck." This last made no sense as a statement to Cook; it was Dan talking to himself.

Cook watched Dan hustle out the front door. He decided he had come to the right house after all. Robbie roused himself, and Cook, at long last, began the climb up the stairs to his room.

Five

According to Robbie, the third floor was originally servants' quarters. The ceilings were lower than in the rest of the house and the floors were of pine rather than oak. Cook found it all comfortably snug. It reminded him of the *Zimmer frei* lodgings he had taken in Swiss villages during a summer of hitchhiking—single rooms in the midst of strange households, where he always had to nudge family photographs aside on the nightstands to make room for his things.

After Robbie showed Cook to his room, the boy engaged him in a brief, almost token conversation, as if he had read in some juvenile book of etiquette that one should chat for sixty seconds with a new guest in his room to make him feel at home:

"When I get a new hamster I'll name him Jeremy," Robbie announced rather flatly.

"That's nice," Cook said as he began to unpack. "You expecting to get one?"

"Yeah. My last one died."

"That's too bad."

"I'll get a young one."

"Oh?"

"So he'll live longer."

"Ah. I thought you were making fun of my little boy's name again."

"I didn't say it was a *little* boy's name."

"That's true, you didn't. You've got a good memory."

"I remember what I say, anyway."

"There's an old saying: 'A liar must have a good memory.'"

Robbie frowned. "I don't get it."

"If he has a bad memory he'll forget what lies he told and end up saying things that don't fit together."

"Oh." Robbie seemed subdued.

"I'm not saying *you're* a liar," Cook quickly added.

"I know. Is that real gold?"

Cook followed his eyes. He was looking at his shiny briefcase latch. "No. It's paint or something."

"Oh." Robbie heaved a leave-taking sigh. "See you later, I guess."

"Okay. Can you tell your mom and dad I have some things to do up here? I'll be down in a bit."

Robbie jabbed a fist in the air and said, "Right on."

Cook wasn't aware he had made a political statement, and he smiled quizzically as Robbie left. He began to unpack. He found two empty drawers in the dresser and half of an armoire free. Apart from these two pieces there was a double bed, a nightstand, a small, ill-painted yellow desk, and a long, overflowing bookcase, which he browsed in between trips from the open suitcase to the dresser. The books were standard extra-room fare: mixed collegiate liberal arts paperbacks, outdated self-improvement texts, and the odd bizarre title like *The Pipe: A Photographic Celebration.* There were also lots of novels by people he had never heard of. But he saw some old friends there, too—Dickens, Jane Austen, Thomas Mann, D. H. Lawrence. God, Lawrence. Did anyone still read Lawrence? He thought of the gamekeeper in *Lady Chatterley's Lover,* with his perennial "fire in the loins."

It always reminded Cook of what they yelled in mines when they blasted: "Fire in the hole!"

His room was long, running nearly the full width of the house, and windows filled most of one wall. In the midst of these was a glass door leading to a small balcony. He was pleased to see that his room faced the street. It would make it easy for him to observe comings and goings, if he needed to.

When he was finished unpacking he took *The Pillow Manual* from his briefcase and sat down with it at the little yellow desk. He reread the cheerless verse from Proverbs on its blue cover, evidently the Pillow Agency motto:

> He that passeth by, and meddleth with strife belonging not to him, is like one that taketh a dog by the ears.

That morning in Pillow's conference room Cook had frowned over this sentence, searching it for hidden encouragement. He had finally given up and tackled the first chapter of the manual—two hundred dense pages on the history of matrimony in Western culture—beginning it with good intentions, then skipping major portions of it, then guiltily going back and skipping them all over again. Thus looping and skipping, like a daydreaming child on his way to the candy store, he had made it to the second chapter, "The Pillow Agency Today"—a title that reminded him of industry films about oil and electricity with lots of zippy music. Here he found names and addresses of dozens of married couples. A single brief comment concluded each entry. "Will get better and better" was the hopeful comment for one marriage. But another read, "Pattern will continue: Bill having affairs, Peggy forgiving him, until death of one or both." Another read, "All this marriage needs is a little more money."

The Wilsons were not listed. Cook assumed this was the

dead file—completed cases. It would be up to him to sum up their lives when he was done—a task that at the moment seemed ridiculously beyond his reach.

Chapter Three, though promisingly titled "Methods," was Pillowesque in its informational stinginess: every page of the chapter was sealed except for the first, which contained an "Unsealing Schedule": "Day One—Read Pages 227–228," "Day Two—Read Page 229," and so on. Pillow had pointed this out to Cook upon tendering him the manual, cautioning him not to read a word of this chapter until he was "on the job site," as he put it, and then to read only what that day's schedule allowed. He warned Cook that the manual was "subject to inspection" to ensure that the reading schedule was being adhered to. At the time, Cook had had a rebellious urge to unseal the whole damn thing right there in front of Pillow, just to see him come apart.

This was Day One, and he was on the job site, so it was time to do the dirty thing. He slid his hand under the first sealed page and popped the pink tab at the right margin, surprised at the pleasure it gave him. He turned to the popped page and read:

DAY ONE

Have a regular social evening.
Demonstrate your conversational competence.
Ask 25 questions.

Cook made a face. "Have a regular social evening" was close enough to "Have a nice day"—or the even more putrid "Have a good one"—to enrage him. There was a bit of a paradox in the directive, too, on the order of "Be spontaneous!" The sentence about his conversational competence instantly made him feel he didn't have any. "Ask 25 questions." Did it matter what they were? An odd exercise, even by Pillow's standards. But at the bottom of the page, Cook noticed a "Turn, please," and he did, for the sealing tab had held two pages, not just one. On this second page were the questions—standard queries about courtship and the like, with instructions that Cook was to put them to each partner while the other one was absent and then to collate the responses. The tape recorder in his possession was to be used for this exercise *only*. The instructions concluded with the promise of a courier to arrive on the following day to snatch the recorder from him, guaranteeing compliance. Pillow ran a tight ship. Cook looked for encouragement there. Didn't methodological uniformity imply methodological soundness? Not really, he said to himself. Shut up, he said to himself.

Cook took the tape recorder from his briefcase. He established to his satisfaction that he could work it (it was a more recent model of the same Sony he had used with tinier informants at Wabash), and he went downstairs for a regular social evening of good old-fashioned conversational competence.

As Cook pushed open the swinging door into the kitchen, where the family was gathered, he experienced a fresh crisis of confidence. He tried to beat it back with an eager display of friendliness, saying, "You've made your house very comfortable." He overdid it a bit, braying the sentence.

"You think so?" said Beth, looking at him from the refrigerator, where she was kneeling and wrestling with a vegetable drawer. "I'm not really happy with a lot of it."

Cook lacked a follow-up remark, as he always did when he was insincere. Dan was standing near Beth, his hands extended toward her in the obvious posture of a man thwarted in midutterance.

"Did I interrupt?" Cook asked. "Sorry."

"That's all right," said Beth.

Robbie said, "It's not all right when *I* do it." He was carrying a tray of plates and utensils from the kitchen into the sun-room at the rear of the house.

"Go on with whatever you were doing," Cook said.

Dan, obeying Cook without acknowledging him, resumed speaking to Beth. Cook stood still and listened. Dan
was telling her about something that had happened at work.
But there was trouble at the receiving end. Beth was not all
there for him. She was moving briskly from station to station: from refrigerator to counter to spice rack to sink, nodding and interjecting "Mm-hmm" and "Wow" at the right
spots, but obviously not listening. Dan began to talk faster
and louder. He gave the impression that he was physically
following her, even though he stood in one place the entire
time. Cook watched and grew agitated himself. Dan's story
climaxed just as Beth finished her work. She picked up a
platter, and with a brief laugh signaling not amusement but
only the end of this failed speech event, she presented him
with his reward: a big raw fish.

Dan accepted the fish without a word and went through
the sun-room and out the back door. If he was angry, he hid
it. If Beth knew he was angry, she hid it. But Robbie, making a trip into the kitchen, sidestepped his father as if sensing
he could easily be bowled over.

Cook remained standing across the kitchen from Beth,
thinking. There was a technical name for what he had just
seen Dan and Beth do, but he couldn't think of it. Beth
turned to see if he was still there, reacted with surprise when
she saw that he was, but quickly smiled and offered him a
drink.

"No, thanks," Cook said.

"First time in St. Louis?" she asked as she turned back to
the counter, where she was chopping something.

"Yes. I've passed through here, but that's all."

"It's a nice city," she said—with emphasis, as if he had
asserted the opposite. "It's a great place to raise a family, and
you can get anywhere in twenty minutes."

"Sounds good," said Cook. He had no family and didn't
want to go anywhere.

"Ooh. Dan didn't take the oven mitt out. He'll probably
need it."

"I'll take it," said Cook, grabbing it from the counter.

"Can you remind him not to overcook the salmon?"

Cook said he would do that. He walked into the sun-room, a large room with an almond-tile floor and a curve of tall casement windows looking onto the backyard. It was obviously an addition to the house, joined to the kitchen by French doors. Robbie was seated at the table with an open book on his plate.

"You've set a very nice table," Cook said to him.

"Give me a break," Robbie said without looking up.

Cook stepped out the back door onto the wooden deck. He trotted down the stairs to the brick patio, where Dan was hunched over a barbecue kettle.

Dan looked up, but just for a moment. He was concentrating hard on the grill. "First time in St. Louis?"

"Yes, not counting the times I passed through."

"Yeah," Dan said sourly. "The Great Flyover." He had been holding a knife and fork poised above the salmon, and now he suddenly plunged them into it, making a deep slice. Cook saw several open scars from previous slices, even though Dan had just put the fish on. Dan was wearing a chef's apron with loops at the waist for utensils. Two spatulas dangled there. Bumptious lettering across the front of the apron read, NOW WE'RE HAVING FUN!

Cook said, "I'm supposed to tell you not to overcook it."

Dan raised his eyes more slowly than Cook would have thought possible without humorous intent, but there was clearly no such intent here—Cook knew this when Dan failed to return his strained grin. He just stared at Cook.

Cook said maybe he would have a look around the yard, and he eased away, casting a final glance at Dan. Hovering over the fish, he looked like a ravenous heron on the prowl in shallow water. Cook wondered why Dan was so tense. Was it Cook's mere presence? Was he angry at Cook for interrupting his story in the kitchen? Or was he angry at Beth for not listening?

"Complementary schismogenesis," Cook said to himself,

softly. That was the name he had tried to remember in the kitchen. In *The Woof of Words*—Cook's surprisingly popular general introduction to linguistics—he had devoted a tidy chapter to this concept, originally developed by some anthropologist whose name he could never remember. Complementary schismogenesis was what happened when person A did something that irked person B, so B did something in response that made A do even more of the thing that irked B, which made B do *his* thing even more, and so on. It could all take place quite unconsciously. The classic metaphor illustrating it involved a married couple under an electric blanket with dual controls that have been switched by mistake. The wife wakes up cold, so she turns the thermostat on her nightstand up; this raises the temperature on her husband's side of the blanket, so he wakes up hot and turns his thermostat (actually his wife's) down, so of course she turns hers up even farther, and so on.

In the kitchen, Dan had had a story to tell. But Beth had had a meal to prepare. Dan talked. Beth cooked. Dan, reacting to Beth's inattention, talked harder. Beth, fighting the distraction, cooked harder. The repulsion was mutual and meticulously balanced. Complementary schismogenesis. It was a killer concept.

Cook walked slowly along the edge of the lawn, looking at the flower beds, which he liked for their signs of nonfanatical maintenance. He appreciated the human touches—the dead marigolds that should have been removed some time ago, the soccer ball lying in the impatiens, smashing them. At the back of the yard he spotted a little cross made of Tinkertoys, with a tiny mound of fresh dirt in front of it. Robbie's hamster.

Cook made his way back to the grill. Dan was still leaning intently over the fish. He suddenly swore and stabbed the fish with his knife, then grabbed at the two spatulas on his waist loops, struggling with them like a double-holstered greenhorn in a shootout. He freed them and wrestled the fish off the grill. He set it on a wooden platter, where it promptly broke into several small pieces.

Breathing heavily, Dan said, "There's a two-second window when it's ready. I missed the window. It's overdone." He laughed bitterly and looked at Cook. "You got a dumbshit cook, it's gonna be a dumbshit meal, right? What's she expect?"

Cook shrugged. "For my part, I don't care. I don't like food much."

Dan frowned. "What do you mean?"

Cook shrugged again. "I just don't like food."

Dan looked wildly perplexed. "So what do you do instead?"

"Oh I eat, like everybody else. But it bores me."

Dan laughed softly. "I'll try to make it interesting for you by giving you a job. I want you to say the fish is perfect. Say it's the best goddamn fish you've ever had."

Cook forced the grin of a jovial conspirator. "All right. I'll do my best."

"Sound like you mean it."

"I will."

"Here we go." Dan led the way up the stairs.

Beth greeted them at the back door and took the platter. "Gee, honey," she said. "It looks like mashed potatoes."

Robbie, still seated at the table, laughed out loud, but his eyes remained on his book. It wasn't clear what he was laughing at.

"It so happens that I *like* mashed potatoes," said Dan. He untied his apron and tossed it on a chair. Beth brooded silently over the fish and set it on the table. As she walked back into the kitchen Dan caught Cook's attention, then rocked his hand back and forth between them, his three middle fingers clenched, his little finger pointing at Cook and his thumb at himself, while he mouthed in rhythm with the rocking of his hand, "You and me, you and me."

Beth came back with a water pitcher and they all sat down.

"Fish," said Robbie, looking at the platter. "Yum.

Yummy-yum-yum-yummy-yummy." He turned away from it and took a big bite of the frozen pizza Beth had baked for him.

"Wine, Jeremy?" Dan held the bottle over Cook's glass, about to pour.

"No, thanks," Cook said quickly.

Dan poured some for his wife as she began to serve the fish. "Beth makes a lovely salmon," he said.

"But you grilled it, honey."

"Yeah, but the seasoning's what's important. That's what makes it special. Give him more, honey. Yeah. Take it, Jeremy. Good. There you are. Now, dig in. Right. Chew it up good. Unh-hunh. What do you think?"

Dan talked the fish right into Cook's gullet. It seemed so bathed in words, and Cook felt so robbed of independent speech, that when he said, "Very tasty," he felt as if the fish were saying it, calling the message back up Cook's throat. He was about to say more, but Beth beat him to it.

"It *is* good," she said, licking her fingers. She had popped a piece into her mouth. "Nice going, honey."

Cook looked at Dan, but his face was surprisingly blank as he poured himself some wine. It seemed to be a joyless moment for him.

"So," said Dan, "what happens, Jeremy? What's on the agenda?"

Cook went on alert. Since Robbie was in the dark, wouldn't it be better to discuss this when he wasn't around? Cook looked at Robbie. He was wolfing his pizza at an astonishing pace.

"There will be a number of activities," Cook said. He let them ponder that word—a distant echo from the daycare center at Wabash. "I'll be letting you know about them as they come up."

"We've told Robbie about the survey you're doing of the language of St. Louis," Beth said to him. But she was looking at Dan.

"Do you know where words come from?" Robbie asked.

"My teacher's always talking about where words come from."

"Sure," said Cook. "That's part of what I do."

"Like, do you know where 'salmon' comes from?"

"No," Cook said flatly. The truth was he hated etymology. People always expected him to know the origins of words and he never did.

"How about 'napkin'?" Robbie said.

"Nope." Once—just once—Cook had been able to give an etymology when called on. It was for the word "starboard"—from the Old English "steorbord," literally "steering side," because the rudder was on the right side of Anglo-Saxon vessels. He had delivered this information at a dinner party, and even though it was solicited, he felt uniquely responsible for disabling the conversation, which limped for the rest of the evening. That was the curse of etymology. It brought an initial rush of elation, but after that came emptiness and despair.

Robbie said, "Do you know anything about parts of speech?"

Cook brightened. "I'm real good at parts of speech."

"We're learning them in school."

"Already?" said Cook. "That's great."

"It's repulsive," Robbie said. This made Cook laugh, which seemed to surprise Robbie, then please him.

"What about tonight?" Dan said to Cook. "What happens tonight?"

Robbie evidently assumed his father's question was meant for him, and said, "There's a Garfield thing at eight-thirty. If I do my book report now, then my *parts of speech*"—he gave Cook a sneer, as if Cook had invented them—"I can just make it."

Dan said, "What about math? Don't you have any math homework?"

"Did it at school."

"Why do they call it homework if you can do it at school?"

"I didn't call it homework," Robbie said coolly. "You did."

Dan looked at Cook and rolled his eyes, as if to say, "Some kid, hunh?" Beth smiled.

They ate silently for a while. Robbie scooted his chair out and said, "Let me know when the activities begin."

"Okay," said Cook.

They watched him carry his dishes into the kitchen. He put them in the sink with a crash and ran upstairs. His footsteps on the stairs made so much noise that for a moment Cook guessed he was angry about something. But a glance at Dan and Beth told him these were just everyday noises.

Dan said, "Jeremy, you sure you don't want any wine?"

"Yes. I'm sure." Cook hesitated. Then, to prevent endless future repetitions, he said, "I don't drink."

"Oh? You got a problem?"

"Honey," Beth said disapprovingly.

"It's all right," Cook said to her. To Dan he said, "I used to have a problem, but now I don't. Which is to say I've got a problem if I drink, which is to say I've got a problem, but for me, not drinking is a smaller problem than drinking."

"Geez, Jeremy," said Dan. "Sounds like you got more problems all by yourself than Beth and me put together."

"What's *with* you?" Beth said to Dan. "You're the one with a problem."

"I'm tense," Dan said. The words exploded, and as soon as they were out he looked spent, defeated.

"I guess we all are," said Cook.

"Not like me," said Dan. He squirmed a bit in his chair. "The man always gets blamed when a marriage is in trouble. It's always the man."

"That's ridiculous," said Beth.

"It's true," said Dan. "People always blame the guy. They always say it was the guy that stunk it up."

Beth looked at Cook, apparently for a comment. He had none. She said to Dan, "Tense or not, you've got to be more careful about talking in front of Robbie. Why did you ask Jeremy what was going to happen right in front of him?" In anger—even mild anger—Beth was not pretty. Cook was disappointed in the change.

Dan stopped chewing. His broad, alert face suddenly looked dumb. He resumed chewing, but more slowly. He took a drink of wine and said, "I figured he could tell us without tipping off why he's really here."

"Couldn't you wait just a few minutes until Robbie was gone?" Beth said.

"I didn't know he was going to dash off so quickly. For all I knew, he was going to hang around us all night."

"In that case we could have sent him upstairs."

Dan took a slow, deep breath. "It's no big deal. Jeremy handled it fine. He's no slouch."

"It *is* a big deal," said Beth. "Robbie is a separate entity. This isn't his concern."

Dan gave Cook a tired look. "My son—the entity."

"You know what I mean," Beth said.

"Okay okay okay. I get the point."

"Good."

Dan seemed not to like that "Good." His body did a slow writhe in the chair. "What if I don't like the alibi we've concocted for Jeremy—the old survey-of-St.-Louis alibi? What if I don't like it?"

"If you want to change our decision about what to tell him, we have to discuss it."

"He's old enough to understand without being upset. I think we should tell him the truth."

"My point is you should have discussed it with me first. You can't just—"

"I'm discussing it now."

"You can't just do it unilaterally."

"I *knew* you were going to say 'unilaterally,'" Dan snapped. "I *knew* it." He put his fork down hard.

Beth stared at him.

"All right," Dan said. "Let's discuss it. I say we tell him."

"I say we don't," Beth said. She turned to Cook. "What do you say?"

"I don't have the foggiest," Cook said. "Can you pass the salad, please?"

"You don't?" Beth said sharply. She seemed annoyed and handed him the salad bowl rather brusquely. "What's the normal procedure?"

Cook saw that he had blundered. "What I meant," he said, "was that it's become a point of dispute between the two of you, and if I told you my view I would be taking sides." Beth stared at him—skeptically, he thought. He decided a change of subject was in order. "Tell me what you folks do."

Beth gave him a blank look. "You mean our jobs?"

"Yes."

"You've got to be kidding," she said. "Don't you know?"

"Not exactly," said Cook, wondering how he had blundered now.

"We spent hours talking with this guy and filling out forms."

"Mr. Pillow?" Cook hoped so. They would think him wonderfully normal in comparison with Pillow.

"No, no. Some other guy from the agency. We spent *hours* on those forms."

"Nothing was given to me."

"Incredible!"

Fortunately, Dan was less outraged than Beth. "If he didn't get them he didn't get them. They probably have their reasons."

"It's ridiculous," said Beth.

"Beth's a music teacher," Dan said.

"Hours we spent on them. *Hours."*

"Really?" Cook said, turning to her. "Do you teach at home or—"

"She teaches at a private elementary school in the city, not far from here."

"What's your instrument?" said Cook.

"It's a *pisser,*" Beth snapped.

"Piano," said Dan. "She's good. I play too, but just for fun."

"But you're good," Beth said, finally switching to their channel. She turned to Cook. "He's good. He just doesn't practice."

"Yes I do," said Dan.

"That's not practicing," said Beth.

"It's not practicing like *you* practice, but it's practicing to me. It's not my *job* or anything."

"What *is* your job?" Cook asked him.

Dan began his answer with a long sigh. "I'm a..." He looked at Beth. "What am I? I never know what to say. I used to be a geographer, but now I'm a printer."

"A printer?" said Cook.

Beth said, "You're co-manager of the business, honey. Come on."

"Right." Dan took a swallow of wine. When he set his glass down he seemed a little surprised to see Cook still looking at him. Evidently for him the subject was closed.

"Dan and my brother run the place," said Beth. "It's a midsize printing plant. My father founded it forty years ago."

"Ah," said Cook.

"Dan does beautiful maps. He's a great cartographer. Decorative ones, funny ones—all kinds. There are some in the living room. I'll show you after dinner. The plant does some map printing, and that's how Dan first got interested in the business." Beth looked at Dan appreciatively. She seemed to be waiting for him to follow up. When he didn't, she turned to Cook and said, "Did you talk at all with the man from your agency who was here?" It wasn't an angry question. She was over that and was looking pretty again.

"No," said Cook.

"So you don't know what he said about Dan and me."

Dan laughed. "Helluva thing."

Beth grinned. "Maybe we shouldn't tell him."

"A helluva thing. Go ahead. Tell him."

"Yeah," said Cook. "Tell me this helluva thing."

Beth said, "He told us there was a horror in our marriage."

Cook's whole body gulped, like a frog's.

"Actually," said Dan, "he said, 'There is a horror at the core of your marriage.'"

"Right," Beth said. "'At the core.'"

"What did you say?" Cook asked.

"What *can* you say?" said Beth. "It was such a shock. Dan made jokes. He said, 'Just one?' And he said, 'Aren't there any on the periphery?'"

Dan laughed. "Helluva thing."

"What is it?" Cook asked. "What's the horror?"

"He wouldn't tell us," said Beth.

"Didn't you ask him? I mean, didn't you insist?"

"Of course! But he wouldn't say."

"But—"

Robbie appeared in the doorway from the kitchen. "Have you guys seen my Leif Ericsson book?" He looked at his parents. There was a pause.

"I took it back to the library on my way to work," said Dan.

Robbie's face collapsed. "But I *need* it. My book report is due tomorrow."

"Tomorrow?"

"I'm *dead* without it." Robbie looked at his mother. "I *told* you I wasn't done with it."

"Don't blame Mommy," said Dan. "I'm the one who took it back. We can go get it now if it's that important." He stood up from the table and looked at Cook. "Want to take a ride, Jeremy?"

"Are you done eating?" Beth said to Dan.

"Yeah." He hesitated. "Are you mad because I want to do this?"

"Why would I be mad?"

"Because it's kind of an abrupt end to the meal."

Beth shrugged.

"What if someone else got it?" Robbie said, a whine in his voice.

"We'll just have to see," Dan said calmly. He turned to Beth. "Leave the dishes for when I get back."

"I'll help," said Cook.

"Honey," Beth said to Dan, "didn't you ask me this morning if you could take all of the books back to the library?"

"I don't know. Did I?" Dan was leaning away, obviously eager to go.

"And I said, 'All of *our* books.'"

Dan gave her a blank look. "Yeah? So?"

"'*Our* books.' Yours and mine."

Dan laughed. "So I'm supposed to know from that that I shouldn't take Robbie's? Geez."

"Yes," said Beth. "That's exactly what I meant. 'All of *our* books.'"

Dan's face darkened with thought, or anger, or both. "'Our,'" he said. "'Our.' It means 'belonging to us,' right? Us—you, me, and Robbie."

"But I didn't mean Robbie," said Beth. "I meant you and me. 'All of *our* books.'"

"You keep *saying* it like I'm suddenly going to be overwhelmed with understanding," Dan said, his voice suddenly higher. "How was I supposed to know you didn't mean Robbie?"

"It's obvious."

Dan groaned.

"'*Our*,'" said Beth. "The way I said it, it makes no sense any other way. Why would I say it like that? Who else is involved? The neighbors? I meant 'our'—"

"In a contrastive sense," said Cook.

This cut the discussion off as effectively as if Cook had produced a battle-ax and sliced the table in half.

"Sorry," Cook said.

"Don't apologize," Beth said to Cook. "You're right."

"Oh," said Dan. "The linguist has spoken? I don't accept that. I just don't accept that."

"Doesn't the library close pretty soon?" said Robbie.

"Yes," said Dan. "*Our* library closes in *our* town at an early *hour.*" This involuntary pun confused him for a moment, but he hurried on. "I'm taking *our* son, a kid that, incredible as it may sound, I often refer to when I speak." He turned to Cook. "Jeremy? Coming?"

"Sure," said Cook. He was feeling rather exhilarated from the direction the conversation had taken. He stood up and said, "Great dinner, Beth." As he joined Dan he said, "You know, this misunderstanding couldn't have arisen in seventh-century England."

"Why?" said Dan. "No local libraries?"

"No, no. Because of the dual pronoun number. I'll explain it. Most languages have a singular and a plural—right? Early Old English had a *dual* number in addition to those. It had one pronoun meaning 'belonging to me,' another—the dual one—that meant 'belonging to the two of us,' and a third that meant 'belonging to the three-or-more of us.' Isn't that something?"

Dan frowned deeply.

"In fact, if you let me think a minute, I can give you the different versions of the whole sentence in question. Listen up, Robbie." Cook put his arm around the boy as the three of them headed out of the room. "I'm going to speak some Old English. Nobody's talked like this for a thousand years."

Six

On the way to the library, Cook was nagged by a fear that he had offended Beth at the end of dinner. He was sure he hadn't *said* anything offensive. All he had done was help translate the devilish pronoun under dispute. He was okay as far as that went. But he couldn't shake the feeling that he had done something—or left something undone.

Could it have been that Dan, Robbie, and he had exited as an exclusive group? A male group? Even so, why did Cook feel guilty? Dan had invited him to come along. Was it Cook's responsibility to leap up and say, "Hold on, now. What about Beth?" Of course not.

He had complimented her on the dinner, so he was covered there. How had she taken his compliment? He couldn't remember, because he hadn't actually looked at her. The truth was he had more or less forgotten her. Should he feel guilty for that? People forgot about people all the time. You talk to Joe, you turn to Frank, you wink at Ellen—you leave people behind when you move on to others. Think of the people he had spoken with in his life and forgotten about. Thousands of them. Was it a huge resentful throng?

One good thing had happened, at least: the linguist had done something linguistic. Who would have guessed that the Old English pronoun system could shed light on a twentieth-century marital misunderstanding? You never knew what might come in handy. The next time they quarreled, all of Cook's Kickapoo might come back to him in a flash and save the day. Who was it who said, "In observation, chance favors those who are most prepared"? Somebody, by God. Maybe Pillow's faith in him was justified. He did have abundant knowledge about language, at least. "At least"? Why "at least"? What else was there but language?

Cook was free to pursue these thoughts because Dan and Robbie were occupied in the front seat of the van by a song on the radio. They beat time to it and sang snatches. Cook watched and thought someone ought to do a study of what bits of songs got sung by listeners and what bits didn't. Was that a linguistic question? You bet it was. Everything was a linguistic question these days. And if it wasn't, he'd make it one.

"You like him?" Dan asked Cook over his shoulder.

"Who?"

"Billy Joel."

"Never heard of him."

Dan laughed. Cook wondered why.

Robbie turned around and looked at Cook. "You've never heard of Billy Joel?"

"Nope."

"Geez," said Dan. "You're serious."

"That's incredible," said Robbie.

Dan said, "He's really a major figure."

This angered Cook. "I'm a linguist, okay? I don't follow this stuff."

"Okay," said Dan. "No one says you have to."

"You ever heard of Elvis?" asked Robbie.

Dan said, "Drop it, Robbie. Here we are." He had pulled the van into the library lot and coasted into a parking space. He turned off the ignition, but the engine continued running in a prolonged fit of coughing. Dan and Robbie joined it in a funny imitation, their shoulders shaking as the van shook. It was obviously something they had done before.

When the engine quieted, Robbie said, "Here's the plan. Dad, you check downstairs at the desk. I'll run upstairs and check there. We'll meet downstairs. Okay? Ooh—and I gotta get a book on hamsters, so my new one doesn't croak on me. I just hope I don't get that witch at the checkout counter." He hurried out of the van and ran full speed to the front doors.

Dan asked Cook if he wanted to come with him or wait. Cook had spotted a bank of pay phones in the brick entryway, and he told Dan he had to make a phone call. Dan looked at him as if for further explanation, but when he got none he just said he and Robbie wouldn't be long and went on into the library.

Cook walked to the phones. He took Pillow's business card from his pocket and dialed the home number given on it. An answering machine came on with Pillow's voice, apparently speaking from the bottom of a well. Cook had experienced slow, self-conscious messages on these things, but Pillow's set a record. Cook told the voice to shut up. He hung up and fished in his pocket for another quarter, this time dialing Pillow's office number.

"Pillow."

This no-nonsense way of saying hello threw Cook for a moment. "Roy? Jeremy Cook here."

Pillow responded with silence. Had he forgotten who Cook was?

"I'm at the Wilsons'," Cook said helpfully.

"Of course you are. I know that."

"I have a question. Is there a horror at the core of the Wilson marriage?"

"Don't be silly," said Pillow. "Of course there is."

Cook flinched as if he had been slapped. "Why didn't you tell me about it?"

"Tell you? Good God, man. It goes without saying."

"It does?" Cook forced himself not to shout. "What *is* it?"

"Just a minute, Jeremy. I've got another call."

Cook started to protest, but Pillow went away and left a

void behind. A minute passed. Then another minute. Cook shouted into the emptiness. A moment later he heard a promising click. Then he heard several clicks bunched together. These climaxed in a dial tone.

Cook held the receiver at arm's length, looked at it, and said to it, "You are a prick."

A black teenager at an adjacent phone raised his eyebrows at Cook.

Cook found another quarter and redialed the Pillow Agency. The line was busy. "Stupid fucking *twit,*" said Cook. The teenager grinned broadly. Cook dialed again and got Pillow, whose first word was "Sorry."

"Right," said Cook.

"It was Mrs. Pillow. I was going to get right back to you, Jeremy. You shouldn't have hung up."

"The horror, Roy. Tell me about the horror."

"After I spoke with Mrs. Pillow and discovered you had hung up, I tried to call you at the Wilsons'. You told me you were there."

"Never mind that. Tell me about—"

"You lied."

Cook wanted to slump to his knees. "I didn't mean I was literally there. I was just reminding you who I was when I said I was at the Wilsons'."

"Reminding me?" Pillow said with a laugh. "You mean you thought I might have forgotten?"

"Yes."

"Lord, Lord, Lord. Insecurity. It's the universal disease, isn't it? Mrs. Pillow and I were discussing this very subject at lunch. We disagreed in our views, but I don't think frank disagreement is a threat to love. Do you?"

"You had lunch with your wife today?"

"Yes. I had prime rib."

"You said you were going to have lunch with me."

"I mentioned in a general way I would like to have lunch with you someday, yes, that's true."

"You said *today.*"

"Oh come now, Jeremy. *You're* the one who said you were at the Wilsons' when you weren't. And you're calling *me* a liar?"

"You said it. You said 'today.'"

"You *heard* 'today,' Jeremy, but I'm sure I said 'someday.' Perhaps you were just hungry."

Cook laughed wildly. "Let's go back to the reason I called. The horror at the core of the Wilson marriage."

"Yes?"

"How can you say 'yes' like that, as if it's an everyday thing?"

"It is, Jeremy. There's a horror at the core of *every* marriage—and it's the very same horror."

"What do you mean? What is it?"

"You have *The Pillow Manual*. It will lead you to it. Are you having a regular social evening?"

"Well, I—"

"Are you demonstrating your conversational competence?"

"Well, I'm—"

"Have you asked twenty-five questions?"

"No, I—"

"You see? There's plenty still to do. My advice to you is to roll up your sleeves and get to work."

"I hate that expression."

"Pardon?"

"'Roll up your sleeves.' I hate it."

"Well, I'm sorry, Jeremy."

"I really hate it."

"I'll try not to use it in the future. If it's on your hate list in *The Woof of Words,* I don't remember it. But may I change the subject?"

Cook was so impressed by this burst of decorum that he said yes.

"I've been going over the questionnaire you filled out this morning. One of your answers puzzled me." Cook heard the rustling of paper. "Here we are. The question is 'Rank the following social situations from *least appealing to you* to *most appealing to you* by numbering them from one *(least appealing)* to ten *(most appealing).*' Do you remember the question, Jeremy? It gives 'cocktail party for twenty,' 'country club dinner dance'. . . ."

"Sure. I remember it."

"I don't think you understood the instructions. You wrote a 'one' next to all of them."

"That's right. They were all 'least appealing' to me."

"But compared to what? What social situation does appeal to you?"

"None."

"Oh come now."

"I mean it."

"Not even 'quiet dinner party for four'?"

"Sounds awful."

"You don't like groups? Is that what you're saying?"

"Yes."

"Do you like people?"

"Of *course* I like people. What do you think?"

"Yes, I can see from your other answers here that you . . . that you . . ." Pillow fell silent. Then he said, "You say here that you've slept with sixteen women in the past five years."

"I wasn't crazy about answering that," said Cook. "I was going to leave it blank, but I was afraid you'd get the wrong idea."

"It also asks how many of them you loved. You did leave this one blank."

"I guess I should have put a zero. The answer is zero."

"And under 'Explain'—the follow-up to that question—you again wrote nothing."

"What's to explain?"

Pillow made a flabbergasted noise. "Frankly, Jeremy, it cries out for an explanation. You slept with sixteen women but didn't find one of them lovable?"

Cook wanted to laugh. Pillow made them sound like

teddy bears. "I think this is my business, Roy."

"It's Pillow business now."

"I didn't love them. What more can I say? I don't know why. Maybe you can tell me. You want to meet them? Want me to hunt them up and bring them by?"

"Do any of them live in the area?"

Cook laughed. His laughter echoed so loudly off the brick and glass walls that two librarians at the front counter looked through the window at him. So did Dan and Robbie, who had just walked up to the counter. "I was *joking*, Roy," Cook said.

"Oh."

"I don't see why you need all this stuff, anyway. You've already hired me, right?"

"Oh, there's no question about that. But I'm concerned, Jeremy. You know how I feel about love."

"Yes. You told me."

"I believe in it."

"I know. You told me."

"I would give my life for it."

"That won't be necessary."

"Love, Jeremy."

"Yes, Roy."

"Trust."

"Yes. Trust."

"We hear those words so often that we forget what they mean."

"Yeah, well, that happens." Cook watched Dan and Robbie check out their books.

"I wish those words were outlawed. Forbidden. We would have to invent new ones."

"A powerful idea, Roy." Cook wasn't the least bit interested.

"The new words would *mean* something. For a while, anyway."

"Ah," said Cook, suppressing a yawn, "but what then?"

"Let's make up new words, Jeremy." Pillow said this with frightening enthusiasm. He made it sound like a child's game.

"I'd rather play Candyland, Roy."

"Pardon?"

"May I change the subject?"

"No."

"What? Come on. I let *you* change it."

"You want to talk about the horror. Time to end our chat, Jeremy. We've come full circle."

"I hate *that* expression, too."

"Sorry. It's purged from my lexicon. I never want to say anything to upset you. To be on the safe side, I'll say nothing more." Pillow hung up.

Cook stared at the dead phone. As he hung it up, Robbie and Dan came out the door. Robbie waved a book for Cook to see and then sprinted all the way to the van. He seemed to run flat out just about every chance he got.

Dan came up to Cook. "We found it. I'm off the hook."

"Which hook is that?" Cook asked.

"Beth's meat hook. She's got one on the wall in every room. Haven't you seen them?" Dan leaned toward Cook, screwed his face up, and piped, "'You've made your house very comfortable'" in blatant mockery of him. "But what about the meat hooks, Jeremy? Eh? What about the meat hooks?" Dan laughed insanely.

For a moment Cook wondered if Dan had had a snort of something in some alcove of the library. He had trouble matching this angry man with the pleasant fellow who had been willing to dash off and fetch his son's book. Cook was so unnerved by Dan's outburst that he could think of nothing to say. He was silent as they walked to the van.

Pillow believed in love. What did it mean? Take Dan. Here was a guy who, if you asked him (or if *she* asked him), would probably say he loved his wife. He might even say he loved her a lot, or a great deal, or a bushel and a peck. But listen to the way he talked about her. Just listen to him.

Seven

"So, you see, it's a bunch of short hops. Norway to the Faeroe Islands. From there to Iceland. Iceland to Greenland. Greenland to Newfoundland. That's how the Vikings did it. It's a lot easier than Columbus's way. If you look at the route Columbus had to take, it's one big scary ocean waiting to swallow you up." Dan looked from Robbie to Beth, who was across the living room. He added obscurely, "Just like Mommy."

"Yeah," said Robbie, looking with fascination at the large globe near the fireplace. "Hop. Hop. Hop." He hopped his fingers along the globe. "My book didn't explain it like that." He gave his father an odd look—more curious than appreciative.

Cook had been watching and listening from the couch. He looked back to Robbie's Leif Ericsson book, which he had picked up from the coffee table. A picture of a Viking stuffing his face with grapes stared back at him.

Dan said, "Time for bed, Robbie."

"Kisses!" Beth called out in a Pavlovian response. She rose from her knees, where she had been shelving records, and kissed Robbie good night. Dan said he would tuck him in. Robbie and Cook said good night to each other.

This left Cook alone with Beth. She sat down in a large

stuffed chair across from him and put her feet up on the ottoman. Cook felt a nudge from "Have a regular social evening"—it was palpable, as if Roy Pillow had slipped his hand underneath him and goosed him. The result was that his mind went blank.

One of the chapters in *The Woof of Words* was devoted to things in language that Cook hated. In it he proudly set a new standard for unapologetic prescriptivist bias. Among the items on his hate list were "arch" as an adjective (he could never remember its meaning), "ombudsman" (an ugly word), "jejune" (it reminded him of "jujubes," a candy that used to stick annoyingly to his teeth), and tediously unclever self-corrections like "famous—or rather *in*famous" and "despite this—or perhaps *because of* this." Also in this chapter were sentences he hated because they were completely predictable once a social role was defined, such as that of first-time guest.

Unfortunately, as Cook now searched for something to say to Beth, he felt straitjacketed by his own harshness on this subject. Two chestnuts from that chapter danced on his tongue, but he couldn't bring himself to say them. The first —"How long have you lived here?"—was dumb not only on grounds of predictability, but because it always clumsily triggered the countercliché, "Do you mean in this house or in this city?" Cook once actually responded to this request for clarification by saying, "Either one"—a blundering admission of insincerity for which he would always feel guilty.

The second—a springtime favorite—was "Are you going anywhere this summer?" This was a decent question, in that it could produce a whole bunch of words on both sides, and Cook was actually preparing to say it, when it suddenly occurred to him that Beth's occupation as a music teacher provided a topic that was consistent with his position on originality and interesting to him as well. Incredible as it seemed, there was promise on the horizon of social interaction without sex and yet without boredom.

Ideas rushed upon him—all the private theories about

music he had entertained over the years. He heard himself blurt out, "What can we learn from the birds?"

"What?" said Beth.

"I mean musically. What kind of scale do birds use?"

"I have no idea."

"I mean . . . Western? Eastern?" He hoped these were different, and that there was only one of each.

Beth shrugged. "Search me."

Cook's topic, launched with such hope, was suddenly stuck in the mud. He was at a loss to develop the question. He had been carrying it around with him, and it seemed to grow weightier every year—every time he heard a goddamned bird, in fact—but now that it was out there, it amounted to nothing.

"Forget that," said Cook. "Here's another question. Are there some composers that are more fun to remember than to listen to?"

"Like who?"

"I'm thinking of Chopin. Isn't he prettier in the mind, in memory, than when you're actually hearing him?"

Beth shook her head immediately, as if she had settled this very question back in junior high. "No," she said.

Cook wanted to defend this point. He wanted to hold his ground. The only defense he could think of, though, was a rather high-pitched "Really?"

"Not for me anyway."

"When I was in college," Cook said, lurching on to his third theory, "I had a Nonesuch recording of Scarlatti harpsichord sonatas that seemed to be an aphrodisiac. Every time I brought a girl to the apartment and played it I . . . I got lucky. You ever hear of that?"

"No, Jeremy," Beth said, smiling. "Word of your good luck never reached me."

"*Domenico* Scarlatti," Cook said, tickled to show he knew there was more than one Scarlatti. Then it struck him as ridiculous to think that a clarification of this could enhance the look of his theory. Theory? Whatever possessed him to think of it as a theory? Everything he'd said suddenly seemed ludicrous. All those years with these paltry ideas, anticipating a thunderous airing of them. What a dunce he was.

Cook sighed. "How long have you lived here?" he asked.

"Do you mean—"

"In this house," Cook snapped.

Beth's eyebrows shot up and came right back down. "About ten years."

"Ten years, eh?" He paused, sighed, and said, "Are you going anywhere this summer?"

"Yes," Beth said, her face brightening. "Dan's taking me to Italy."

Cook quickly dismissed the memory of his own failed sentences in order to recoil inwardly at hers, with its central idea of the husband "taking" the wife somewhere. Cook had never understood this concept. Didn't Beth know where Italy was? Did Dan have to show her? Or did she mean that Dan would be piloting the jet to Rome? Or did she antici-pate a crippling disease overcoming her, and Dan literally wheeling her all over the peninsula? What did it mean?

Cook realized Beth had been speaking while he had been privately abusing her sentence. Now she stopped and looked at him. She had probably talked about Italy, but he didn't want to risk a follow-up remark that didn't follow up. He opted for spontaneity, lunging at the first idea that popped into his head. "When did Robbie's hamster die?"

Beth hesitated. Perhaps she was seeking a link between Dan's husbandly shepherding of her to Italy and a dead ro-dent. "Last week."

"I see," Cook said—a remark so intelligent that it created a long silence, during which Dan returned from putting Robbie to bed.

Dan looked at the two of them and called attention to the deathly stillness in the room by stopping in his tracks and saying, "Don't let me interrupt! I don't want to interrupt! Go right ahead!" Dan laughed riotously at his joke and sat down on the couch. Cook and Beth exchanged glances.

Cook leaned forward and took a Hershey's Kiss from the bowl on the table. It must have been his tenth one, at least. Ever since he had quit drinking he had been a slave to sweets. His solution was never to buy candy. But as soon as they returned from the library, Beth had set this bowl right in front of him.

"Want me to put some music on?" Dan said, standing up again.

"Sure," said Beth.

"What would you like?"

"Anything you want," said Beth. "But not reggae, okay?"

Dan tensed. He said, "What, then? Just tell me."

"Whatever you want. Only not reggae."

Dan got a crazed look on his face. He turned to Cook. "Any suggestions?"

Cook felt much more relaxed now that Dan was back. "Do you have any Karl Ditters von Dittersdorf?" he asked. He had always loved this man's name.

Beth said, "As a matter of fact we do. I'll get it." She stood up.

"Helluva request," Dan muttered as he sat back down. Under his breath he said, "Whatever you want, only not reggae. Anything you want, only not what you want."

"Oh, stop," Beth said calmly as she looked through the records.

"You like reggae?" Dan said to Cook.

Cook, observing a private rule to be frank about his ignorance on any subject, said, "I don't know him."

Dan gave Cook an odd look, but he said nothing. A string quartet started up. "So," Dan said, starting fresh, "welcome to the City That Hates Itself."

"Don't listen to him," Beth said as she sat back down. "St. Louis used to be called that. Now it's just the City That Dan Hates."

"Are you both from here?" Cook asked.

"Beth is," said Dan. "I'm from San Francisco."

"Really?" said Cook. "I'm from Monterey originally."

"No kidding?" Dan was visibly excited. He looked at Beth. "Monterey."

Beth raised her eyebrows and smiled slightly.

"You never meet anyone from California out here," Dan said to Cook. "The California orientation is longitudinal. It shows up on preference maps that show where people would like to live. Most people like their own latitudes— Minnesotans like the upper Midwest, Southerners like the South. But Californians are different. They like their longitude—anywhere on the west coast, from Vancouver to Mexico."

Cook nodded. "You're right." Whenever his parents had traveled anywhere, it was always north or south, never east. And when he went to Indiana, his friends treated him as if he were a missionary who had taken bizarre vows. "Why are *you* here?" he asked.

"Graduate school—Washington University. And Beth wanted to come back to her hometown, so it worked out well."

Cook always had a hard time processing people's thumbnail biographies. They swallowed up the years so fast that they left him feeling mentally slow. "You didn't meet here?"

"No. We met in college. U.C. Santa Cruz. Hell, right across the bay from you, Jeremy."

"Ah," said Cook, his eyes going to one of the wall maps Dan had drawn. He had studied it earlier, when he was alone in the room for a moment. It was a comic decorative map of a seaside area with architecture drawn in exaggerated style. He had *thought* it was the Santa Cruz Boardwalk, but he couldn't believe he would find it here, on a St. Louis wall.

Dan said, "We met in college and got married the year after we graduated. We knew we had a sure thing. Right?"

Beth gave him a neutral look.

"Maybe not a sure thing," Dan said. "A probable thing." He sighed. "Maybe an iffy thing. Maybe a—"

"How about you, Jeremy?" Beth asked. "Where have you been between Monterey and St. Louis?"

Cook told them about his years—many years—at U.C. Berkeley, where he had enrolled as an ugly, bewildered freshman and emerged as a good-looking Ph.D. in linguistics. He told them about his work at the Wabash Institute. Beth listened closely—so closely she made Cook a little nervous. She asked him how old he was, and he told her: thirty-two. Her response was a frown.

Dan said, "I'm thirty-four. Beth's thirty-three. She's sandwiched in between us."

While Cook's mind filled with a specific but improbable image, Dan suggested he and Cook try to find a link in their past that spanned the seventy-five miles or so separating their hometowns. But several minutes of questions about possible mutual acquaintances or jointly attended events produced nothing. They ended up reminiscing over old Art Hoppe columns in the *San Francisco Chronicle*.

Then Dan said, out of the blue, "This isn't Dittersdorf."

Beth made a slight scoffing noise. "Sure it is." She pointed to the album cover at the end of the living room, which she had left propped on a shelf and facing out, like a record store clerk. "See?"

Dan shook his head. "It's Haydn. It says Dittersdorf, but there must be some Haydn on the record, too."

"That's impossible," said Beth. "We don't have any records like that. Jeremy, this is Dittersdorf, isn't it?"

Cook furrowed his brow. He had no idea. He just liked the guy's name.

Dan said, "It's Haydn. There's this thing that Haydn does. I just heard it."

"What thing?" Beth said.

"I don't know. I can't describe it. You're the one who knows stuff like that."

Beth stood up and went to the album cover, saying under her breath, "This *thing*." She looked at the cover and waved it in the air. "It's all Dittersdorf," she said. But she gave Dan a kindly look, as if to say she wouldn't hold his error against him.

"Check the record," said Dan.

Beth flashed a number of responses in quick succession: irritation, then realization that Dan could be right after all, then something deeper—something worse. Dan started to stand up, but she said, "I can check it," and he sat back down. Beth took a long time reading the record label as it went around the turntable. Then she went to a row of records in the bookcase, and after a moment's search she took one from the shelf. She slid the record out of it, read the label, and said, "You're right. The last person to play these put them in the wrong covers." Her voice was slightly thinner.

Dan reached over and tapped Cook's knee familiarly. He whispered so softly that Cook barely heard him: "She's mad now. She'll take it out on us."

Eerily on cue, Beth turned and said to Dan, "Did you have both of these out at the same time?"

"I don't think so."

"Well, someone did." Beth turned to Cook. "Why didn't *you* notice it wasn't Dittersdorf, Jeremy? You're the one who requested him."

"Well, actually..."

"You want me to put him on?" She held the true Dittersdorf record up.

"No, no," said Cook.

"You want it, you got it," she snapped, and she switched the records.

Cook sat very still, hoping this incident was over. Beth seemed to be making an awful lot out of it. Another string quartet began, indistinguishable to Cook's ear from the previous one. Under cover of the music, Dan whispered to Cook, hissing ominously: "She's not done."

Beth returned to her seat. She looked at Cook and asked, "Are you married, Jeremy?"

"No."

"Ever been?"

"No."

"Ever come close?"

Cook thought. Paula. Yes. He thought some more. No. He sighed. He thought of Pillow's questionnaire—sixteen unlovables bedded in five years, zero lovables. He hadn't been able to bring himself to write "one," for Paula. But maybe he was just mad at her for leaving him. Maybe he was crazy in love with her. He sighed again. He hated entertaining the opposite of the thought he had just been entertaining. It made him feel as if anything could be true.

"Must be a toughie," Dan said.

Beth didn't smile. "The answer's probably no, only he doesn't want to admit it."

"I imagine he was pretty isolated in Indiana," Dan said. "Out in the country and all."

"But what about Berkeley? He was there for—what did he say? Eight years?"

"Yeah," said Dan, "but college is different. He probably came close in Berkeley, but then backed off, and out in Indiana, when he might have been more interested, it was slim pickings."

Beth gave Dan a cool look. "Sounds like a version of your life the way you wish it had happened."

"Not really," Dan said.

"Don't you wish we had only 'come close' in Santa Cruz?"

"I wasn't saying that."

"Sometimes? Don't you wish it sometimes? You can tell me. It's not a crime to think it." Beth looked at Cook. "We haven't forgotten about you, Jeremy. Just speak up when you're ready to answer."

Cook nodded. He had an urge to remain silent that went beyond his memory-bag of regrets over Paula. Simply put, he wanted to go on watching them.

"What would have happened?" Dan said. "I mean if we had only come close. What do you think?"

"You would have still come to St. Louis," said Beth. "To Wash. U."

"Yeah." Dan laughed. "And you would have come back, too. We'd have run into each other all the time."

"You'd have been unhappy."

"You think so?" Dan said, surprised. Then, resigned, he said, "Yeah. I'd start looking for you. I'd call. We'd get together. Jesus. It's like a story where a guy tries to change his life by tinkering with his past, only it comes out the same." He took a quick breath. "Wait. Would you have lived at home?"

Beth thought. "For a while. Until I found a place."

"Yeah. Okay. I would have met the whole gang and seen 'em in action. We wouldn't have gotten married after all." Dan grinned.

Cook expected Beth to react angrily to this slight to her family. Instead, she laughed softly. She looked at Cook again. "Well?"

Cook swallowed. He cleared his throat. "There was a woman named Paula." This sentence had the ring of a prelude. Indeed, it *was* a prelude. But he had no idea what to say next.

"Yes?" said Beth.

Cook shrugged.

"Come *on,*" Beth said, almost bullying him.

"The man's in pain," Dan said. "Lay off, honey."

Beth folded her arms across her chest. "I want to get some idea about what he knows. This is serious." She looked at Cook. "There's a lot at stake here."

Cook said, "I know there is."

"Dan and me. Robbie."

"I know."

"Our whole lives are at stake."

"I know that," said Cook. "You think I don't know that?"

"This is it. This is the only kind of counseling I could get Dan to agree to."

"Yeah," Dan said. "I think it's a great idea." His tone was

strangely upbeat, at odds with Beth's intensity. "The guy lives in. Right underfoot. I think it's terrific."

Beth said, "So I jumped at the idea—I was desperate!— but now that you're here, I don't know. A *linguist?* And a *man?* I was told we'd have a woman. And a thirty-two-year-old bachelor? A bachelor who's never even come close to marriage, or if he has, he's too tongue-tied to talk about it? What can you possibly know about commitment?" She looked at Cook. Then, as a new thought seemed to strike her, she said, "You're not gay, are you?"

"No."

"You could tell us."

"I would. I'm not."

"It would be much better if you were. That would be fine."

"I'm not."

"Blast the luck!" said Dan.

"Listen," Cook said. "Let me say something." He took a deep breath. "You've got a point, Beth. I don't know what I know about commitment. But the question is what do I know about language. You two need to learn how you behave verbally with each other. I can tell you. I really can."

"I believe you, Jeremy," Dan said. "I'm glad you're here."

Beth could have said something nice. But she didn't. She just sat. Cook wished she hadn't done that.

He also wished he didn't have to administer the cursed questionnaire from *The Pillow Manual*. It was getting late, and he was afraid Beth would complain when he brought it up. But he had to—it was a Day One assignment.

"I'm supposed to ask you some questions," Cook said. "They're up in my room."

"Good," said Beth. "Let's get cracking."

Cook tried not to look surprised. "Who wants to go first? I have to ask each of you separately."

It was established that since Dan would be rising early to take Robbie to school, he should go first. As they discussed this, Cook was surprised to learn that Dan would be coming back home in the morning instead of going to work. He had arranged to take some time off and would be home for as long as he could manage. Also, the school where Beth taught had just completed its term. Cook, Dan, and Beth would simply be there—would simply *be*.

Cook went upstairs for his tape recorder and list of questions from *The Pillow Manual*. He reviewed his performance thus far. He couldn't really say he had had a regular social evening. In the normal course of things, a hostess wouldn't challenge a guest's capacity to make a loving commitment. As for demonstrating his conversational competence, he had been a perfect antihero. Every time he had opened his mouth he had felt like Harpo Marx honking his horn. There remained the twenty-five questions. With luck he would ask them without losing much more of his face, and the sun would set on Day One.

He returned to the living room, where Dan awaited him with his hands folded on his lap like a good boy. While he put the questions to Dan, Beth busied herself with some laundry in the basement. When it was her turn, Dan showered and went to bed.

When Beth's turn was over, Cook said good night to her and, mindful of the courier due the next day to take the tape recorder, stayed up until nearly three in the morning transcribing the responses, editing them (including one major cut), and collating them. To what end he did this he didn't know, though he assumed it was so that he could study them someday.

This was what he got:

Q: How long have you been married?
DAN: Eight and a half years.
BETH: Eleven years.

Q: Describe your courtship.
DAN: Well, we met at a party. We hit it off right away. It was kind of neat—you know how a party has a flow and you

drift around and get interrupted and separated from people all the time? Whenever that happened to us we made a
conscious effort to get back together. It was clear what
was going on. It was kind of exciting realizing that. I
asked her if she wanted to come over to my place, and she
said sure, and that was that. *(Pause)* Is Beth gonna listen
to my answers? *(Pause)* You don't *think* so? You don't
know? That's pretty bizarre.

BETH: He pursued me. *(Laughs)* It's funny how traditional it
was. We met in our senior year, and Dan kept asking me
out and I just kept going. As I look back, I think I fell for
him for the wrong reasons—he was good-looking,
funny, lively. Not *wrong* reasons, exactly—just insuffi-
cient reasons. But underneath that there were some right
reasons that I didn't even know about, and those are the
things I've come to love about him. I almost feel lucky
about that. I sure didn't plan it. I didn't know *what* I was
doing. Say, does Dan get to hear what I say here? *(Pause)*
You don't? Who's running this show anyway?

Q: Was there a formal proposal of marriage?
DAN: You mean, like down on my knees? Or do you mean
one of those cute things like hiding the engagement ring
in the dessert or something? Don't make me sick.
BETH: No.

Q: How did you decide to get married?
DAN: Beth pushed for it. It was in our fifth year of school.
Beth was getting her teaching credential, and I was picking up some courses in economics—I didn't know what I
was going to do, professionally. We were living in this
great little cabin in the Santa Cruz Mountains. It was an
unheated place, colder than hell on winter mornings. Her
folks were antsy about our living together—our "situation," they called it. They'd complain about it every time
Beth talked to them on the phone, and she started stewing
about it, and she *kept* stewing about it, so I finally said

what the hell, what's the difference? And we got married.

BETH: Dan will say it was because of my folks, but it wasn't. That's just an idea he's stuck on. Basically we picked a date together. We both wanted it.

Q: What quality do you like most in her/him?

DAN: Her warmth.

BETH: He's a great father.

Q: What quality do you like least in her/him?

DAN: Her coldness.

BETH: He doesn't know how to be a husband.

Q: How important is it to you to understand the inner life of your spouse?

DAN: Hey. That's an interesting question. Sure, I'd like to know what makes her tick. Why not? Couldn't hurt.

BETH: Are you kidding? What else is there? I think about Dan almost as much as I think about myself.

Q: Who initiates most of the talk?

DAN: Who initiates it? I guess sometimes I do and sometimes she does. It's pretty even.

BETH: Me.

Q: Describe a typical good talk.

DAN: We both come home from work in a good mood and tell each other funny stories about what happened that day.

BETH: I feel horrible and he says exactly the right thing to make me feel better.

Q: How often do you have a good talk, as you have described it?

DAN: Not for years.

BETH: Never.

Q: Describe a typical bad talk.

DAN: Sure. I come downstairs for breakfast and say good morning and she blasts me.

BETH: I have something important to say and he cuts me off.

Q: What are your fights like?

DAN: Unsatisfying. When I'm right, she can't stand it, so she leaves the room, right in the middle of what I'm saying. I hate that. Why does she do that?

BETH: They hurt. They make me ache from top to bottom. They make no sense. We'll both think we're right, and sometimes I think we *are, both* of us. We need someone to sort it out. We're stuck.

Q: Do you ever enjoy fighting?

DAN: Well, maybe I would if she didn't always leave whenever I make a decent point.

BETH: Anyone who could ever enjoy fighting is sick.

Q: Who wins?

DAN: Excellent question. Excellent. (*Pause*) I don't have an answer. (*Laughs*) I was going to say sometimes I win and sometimes Beth wins, but then I realized that when *she* wins, I'm still pissed off and I still think I'm right, deep down, and she's probably the same way when *I* win. So nobody wins, I guess.

BETH: The way I see it, you both win or you both lose. If anything gets resolved, you both win. If not, you both lose.

Q: What's your sex life like?

DAN: Ah. I knew you'd get to this. And I want to hear all about yours at the earliest opportunity. Ours is excellent. No problem.

BETH: It's surprisingly good. We got in the habit of good sex when we were getting along, and it's carried us through these times.

Q: How often do you have sex?

DAN: Oh... twice a week?

BETH: Once a week.

Q: Are you sure?

DAN: Yeah. Pretty sure. I think so. Why? Does that sound odd? That's average, isn't it? From everything I've read, it's average. Isn't it?

BETH: Like clockwork.

Q: Are you happy with that frequency?

DAN: Funny question. Yeah, I guess so. It's something we've settled into, so we must be. Sure. Why not?

BETH: No.

Q: Who usually initiates sex?

DAN: You know, it's funny. We've fallen into kind of a routine. We'll be in the bedroom watching TV, and we'll be fooling around, and then we'll *really* fool around. Sunday night especially. During *60 Minutes*—it seems to happen a lot during *60 Minutes*. Robbie's always watching Disney in the den, and if we don't tell him to turn it off when it's over he'll just keep watching whatever's on, so... What was the question? Oh—who initiates it? Well, the way I've described it, it's mutual. I'd have to say it's mutual all the way.

BETH: Morley Safer.

Q: Do you both reach orgasm regularly?

DAN: Helluva question. The answer is yes.

BETH: We're very efficient.

Q: Who reaches orgasm first?

DAN: Oh... Beth, I guess. Yeah. Beth.

BETH: Me.

Q: Why?

DAN: It's just something we've decided to do. We like it that way, I guess. Seems to work. Why mess with a good thing?

BETH: Dan hates to go on with it after he's finished, so I always go first.

Q: Do you talk during sex?

DAN: Talk? Not really. What's to say?

BETH: No.

Q: How has sex changed for you over the years?

DAN: Wow. That's a biggie. Let's see...How has it changed? Lemme think. Hmm. Maybe less often, you know? But better. More quality time, you might say.

BETH: When I met Dan, I had a history of meaningless sex. Lots of it, but no real closeness. With Dan, at first I thought I was getting that closeness, but looking back on it now, I don't think I was. I *thought* I was, so it *seemed* better, and it probably *was* better, too—better than what I was used to, anyway—but now I know that it wasn't the true thing. We were so young, such strangers to each other, I don't see how it could have been intimate. It's become more intimate since, over the years, and that's made it a lot better. It's not *perfect,* but it's better. It's changed in other ways, too. I find I require, or *desire,* a longer warm-up period. My ideal sexual experience would annihilate the concept of time. I'd like more dynamics, more rises and falls, more subplots to go with the main plot. I like to be surprised once in a while. My orgasms used to be tenser than they are now. I used to have to work for them. Now, if I'm relaxed enough, which I usually am, they just come of their own accord. It's nice that way, very nice. As for Dan, he's very good in bed—always has been—but he seems less overwhelmed by it all now. His climax is just this thing that happens. He doesn't buck and snort like he used to. He says it's just aging—physiology—and he's probably right. He peaked sexually at eighteen or something, when I didn't even know him

—too bad!—and I'm still moving to my crest. It's just getting better and better for me. I can't seem to get enough, to be honest. So—does that answer your question?

Q: What does he/she do that bugs you?

DAN: Gee. I don't know. I'm not sure it's even worth talking about. I suppose I could name a few things, if I think about it. Let me think. (*Pause*) Well, I guess I could say something about the mail. She never puts it in the same place. When I get it from the mailbox I always put it right there on that table in the entryway. When she gets it there's no telling where it'll end up. On top of the piano. On the toaster oven. Under the newspaper. It's like an Easter egg hunt. I hate it when she beats me to the mail. Hate it. And she never really goes *through* her mail properly. You know what I mean? Me, I have three categories. Pitch, read now, read later. She doesn't have any categories, as far as I can tell. She just shuffles it all around and leaves it, and important stuff gets lost and the junk mail kicks around the house till next Christmas. Another thing —when she sends mail, she never puts the zip code on it. I shouldn't say *never*—I don't want to be unfair—but she leaves it off more often than she should. And she'll stick it out in our mailbox, wedging it under the lid, instead of walking down to the corner with it. A good wind comes up and that baby's gone, blown away and lost in the ivy. Give Beth a letter to mail and the odds are no better than fifty-fifty that it'll make it to its destination. (*Pause*) Well, that wraps up the mail, I guess. You see, to answer your question, I decided to break it down room by room— what is there in each room that reminds me of things she does that bug me. I started on the front porch, where the mailbox is. Now we can move on to the interior of the house . . . [twenty-two minutes not transcribed].

BETH: He knows exactly what I want but he won't give it to me. (*Pause*) What are you waiting for? Next question, please. Oh, we're done? Hmm. Well, I can't say this is the most useful exercise I've ever engaged in, but we'll see what happens, I suppose. Good night, Jeremy.

His transcription and collation concluded, Cook slammed his pen down, groaned, and went to bed.

But when his head hit the pillow his mind took off, hurtling and stumbling through the events of the evening, from his arrival right through to the end. He jumped back up, turned on his light, and went to his desk. He took a yellow legal tablet and wrote a heading across the top of it: THE HORROR! Underneath this he entered a simple declarative sentence.

Then he went to bed—and to sleep.

Eight

"She's a bitch, Roy."

"What?"

"She's a bitch."

"Oh come now."

"That's the horror, isn't it? She's a bitch. But you said it's the same horror in every marriage. Is the woman always a bitch?"

"Oh my," Pillow said. "Oh my."

"That's it, isn't it?" Cook stretched the long phone cord from the third-floor landing to his window. He looked out to the street below, where Beth was vacuuming her car. He wanted to be sure she was still there, out of earshot. "That's the horror, isn't it?"

"No."

"No? Listen. She kept attacking me last night. Said I didn't know beans about commitment."

"Mmm."

"And when she had the chance to say something nice, she passed it up. She held back. It was obvious what she was doing. In sum—a bitch."

"Mmm."

"She overreacts to everything, she complains, she—"

"We do not accept bitches, Jeremy."

"What?"

"The Pillow Agency does not accept them."

Cook tried to clear his head. He wished he had had his morning coffee before calling Pillow. "What are you saying?"

"We don't do bitches. You can't save a marriage with a bitch in it."

"But how do you identify them? How do I know your idea of a bitch is the same as mine?"

"Don't do that, Jeremy. Don't say we speak a different language. Don't."

"Hey. She's vacuuming *my* car now," said Cook, for she had opened the door to his Honda Coupe and was doing just that.

"There, now," said Pillow. "That doesn't sound like something that a *bitch* would do. That's not *bitch* behavior."

Cook marveled at Pillow's concrete sense of this word. Pillow seemed to know what a bitch was the way Cook knew where his socks were. Cook kept his eye on Beth. She was hunched down, really going at it to clean the floor of his car, sucking up the trash of his private life.

"It's a shame you won't be able to thank her for the nice favor," said Pillow.

"What? Why not?"

"Haven't you read 'Day Two' yet?"

"No, I haven't. I just—"

"Well, you know where to find it. Now, Jeremy, I must say something to you. You know I have fond feelings for you."

Cook stifled a yelp.

"I *do* enjoy chatting with you," Pillow continued, "but— how shall I say it?—you *have* been calling home rather a lot. Read 'Day Two' and..." Pillow stopped and said in a sharper tone, "You didn't just get up, did you?"

"Well, actually—"

"You aren't still in your pajamas, are you?"

"Of course not," said Cook, yanking his hand out of his

pajama bottoms, where he had idly been playing with himself.

"I hope not," said Pillow. "It's almost eight-thirty. Time to go to work. I'll initiate our next contact, when it's time for your date."

"My date?"

Pillow was silent.

"What do you mean, Roy?"

"I've arranged a date for you," Pillow said matter-of-factly.

"With a woman?"

"Don't sound so surprised. What do you think we took that blood sample for? What did you think?"

"I didn't think *anything*. I had no idea. Christ, Roy, I can't buy this at all."

"How's that?"

"I don't do blind dates. It's that simple."

Pillow gave an indignant snort. "I wouldn't call this a *blind* date, Jeremy. That would slight the research that has gone into it, wouldn't you say?"

"But what's the point?"

"Ah. Let me ask you this: What is the point of the Pillow Agency?"

"That's easy. To drive me out of my mind."

Pillow paused, as he did with all of Cook's sarcasms, in sober consideration. "I don't quite follow, Jeremy."

"Okay, okay. The point is to save marriages."

"Yes. *Yes.*" Pillow fell silent. Evidently he got stuck gazing on the beauty of this vision. "And to save them we must understand them. Marriage is . . . Well, what's the etymology of 'marriage,' Jeremy?"

"I don't know."

"Neither do I. Never mind. If we are to understand marriage, we must know who fits best with whom—an empirical question subject to experimental inquiry. The linguists on the staff normally cooperate in this endeavor by dating subjects I've selected for them. I hope you will cooperate, too."

"Absolutely not."

"Come again?"

"I won't even come once, unless I do it by myself, because the answer is no."

"You've managed to confuse me, Jeremy."

"No."

"No?"

"No."

"If you say no, I'll have to fire you."

"What?"

"This aspect of our work is that important to me. I'm fond of you, Jeremy—*very* fond of you—but I'll drop you like a rock if I have to."

Cook wanted to bite the mouthpiece off the phone and spit it to the floor. "You're a freak, Roy. Do you know that?"

"Don't say anything you'll regret, Jeremy."

"You're totally weird. You're a dip and a doofus."

"Mmm."

"I hate working for you."

"I shall be in touch about the day and time."

"And you *still* owe me an apology, goddammit. For the way you reacted when I told you—"

"Shame on me," Pillow said, so quickly that Cook barely understood him. "I was *so* nervous. I was afraid you would turn us down. Shame on me."

"Nervous? But—"

"I'd followed your work for years, Jeremy. I was scared to death of you."

"But you were *mean* to me. You acted like you wanted to withdraw the job offer."

"Yes! That's the devil of it. That's what insecurity does. I was convinced that the Pillow Agency was so *beneath* you, and you were so . . . so exalted, that when I saw that little bit of tarnish on you, yes, I became mean. I thought, 'Why, I'm not as bad as I thought I was. *He's* the bad one.' I became unkind. Then, over the weekend, I gave myself a good talking to and sorted things out. When you reported for work Monday morning, I was the happiest of men."

"Good God," said Cook. "I had no idea."

"Insecurity, Jeremy. The family of civilized man is bound in a chain of events linked by insecurity."

"But why didn't you tell me any of this before?"

"You're right, I should have, I'm sorry, I'm sorry." Pillow was chock-full of anguish. "I was ashamed to. Oh, shame upon shame! Such a fraud! Such a hypocrite! Here I am preaching communication, and I can't even—" He broke off. "I can't—" The next sound was Pillow's phone rattling into the cradle.

Cook hung up the phone and carried it back to the table on the landing. Pillow wouldn't have to worry about any more phone calls from him for some time.

He took another look out the window. Beth had finished vacuuming and was coiling up the extension cord as she headed back to the house. What an odd thing to do, Cook thought—vacuum his car. Was she often moved to spontaneous charity like this? Did that mean she was *not* a bitch? Or was she a bitch and a snoop too? And what had Pillow meant when he said Cook wouldn't be able to thank her?

He went to *The Pillow Manual* and popped the second seal. There was his answer:

DAY TWO
Watch. Say nothing.

"Okay by me," Cook said aloud to himself. "I mean, what the hell, hunh? Why not? You bet. Hey, go for it." In anticipation of his day of speechlessness, he continued talking to himself in this idiotic vein while he showered and dressed for breakfast.

"It's useless," said Beth. "Save your breath."

"What do you mean?" said Dan.

"He's not talking."

"How come?"

"I don't know. Part of the routine, I guess." Beth bent close to Cook, who was seated at the kitchen table, and said loudly, "Part of the routine—right, Jeremy?"

Cook leaned back a bit from the force of her voice and nodded. He had been using nonverbals with her all through breakfast. He hoped they were allowed.

As she carried her dishes to the sink, Beth said, "By the way, Jeremy, I ran the vacuum cleaner through your car. I figured since I had it out I'd go ahead and do it. I hope that was okay."

Cook nodded and gave her a smile.

"I'm afraid I accidentally vacuumed something out of the little tray in front. It was metal—I could hear it go up the tube. Was it something important?"

Cook's smile faded.

"It *is* important, isn't it?" she said. "Hell, I'm sorry. I'll fish it out of the bag. I should be able to find it in there. What is it?"

Cook shook his head. The one-year anniversary of Paula's exit from his life was coming up in a week. He had been waiting until then to part with this little relic—a tiny heart-shaped earring of hers that had been rattling around in the tray for fifty-one weeks. He might as well let it go now.

Beth was looking at him curiously. He shook his head again. She shrugged and turned to the sink.

"Okay," Dan said. Cook had observed that this was his favorite transition word. He sat down at the table and looked at Cook. He seemed about to speak to him, but then he turned toward Beth. "Honey, you forgot Robbie's Hershey Kisses. He looked through his lunch in the car and said they weren't in there."

"I couldn't find any," Beth said. "I thought he took them with him."

"Nope," said Dan. "He was pretty upset. Dessert's important to him."

"I know that. But they're just not here."

Cook's face was buried in his coffee cup. The brutal truth was that in the course of his long night of tape transcription he had plundered the Hershey Kisses, emptying the bowl in the living room into his pockets before going up to his room, and then tiptoeing back down later for the half-full bag in the kitchen.

Dan was looking at Cook as if he were a sculpture. "This is neat. You going to just hang out and watch us?"

Cook nodded.

"We just go about our business?"

Cook nodded.

"How long you gonna be like this?"

Cook thought. He made a circle by bringing his cupped hands together. He made this circle rise from a point to his left, just below the table, in an arc that ended below the table again to his right. He felt like a dumb Indian in a dumb movie.

Dan's grin grew as Cook's little sun rose and set. "Great," he said. "Okay. Let me bring you up to date. I just took Robbie to school. This is his last week. Beth's got a couple parent conferences this afternoon. Me? I'm here, at your service." Dan's smile faded a bit as he ran out of gas. He looked at Beth. "You know, I have this urge to tease him. I can't take him seriously like this."

"I know," Beth said over her shoulder. She rolled the portable dishwasher from the sink into a little storage closet. Its wheels screeched horribly.

Dan scooted his chair back from the table. "Okay. I've been wanting to clean up the basement. That's the plan." He stood up.

Beth turned around. Her face was blank but her mouth was slightly open.

Dan seemed to sense something was amiss. His motions suddenly became less fluid as he eased away from the table and headed for the basement door.

"You're kidding," Beth said.

"Me?" said Dan, stopping. He looked at Beth. "I'm not kidding. It's a mess down there."

"I can't believe you."

"Why not?"

She shook her head. "You overwhelm me," she said softly.

"You overwhelm me too, honey. Now can I go clean the basement?"

"You go to hell." She said this sternly, but then her lips quivered and she seemed about to cry.

"Hey," said Dan, going to her. "What am I missing here? Come on. I'm sorry if I missed something. Tell me."

Beth said, "You're missing the whole point. Why is *he* here?" She jabbed a finger at Cook. "He's not going to learn anything watching you move a bunch of junk around."

"Yeah," Dan said slowly and thoughtfully. "He's here to watch us talk. I guess I could talk out loud while I work. Would that be okay, Jeremy?"

Cook held his body language in check, declining to respond. He didn't want to be part of Dan's plunge onto the rocks. It was as if Dan were *trying* to be stupid.

"He's supposed to watch us *together!*" Beth yelled. "Jesus Christ!"

"Okay okay okay," Dan said in instant surrender. "I was just in the mood to clean the basement, all right? You know what it's like to be in the mood to do a rotten job? You've got to take advantage of it. There's a lot of work to do around the house—"

"How about working on our marriage?"

"Fine. We'll do something together."

Now that she had him, she didn't want him. "Forget it," she said, turning back to the sink. "Do whatever you want."

"No, honey," Dan said, reaching for her. "Come on. Don't do that. You're right—we'll do something together."

Beth let him hold her, though she seemed a little stiff. "I just can't *believe* you sometimes," she said.

"I know. I'm awful."

"So what do we do?" Beth said, easing away from him.

Dan went slowly back to his chair as his mind lumbered into action. Total redemption required that he propose a common activity acceptable to Beth but not wildly out of character for him, for then his proposal would seem insincere. Cook figured he was a goner.

"I don't suppose you'd want to help me clean the basement."

"No."

"It needs to be done. We could do it together."

"No. I'd hate that."

Dan had regained some ground there. Cook was sure of it.

"Yeah," said Dan. "I guess it's not very romantic."

Cook held his breath. But Beth said nothing.

"Shopping?" said Dan.

"I'd *love* to," said Beth, showing more feeling toward the subject than Cook would have thought possible. "But you'd hate it."

Dan got a sadly crazed look on his face, and he whined plaintively, "Can't we meet somewhere between shopping and cleaning the basement?"

Cook found the silence generated by this question deeply discouraging.

"It's a lovely day," Beth said, her eyes drifting to the window.

"Want to go for a bike ride?" said Dan.

Beth smiled. *"Great* idea."

"Good," said Dan.

They turned and looked at Cook. He was obviously bikeless. Their stares made him feel like an obstacle to their reconciliation.

Beth said, "Robbie's bike?"

Dan shook his head. "Too small."

"Could he trot alongside?"

"He doesn't strike me as a trotter. You a trotter, Jeremy?"

Cook shook his head.

"How about Ron's bike?" said Dan. "Can you call Mary?"

"Could you call her? I don't feel like talking."

"You don't have to talk," Dan said. "Just ask if we can borrow Ron's bike."

"You do it, honey. I'd have to talk."

"Why would you have to talk?"

"I just would."

"*Why?* You just say, 'Hi, Mary. Listen. We have a friend here who needs to borrow a bike. Can we use Ron's?'" Dan's wooden delivery seemed to ridicule Beth for failing to recognize how little would be required of her. Cook tensed, expecting her to retaliate. But she didn't get angry at all.

"Just do it. As a favor. All right? I've got to change." She left the kitchen and went upstairs.

Dan looked at Cook. "She'd have to talk. Figure that out." He got up and dialed. While he waited for an answer at the other end, he said to Cook, "They're neighbors, across the street. Hey—I should have had *you* call. I'd like to see you act it out over the phone, without speaking." Dan threw himself into a violent charade to suggest this, then abruptly stopped.

"Hi, Mary. Listen. We have a friend here who needs to borrow a bike to take a ride with us. Can we use Ron's?" He winked at Cook, apparently to show him how easy it was. "An old friend from college . . . Yeah . . . Santa Cruz, right . . . No, first time in the Gateway City . . . Yeah. Anyway, listen . . . Yeah, we're about to go out and . . . It's a *great* day. Sure is. Listen, can we borrow Ron's bike? . . . Oh? You have to do that? . . . Okay. We'll be here. Bye."

Dan hung up and said to Cook, "She's got to call her husband for permission. Jesus." He sat down at the table. "She'll call back." He sat still for a moment, then stood up and went out the swinging door to the bottom of the stairs and yelled the news to Beth. Cook heard a faint, obscure response. Dan returned and sat back down. He drummed his fingers on the table.

"Doesn't that strike you as bizarre? That she would have to get his okay?"

Cook shrugged.

"I mean, if they called here to ask for *my* bike, Beth'd say, 'Sure, take it, have fun.' What's the big deal?" He looked at Cook's cup. "More coffee?"

Cook nodded.

"A bike," Dan said as he took Cook's cup to the coffee maker and refilled it. "What can you do to a bike?"

Cook was silent on the subject.

"The guy—Ron—is a bike nut, so maybe it's an expensive one." He set the coffee in front of Cook. "He's a fusspot. Maybe all bike nuts are. You think so?"

Cook tried to signal fairly strong agreement, wanting to make it clear, however, that his agreement was based not on actual experience with bike nuts but merely on a lifelong partiality to hostile generalizations. It was a tough concept, and he almost threw his neck out trying to convey it.

"I wish to hell she'd call. Jesus. You see a pattern here, Jeremy? My wife won't let me do what I want to, so I commit myself to a new want, which I don't really want, but in time maybe I will, because if you can train a dog, you can train a husband, right? So I call Mary, and *she* won't let me do my new want, which I don't even want anyway." He froze and studied the phone, as if he could make it ring that way. When it didn't, he walked to the window and looked out onto the backyard.

"'Work on our marriage,'" he said. "I'm working. Look at me. I'm working right now. I'm working so fucking hard I—"

The phone rang and Dan grabbed it and said hello. His shoulders sagged. "Hi, Rose... Yeah... Hey, I'm sorry I left you hanging on so long yesterday. The doorbell rang and I had to answer it... Yeah, just for a couple days. To fix up the house, spend some time with Beth, you know. Lemme get her." He set the phone down, grimaced, and went to the bottom of the stairs, where he yelled at the top of his lungs,

"Beth! It's your mom!" Beth called out something in response, and Dan muttered and returned to the phone.

"She'll be right here, Rose." He added with a laugh, *"Honest. I promise.* Yeah. Bye." He set the phone down and said in a whisper to Cook, "I'm gonna go across the street and see what the story is. When Beth picks it up in the bedroom, can you hang this up?"

Cook nodded and watched him go. He sipped his coffee. The kitchen was wonderfully quiet with Dan gone. Cook's eyes came to rest on the phone. He wondered if Beth and her mother were going to say anything interesting—about Dan, for example. You never knew where data might lurk. He slipped out of his shoes and tiptoed to the phone. It was a wall phone, and Dan had hooked the receiver precariously on the top of it. Cook didn't touch it, for fear of making noise. He contented himself with snuggling up close to it. Despite his necessary distance from the earpiece, he could hear Beth's mother breathing as she waited for her daughter. Inhale, exhale. Inhale, exhale. He listened, feeling that they were becoming intimate, in a sense—though in what sense he wouldn't have been able to say.

He heard a door open upstairs, followed by footsteps and the click of the extension. Then he listened hard.

"Got it!" Beth yelled.

Cook lurched away from the phone.

"Got it!" Beth yelled again. "Hang it up!"

He rattled a kitchen chair noisily at the table, then stomped to the phone, which he hung up definitively.

No eavesdroppers down here, lady. Not a one.

The three of them rolled through Forest Park, Dan in the lead, then Beth, followed by Cook, who kept falling behind. Mr. Bike across the street had been unreachable at the office, so Mr. Bike's wife had donated her own vehicle to the cause. It was a three-speed clunker, festooned with plastic flowers and laden with so many wire baskets that Cook felt as if he were riding a cyclone fence. One of the pedals developed a slip shortly after they set out: on every revolution Cook's right foot coasted freely for several inches before engaging again in any kind of useful propulsion. He had an urge to hop off the bike and give it a shove out into the street traffic.

Dan seemed to be having a hard time throttling down, and he pulled ahead even farther. Beth dropped back and fell in alongside Cook. She apologized for the condition of his bike and offered her own to him. He shook his head and struggled manfully on.

"Look at Dan," she said. "I swear. He's just dying to go faster. He hates slow bike rides. I used to think it was just a male thing—a fascination with speed. But I know better now. I can't talk if we go fast. So we go fast." She sighed. "Control. It'll get you every time." She glanced at Cook. "I'm surprised you didn't ask any questions about it last night in your questionnaire. Who controls things? That would be a good question." She looked ahead at Dan, who was pulling away so gradually that it was hard to tell he was doing it. "Dan hates being in the car with me because I've got him trapped. That's what he'd say. Just ask him. Why'd he marry me if he doesn't want to talk to me? Who am I supposed to talk to?"

They rode on in silence for a while. "What he does," Beth went on, "is he declares certain subjects forbidden. I can't tell him my dreams in the morning. Too boring. I can't talk about problems at my school for too long—I reach his limit real quick there. Even stuff that concerns *us*. I like to talk about the future, sort of dream out loud, fantasize. Nope. Nothing about the future, except for short-term stuff, like upcoming trips. Oh, Robbie's education—that's another exception. We can talk about that. But not about me, not about my hopes." She laughed bitterly. "I guess his goal is to eliminate all topics, one by one, until nothing's left, and I'll be mute. His father—that's another forbidden subject. He's all alone. Dan's mother died a couple years ago, and he lives in an apartment in South San Francisco. He's retired—used to be a Muni bus driver. Now he never sees anybody. He's a total recluse, the unhappiest man I know. Can't talk about him, though. Dan says it's a hopeless case, there's nothing he can do, so no more talk about it. The subject is closed."

Beth's voice had become slightly hoarse—with unhappiness, Cook guessed. He looked ahead. Dan was so far in front that the dips and bends in the bike path kept taking him out of view.

Beth heaved a huge sigh and made a valiant shift of subject, pointing out the houses across the street from the park —some of the finest houses in the city, she said. She called them "mansionettes" and said most of them dated from the turn of the century. She named the styles for him: Italianate, Georgian, Greek Revival, and when all else failed, American Eclectic. They were all set well back from the road. Cook noticed that there was absolutely no sign of life about them —no little children playing on the grass, no one unloading groceries. The houses seemed to exist independently of people, just for themselves.

Beth said, "Look at that one—the French one with the porte cochere."

Cook plumbed his Romance vocabulary and figured out that she meant the gray limestone house with the little drive-up porch on the side: the coach-port. It had forbidding lines and a yard heavily shaded by trees that looked like magnolias. Did magnolias grow in St. Louis? He turned to Beth, wishing he could ask her.

She was crying. Her bike began to weave.

"What is it?" said Cook. "Stop, Beth. Stop your bike."

She came to a jerking halt, nearly tipping over when she put her feet down before the bike had completely stopped. She looked ahead. Dan was well out of sight now, long gone. She began to cry more heavily.

Cook stopped beside her. He said, "Maybe he's just gone ahead a bit and he's waiting for us. He's probably waiting. Don't you think so?"

Beth cried. He reached out for her. As they awkwardly straddled their bikes, he held her against his shoulder, letting her cry there and patting her back. It was all he could think to do.

Nine

"He's a prick, Roy."

"Oh come now."

"I mean it. He's a prick."

"No pricks allowed, Jeremy. Pricks need not apply. The Pillow Agency will not have them. You can't save a marriage with a bitch *or* a prick in it."

"Yeah? What if one slipped through?"

"Out of the question. Hang on." Pillow put Cook on hold before he had a chance to protest. As he stood at the pay phone in the restaurant entryway, he kept his eye on the rest room door for Beth. At her suggestion, on their way home from the park they had stopped for coffee at this place —a Greek restaurant named Zeno's. But as soon as they sat down, Beth had gone into the bathroom. This had left Cook with limited options—sitting alone at a restaurant table, which he always hated doing, or . . . calling Roy Pillow? Incredible as it seemed, talking to Pillow was actually preferable to conspicuous solitude.

Pillow came back, armed with a witticism: "You must be on a different calendar than mine, Jeremy."

"How do you mean?"

"Has a great deal of time passed since you last telephoned, by your reckoning? By mine, it's been just a few hours."

"Good, Roy. Very clever."

"I shall say goodbye now."

"Wait, Roy. I've got an unhappy woman here."

"Mmm."

"What should I do? And don't tell me the goddamn *Pillow Manual* will be my guide."

"Speaking of which, you shouldn't be talking, even to me. You must foster the observer's attitude. That's the ticket. Goodbye, Jeremy."

Cook swore, sighed, and returned to his table. Beth was still in the bathroom. If she didn't come out soon, he would have to send someone in there to check on her. This was something he had never done before, but things like this probably happened when you got involved with people. You had to ask strangers to go into the bathroom for you.

The door to the kitchen was right behind him, making him jump every time it swung open. He could switch tables, but then to the other patrons he would look like a malcontent as well as a loner. What were all these people doing in a Greek restaurant at ten-thirty in the morning? Didn't they have regular jobs somewhere? Were they all Pillow agents? He looked at the menu cover. Zeno's. There couldn't be a real Zeno in the kitchen. Some classics-loving show-off had named the place. Cook wished a Chapter 11 on him.

Thoughts of bankruptcy led Cook naturally enough to his sex life. It had been nearly four months since he had had one. Could he still do it? He reviewed it, the way one might recall how to change a tire before a long trip, reminding oneself where the important tools were and brushing up on points of access, safety procedures, and the like. Yes, he could remember it—just barely. But how could he apply this fading knowledge? He knew only one woman within hundreds of miles, and he was supposed to be saving her marriage.

Of course, there was the date Pillow had threatened him with—a prospect he had successfully kept out of his mind for at least five minutes. Cook had been on one blind date in his life. It was in college. By any measure, it was not a success. He recalled its climax, an hour or so into it. He had been walking with the girl and another couple on a sidewalk bordering a large, dark, empty field. Without a moment of thought, as if he were controlled by aliens who had wired him up, Cook had bolted, sprinting across the lot at top speed and disappearing into the night. For lasting guilt, there was no single act in his life, from birth to the present, that he regretted more than this one.

A waitress came to his table and he ordered a cup of coffee. He took a sheet of yellow legal paper from his pocket and unfolded it on the table. Under the heading THE HORROR! was the terse hypothesis he had written the night before:

She's a bitch.

He studied it for a minute, then crossed it out and entered a new one:

He's a prick.

Pillow had denied the claim, but Cook had no reason to trust Pillow's judgment. In fact he had ample reason to *dis*trust it. And he had the vivid memory of Dan pedaling off toward the horizon, lifting his butt up smartly from the seat, the better to pump and put distance between himself and his wife. If Dan was going to pass the prick test, he would have to do it on his own, without Pillow's help. Until he did, this sentence summed up the Wilson marriage.

He folded THE HORROR! and put it back in his pocket. It was good that he did this, because a moment later Beth appeared and sat down at the table. Cook's coffee came at the same time. Beth ordered one for herself. Then, frowning unprettily, she asked Cook why he hadn't ordered for her. Cook gave a guilty shrug. He felt just as he had felt after dinner, when he was worried that he had offended Beth by going to the library with Dan and Robbie. This time, though, annoyance followed hard upon the guilt. What was her problem, that she kept making him feel this way?

Beth said, "There's something you should know." She held him in her gaze. "My parents have money." She looked at Cook strangely, almost defiantly. It was as if she had told him a different kind of secret—that she was a paroled murderess, or a former man. "That French house I showed you, with the porte cochere? I grew up there." She smiled slyly, as if amused to have tricked him by holding back this information. "They don't live there anymore—they've moved to West County. Anyway, there it is. They have money."

She was waiting for a response. Cook's main thought had nothing to do with money. He wondered what it would be like to live as an adult less than a mile from one's childhood home.

"It's not an issue for me," Beth said. "It's absolutely not. But it is for Dan. He says money's at the root of all of our problems."

THE HORROR! wanted to leap from Cook's shirt pocket. It begged for revision.

"They've helped us financially," Beth went on, "but no more than most parents help their children. Well, maybe a little more. They helped us buy our house. They help with some of Robbie's expenses, like camp, through a trust fund. But they never, *never,* throw the help they've given us in our face. Dan's just waiting for them to do that. He's poised, ready to spring at them when they do."

Her coffee came, and she sipped it and looked at Cook. "So. There it is. Money." She sighed and made a sour face. "I hate this. You're impossible to talk to." She looked away, out the windows, at the traffic.

Cook sipped his coffee. Beth looked back at him and said, "Does it seem to you that Dan indulges Robbie?"

Cook raised his eyebrows.

"The way he jumped up from the table to take him to the library last night. Do you think that's healthy?" She shook her head, apparently dissatisfied with the way she was putting it. "He's always going out of his way to do things for him. Of course, it's terrific for Robbie, but from my point of view...I feel like he takes better care of Robbie than he does of me." She seemed a little embarrassed to be saying this. She looked away again, out the window. Cook waited. She looked back at him.

"When I showed you my old house across from Forest Park, I had a memory of being a little girl there—of looking out my bedroom window at the park, and thinking how I would be married someday, and how I'd be walking with my husband on the bike path, and I'd point out the house and surprise him by telling him I grew up there, and he'd be amazed and say, 'Really? That's interesting. Tell me about it.' It was an important fantasy to me. But the reality turned out different. When Dan and I came to St. Louis for the first time, my folks were still living there, and when Dan saw the house he didn't show any of the interest I'd expected. He didn't have any *curiosity*—he didn't ask which room was mine or if I played in the park or anything like that. He just looked at the house for a long time from the car, without getting out, and he said, 'This is gonna be a problem.' I had no idea what he was talking about." She took a deep breath. "Anyway, all that kind of came over me. Sorry."

Cook made a sympathetic face. It felt a little funny to him, but he held it as long as he could.

They walked their bikes home, through a lively area of shops and restaurants that Beth referred to as "the Loop." When they entered the gate into Dan and Beth's neighborhood, Beth looked up and saw something that made her gasp softly. "Ooh," she said. "The roofers. Shit. I forgot." She hopped on her bike and took off down the sidewalk. Far ahead, Cook could see a pickup truck parked in front of Dan and Beth's house.

He got on his crippled bike and pedaled to catch up with

Beth. The truck was facing them, with the driver's side against the curb. This gave it a faintly illegal look. It listed heavily to the curb side under its load of two ladders and several men, who seemed to be hanging all over it. They watched Beth approach. Cook was behind her, and he felt their eyes switch to him. He could feel their admiration for his nicely decorated bike and their deep respect for him as a man.

Beth stopped her bike at the driver's door and said, "Are you Mr. Farmer?"

Cook heard murmured denials. They were not Mr. Farmer. They were Mr. Hanke.

Dan suddenly appeared from around a corner of the house. With him was a shirtless man—the chief Hanke, presumably. Dan brightened somewhat to see Beth and Cook. He excused himself from the man and walked toward Beth, who seemed a little confused and met him on the sidewalk. Cook, sensing speech was about to happen, laid his bike down in the ivy and drew close.

"I got a bid for the roof repairs," Dan said. He glanced at Cook but showed no sign of recognition. "They'll do it for eight hundred."

"Let's get another bid," said Beth.

Dan immediately tensed. "They're here," he said slowly. "They can do it now. It's hard to get these guys to show up. That's half the battle."

"I've got another roofer coming today," said Beth. "Let's see what he says." She spoke evenly, but not peaceably.

"You called a roofer?"

"Yes."

"How do you know he's coming?"

"I don't. I'll go in and call him right now to make sure. Okay?"

"I kind of told this guy he got the job," said Dan.

As if to underscore this, the Hankes began to detach themselves from their truck. They had a uniformly skinny, stringy-haired look. They moved slowly and in complete silence. Cook found this eerie until he identified it: experience told him this was the reluctant, wordless, life-cursing behavior of souls who were deeply hung over.

"Tell him we haven't decided," said Beth. "Tell him we'll have to get back to him to let him know."

Dan pressed his lips together. He inhaled sharply. He sighed. He did everything but refuse.

"You should always get two bids," said Beth.

"I know," Dan said wearily. "You think I don't know that? But they're here, and it's a reasonable bid."

"What do you know about them?" asked Beth.

The clang of a ladder as it banged from the truck onto the pavement made them all jump. "They're *here*. That's what I know."

This distinction suddenly disappeared with the arrival of the second crew—the Farmers—whose truck was slightly newer than the Hankes'. It came from the other direction and parked along the curb directly in front of the Hanke truck, front bumper to front bumper. Dan, Beth, and Cook watched them come to a stop. So did the Hankes. Cook thought the two crews would buddy up to each other and talk shop, but there was none of that. Just dull staring. The two gangs—five Hankes and four Farmers—looked heavily sedated.

Beth hurried to the Farmer truck, introduced herself, and asked who was in charge. As she talked with them, Dan's roofer, perhaps fearing an erosion of his support, looked questioningly at Dan.

"We seem to have a little problem, Mr. Hanke," Dan called to him. "Bear with me a second, will you?" Then he went to Beth and her crew. Cook stuck close to Dan.

"Howdy," the man behind the wheel said to Dan, his face reddening with a broad grin. He thrust a hand out the window past Beth. He was a large, barrel-chested man. The Farmers seemed to eat better than the Hankes.

"Mr. Farmer wants to give us a bid, honey," Beth said

brightly, as if his willingness to do this were a pleasant surprise.

Dan said, "Okay. Let me handle it, though, for the sake
of consistency. I want to be sure his bid is based on the same
repairs. If it's not, we're going to get even more balled up
than we are."

"Good thinkin'," said Farmer.

Beth accepted this as a nonusurpation of her authority. As
Farmer got out of his truck, Dan went back to Hanke and
asked him to bear with him while he got another bid.

Hanke, far from expressing disappointment, grinned and
nodded rapidly, as if driving a nail with his chin. "Don't I
know about *that*. Got to please the wife. Don't I know about
that." He drifted back to his own crew and gave them an
update.

Dan and Farmer toured around the outside of the house.
Farmer carried his extra weight awkwardly, reminding
Cook of Ariel Sharon, with whom Cook figured he shared
little else. Dan pointed to several places where the roof
leaked. Farmer listened actively and sympathetically. He said
he wanted to see the leakage points from inside.

"We're gonna go inside," Dan called to the Hankes from
the front steps. "Bear with me, okay?" As often happens
when a group is addressed, no single person took responsibility for the role of hearer, and Dan's plea was answered
with stares.

They stomped around inside for a while, where Cook, in
the closer confines, reassessed Farmer's enthusiasm: the guy
stunk of booze.

When they came out, Farmer went to his people for a
conference. Dan, Beth, and Cook were left alone for the first
time since they had been in the park.

"Where'd you two go?" said Dan. "I turned around and
you were out of sight. I looked all over for you. Did you
take a different path?"

Beth said, *"Yes."* Then she said, more coolly, "Did your
man go inside the house?"

"No."

"Hmm. My man seems to know what he's doing."

While her man, Farmer, continued to consult with his crew, Dan's man, Hanke, sidled up to Cook, gave him a looking over, and said, "You a roofer, too?" He said it very softly, evidently not wanting Dan or Beth to hear. His strange assumption seemed to be that if Cook *was* a roofer, Dan and Beth might not know it, and he didn't want them to find out.

Cook shook his head and said he was just a friend. Hanke nodded and went back to his crew and conferred with them. Perhaps there was a ground swell of curiosity about the silent stranger.

Farmer returned to Dan and Beth. He talked at length about the difficulty of doing this, the near-impossibility of doing that, and the superhuman efforts required to do the other. He slapped himself sharply on the belly with both hands and bid the job at seven hundred dollars.

"That's a hundred dollars less," Beth said right away.

"I know," Dan said testily. "Isn't subtraction wonderful?" He turned to Farmer. "Can you do it today?" He sounded hopeful for a yes, but Cook knew he wanted a no. Dan wanted to win, and winning meant getting *his* guy, Hanke, up on that roof, even if it cost an extra hundred dollars.

"Sure can," said Farmer. "If we get started now."

"Do you have references?" said Dan.

"References?"

"People you've done work for that could recommend you."

Farmer gave this some thought. "We're just startin' out in the business. But we'll do you right. Don't worry about that."

Beth said to Dan, "Do *yours* have any?"

Dan called out, "Mr. Hanke, do you have any references?"

"Yeah," Hanke said, taking a step forward. "There was that guy over on...over on..." He faded out, then came back. "He was a doctor. I forget his name."

Dan turned to Farmer. "What kind of guarantee can you give against future leaks?"

"One full year," Farmer said proudly.

"Three years," Hanke called out.

"Five years," Farmer countered.

"A lifetime," said Hanke. "The lifetime of the house or the owner—whichever comes first."

Cook decided he would rather fall from the roof and land on his head than try to process this sentence. He reached out and put one arm around Beth, and he put his other arm around Dan, and he said, "Can we step aside a moment? Can we do that?"

Dan looked at Cook as if he had spoken in the Icelandic dialect of Schnorrfark. Frowning, he turned to Farmer and Hanke and asked them to bear with him a second. Cook took Dan and Beth down the sidewalk a ways.

"There's an old saying in *The Pillow Manual*," Cook said sagely. "To wit, 'A divided marriage is an inefficient unit.' Dan, Beth—what we have here are two roofing crews. One is certainly drunk, and the other wishes it were. Both will take your money and do nothing for your roof but harm it. Send them home. Get someone who doesn't have amnesia about his references. Get someone who doesn't promise guarantees that are a thousand times longer than he's been in business. Do it right."

He left them there and went inside the house.

There immediately followed a period of small rebellions. After Dan dismissed both roofing crews—a treatment that surely must have perplexed them—he stomped down to the basement without a word and began to clean it, emphasizing demolition in the early going. Beth went right to the piano and practiced the same four or five nerve-jangling measures over and over. Cook, after a few minutes of aimless wandering on the first floor, became fully aware of the hostility

Dan and Beth felt not only for each other but—at the moment, at least—for him as well, and he withdrew to his room. Singing obscene lyrics to go with Beth's music, he sat at his little yellow desk and tore into the forbidden, sealed portions of *The Pillow Manual*, slipping his flat hand in at the bottom of each page and whacking the tabs apart with sideways karate chops.

But having done this much, Cook slammed the manual shut without reading a word. If he failed with the Wilsons, he wanted it to be Pillow's failure, not his own, and that meant sticking by the rules. As for his lapses into speech—in the park with Beth and just now with both of them—he felt he hadn't done anything wrong. He had had no choice, really. Only a clod would have withheld words on those occasions.

Beth's practicing came to an end. Cook heard footsteps on the first floor, then on the second, in the master bedroom directly below him, then on the first again. The front door opened and closed. He looked out the window and saw Beth get into her car and drive off. He remembered Dan mentioning some parent conferences she had to go to.

Cook wandered down the stairs to the first floor. He went to the piano and turned on the small music light. The sheet music was open to a piece by Darius Milhaud. Cook had retained very little from his three years of piano lessons as a boy—mainly memories of the neighborhood dachshund that chased him to and from each lesson, and of his piano teacher's husband lurking out of sight in the kitchen and constantly clearing his throat, as if in comment on Cook's playing. But the three years of piano had been followed by five years on the trumpet, so he could still read music, at least in the treble clef. He plinked a few notes. They sounded fairly right. He plinked them again.

"I don't have to listen to that shit from *you*," Dan shouted from directly below.

Cook's hand froze over a D-sharp, his eyes stuck on the music. It slowly dawned on him, as he wondered what to do next, that the treble and bass clefs of the piece were written in different keys; the former had four sharps, the latter three flats. He had never seen anything like this before. He pointed to it and whispered to the floor, "This sums up your marriage, asshole."

"Sorry!" Dan called. He followed it up with some mutters. His apology seemed genuine and spontaneous. He couldn't possibly have heard Cook's comment. Cook decided to see what he was doing.

"You're right," Dan said to him before he was all the way down the stairs. "You're right you're right you're right. We *are* inefficient." A bare bulb shone brightly in Cook's face, and he couldn't see Dan clearly. He moved around to get a better view but immediately bumped into a standing roll of tin. Dan stood in a small clearing in the center of the basement, surrounded by junk that was piled halfway to the ceiling. He threw a cardboard box to the floor and stomped it until it was small enough for him to fit it into a trash bag.

"We're ridiculous. I was in the middle of Forest Park when I remembered the roofers were coming, and I shot right back here. I'll bet Beth forgot about *her* roofers until she saw mine. Am I right?"

Cook nodded.

"The question is, why didn't I tell Beth I'd called a roofer? Why didn't she tell me *she'd* called one? I'll tell you why: we were fighting. When you're fighting you don't want to say, 'Hey, honey, guess what? I called a roofer.' There are gaps like these all the time around here. Complete breakdowns. Anyway, thanks. You were right."

Dan stretched an arm out, inviting Cook to survey the basement mess. "You get married and have a kid, next thing you know you've got a basement that looks like this." He picked up a box. "Look. Robbie's car-seat box. It's been down here for ten years. The box is here and the seat's hanging over there somewhere. What sense does that make? Jesus. Our whole life is down here." He looked around. In the harsh light of the bare bulb his face looked angry, but when he spoke, his tone was not. "Look at that. The gates to keep Robbie from falling down the stairs. I labeled them and taped the screws to them and saved them for our long-awaited second child. But we fought too much for that. Beth said no more until we worked things out. Helluva policy." He pointed to a corner of the basement. "Old drywall, piles of it, crumbling, mildewed. That's gonna be fun to clean up. I'll probably get some lung disease from it. Over there's our kitchen table from our first apartment in St. Louis—an old cable spool. It's got knotholes in it that your dinner would drop into and just disappear in. Do I miss those days? Hell if I know. Our early years are a blur. Here." He threw Cook a box. "Smash this if you want to help. Stomp it into as small a piece as you can."

For a while they worked in silence. Dan seemed to be working outward from the center—as good a plan as any.

"Want to know why I'm doing this? In case we sell the house. That's right—I'm preparing for our divorce. If it comes to that, I don't want to spend time here sprucing the sonofabitch up. I want it to be all ready, so I can make a clean break. Does that surprise you? I mean, that I'm planning for it?"

Cook's foot had broken through a box and was stuck. He yanked it out and almost fell down in the process.

"You're real good at this, aren't you?" Dan laughed. "Look at this. A sewing machine. Used once, maybe. She never sews. You sew? You want it?"

Cook shook his head.

Dan set the machine to one side. "I'll just put it here so I can trip over it later. That should be fun." He sighed. "That's why the roofers were here. Getting the place ready for the old heave-ho, just in case. I wonder if Beth thinks I'm doing all this for general improvement, or what. It makes her happy, I know that much. She'll look down here and say, 'Great job, honey.' And I'll think yeah, sure. But it's got to be done. We've got to be ready to sell it. If we kept it, Beth'd stay here and I'd be in an apartment, but the sonofabitch'd need repairs—it *always* does—and *she* couldn't do them, so she'd call me, and I'd come trotting over with my little toolbox . . . When I think about that, I say no way. No way."

Ten

When they took a break for lunch, Cook went to the refrigerator, planning to throw a dry, minimal sandwich together and get through it as quickly as possible. Dan told him to sit down and said he would fix both of them lunch. Cook gestured that he wanted to help, mainly by clutching at his heart and throwing his hands out from it—not exactly American Sign Language, but it did the trick. Dan pointed to a tall oak hutch across the kitchen and told Cook the seasonings to get from it.

As Cook tracked these down and delivered them, Dan went to the food processor, put two slices of bread in it, and created bread crumbs. Cook almost yelped like a savage at the sight. Then Dan got some milk and some things that he called turkey fillets out of the refrigerator. He poured a small amount of milk into a bowl—Cook knew not why—and took the seasonings Cook had fetched and added them to the bread crumbs, not measuring them but just shaking them in with a hey nonny-nonny. He stirred these up, making a pretty speckled sight. Then he dunked the turkey fillets into the bowl! Cook was sure now that Dan was playing, just horsing around with the ingredients until Beth got home. When she did, she would yell at him and chase him out of the kitchen.

But Dan pressed on as if his actions were in the service of some goal he had envisioned from the beginning. He set the moistened fillets into the seasoned bread crumbs in such a way that the crumbs actually *clung* to the fillets, as if by magic. Then he set these into a skillet, which was somehow already at hand, hot, oiled, and ready. As Cook watched the fillets begin to sizzle, the word "breading" leaped to his mind. Seeing its etymology reenacted before his eyes gave the event a wholeness and a beauty that made him feel unworthy.

On a separate burner, Dan heated up some succotash. Succotash! Cook liked the word almost as much as he liked the name Karl Ditters von Dittersdorf. He even liked the food itself. But he hadn't eaten it in years. That was part of his food problem. He forgot about foods and tended to fall back on the same two or three dishes over and over.

A hot lunch. Cook hadn't had a hot lunch outside of a restaurant since the time his mother—herself no ace in the kitchen—had heated up some canned soup for him when he was sick. Dan and Cook sat down to eat at the round glass table on the deck. Three minutes after they had started, Cook was done. Dan stared at him in wonder, his mouth halting in midchew. Cook wished he could explain. Awful food—his regular fare—was best eaten fast. This meal deserved to be eaten slowly, but Cook always went on automatic as soon as a fork was in his hand. He rubbed his tummy for Dan.

Dan smiled tiredly and said, "Shut up." Then he said, "Beth's the real cook. She's great. Never makes the same thing twice—and I wish she would, because it's always good and sometimes I'd like to have it again. The problem is that she wants me to love cooking the way she does. She sees it as a way we could be together. She's got this fantasy of us cooking and giving great dinner parties. It's got a couple of flaws, though: I don't like parties and I don't like cooking. So she's got another fantasy, only I'm not in it. She dreams about a perfect guy who cooks with her all the time.

They go through cookbooks together and get all excited, and they go shopping for stuff at little ethnic food stores, and they spend the whole day working on these complex dishes, sipping wine and giggling through it all." He paused. "But I comfort myself, because you wanna know what this fantasy guy is like outside the kitchen? You wanna know?" Dan got a wild look in his eyes. "He's a fucking *bore.*" He laughed uproariously and settled down and ate in silence for a while.

Then he said, "I just realized something. The first time I had her over to my apartment, I cooked her a meal. Geez. I probably gave her the wrong idea. She probably thought *I* was the fantasy guy. But she tricked me, too. Our whole marriage is based on a geographical mistake. There I was, in Santa Cruz, as provincial as all native Californians are, and along comes Beth. From St. Louis! I said to myself, anyone who goes to college two thousand miles away from home has got to be an independent woman. So I fell for her. It was an ignorant thing to do. I didn't know how common it was for midwesterners to leave their home states for college. I was used to the California model— staying there. I drew a false conclusion about her. She's not independent at all. She's the most dependent, traditional, needy—"

A knock on the wooden gate at the corner of the house made him stop. A woman's voice called out, "Beth? Dan? Yoo-hoo. Anybody home?"

"Come on in, Mary," Dan called. He didn't seem to mind the interruption at all.

The gate rattled as she struggled with the latch. Cook turned around to see what kind of woman actually said "Yoo-hoo." Would she look like her bike, with streamers and baskets hanging all over her?

She did not look like her bike. But she grabbed his attention for another reason. She was Miss St. Louis Hot Pants. Cook hadn't seen shorts like those for quite a while. "Yoo-hoo, turn around, please," he wanted to say, so he could inspect her rear, and she obliged, though her own reason for doing so was to close the gate after her.

She trotted up the stairs. "I saw my bike lying out in front and got worried that something happened," she said.

Cook smacked himself on the head and was about to apologize for leaving it there, but he couldn't get the words out in front of Dan. Such a good little Pillow agent.

"I'm sorry, Mary," said Dan. "We've had a busy morning. I should have returned it."

"It's all right," she said.

Cook liked her a lot. Her face didn't add to her hot pants, but it didn't detract from them either. She was a little too old for hot pants, but that made them even more exciting to him. What a day! A hot lunch, and then hot pants!

Dan said, "Mary, this is the college friend I told you about. *Say hello,* Jeremy."

"Hello," said Cook.

Mary smiled. "Are you here for long?"

"Mmm." Cook looked at Dan. "Couple weeks?" he said.

Dan's eyebrows shot up. "Not if I can help it."

They laughed all around. Mary said to Cook, "You'll be here all alone if you stay that long." She turned to Dan. "Aren't you leaving next week?"

"Yep. A week from yesterday."

Cook frowned in surprise. Was this the trip to Italy? In less than a week? Why hadn't anyone told him?

"Got your passports?" Mary asked.

"Yep."

Cook wondered if he would be done with his work by then. He wondered if he would even have *started* by then. Did Pillow know about the trip? He must not have, or he would have mentioned it. But wasn't Pillow's special gift *not* mentioning things? Cook decided to stop thinking about Pillow.

"When's Robbie's camp?" Mary asked.

"It starts the day we leave and ends the day after we get back. We planned it so they overlap exactly."

"Sounds like you've got it all together," Mary said playfully. People in hot pants, Cook observed, could get away with saying unfunny things playfully.

Mary suddenly seemed a little self-conscious, perhaps because Cook was so silent. She said, "I'll get along and let you two reminisce about your wild past."

Dan thanked her for the bike. Cook smiled. She turned to go. Hot pants!

Cook stood up and went after her. He could feel Dan looking up in surprise. He reached her at the gate. "There's something wrong with your bike," he said.

"Oh?"

"Let me show you." He followed her hot pants out of the gate to the bike, which she had leaned against the side of the house. He lifted it by the seat with one hand and made the pedal go around jerkily with the other. "See that?" he said to her hot pants, for he was bent over and looking right at them. "See how it clunks?"

"Oh, yes," she said.

"Let me take it into the shop for you. I should do that. It happened while I was riding it, after all."

"I couldn't let you do that," she said. "Forget it." She put a hand on his shoulder.

FIRE IN THE LOINS!

"Stand up," she said. "There's something I want to tell you."

FIRE! But she's married, Cook said to himself, and the fire died down. But her husband is a bike nut, he said, and the flames leaped back up.

"I know who you are," Mary said matter-of-factly. "Beth told me about you. I hope you can help them. Let me know if there's anything I can do."

At this reminder of his professional obligation, her hot pants seemed to unfurl and suddenly cover her legs all the way down to her shoe tops. Cook sighed. Then he thought about her offer. *Could* she help?

"You can answer a question for me," he said. "Has Dan ever made a pass at you?"

She was only mildly shaken. "No," she said.

"How long have you known him?"

She thought. "Three years." She smiled. "It's funny, now that you mention it. Dan makes sexual jokes all the time, but only when Beth is around. They aren't *flirting* jokes at all. I mean, they aren't about me and him, as if he's hinting at something. Actually, they're about him and Beth more than anything else. Beth doesn't seem to mind. She usually laughs, in fact. But when he's alone with me he doesn't do it. He's almost formal." She tilted her head to one side and looked at Cook. "Why do you ask?"

"Just curious."

"It's a good sign that he hasn't, isn't it?"

"I think so."

"Ron would kill him if he did. He would just kill him."

Cook swallowed. "Does Dan know that?"

"No, no. Dan wouldn't fool around. He just wouldn't. I know the type."

Cook nodded soberly, implying he knew the type, too. His eye fell on her bike. "Can your husband fix this?"

She smiled ruefully. "Yeah. I wish he spent as much time on me as he does on these bikes."

The siren call of hot pants was faint this time. Cook thanked her and said goodbye.

Dan had returned to the basement, where he was working to the sound of some music Cook was unfamiliar with. Instead of joining him right away, Cook went into the dining room, took THE HORROR! from his shirt pocket, and opened it on the table. He crossed out his most recent theory—"He's a prick"—and entered a new one below it: "Money."

A number of things led him to do this. Above all, Dan simply didn't seem like a prick. Occasional prickishness toward Beth did not make him a permanent prick. And he hadn't been a prick during the crisis with the roofers; that had been painful for both Dan and Beth, and true pricks didn't feel pain. Also, a prick would have made a pass at Hot Pants. Cook had come close to doing so, and had felt more like a prick the closer he got. Dan was unhappy—of this Cook was sure. But he wasn't a prick.

Money. Cook sat and studied the word while Dan stomped boxes and called out snatches of lyrics. Since money was something Cook seldom thought about, it took some effort—like fashioning a long sentence in a foreign language. Dan and Beth were certainly well-off. No—that suggested too much money. They were comfortable. No—too little. Quite comfortable. Yes. Quite comfortable. The house was way oversized for them: six bedrooms for three people, and more chairs and sofas and tables than ten of them could use. Their two cars seemed fairly new, though Cook hadn't looked at them closely or noticed the make of either. Beth, being a schoolteacher, probably didn't earn as much as Dan did as co-owner or whatever he was of this printing plant he didn't seem to want to talk about. The plant, though, came from Beth's family. Was that important?

Cook leaned back in his chair and stared at the ceiling. Money. He reviewed the strained moments he had witnessed thus far to see what role it played: (1) in the first conversation Cook had heard after his arrival, Beth had briefly chided Dan for abandoning Cook to watch the ball game on TV, for letting the cookies burn, and for leaving her mother hanging on the phone; (2) there had been the snap and sizzle of complementary schismogenesis in the kitchen when Dan had wanted to talk and Beth had wanted to cook; (3) Beth had chided Dan at dinner for being indiscreet about Cook's function in front of Robbie; (4) Beth had chided Dan for not understanding what "*our* books" meant; (5) Beth had been peeved by Dan's identification of the alleged Dittersdorf quartet as a Haydn; (6) Beth had chided Dan for wanting to clean the basement instead of working on their marriage; (7) Beth had cried at the next display of Dan's dodge-'em attitude, when he pulled away from them on the bike path;

and (8) they had played tug-of-war over the two roofing crews.

Cook found his review a little discouraging. So many flash points reached in so little time—about eighteen hours. And Beth certainly did a lot of chiding, didn't she? And where was the money in these disputes? Cook couldn't find any—not even pocket change.

The doorbell rang. Cook put THE HORROR! back in his shirt pocket and went to the door. It was a tense, goateed courier, who told him he had a pickup to make for the Pillow Agency. Cook stared at him in wonder, then realized what he wanted and went upstairs and got the tape recorder. Beth drove up as the courier's van pulled away. Cook watched her get out and open her trunk. He went down to help her with the boxes she was taking out. She told him her classroom at school was being replastered and she had to get her personal items out of there for the summer. They made three trips from the car to the storage room on the third floor, carrying boxes of books, music, and small percussion instruments—triangles, castanets, maracas—that rattled pleasantly in transit.

All the while, Cook stayed behind Beth and kept a close eye on her, in part because he was still warming down from Hot Pants, and in part because he had always been a sucker for short jeans skirts like the one Beth was wearing. There was something about them—something having to do with *access*. Regular jeans were closed to him, whereas jeans skirts were open. Because the two garments were related—cognates, as it were—the idea of access always came as a nice surprise, like a forgotten holiday popping up on the calendar. And Beth's legs, which were girlishly muscular rather than the thin, elegant things destined for hosiery, were just right for a jeans skirt.

When they came back downstairs from their last trip, Beth gave Cook a nice smile and thanked him for his help, which immediately made him feel guilty for viewing her sexually. She said, "Geez. He's listening to reggae again.

Every chance he gets . . ." Her voice trailed off and she went into the kitchen.

Cook went back down to the basement. The cleared circle was much wider, and when Cook resumed working he noticed that the junk was more varied. He would hold up objects for Dan's judgment—should they be kept or thrown out? Dan looked at them: tarnished silverware, a toaster oven, a dented brass chandelier with cut-glass pendants. "Pitch," he would say. The overriding principle was "pitch."

The basement door opened and Beth came down the stairs. Beth and Dan's last contact, about the roofers, had ended ambiguously, with no clear winner or loser. Cook wondered how they would be with each other now.

Beth sat down on a lower step and watched them. Dan turned off the music. She said he didn't have to do that, she didn't mind it. But Dan said he was about to quit for the day. Beth said the basement was looking great. Dan asked how her conferences had gone. She said fine—two more and she would be done for the year. She reminded him that tonight was the last night of a German film they had wanted to see at the Tivoli, and she said that Tommy's mother had agreed to have Robbie over if they wanted to go to the seven o'clock show. Did they? Dan said sure.

This was all friendly enough. Functional but not cold. To Cook it sounded like everyday stuff.

"I guess Jeremy's coming, too," Dan said. He began to turn off the basement lights, pulling one bulb string after another. "You can't get shed of him, as they say in these parts. Oops. Sorry." He looked guiltily at Beth. "I didn't mean to make fun of St. Louis. It's a city on the comeback, a great place to raise kids, you can go anywhere in twenty minutes, it has a great—"

The doorbell rang. "That's Robbie," said Beth, pretty much ignoring Dan. "He's lost his key again. I'd better get him started on his homework if he's going over to Tommy's. We'll eat at six, guys." She went up the stairs.

Dan looked after her. "Hmm. 'Guys.' She usually reserves

that for Robbie and me. You're one of the guys, Jeremy. What do you think of that?"

Cook showered and dressed for dinner, choosing one of two identical pair of khakis and one of the six knit shirts—all primary colors—hanging in his armoire. He hurried with his socks and shoes, not because he was late but because he heard some lively piano playing and wanted to get nearer to it.

It was Dan, playing without music—a ragtime piece Cook didn't recognize, which is to say it was not "Maple Leaf Rag." Cook approached and listened for a while. He felt a tap on his shoulder and turned around. Beth was holding out a closed fist, indicating she had something to give him. He automatically extended his hand, open under her fist, and she dropped a tiny heart-shaped earring into it.

"Something told me you wanted this," she said.

Cook smiled his thanks and pocketed the earring.

"What a blusher you are!" said Beth, and she laughed lightly and went up the stairs.

When Dan finished the piece, Cook urged him to go on playing, but Dan sprang to his feet, as if energized by the music, and said he was going to watch the news. He invited Cook, and they went upstairs to the den. Beth joined them on the couch, and Robbie, drawn by the TV noise, came in and sprawled across the floor. Cook surveyed the scene— the Wilsons at home, he figured, as they basically were when he wasn't around.

They watched the last few minutes of a local news broadcast, with Dan making wisecracks all the way through it. For the network newscast at five-thirty, Dan was commander in chief of the remote channel changer, and he danced from NBC to CBS to ABC, fleeing commercials and reports he found boring. Robbie preferred the commercials to anything else, and when they came on he would yell "no no no" or "you'll like this, you'll like this," but Dan would zap them. Beth didn't seem to mind his channel-changing at all. Cook, however, was nearly unhinged by it. He had to fight the urge to wrestle Dan to the floor and take possession of the remote changer. He wasn't opposed to the channel-switching as such. He just wanted to do it himself.

At dinner Cook marveled to find garbanzo beans in the salad Beth had made. Succotash, and now garbanzo beans! It was really amazing what people could do with food when they put their minds to it. He rubbed his tummy in approval for Beth.

She rolled her eyes and said, "You getting your tongue back tomorrow?"

Cook nodded, even though he didn't actually know this.

"You said there'd be activities," Robbie said. "Some activity. Hunh! There's more activity in a . . . in a . . ."

"In a graveyard," said Dan.

Robbie thought this was the most hilarious thing he had ever heard. But he abruptly sobered up and said, "Uh-oh. There's one more little bit of homework I've got to do. Parts of speech." He glowered at Cook. "We're on prepositions."

"Ah," said Dan. "'To.' 'For.' 'In.'"

"Yeah, yeah," Robbie said impatiently. "I've got to find a sentence with one at the end of it."

"A sentence ending with a preposition?" said Dan. "I always thought we were supposed to avoid those."

"Yeah. She said that, but she wants us to have one anyway. I don't know why."

Beth said, "Maybe so she can teach you how to say it differently."

"Whatever," said Robbie. "I need one." He looked from his mother to his father. Then he looked at Cook. A colleague of Cook's had once said that a true linguist always had an example handy, no matter what the construction.

"Well?" Robbie said. "You guys got one?"

"I'm thinking," Dan said, making a strained face.

Beth, too, was frowning in thought. She laughed. "It seems like they happen all the time when you don't want them to, but thinking of one is—"

" 'Look *out!*' " said Dan.

Everyone stared at him.

" 'Look *out.*' 'Come *in.*' 'Roll *over.*' "

"Hey," said Robbie. "Great." He bolted from the table, shaking the water glasses, and grabbed his notebook and pen from the kitchen hutch where he had left them.

Beth said, "I don't think those are prepositions."

"Hunh?" said Robbie, looking crushed as he came back to the table.

"What do you mean?" Dan said.

"They seem different." Beth threw a glance at Cook.

"How do you mean, 'seem different'? *In, out, over.* They're prepositions."

"But they seem different."

Dan's face went a little wild. "You can't just sit there and say they seem different. You've got to support what you're saying. You've got to—"

"Okay, okay. Calm down. For one thing, there's no other way to say them. With the kind of sentences Robbie's talking about, you can always say them differently by moving the preposition around."

Dan wasn't having any of this. "Write them down, Robbie. They're fine."

"I'm not gonna write them down if they're wrong," Robbie said flatly. "I'll look like a fool. You want me to look like a fool? Is that what you want?"

"You're not going to look like a fool," said Dan. "They're good enough examples."

"Oh, great. Now they're just good *enough.* Come on, Dad. I want to take a really good one in."

"They don't have objects!" Beth said proudly. "That's it. Prepositions always need objects."

"It's understood," said Dan. "It's an understood object."

Cook nodded to himself. He knew this was coming. Understood material—the last refuge of a grammatical scoundrel.

"'Look out'?" said Beth. "What's understood in that?"

"'The window,'" Dan said soberly. "The full sentence would be 'Look out the window.'"

Beth laughed. "You mean when I say 'Look out,' I always mean 'Look out the window'?"

"Not always," said Dan. "It could mean 'Look out the keyhole,' or 'Look out the periscope.'"

Beth gave him a gently disapproving look. "I thought you were being serious," she said.

"Maybe something *is* understood," said Dan, his excitement showing that now he *was* serious. "'Your eyes.' When we say 'Look out,' we're saying 'Look out your eyes.'" Dan looked at Cook, who stuck his lower lip out, as if in thought. The theory was worth that, at least.

"So is it good or not?" Robbie said.

"No," said Beth.

"No," said Dan, surrendering with a little laugh. "Come on, Jeremy. You can help us here. Just one example?"

"Be a sport, Jeremy," said Beth.

"Yeah," said Robbie. "You're really needed now, and you're just *sitting* there. You're being a little e*xtreme* with this silence of yours, you know."

Cook had already spoken up for Dan and Beth that day. He figured Robbie had a turn coming, too. He cleared his throat. He spoke:

"A little boy was upstairs in his room. It was nearly bedtime, and he was waiting for his father to come read him a story, as he did every night. He went to the top of the stairs and waited. In a few minutes he heard his father coming, and he got excited. But when he saw the book his father had chosen, he was disappointed. It was a book he didn't like at all. He said to his father—now listen to what he said, Robbie—he said, 'What are you bringing that book that I don't want to be read *to from out of up for?*'"

"Oh, *wow!*" said Robbie, his eyes widening as he began to scribble it down. "Say it again. Say it again. Say it again."

Cook and Dan cleaned up from dinner. Beth went to the piano and played some Gershwin—"Who Cares?" and "The Man I Love." She played very well but quite slowly, as if she heard things in the music that made her pause and listen before going on. A little later, they walked Robbie down to his friend's house and went on to the theater, which was right around the corner in the Loop. It was nearly empty. Beth sat between Cook and Dan. As they waited for the film to begin, Dan said he hoped that he and Beth wouldn't fight about it. Cook frowned a question, and Dan said, "We see a movie, we fight about it. You name it, we've fought about it."

Beth said, "He can't name it, honey. He can't talk."

"You name it then," Dan said.

"*The African Queen,*" said Beth. "We've never fought about *The African Queen.*"

"We've never seen it together."

"Yes we have," said Beth. "On TV."

"I don't think so."

"Sure we have."

"When?"

"A couple years ago. We watched it in the sun-room just after it was built. I remember thinking it was the first of many movies we'd be watching in there."

Dan shook his head. "I don't remember."

Beth sighed. "How about *The Sting?* There's a movie we both liked. We didn't argue about that one."

"We argued about the music," Dan said.

"We did?"

"You liked it, I didn't."

"But it's ragtime music," said Beth. "You like it. You *play* it."

"But I don't like it orchestrated. It's meant for solo piano. We had this big argument about it."

"*Terms of Endearment,*" said Beth, forging ahead. "There's no way we could have argued about *Terms of Endearment.*"

"Let's see," said Dan, his face showing a little nervousness. "Let me think. That's the one where..."

Beth laughed and turned to Cook. "My favorite movie, and he doesn't even know what it's about. This happens all the time."

"I confuse it with *Tender Mercies,*" Dan said.

"They have nothing in common," said Beth.

"It's the titles. They sound so alike. The consonants and vowels." Dan brightened and looked at Cook. "Hey—linguistics. Help me out. Aren't they similar?"

Beth laughed. "You don't need him to tell you that. Of course they're similar. But you're the only one in the world who confuses them because of it."

"Which one was Jack Nicholson in?" Dan said to Beth. "Come on. Tell me that much. Was it—"

"Oh shut up."

"Let me try to think of one," said Dan. "Let's go at it geographically. We both like Venice, right? How about movies set in Venice?"

"*Blume in Love,*" said Beth, glancing at Cook, a smile flooding her face. "Now *there's* a movie."

"*Don't Look Now,*" said Dan.

Beth's smile faded. "I name a love story, he names a horror movie."

"A love story?" Dan frowned. "*Blume in Love?* Which one is that? I always confuse it with..." He caught himself—caught the imminent reprimand—and mumbled something.

"What?" said Beth.

Dan cleared his throat. "I always confuse it with *Klute.*"

"God!" Beth said, raising her hands in despair. "I can't believe it."

"They sound alike," Dan protested. "The long *u.* The *l.*"

"Can you believe him?" she asked Cook. Then she gave him a skeptical scrutiny. "You haven't registered a reaction to any of these movies. Have you seen any of them?"

Cook raised a single finger.

Beth laughed. "One? Which one? Let me guess. *The African Queen?* The oldest one?"

Cook nodded.

"Geez," she said. "Where've you *been,* exactly? You're like someone from another planet."

"Brother from Another Planet," said Dan. "Now *there's* a film."

Beth was watching Cook. "I suppose you haven't seen that one, either."

Cook glumly shook his head.

"What's the story with you?" she said.

"Hey," said Dan. "Let's get Jeremy, hunh?"

"I mean it," she said, turning to Dan. "I can't figure him out."

"I think it's linguistics," said Dan.

"What do you mean?"

"Everything takes place on two levels for him. He's on the other level as much as he's on ours. It makes him seem strange. But he's just thinking."

"Is he?" said Beth, turning back to Cook and staring at him. "I wonder."

But she had to stop wondering, and stop staring, because the lights went down.

It was quite a film. Cook squirmed for two hours as he watched a potato-faced German do all sorts of damn fool things, some of them criminal, for no apparent reason and with no sign of emotion. It was wholly without meaning. Cook's only comfort was that nobody talked excitedly at the dinner table and waved their utensils around, the way they always did in French movies. He really hated that. When he sensed that the potato-face was nearly done with his deeds, a familiar dread swept over him: *When the movie ended he would have to say something about it, or look stupid.* But then he remembered his privileged muteness, and he rejoiced. He relaxed so thoroughly that he dropped off to sleep.

When he awoke to the rolling credits, Dan and Beth were

standing up. They were silent—all the way out of the theater, down the sidewalk, and around the corner to their street. It was an ambiguous silence. Had the film baffled them speechless? Were they ostentatiously avoiding an argument? Or were they mocking Cook? He never found out. When they reached Robbie's friend's house, Dan and Beth burst out laughing, apparently at their silence, but they said nothing that explained it.

Robbie was in a lively mood and he chattered all the way home. He told his parents that they had done *exactly* the right thing in not buying him a Nintendo, because he could play on Tommy's whenever he wanted to, and it was *so* expensive, and it was almost *too* much fun, really, and if he had one he'd be addicted to it for sure, and he was glad *not* to have one. To Cook's ears, it sounded as if Robbie would positively kill for this thing, whatever it was. Still, Cook thought, sour grapes was a defense mechanism we all had to learn sooner or later. He was a little surprised at Robbie's precocious mastery of it. Maybe only children were like that, though.

Then Robbie said Cook's preposition sentence and laughed. He said he was going to send it in to "Our Own Oddities" and win ten bucks. Dan explained to Cook that this was sort of a contributors' "Ripley's Believe It or Not" in the *Post-Dispatch,* and Robbie had been submitting items to it for years—banal coincidences from his life, pictures of oddly shaped vegetables, that sort of thing. As soon as they got home, Robbie asked Dan to help him write it up. Beth said it was getting late, but Dan said they could whip it off on the word processor, and he and Robbie went to the computer in the corner of the dining room. Robbie loaded the program and Dan typed it for him, talking him through many of the commands as he used them. They ran the printer and checked the result, and then Dan took Robbie up to bed.

Beth went upstairs to kiss Robbie good night. When she returned she put on a CD and stretched out on the couch with her eyes closed. To Cook the music sounded like the score for some movie about space travel he had shamefully neglected to see. When Dan came back downstairs he read the sports page and mumbled. It was obvious that neither of them was interested in producing any more data. This suited Cook, who was surprised at how worn out he was from just one day of "Watch. Say nothing."

Dan put the paper down and announced he was going to bed. Beth rose from the couch and turned off the CD player. Cook, who had been sitting quietly, awaiting developments, stood up. They all looked at one another.

"Beth and I were talking a little bit about this, Jeremy." Dan nodded to himself, looking sure of what he was about to say. "We think it's okay. I mean, it's okay."

"Yeah," said Beth. "It's okay."

They spoke heartily, with lots of nods and warm looks. If they felt that good about it, Cook wondered why they didn't just pick stronger words and save themselves the wear and tear of body language. But maybe they couldn't. Maybe this was the best they could do.

At any rate, Cook went to bed with an actual smile on his face.

Eleven

"It's good to hear your voice this morning, Jeremy."

Cook, freshly showered and wearing a towel around his waist, had just opened the bathroom door on the third floor and found Dan on his knees with a pallet of plaster, filling cracks in the wall on the landing. Cook gave him a curious look. Good to hear his voice? What had he meant by that?

Dan sat back on his heels, remaining on his knees and looking up at Cook. "Lots of people sing in the shower, but I guess linguists *talk* in the shower. And a funny kind of talk it is, too. 'If Dr. Cook knew anything about Timbuktu...' That was it, wasn't it? It came and went, out of the blue."

Cook smiled vaguely, trying to be friendly. Fearing this might not be enough, he threw his head back and laughed before hurrying on to his room, postponing the conclusion that he was losing his mind until he had tried to figure this out. Self-speech in the shower fell within his range of sane behavior, though it did push the envelope a bit, as he hated to say. What worried him was (1) he couldn't remember having said what Dan said he said, and (2) it made no sense to him. He cared nothing for Timbuktu; it was as remote from his thoughts as it was famous for being from everything else. And *"Dr.* Cook"? Was he so insecure that he had to proclaim his credentials to the shower walls?

Dim signals began to tap in memory's vault. Dr. Cook—a figure of fairly recent derision in linguistic circles, if memory served, and it did, damn it. "If Dr. Cook knew anything about *Kickapoo*..." That was one of F. F. Sweet's memorable sentences—or part of one. How had it concluded? "... then he wouldn't be the sidewalk turd that he is"? Cook couldn't remember. It didn't matter.

Yes it did. Why hadn't he kept Pillow's copy of the journal instead of *shafting* it? He should be studying the article so that he could write a defense of himself.

No he shouldn't. It didn't matter.

Yes it did.

No it didn't.

Repression was good, almost as good as death, but unlike death, it leaked. His volubility in the shower demonstrated that. But it didn't follow that he should give himself over to this fight. That would be a backward step both scholastically and developmentally. He should let it go. In time, the rupture would heal and the leaks would stop. The self-speech would disappear from his waking life and fade to passing mutters, obscene and flecked with spittle, from deepest sleep.

Cook dressed quickly. Earlier, when he had awakened, he had put off reading "Day Three" so that he could shower with a clear head and think about his silent but eventful Day Two. Now, eager for new orders, he opened *The Pillow Manual,* remembering with shame his violent deflowering of it the day before and taking care not to expose any pages other than "Day Three."

His experience with the daily instructions led him to expect a brief, forceful command. This one was brief to a fault:

DAY THREE
Pillow.

"Pillow"? What about him? Was he going to drop by and handle things today? If that was the message, this was a hell of a way to express it. Or could it be the regular English word with a meaning Cook didn't know about? It was possible. Words confused Cook more often than they should have, considering his field. He could never remember what "moue" meant. Or "a dog's life"—were dogs seen as leading cushy lives or tragic ones? He had no idea.

He tracked down a dictionary on the bookshelf and looked up "pillow," but he found no surprise meanings there. So he sucked it up, as they said—whatever *that* meant —and called his evidently eponymous boss.

"Roy?"

"Jeremy? Again? Absurd!" Pillow hung up.

Cook stared at the dead phone in his hand. He thought of that area of the human body, both male and female, defined by an arc sweeping down from the navel, around and up the backside to the tailbone. He ran through all the nouns for things found and produced there. He had such a good time that he misdialed Pillow's number and had to redial. When he reached him, Pillow gave him the quick pick-up-and-hang-up treatment Cook had seen him perform in his office.

Cook took the phone back to the landing and set it on the table. Dan had left the third floor, taking his tools with him. Cook wandered out onto his little balcony for some fresh air. What was he supposed to do all day? Stuff pillows with Dan and Beth? Have a pillow fight? Gather all the pillows in the house and have an orgy on them?

Through the trees in the small park across the street he spotted a flash of bright orange—Hot Pants semaphoring to him as she bent over a lawn sprinkler. His hands formed two buttock cups and contracted rhythmically. It struck him that his sexual despair was greater than it had ever been, even though this dry spell was by no means the longest of his adult life. The reason, he guessed, was Beth. It wasn't just the fact that he often imagined making love with her, but also that he was in her house with her, seeing her, brushing by her, moving in an orbit with her—in short, occupying the same physical space, outside the bedroom, occupied by the man who *could* make love with her, and did, once a week. (He believed Beth's frequency report over Dan's.) Although Cook's relationship with Beth necessarily took place on the barren turf of asexuality, he had come to feel that he and Dan "shared" her. A bizarre feeling—he knew it—but he couldn't help it.

He looked to his right, and his eyes met those of an old man in the front yard of the house next door. "Hi, Dan," the man called up to him in a liquid growl, and Cook waved. Dan had mentioned this neighbor to Cook the night before. He was eighty-five years old and had lived in the house since his birth, the only such resident of the neighborhood. "Friendly and foulmouthed," Dan had said of him. Cook stood waiting for the man to yell, "Hey, you dick, you're not Dan, you fuck!" But he just went back inside. Cook did the same.

When he went downstairs he found that the obscurity of his instructions for the day would pose no immediate problem, for the house was empty. He walked from room to room, finally spotting a note on the table in the sun-room:

> To the cunning linguist—
>   I'm at the hardware store—back in 45. Robbie's at school. Beth ran off with a roofer.
>
>   Yours in Christ,
>   Dan

In *The Woof of Words,* Cook treated English constructions likely to arise when a speaker was eager to deny intent, such as "happen to": "I happened to get drunk and kick my wife down the stairs." Another was "end up," as in "I ended up torturing heretics for a living." He thought about these when he found himself, in the course of a time-killing stroll after breakfast, at the library, where he ended up at a computer terminal and happened to type in the name of F. F. Sweet.

Cook seriously doubted that F. F. Sweet had written a book in his carping career, but it was worth a try. His dim hope was to find F. F.'s soft underbelly, something to initiate a revenge strategy that wouldn't require him to hunch over a Kickapoo grammar for six months. After typing the name, he punched "Return" and blinked with surprise to see that the computer for the library's holdings recognized the bastard as a bona fide author. He punched another button, and one title came up on the screen.

"No," he said. It couldn't be. He turned to a nearby reference librarian, asked her where he might find the book, and said "No" to her when she told him. He said "No" as he walked up the stairs and again when he entered the children's section. A few mothers and fathers were there, browsing the shelves while their children roamed. Cook went to the wall where the picture books were shelved and worked his way down the alphabet to "S." He recognized the spine right away and grabbed the book, glared at it, read the author's brief biography with disbelief, and wedged it back on the shelf, out of order and backward—his first counterblow.

Cook's experience at the Wabash Institute had taught him to divide the world of young children's books into two categories—those that were also fun for adults and those that were not. The worst ones could bring adults to their knees in weeping pleas for mercy. The worst of the worst was *A Valentine for Val,* text and illustrations by F. F. Sweet.

Cook knew the plot well, though he had never paid attention to the author's name until now. Val was a little Indian boy who couldn't handle Valentine's Day. Every year he bought big bunches of valentines, but he never sent them out and never received any. Then one Valentine's Day he decided to send his accumulated hoard all at once to all his friends. He went to the post office and mailed them. When he got home, the mailbox outside his tepee was overflowing. It contained exactly as many valentines as he had sent out.

Flaws: kids of picture-book age didn't know what the hell Valentine's Day was; Val was a stupid name; Val's identity as an Indian never really came across; an inordinate amount of time was devoted to the trip to the post office; no motive was established for Val's sudden decision to mail the valentines; there was no evidence that Val had any friends to whom he could send valentines or who might be expected to send him any; since he received more than one valentine, the title was wrong; a young auditor could easily be confused and think that Val mailed all the valentines to himself; the art was for shit.

A Valentine for Val must have disappeared from the Wabash Institute a dozen times during Cook's tenure. He was responsible for many of its disappearances, but not all of them—the other linguists despised the book as well. After every disappearance there would be a merciful respite from Val, until a well-meaning parent—most often some sappy father—would make a gift of a copy. Thanks, pal.

Cook grabbed the book again and reread the biography. It described F. F. Sweet as "an Indian buff who lives in Washington, D.C., with his eight cats." Indians, Washington, D.C.—it *had* to be the same guy, and the sum of his publications was apparently *A Valentine for Val* and "Why Jeremy Cook's Theory of Kickapoo Adverbs Is Preposterous." The biography said he was "hard at work on a sequel to this volume." It had been ten years since *A Valentine for Val* was published. F. F. must have hit a block. But Cook had an idea for the sequel. The story would open where the previous tale left off. Val eagerly opens the envelopes, only to find they're all filled with unspeakable horrors, sent by a deeply injured, justifiably angry, and incredibly relentless enemy; as a result, Val has a nervous breakdown and mopes around the tepee for the rest of his life. *A Valium for Val.*

The question was this: what real mayhem could Cook create from his discovery of F. F.'s authorship of this book? The answer came easily: none. Cook knew no editors of relevant journals, and even if he did, who would want to publish a hostile review of a popular ten-year-old picture book? Cook's honesty would have killed such a plan anyway. After all, the book worked. The kids at Wabash cried their fool heads off for it every day. In other words, in moments of leisure F. F. Sweet could take pride in his book—when he rocked on his Washington, D.C., porch, for example, or when he fed his eight stupid cats. And there was nothing Cook could do about it.

"Jeremy! Hey! What are *you* doin' here?"

Cook was down so deep in his private world that he was slow to rise to social competence. Robbie stood there grinning at him, his knapsack slung over one shoulder in collegiate fashion. A cute blond girl—perhaps a classmate—passed by Robbie and gave him a lingering look. Through her eyes, as he searched for a way to explain his presence, Cook saw that Robbie was in fact a very handsome boy. He was also funny and even charming, in his way. He seemed entirely comfortable with himself. As for Cook, he felt stuck right where he was, in the picture-book section.

"Those books are all for little kids," Robbie said. "What are you doing?"

"Oh, I'm just confused," said Cook. "What are you up to?"

Robbie looked over his shoulder, watchful of being overheard. "It's a library day. My school's just down the street, and we come here a couple times a week. We're coming a lot this week, because school's almost over and my teacher's pooped and she's run out of ideas."

Cook laughed.

Robbie said, "I'm looking for a book on knots. For my summer camp. Last year they taught us all these *great* knots, I mean *great* ones, but I forgot all of them. Then I'm going to get a book on stars. Last year there was a guy in my bunk who knew all the constellations. I didn't know a single one. I hated it that he knew all that and I didn't. I'm going to nail those suckers down cold." He set out down a row of stacks. He looked back at Cook as if wondering if he wanted to come along, but Cook just waved and headed for the stairs.

• • •

Neither Dan nor Beth had returned home. Cook went up to his room. He figured enough time had passed for him to call Pillow and maybe even get a few words in before Pillow hung up on him.

When Pillow answered, Cook blurted out, "What does 'Pillow' mean?"

"A pillow is a soft cushion for the head. It can also be merely decorative, as one might find on a settee, or a—"

Cook burst out laughing. Pillow had answered as automatically as Mr. Memory in *The Thirty-Nine Steps*.

"Did something amusing just occur where you are, Jeremy?"

"No, Roy. Not at this end. Listen: 'Day Three: Pillow.' What the hell?"

Pillow gasped. "You're on Day Three already?"

"Of course I am. It's the third day."

"Oh my. You don't understand. Oh...So fast. Day Three. Good Lord."

"I'm just following the unsealing schedule. It's Day Three. What's the big deal?"

"But you're taking the meaning all wrong. Don't you see? 'Day' in *The Pillow Manual* has nothing to do with the 'day' you might use in casual conversation. It means something entirely different. It means a unit of time that lasts for as long as you want it to. I assumed you would stay with the 'Day Two' instructions for *much* longer than you have. Do you remember those instructions? 'Watch. Say nothing.'"

Cook laughed. "Yes, Roy. I remember. It was only yesterday, after all. Oops! Does 'yesterday' mean something different to you than it does to me?"

"What a funny idea, Jeremy. Why do you say that?"

"Listen, Roy. If you give me the word 'day' I'm going to think 'twenty-four hours.' So would anybody else. I can't believe the rest of the staff understands it the way you mean it."

"Well, they usually don't, at first. They show a peculiar

tendency to make the same mistake you made. It's a source of vexation to me."

Cook closed his eyes and shook his head slowly. It felt like an action he had never performed before. Pillow was driving him to new behavior.

"So what's the point, Roy?"

"The point is you haven't husbanded your time and resources. You've—" Pillow paused. "Where does that come from? 'Husband'—the verb."

"I don't know."

"Does it come from the noun? But where does the noun come from?"

"I don't *know.* Look, are you saying I've gone too fast?"

"Do you feel that you have?"

Cook considered this. "I've got nothing to compare it with."

"Mmm. Do you feel that you've gotten all that one can get out of 'Watch. Say nothing'?"

"Who knows? I could do it again today, if you want."

Pillow made a scoffing noise. "It's a bit late in the game for *that,* Jeremy. You've already read 'Day Three.' You can hardly go back to 'Day Two' when you've read 'Day Three.'"

Cook was beginning to think that the Pillow Agency ran a forty-week boot camp that he had somehow missed out on. He decided to match Pillow's perpetual obscurity with some of his own: He would not tell Pillow about Dan and Beth's upcoming trip, which he was now sure Pillow was ignorant of, considering how languorously he expected Cook to operate. Cook would drop a mention of the trip on him one day as if it were shared knowledge, and he would listen to Pillow bluster about how he had no idea, how he should have been told, and Cook would just say, "Oh come now."

Cook said, "I guess my only choice is 'Day Three,' then. 'Pillow.' What's it mean?"

"Ah," Pillow said with frightening pleasure. "'Pillow.' It's a crucial step in the process. It's a verb: 'to Pillow.' 'I Pillow. You Pillow. He Pillows.'"

"In Black English, 'He Pillow,'" said Cook.

"Quite right. The past tense is 'Pillowed.' The past participle is 'Pillowed.' The—"

"It's a regular verb. I got it, Roy. What's it *mean?*"

"Well, basically it means to stop the action and demand meaning. You've been a quiet presence in the house so far, Jeremy. You've been lying low. Now it's time to speak up. Suppose that the husband or wife says something that strikes you. Maybe it's a little bit off. Maybe it's a little askew, a little unexpected, a tad cryptic or disproportionate. You slam on the brakes. You stop everything and demand meaning— *full* meaning. You may also ask for an explanation of the timing of the utterance, the style, diction, accent, register, prosody, intonation, pitch, and tempo. That's Pillowing. Do that, and you're Pillowing."

Cook actually felt something like respectful interest. He said, "I just stop them, right in the middle of whatever they're saying?"

"When the fancy strikes you, yes. You may do it when they're talking to you or when they're together and you're just observing—either way. When they're together, listen for snaps."

"Snaps?"

"Yes. When one marriage partner snaps at the other, Pillowing is indicated. It's important to stay on them, Jeremy. Don't let up. Demand meaning until you're satisfied."

"It sounds like I'm going to be a pest."

"Mmm. Pest. I don't like that word. I prefer gadfly, in the Socratic sense. Or noodge. Be a noodge. That's a Yiddish word—"

"I know it, Roy. I know the word."

"Good. To Pillow is to be a noodge."

"Okay. Any other guidelines?"

After a short pause, Pillow said, *"The Pillow Manual* will be your guide."

Cook frowned. "All *The Pillow Manual* says is 'Pillow.'"

"That's right. Don't you get my meaning, Jeremy? I was trying to answer your question by saying no somewhat creatively."

"Oh. I see. Uh, Roy?"

"Yes?"

"You don't have to do that, you know. Speak creatively. It's coals to Newcastle."

"You think so? Why, thank you, Jeremy. I'm quite flattered. What a pleasant note to say goodbye on. What a pleasant note indeed. But before I go, I want to tell you that your date is ready."

Cook closed his eyes and shook his head slowly.

"Shall we say . . . five-twentyish?"

"You mean *today?*"

"Today."

"Oh God."

"Courage, Jeremy."

"And if I refuse?"

"We've been through this. It was most unpleasant. I'm still healing from that unpleasantness."

Cook sighed. "There's only one reason I'm willing to agree to this, Roy. It's the Wilsons. I like them. I want to help them. You probably calculated it that way, didn't you? You deliberately didn't tell me about this dating business until I became involved with them."

"That's dangerously close to being an unpleasantness, Jeremy. Please, be careful. Now, she will pick you up there at the job site. Isn't that nice?"

"Tell me about this babe. Where'd you find her?"

"No, no. Mum's the word. Surprise is nine tenths of pleasure."

"I hate surprises."

"Oh? Well then, I'll say this much: remember what they say about opposites."

"Opposites?"

"Yes. What do they say about them?"

"I don't know. That they attract? Is that it?"

Pillow laughed. "You've got it, Jeremy. You're way ahead of me."

"Really? Why do I feel I'm always behind you, Roy? With my face stuck deeply up your ass. Why do I feel like that?"

Pillow paused. "That's not a very attractive image, Jeremy. It's a rather unpleasant one, in fact. I hope you can say something pleasant now, so we'll be able to say goodbye on a happy note. I hope you can do that."

Cook brought all of his previous day's experience in taciturnity to bear on this moment. He was supremely, eloquently silent. Pillow hung on, waiting for speech. Cook kicked off his shoes and made himself comfortable. There was no telling how long this would last.

Twelve

"**I** Pillow. You Pillow. He Pillows."

Cook recited this conjugation in rhythm with his steps as he came down from the third floor. Through his window, while clinging to the receiver, he had seen the two subjects of imminent Pillowing return—first Dan, full of energy, hauling large rolls of something over his shoulder from the van to the front porch, then Beth, who moved heavily as she walked from her car to the house, carrying two bags of groceries and looking tired. (Cook's standoff with Pillow ended just as Beth drove up, but with no clear victor. As they breathed at each other, a call-waiting signal came in at Pillow's end. Without a word to Cook, Pillow put him on hold and took the call. Cook pretended that Pillow had thereby conceded and immediately hung up his own phone.)

"I Pillow. You Pillow. Hi, Beth."

She was holding the grocery bags and looking at him curiously from the bottom of the stairs. "Ah," she said. "You're back in the world of the speaking. Good." She groaned. "Jesus, it's hot." She headed for the kitchen. Cook followed. She was apparently unaware he was behind her, until the swinging door banged into him. When she turned around he assumed it was to apologize. But instead she just frowned.

"Can you put the milk in the refrigerator?" she said. "I'm wiped out." She set the bags on the counter and went into the sun-room, where the air conditioner was on. She shut the French doors behind her and threw herself into the recliner.

Cook bristled—not at Beth's words but at the way she had said them. He hated "entitled" people, and she had just acted entitled. As he took the milk from one of the bags and opened the refrigerator, he struggled to match this impression with his overall view of her. The day before, she had spontaneously vacuumed his car. Entitled people didn't do things like that. And they didn't root through vacuum cleaner bags for mementos after being told not to bother. Still, right now he had a bad feeling—the resentfulness of grudging servitude—and while it wasn't the same bad feeling he had already known with Beth (guilt for having let her down in some way), it was a close kin to it. He slammed the refrigerator door shut, threw a scowl through the French doors at the top of Beth's head, just visible over the recliner back, and went to see what Dan was doing out in front.

"It's a monster, Jeremy," Dan called to him from the street. He was untying the rope holding a long ladder to the top of the van. "A sixty-footer. I've rented it to do the roof work myself. There's a high school kid down the street who helps me with stuff like this. I'll call him."

"I want to help," Cook said, walking toward him.

"No. It's a monster."

"I want to."

Dan shook his head. "You'd hate it."

"Let me help."

"Okay, then. Stop lollygagging and get your butt over here." Dan laughed.

Cook walked to the front of the van, where the ladder projected over the hood, and began to untie the knot at the other end of the rope. Dan explained that he had done some investigating around the neighborhood and learned that leaking tile roofs such as his were best treated "holistically"

—by removing the tiles, replacing the underlying tar paper, and reinstalling the tiles. He said he would start on the dormer over Cook's room.

"I should tell you something," Dan said. He was gathering his end of the rope into tidy long loops. "Beth and I had a fight this morning."

"What about?"

Dan scrunched his face up. Before he could speak, Beth called from the front door, "Honey! Phone. It's Bruce."

Dan made a strange, deep noise and went to take the call. Cook gathered the rest of the rope. Dan came back out and called to him, "Take a break, Jeremy. They need me at work, believe it or not. We'll get the ladder later. I've got to go change."

"Why wouldn't I believe it?"

Dan went back inside. Cook wasn't sure if Dan had heard him. He hurried to the house, leaving the coil of rope on the front porch, and went upstairs, arriving at the second floor landing just as Dan closed the bedroom door.

Cook walked up to the door and knocked. "Why wouldn't I believe it?" he asked.

"You come in here and you're gonna get bare-assed."

"I'm used to it," said Cook, sounding like a wily veteran of many campaigns in discordant households, though in truth his only experience in this line had been glimpsing the bare bottoms of babies at the Wabash Institute. "Why wouldn't I believe it?"

Dan laughed in a strained soprano—an awful laugh.

"Tell me about your work," Cook said. "You haven't said a word about it." He heard the opening and closing of dresser drawers.

Dan said, "The contract with your agency said the bedroom was off limits."

"Come on. Talk."

"Fuck off."

Cook stared at the wood grain of the door. He finally went downstairs and opened the French doors into the sun-room. Beth turned and looked at him. Before he had taken a step, she said "What" in a low, short voice. Semantically it fell somewhere between "What do you want?" and "Get out." He got out.

He wandered until he came to rest in front of the living room window, where he stared out at the park. He heard Dan hurrying down the stairs, and he watched him go out the door toward the van. But then Dan stopped in his tracks. He turned around, came back inside, and went through the kitchen to the sun-room. Cook was right behind him as he opened the French doors.

"Honey," Dan said, "can I take your car?"

Beth looked up from the recliner, where she had been reading a magazine. "Close the door. You're letting the air out."

Dan obeyed, letting Cook squeeze in behind him without exactly encouraging him to. "I need your car. I'm kind of in a hurry."

"When are you going to put the air conditioner in the bedroom?" Beth asked.

"Soon. Listen, the van—"

"There's no privacy here. I want a room with an air conditioner where I can get some privacy." She managed to say this without looking at Cook.

"*Okay.* I'll take care of it as soon as I can. I've got about six different things going on. The van has a loose ladder on it. I need your car."

"Can't you take it off?"

"I'll get all pitted up."

"Why didn't you take it off before you changed?"

"Because I *forgot.*" Dan took a deep breath. "Look, do you need your car?"

"I'm not sure."

"What is there that you might need it for?"

"I don't know."

"Do you have any specific plans?"

"No. I just like the option of being able to go somewhere if I want to."

"I *knew* you were going to say 'option,'" Dan said, stamping his foot. "I *knew* it."

Beth stared at him.

Cook said, "I have a number of questions I would like to ask at this point."

"How about some answers?" Dan snapped at him. He stormed through the kitchen. Cook glanced at Beth. She watched Dan impassively. Cook followed Dan, and from the porch he watched him haul himself onto the roof of the van, squat down, and heave the ladder off it with a huge groan. It landed in the ivy with a clang, making several of the neighborhood dogs bark in protest. Dan jumped down, got in the van, and drove off.

Cook went back into the sun-room. Beth was reading her magazine, but turning the pages at a speed that suggested she was getting little pleasure from it.

Cook sat on the arm of the couch. "Why did you give Dan such a hard time about your car?"

"You heard my reason," she said without looking up from her magazine.

"Were you mad because your brother ordered him to come in to work?"

"Bruce doesn't *order* him to do things. They're partners."

"Do you mind that he went?"

"Why would I mind?" She turned a magazine page impatiently.

"Because he's supposed to stay here and work on your marriage."

She gave a little snort.

"Dan said you had a fight this morning. What was it about?"

"Do you mind?" Beth said nastily. *"Do you mind?"*

This clearly meant "Get out," so he did, wondering as he

closed the doors behind him how he was supposed to Pillow if everyone refused to talk to him.

He went up to his room. It was hot and stuffy. He threw open the balcony door in hopes of a breeze. Beth's complaint about the air conditioning had struck Cook as another example of entitled behavior, but now he found himself wondering when Dan would put one in *his* room. Which proved . . . something. That there were many sides to the arguments in this house, he supposed. And that as much as he hated to do it, he would have to be open to entertaining the opposite of the view he had just entertained.

He stepped out onto the balcony. Through the trees a flash of orange caught his eye as it went around a corner of the house across the street. He sighed. The phone rang. Beth got it after one ring. A minute later, she went out the front door, carrying her purse. She walked quickly to her car and drove off—exercising her *option*.

Not quite an hour later, Cook looked up from the novel he had been trying to read. He heard the crunch of acorns under tire wheels slowing in front and the slamming of a car door. He looked out his balcony door and saw Beth walk into the house. A moment later, some mildly dissonant music drifted up the stairs. He considered going downstairs, but fearing another dose of *"Do you mind?,"* he closed his door against the music and went back to his novel.

About a half hour later, he heard another crunch of acorns. He set his book down and went to the balcony. Dan's van was back. Cook watched him get out and walk to the house. Cook picked up his book and inserted the old postcard from Paula that he always used as a bookmark. Then he headed downstairs.

The piece that Beth was now listening to was by some heavy German, and it had been trying to climax for several minutes. Cook had heard it begin to end from his room, and now, finally, it did, just as he reached the bottom of the stairs. Beth and Dan were in the living room, and they had been talking loudly over the music. They probably hadn't heard him approach, and because they were at the far end, near the dining room, he was just out of sight in the entryway. On impulse he froze in his tracks with the final chord.

"...kind of thing Bruce *always* does," Dan said. "But I think it'll be okay. Where's Jeremy?"

"Up in his room."

"What'd you two do?"

"Nothing."

"You didn't talk?"

"Not really."

"Do you think he's learning anything?"

"I don't know. Bits and pieces maybe."

"What's the activity today?"

"Search me. He's been asking questions. Maybe that's it."

"Sounds dumb."

"Yeah."

There was a pause. Cook barely breathed.

"I like him," Dan said brightly. "Do you still think he's odd?"

"Yeah," said Beth.

There was another pause.

"Yeah," Dan said, apparently having thought his way to agreement.

"I can't get a handle on him," said Beth. "Is he out of it because he's an intellectual, or is he just out of it?"

"I didn't tell you," said Dan, "he'd never heard of Billy Joel."

"You're kidding."

"We were listening to a tape in the van. He'd never heard of him. And he thought reggae was a guy."

"What guy?"

Dan laughed. "Nobody in particular. He just thought it was the name of a guy."

Beth chuckled. "Have you noticed how he wears the same clothes? He's worn those khakis three days now."

"Are they dirty?" asked Dan.

Cook looked down at his pants.

"I don't know," said Beth. "That's not the point. He just—"

"He told me he hates food."

"What?" said Beth.

"Doesn't believe in it. Wants nothing to do with it."

"Yeah? Seems to me he's been chowing down pretty well at the table. Listen, have you heard him talk to himself?"

"No," said Dan. "Wait—yeah. In the shower."

"What'd he say?"

"Something about Timbuktu."

"He was talking about pillows when he came downstairs this morning."

"Really? Doesn't he have a pillow on his bed?"

"Of course he does."

"Why was he talking about them, then?"

"How should I know? He talks to himself so much he's probably run out of subjects."

"Hey, I've got an idea. Robbie should send him in to 'Our Own Oddities.'"

Beth laughed loudly. "That's *funny,*" she said. This was followed by some kissing noises.

The phone rang.

"Probably Bruce," Dan said. "He was going to call if he ran into any more trouble." Dan made the same strange guttural noise he had made earlier, when Beth had called him to the phone. Cook recognized it this time: it was the name "Bruce" pronounced with a rasping elongation of the vowel. Dan went through the dining room into the kitchen. Cook listened from the entryway.

"Hello?" Dan said. "Hi, Rose. . . ." A fall in Dan's tone made Cook visualize a shoulder sag. "Yeah," he continued. "I'm home again. Home again, home again, hippety-hop. . . . Yeah, working on the house, spending some time with Beth. I'll get her." Cook heard the receiver clang on the floor, as if Dan had more or less tossed it there.

Cook decided to reveal himself at this point and walked

through the entryway into the living room. Beth had gone to the radio and turned it on, and some screechy high strings were a nice background to the terror on her face when she turned around and jumped at his sudden appearance.

"Sorry," he said.

She gave him a funny look. Dan appeared from the dining room, gave Cook his own look of mild surprise, and told Beth her mom was on the phone.

As Beth left the room, Cook said, "She seems to call a lot."

"Once a day," said Dan. "Just like a vitamin. The thing is I always seem to be the one to answer it when it's her."

"How do you two get along?"

Dan shrugged and leaned against the fireplace mantel. "She doesn't know what to do with me. She likes me, I guess, but she probably finds me a mystery."

Cook was surprised at Dan's answer. It wasn't strange that he gave just one point of view about the relationship, but it was strange that he gave *her* point of view instead of his own.

"How do you feel about her?"

"Don't ever ask me that question."

"Why not?"

"Because a husband sees his mother-in-law as the essence of his wife's rotten qualities. Whenever Beth is a bitch, I'll think, 'Hi ya, Rose.' Or I'll hum 'Mighty Lak a Rose.'"

"But what about Beth's good qualities? Can't the mother-in-law get credit for those?"

"Nah. I see those as spontaneous. That's who Beth would be *all* the time if her mother hadn't messed her up."

"That's probably not fair to Rose."

"Who cares about being fair to Rose? I'm not married to Rose."

Cook thought about this. "I see. Yes, that makes sense. It exonerates Beth. It's a way of preserving your marriage."

Dan gave Cook a goofy look. "Now why would I want to do a damn fool thing like that?"

Cook laughed lightly. They had both been standing, and he sat down on the couch. "What happened at work?" he asked.

Dan had moved as if intending to sit down as well, but he suddenly converted his motion into a mere pace, with an awkward hitch at the moment of shift. "Just a little problem that needed some attention."

"Ah," said Cook. "That roots it firmly for me. I know exactly what you mean."

Dan gave him a quizzical look. A silence fell.

Beth came back into the room. As she sat down, Cook said to her, "I'm experiencing topic failure."

"Sounds bad," said Beth.

"I was asking Dan about his work—"

"'Topic failure'?" Dan interrupted. "Is that a standard term, or did you make it up?"

"You're just changing the subject," Cook said.

"I'm changing the subject," Dan admitted. "But I'm not *just* changing the subject. I'm interested."

Cook hesitated, then decided to go along, for the moment. "It's standard. It's what happens when someone raises a topic and it gets a minimal response—or none at all." He looked at Beth. "It happens to women a lot."

"I know," she said.

Dan said, "You mean, like out in the world? At parties? That sort of thing?"

"No," said Cook. "In the marriage."

Dan looked pained by the idea.

"Women work hard at conversation," Cook went on. "They're always putting forward topics for discussion, a lot more than their husbands do, and the topics fail more often. They just die. You read transcripts and you get the impression of big brutes just mumbling while their wives work like the devil at making a conversation."

"Tell me about it," Beth said sarcastically.

Dan pursed his lips. "Maybe the women's topics aren't as interesting as the men's."

Beth made some noises.

"No," said Cook. "Sometimes a husband and a wife will raise the very same topic in the course of a conversation. When the wife raises it, it dies. When the husband raises it, it takes off. It all has to do with the spouse's response."

"Do you see that happening here?" Dan asked.

"Why don't you ask me?" said Beth.

"I'm asking him."

"Why don't you ask me?"

"Because you'd just bitch me up."

"You're right. I would."

There was a pause. Cook waited a moment, then said to Dan, "I haven't observed it here, but I haven't been looking for it either."

Dan made a face. "That doesn't tell me much. Look, if it was a glaring problem—if I ignored Beth all over the place —you'd have seen it, right?"

"Probably," said Cook. He sensed a rising protest from Beth and quickly added, "But if Beth feels ignored, that's significant."

Dan laughed unpleasantly. "Which way are you going to have it?"

"What?" said Cook, even though he had heard and understood him.

Dan groaned and stared out the window. "*This* topic has failed. I'm going to go change. Then I'm going to work on the roof. I get pleasure out of tangible achievements. Roof work—that's where you'll find true happiness."

Cook watched Dan head for the stairs. He waited, and when he heard Dan's footsteps overhead, he said to Beth, "I can't get him to talk about his work."

"I don't know why not," she said. She gave Cook an indifferent look, as if the issue didn't concern her.

"Where did you go in your car after the phone call?"

"To the record store. A new Bartok CD I've been waiting for came in." She laughed. "What did you think? I was off having an affair?"

"No no." Cook hoped he sounded convincing. The idea had indeed occurred to him.

"Yes you did."

"No I didn't."

"Only a man would think I was having an affair. Relax. I don't operate that way."

"Of course you don't. Another question. What did you and Dan fight about this morning?"

Beth sighed. "I woke up feeling discouraged about us. Dan can read my moods—it's one thing he's good at—and he got mad. Said he could tell I was having a 'bitch attack.' That's what he calls them. He says I'm moody. But people are moody for reasons. It's because of thoughts they have. Something suddenly starts bothering them. He doesn't understand that. He never says to me, 'What's bothering you? Tell me what's bothering you.'"

"He doesn't?"

Beth gave Cook an unpleasant frown. "You say that like you've heard him do it. Don't you believe me?"

Cook shifted in his seat. "It just seems odd that he wouldn't ask."

"He's too busy getting mad."

"Okay. Another question. Considering how he stormed out of the house when he went to work, I expected the two of you to be arguing when I came downstairs. How did you patch things up?"

"We just started talking."

"That's it?"

"Sure. Why are you so surprised? Is this stuff *that* foreign to you?"

"No. I just—"

"Didn't you ever do that with your old girlfriend— what's her name? Didn't you ever end a fight just by talking about something else?"

"No," said Cook, suddenly angry. "Never. I think it's a stupid way to end a fight. And this stuff isn't *foreign* to me, damn it. We lived together for a year."

Beth's eyebrows shot up and down once, quickly. "I didn't know that. A year. That's a good start, at least."

"What—you pulling rank now because you and Dan have been together longer?"

"Not at all. Don't get so testy."

"Why don't you go on TV so you can get some applause for it?" Cook felt as if *he* were having a bitch attack—and he rather liked it.

"*What?*" She seemed baffled.

"You know what I'm talking about. People on TV, like contestants on a game show—when they say, 'Herbert and I have been married forty-seven years,' everyone claps. I hate that."

"You should love it," Beth said.

"Love it all you want. I hate it."

Cook fell silent. Dan had come into the room during this exchange. As he watched, he made no effort to conceal his amusement. He looked at Cook and said, "Topic success?"

Cook stood up.

"If I might change the subject at this juncture," Dan said, pronouncing the words fastidiously. "Jeremy, do you still plan to help me or should I—"

"I'll help," Cook snapped. "I said I would."

Dan grinned. "Good man." He seemed exhilarated by Cook's flare-up with Beth. He led Cook outside. "Hey," he said. "Some damn fool threw the ladder in the ivy. Pretty silly, hunh?"

"Listen," Cook said. "Since I'm helping you, you help me. Answer some questions about your job, for Christ's sake."

"Three," said Dan. "Since you put it that way, I'll answer three. Three questions for the sake of our three-personed God. Ready? Go."

"Well, did you start your present job right from college? I don't even know that."

"No. I went to a place called the Defense Mapping Agency. It's in the city—'Right here in St. Louis,' as Judy

Garland says. You ever see that movie?" Dan's manner was bright, but falsely bright.

"And you went from there to Beth's father's and brother's place, I take it. What's the name of it?"

"The name of it? It's 'Beth's Father's and Brother's Place.'"

Cook cocked an eyebrow.

"We're going to change the name, though. I'm insisting on it. I've told them to change it or I would *walk*. That's the hard-ass expression—*walk*. So they've caved in and met my demands. Now it'll be 'Dan's Father-in-Law's and Brother-in-Law's Place.'" Dan gave Cook a strange, almost mean look.

"I don't get it," said Cook.

"I don't either."

"What?"

"Is that your third question?"

"No. It's this: How do you feel about what you do for a living?"

Dan took a deep breath, puffing his chest out more than Cook would have thought possible. "It's a family business. But I'm not family and I'm not a businessman. That about sums it up." He looked at Cook. "You want more? Okay. I joined the business for the money and for the novelty of it. What Beth said about it fitting in with my cartography was bullshit. There was no continuity at all with what I'd done before. I was burned out on my job and my dissertation— never finished it. I felt like a failure. It was a scary time. Beth's father and brother invited me into the business, and I threw myself into it—you know, acting on panic. I had to prove myself. And I did—I really did. But..." He had grown animated, but now he sagged. "I hate it. It's a bore. I don't want to live the rest of my life playing buy low, sell high. You know what I mean?"

"Does Beth know how you feel?"

Dan smiled oddly. "One would think so."

"What's that mean?"

"Just what it says. Look, I think you're on your fourth or fifth question."

"Earlier, when you said 'believe it or not' about your being needed at work, was that a reflection of how you—"

"Stop. No more. Time for work."

"But—"

"Time to play roofer. Do you want to be Hanke or Farmer? Farmer was drunk, so you better be Hanke, in light of this big problem of yours."

"Oh, fuck off," Cook said, and Dan laughed and they went to work.

After a titanic struggle to get the ladder from the street up against the house, Dan climbed it to the roof of the dormer over Cook's room. From there he handed tiles down to Cook, who was more safely installed on his little balcony, stacking them. Dan seemed energized by the work, and he made constant wisecracks from his perch and sang snatches of songs Cook failed to recognize.

When Robbie came home from school he yelled with delight from the sidewalk at the sight of his father on high. He hurried upstairs and came out on the balcony and asked if he could join him. Dan said no, out of the question, it was too dangerous. Robbie whined. Then he complained about the Hershey Kisses—*two* days now without dessert at school. It was a crime! he said.

Cook manfully explained that he had eaten them. He apologized and promised to buy Robbie a bag. Robbie frowned and said, "Nice move. Mom and Dad blamed me. I *told* them I didn't do it." He held his frown, then suddenly broke into a grin and said, "Hey, this is great. You know what the worst thing about not having any brothers or sisters is? It's getting blamed if anything's wrong. When my friend Tommy does something, his mom and dad can never figure out if it was him or his brothers or sister that did it. But here, I'm always the guilty one. But that's all changed now. With *you* here, if you do stuff like this, Mom and Dad won't know who to blame. How long you staying for?"

Cook laughed and said he didn't know. They went to work. Robbie helped Cook stack the tiles. The balcony had grown crowded with them, so Cook handed them from there to Robbie in his room, and Robbie put them in a corner. Cook noticed Robbie's eyes roaming over his desk now and then, apparently looking for clues to the linguist's activities. Finally, Robbie grew tired and went downstairs.

A bit later, while Dan was resting—straddling the dormer ridge and facing forward, as if he were about to ride the entire house off into the sunset—he looked down to the street and said, "Who's that?"

Cook looked over the balcony wall and saw a white car of some kind. (Cook hadn't been any good at identifying cars from a distance since Corvairs had disappeared from the road.) It was parked behind a pin oak at the curb, exactly at a point where the trunk of the tree obscured the driver's seat from his view. But an arm appeared—a long, thin arm— then an entire person: a tall blond woman in a tight white dress that showed a lot of skin above and below it. She stepped from the car and looked at the house, her eyes rising slowly, as if they were mounting the ladder rung by rung, until they reached Cook's eyes and locked on them.

Cook jumped back with a frightened shout. He looked at his watch. Five-twenty. Five-twenty*ish*. He could hear Roy Pillow saying it. But Pillow said it with difficulty, because Cook's hands were around his throat, choking the life out of him.

Thirteen

Cook scampered around his room, peeling his dirty clothes off as if they were on fire. He dashed to the bathroom, splashed water all over himself, and hustled to his armoire to grab a clean shirt and pair of pants. Meanwhile, Dan had yelled greetings to the woman from the roof and was making progress in establishing who she was. He shouted down that he was surprised to learn Jeremy had a friend in St. Louis. Cook listened for the mystery woman's response, but it was minimal. Dan continued to bellow in a friendly way.

Cook groaned, grabbed his coat and tie, and hurried out the bedroom door, dressing as he ran down the stairs. Beth was just crossing the entryway to the front door, drawn by Dan's shouting from above. Meanwhile, Robbie, installed at the living room window, hollered, *"What a babe!"*

"Quick!" Cook said as he hurried to beat Beth to the door. "A nice restaurant nearby. Quick!"

"What?" said Beth.

"Name me a nice restaurant. Quick!"

"Well, there are lots of *good* restaurants in the Loop," Beth said thoughtfully. "I don't know what you mean by nice, but—"

"Vava voom!" Robbie sang out.

"I want fancy," Cook said to Beth. "Expensive. Come *on.*"

"Well, there's Topper's in Clayton," said Beth, a little flustered. "What's going on?"

"How do I get there?"

"Mucho foxo!"

"Robbie, stop that shouting!" Beth yelled. Frowning, she gave Cook directions to the restaurant. Cook flung open the door, shot out, and slammed it shut behind him.

The mystery woman stood on the porch like some six-foot trophy permanently anchored there. Six-foot? Yes. She went up, and she went out as well. She wore a white leather dress with no straps or sleeves or belt or anything. It seemed suspended by its own devices—though he knew it was *her* devices doing it. Their eyes met and Cook's immediately glanced off in an awkward ricochet. He couldn't look at her face. It was like looking at the sun.

"Are you..." he began, but stopped short. Christ, how should he put it? "Do you come from Roy Pillow?"

Something unusual happened to his words. They didn't reach her. He could almost see them—a continuous stream flowing from his mouth, straight and well propelled at the outset, but then falling at her feet. Granted, his question was odd—his syntax was that of an international spy, or a Free-mason deep in a ritual. Still, he had never experienced such a blunt nonresponse.

"Your collar is all funny," she said. Her voice was flat, but because it came from her it attacked him behind the knees, making him jelly-legged. He reached up and found that one side of his jacket collar stuck up like a cowlick. He straight-ened it.

"Is that better?" he asked. It was an intimate thing—the little comment, the correction, the reinspection. Here, now, it was grotesque.

"I'm Jeremy Cook," he said. His name suddenly sounded funny to him.

"I want to learn all about you," she said. This was a lie.

Cook knew it from her vapid tone as well as by pure deduction: no one who looked like this could ever want to learn anything about him.

He suggested they go to Topper's. She said "All right" so flatly that it barely carried meaning. As they walked down to the front sidewalk he peeked at her dress. It stuck out all over—so much that it seemed animated. He imagined it moving of its own accord, with her coming along with it. On the sidewalk, he looked at her car—a Mercedes-Benz convertible with the top down. He looked at his battered Honda Coupe. "My car's in the shop," he said. "Can we take yours?"

She agreed to this but remained standing. Cook wondered what was wrong with her. Didn't she fit in her car anymore? Had she grown since she arrived? Then it occurred to him that she wanted him to drive. But why didn't she just get in on the passenger's side? Ah—she must have been waiting for him to open the door for her. Cook remembered how his father used to do this for his mother, and working from that distant example, he hopped to it.

"Hey, Jeremy," Dan yelled from the roof. "Why aren't you taking *your* car?"

Cook scowled at him as he walked around to the driver's side. His eyes dropped from Dan to Robbie, who was still at the front window, and then swung over to Beth, whose face was at a small window high up in the front door.

The keys were in the ignition. Cook studied the controls and started the car. Dan yelled something and the woman turned to look up at him, but Cook gunned the engine and pulled away. He immediately got lost in the circular confusion of the neighborhood, and before he knew it he was cruising down their street and past the house again—past a grinning, bellowing Dan.

When they were out of the neighborhood, Cook struggled toward conversation, fighting its two deadly enemies, fear and lust.

"Are you from St. Louis?" he asked. This was as close as

he could get to his real question: "Where in the hell did Roy Pillow find *you?*"

She said yes.

"Born and raised here?"

She said yes.

"Do you like it?"

She said yes.

Cook drove. She sat. She didn't exactly take the old conversational ball and run with it—she took a sharp needle and popped it and made him go find another one. He took a deep breath and had a thought that angered him slightly, but it calmed him, too: because this woman didn't react normally to him, he had gone on a search for new ways to be and he had lost himself in the process. He would have to stop doing that, stop losing himself. But he would still try to meet her where she was, even if she occupied such a tiny iota that there was barely room for him there.

"What do you do?" he asked.

"You know what I do," she said.

Cook became engorged. His whole body swelled, as if transfused from a hidden blood supply. His face and everything below it reddened, stretched, and throbbed, until he felt that to observers on the sidewalk it must look as if a tall penis with arms were driving the car.

But maybe she had meant something else—something other than that she was a million-dollar hooker hired by Pillow for Cook's pleasure.

"Of course I know," Cook managed to say, "but I want to hear it from your lips."

"I'm a model," she said—brightly? Peevishly? Neutrally? He couldn't tell how she said it. She didn't say things in any way at all.

A model. Cook pulled up to a stoplight and looked at her out of the corner of his eye. She had a curious cleavage. In addition to being beautiful, it looked muscular, as if her breasts could perform work. He wondered if they could hold up an umbrella.

"A model," he said. "That must be interesting." His true thought was "That must be awful," but he owed her a lie, to match hers about wanting to learn all about him.

Luckily, Topper's wasn't far away, and he located it and found a parking place down the street. He remembered to hop out of the car quickly and open her door. His reward was an optimal view of her tits. They seemed even larger from above. Then, as they walked, he sneaked another peek. They looked different again! He wondered if this was why men looked at tits more than once: they were secretly hoping they might change. He remembered reading somewhere that America was moving into a tit period, with more and more women simply buying new ones. Were hers store-bought? He had no idea. He wondered what the next stage would be—buying tits that actually did change? Tits for all occasions. Maybe inflatable ones. That way, sometimes they would be small and tasteful—for trips to the library, say, or for funerals—and other times they could leap right off the map.

The restaurant was at the top of an office building. As Cook steered her to the front door, she burst into speech: "I'm hungry."

Cook nodded. He thought about her sentence, which, owing to its rare spontaneity, he analyzed rather more than it could stand, like a psychoanalytic critic scrutinizing a knock-knock joke.

She spoke again: "This window is in need of repair."

A big piece of duct tape was plastered across a front window of the building. "It certainly is," Cook agreed as he opened the door for her.

"This building is tall."

Cook decided that the sensory world was her forte. She saw and she heard, and she gave a swift and honest account. This was where he would meet her. "'Tall' is a perfect word for it," he said.

"It's cool in here," she said.

"Yes," said Cook. "Cool in here, and warm outside."

The elevator came and they got in.

"The *top* button," she said. "For *Top*per's."

Humor! A nice surprise. That raised lots of possibilities. Cook laughed lightly as he punched the top button.

The maître d' greeted them with such warmth that Cook assumed he and his date must have been acquainted. Cook wondered if she had some personal connection with the restaurant—relatives who owned it, perhaps? Was that why she had responded so flatly to his suggestion that they go there? Given her remarkable gift of humor, had she hidden this connection in order to surprise him later? Now, or soon, would she reveal all, and would they laugh and have a helluva good time?

He turned to her, his hope for their relationship on the rise. But her face was as empty as a galvanized pail fresh off the assembly line. Cook sighed and followed the maître d' to their table. The man did an unusual thing—he walked backward all the way from the door to their table, negotiating a right-angle turn without even looking over his shoulder. Cook burst out laughing and automatically looked at his woman for a like response. He got none, of course.

These back-to-back disappointments made him see her in a new way. He saw her as MADE FOR FUCKING! That was all she was good for. She wasn't a hooker, but she was still MADE FOR FUCKING!

When they were seated, she said, "Tell me *all* about yourself."

Cook pressed his lips together. He rallied against his new view of her. What if she *was* sincere? What if she really *did* want to learn all about him?

"I'm a linguist." He searched her face for a sign of recognition. It was as expressionless as the huge round curve of her breasts. "I'm a specialist in language."

"Oh, I'll *bet* you are."

Cook pressed on. "I do linguistics."

"Oh, I'll *bet* you do."

Cook frowned. "Linguistics is the scientific study of language," he droned. He looked around at the nearby tables, fully expecting to see red-faced patrons who had overheard this stifling laughter behind their hands.

"Tell me about your magazine," she said.

"My magazine?" Cook frowned. "I've published some stuff in linguistics journals, if that's what you mean."

A wave of irritation crossed her face. "You keep saying that word. I mean your new fashion magazine."

Disaster lay ahead. What idiotic cover story had Pillow concocted? "Tell me what you know," Cook said.

"Well," she said with a little smile, making nice, "I know that you're from New York. I would have known it anyway just from the way you're dressed. The wonderful way you mix these old styles—you must be two years ahead of us out there. Anyway, I know you're gathering material for a new fashion magazine. I know your first issue is going to feature models from different parts of the country. I know I'm lucky enough to be a candidate for the St. Louis slot." She breathed deeply.

MADE FOR FUCKING!

"It's amazing what you know," Cook said.

"Yes. Isn't it?"

MADE FOR FUCKING!

If that was what she was made for, shouldn't he help her fulfill her destiny? Even under false pretenses?

MADE FOR FUCKING!

He sighed. "You are about to be outraged," he said— quickly, before he could change his mind.

"Roy. One question: what the hell?"

"Ah. Jeremy. Tell me about your date. I'm just dying to hear all about it." Pillow sounded like a nightgowned sorority sister hopping on the bed.

"What the hell, Roy? What was your thinking?"

"'Opposites attract.' What else? I wanted to put it to the test. I assumed you knew that."

"Yeah, but how is she my opposite? Am I ugly? Is that it?"

"Oh, Jeremy." Pillow used a tone Cook hadn't heard from him before—one of jocular affection. It was quite frightening.

"I'm serious. How is she my opposite?"

"Well, since you brought up her looks, there *is* a difference there. She knows she's good-looking."

"Yes?"

"And you don't. It's that simple."

"I don't know she's good-looking? Of course I do. My pecker was straining in my pants like a dog on a tight leash."

"No no no," Pillow said quickly. "You don't know that *you're* good-looking."

Cook fell silent. "Oh," he said stupidly. And, still more stupidly, "You think I'm good-looking?"

"Yes," Pillow said in a quick mumble. "But there are more important differences. She's very dumb."

"Yeah. Eventually I figured that out."

"Eventually? It should have been obvious immediately. I'm not talking about cultural literacy in any ambitious sense, Jeremy. I'm talking about two plus two." Pillow cleared his throat. "So," he said in a bright way—a new beginning—"how was it?"

Cook laughed. "It was awful."

"What?"

"The worst time of my life."

"Oh come now."

"Outrageously bad."

"Well, how was sex?"

"Sex?"

"Yes. Surely there was sex."

"Nope."

"Oh come now."

"Nope."

"Doggone it, Jeremy," Pillow said, resorting to strong

language. "This throws everything into a cocked hat. You led me to believe there was always sex, regardless of your feelings."

Cook groaned. "Roy, get in the picture, will you?"

Pillow said nothing for a while. Then: "Go ahead."

"What?"

"Give me your report."

Cook laughed. "I just did. It was awful. End of report."

"Go ahead."

Cook felt his jaw tighten painfully. He made it relax. "You want to know what happened, sort of step by step?"

"Go ahead."

An idea suddenly struck Cook that explained everything: Roy Pillow was not a free man; he was following the dictates of another manual—a *Super Pillow Manual*—which ordered him to do odd things to Pillow agents, like say "Go ahead" over and over. Or "Oh come now."

"We went to dinner. She told me who she thought I was. I told her the truth." Cook waited a moment for Pillow's response. Hearing none, he *went ahead*. "She didn't believe me. Then she did. Then she cried, and she and her tits got up and left. End of date. End of report."

"Did you go after her?"

"No. After a suitable interval, I left the restaurant and walked home."

"What did you learn?"

"Learn? Well, I guess opposites don't attract, eh? At least I didn't attract her—despite my renowned good looks. Once she learned I wasn't this big-shot fashion guy, she dumped me."

"But didn't she attract you, Jeremy? You mentioned . . . something."

"Yes." Cook sighed. "I'm hopeless."

"No you're not."

"She was gorgeous. I couldn't help it."

"Don't be so tough on yourself."

"For a while I even made her into something she wasn't. I

saw this witty, observant person inside her dress, just because... because of her dress."

"You wanted to connect. That's all. You wanted to make a human connection."

"Did I?" Cook asked—with hope.

"You imagined her into someone you could truly be with."

"You think so?"

"You wanted a relationship. I say hurrah to that. Hurrah for Jeremy. Now, what else can you tell me?"

Cook thought. "This 'opposites attract' thing. Surely it doesn't mean people with opposite *values*. It can't mean that."

"Did you learn that from your date?" Pillow asked sharply.

"No," said Cook, a little puzzled. "Not really."

"Then I don't want to hear it. What did you learn from your date?"

"Well, she tolerated me less than I tolerated her. I was willing to hang in there and see what happened, but once she found out who I was she left. So she was less flexible than me. I guess you could say she had less range."

"Yes, yes," Pillow said impatiently. "But there's nothing new there."

"What do you mean?"

"It's something I've known for years. People like her are doomed."

"Why?"

"I've told you that you can't save a marriage with a prick in it, Jeremy. Or a bitch. *Or a dumbbell.* Add that to your list." Pillow sighed. "Your report is wandering far afield and telling me nothing new." He paused. "Your report is over. Do me a favor in the future, Jeremy. Try to have sex."

"Geez, Roy. I'm always trying."

"I suppose you're going to want a hint again," Pillow said petulantly. "Let me think."

"A hint? What do you mean?"

"I've got it. Birds of a feather, Jeremy."

"They flock together. So what? This isn't a hint about another date, is it?"

Pillow laughed.

"Is it?"

"You're way ahead of me, Jeremy. Way ahead of me."

"No I'm not, Roy, you sonofabitch. I'm still behind you, with my face—"

But Pillow had hung up.

Fourteen

After his date and his phone call to Pillow, Cook had a deep hunger for human contact. He wandered downstairs in search of Dan, Beth, and Robbie. But the house was empty, just as it had been on his return from Topper's.

He found a note on the table in the sun-room.

> To the cunning linguist—
> If there is life left in you after your outing, come watch the Mound City Printers kick the Loop Merchants Assn.'s butts all over Hadley Field. Go left at Delmar, then right on Kingsland. The field's on your right—a 20-min. walk.
>
> —Dan

A map accompanied the note, done in the decorative style of the maps in the living room. In this case the motif was baseball. Street names were written on oversized pennants that appeared to be stuck on street corners, baseballs could be seen flying dramatically across the sky, and the entire map was bordered by a filled grandstand, as if the Loop were one big ballpark.

Cook reread the note. The Mound City Printers. *Finally* he knew the name of Dan's business. The map and note reminded him to do something he had been meaning to do since his talk with Dan on this subject. He took THE HORROR! from his shirt pocket and unfolded it before him.

> ~~She's a bitch.~~
> ~~He's a prick.~~
> Money.

Cook had been asking himself some questions. What kind of man avoids talking about what he does for a living? What kind of man fails to finish a dissertation, burns out at his first job, and hates his next one? He crossed out the third entry and wrote down a new one:

> He's a failure.

Cook stared at this. He felt brutal for writing it—something he hadn't felt, oddly enough, with "She's a bitch" or "He's a prick." But he would let it stand. He folded the sheet and put it back in his pocket.

"Hum baby hum baby hum baby."
  "Pick me up, Bob, pick me up."
  "Pull hitter pull hitter."
  "Pick me up."
  "Hum baby hum baby hum baby."
As Cook approached the softball diamond he felt a linguistic panic attack: speech was occurring that meant nothing to him. He rallied and fought it. He reminded himself of all that he *did* know, and he dismissed the men and women on the field as a bunch of yahoos. This made him feel better.

Across the diamond he saw Dan, orange-shirted like the rest of his team. He was standing in front of the team bench, demonstrating a batting stance and wiggling his rear end rapidly. Some of his teammates laughed, Beth among them.

Robbie sat at one end of the bench, wielding a pencil and

calling out something, though to whom he was speaking wasn't clear. Dan sat down on the crowded bench. He began to scoot energetically toward Robbie, making everyone between them scoot, and the domino effect bumped Robbie off the bench onto the ground. He got up grinning and protesting. From the look of things, the Mound City Printers were a fairly irreverent bunch. The Loop Merchants Assn., out in the field, seemed distinctly more serious.

Robbie looked around, apparently to see if anyone had witnessed his embarrassment. He spied Cook and waved. Beth noticed this and turned and waved, too. Cook began to approach, but he imagined a flurry of introductions and questions about who he was. He stopped at the small aluminum bleachers behind home plate and sat down there—the only spectator at the game. Robbie hustled over to him.

"Seven to four, our favor, one out in the bottom of the third," Robbie declared, "in the second game of a twi-night doubleheader."

"I'm not much of a fan," Cook said, wanting to put a quick end to this talk. He added, "But I do know who Elvis is."

Robbie gave Cook a funny smile and sat down beside him. "I'm the official scorekeeper," he said, "so don't mess with me." He showed Cook a sheet filled with diagrams and scrawls. It looked like a lost astronaut's daily log. "I helped us win the first game. Caught one of their players trying to bat out of order."

They watched a Mound City Printer get a hit. The next one made an out, and Beth came to bat. Cook thought she looked sexy in the batter's box and wished he could tell her so. He noticed, though, that she swung stiffly, like a gate.

"Doesn't break her wrists," Robbie said, as if he knew what Cook was thinking. On her next swing she blooped the ball over third base for a hit, and Robbie hollered and cheered and marked his scorecard with a flourish. Cook clapped politely.

"Watch Dad," Robbie said, for his father had stepped into

the batter's box. "He likes to go the other way."

To Cook's ears this sounded like a statement of sexual inclination, and he watched with interest. But all Dan did was smash the ball over first base, where Beth was standing. She jumped back from it as it flew by, then headed for second base and on to third. Dan pulled into second.

Robbie hollered some more. When he settled back down, he said, "The women hate to bat right before Dad, because he always hits it that way. If they get on first, they have to be on their toes. They take turns batting before him. It was Mom's turn this game."

"Don't men ever bat before him?"

"Can't. The batting order has to be man, woman, man, woman, man, woman, man, woman, man—"

"Ah. I didn't notice."

"Stick with me, big guy. Oh, rats." The next Mound City Printer had hit a pop fly to left field.

The teams switched places. Dan swung by the stands when he came in to get his glove, but he didn't stop. He just waved to Cook and trotted out to play shortstop. On his way he said something to the ump that made him laugh. Dan seemed full of life out there, almost ridiculously happy. Cook watched Beth walk out to right field. She chatted on the way with the second baseman. She seemed to be enjoying herself, though not at Dan's manic level.

They watched the Loop Merchants Assn. fail to score, and Dan's team came in to bat again. Dan and Beth came over to where Cook was sitting, which pleased him until he realized a specific curiosity drew them.

"What happened to, uh . . ." Dan began, shaping his hands roundly in the air before him. He seemed about to elaborate on this gesture when Beth interrupted.

"Your date," she said.

Cook sighed. "She wasn't a date. She's . . . a linguist."

Beth laughed. "A linguist?"

"I was interviewing her for a position."

"Yeah, but *what* position?" said Dan. This made Robbie

laugh, which made Dan look at him with surprise.

Beth said she sure didn't *look* like a linguist, and this launched some silly talk about what a linguist looked like. Cook began to fear they were going to talk about his clothes again. But another member of the team approached—a soft-faced man with large eyeglasses and a sad, full-lipped smile.

"This your old college pal, Dan?" he said.

"Right. Jeremy, this is Bruce—Beth's brother."

Cook perked up and shook hands with him. Bruce gave Cook a complicated scrutiny. It felt aggressive to Cook, and yet Bruce seemed to pull back shyly at the same time.

Bruce said, "Dan must have missed you all these years, the way he's taking time off to be with you." Bruce looked at Dan quickly, as if he expected protest. "I know, I know. You haven't had any time off in a year and a half. I know." He looked back at Cook. "And then they're off to Europe, leaving me all alone in the shop for two weeks!" He grinned. "That's okay, though. Old Danny boy never takes Beth anywhere." Bruce laughed at this, though in a strained way that made it hard for Cook to respond genuinely. Bruce seemed to want to be a regular guy, a joker, but it didn't work, exactly. Beth got called away by one of her teammates on the bench, and Dan said he had to go coach and trotted over to the first-base coach's box.

This left Bruce with Cook and Robbie. Cook didn't feel like entertaining questions about his and Dan's mythical college years together, so he made a point of beating Bruce to the next sentence. "Quite a team you've got," he said.

"Yeah," said Bruce. "Thanks to Dan. We're going after our third trophy. It's good for morale. We have a good time."

"Is everyone on the team connected with the business?"

Bruce took this idle question as a request for a breakdown of the team's roster by job description, which he gave to Cook, starting with the batter in the box and working his way down the bench—there were printers among them, salesmen, secretaries, a custodian, and two or three spouses, like Beth. It was a tedious recital. By the time Bruce finished, two batters had made outs and two had reached base, and it was his turn to bat. He assured Cook it had been good talking to him and went to bat and popped up for the third out.

As the Mound City Printers took the field, Robbie marked his scorecard and said, "You knew my dad in college?"

Cook put himself on alert. "Sure. Didn't he tell you?"

"That means you knew Mom, too. They were in college together."

"Yeah. I didn't know her as well, though."

Robbie was silent for a while. Dan had taken over pitching, and they watched him toss some warm-up pitches to the catcher. The first batter came to the plate, but after a couple of pitches a player on the opposing team stood up from the bench to make a complaint. Cook heard him yell something about an arch, and he asked Robbie what the problem was.

"He wants Dad to lob the ball more. Dad's coming in too flat."

The man had meant to say "arc." Dan's first baseman, a woman, picked up on the mistake and yelled at Dan to put more St. Louis Arch on the ball, and Dan laughed, and the third baseman, a man, yelled, "Yeah, Dan. Put some more Jefferson Expansion National Memorial on the goddamn ball," and Dan laughed again. The entire infield took it up, and they urged Dan to put all sorts of St. Louis landmarks on the ball. The joke seemed to escape the Loop Merchants Assn. player who had lodged the complaint. He just watched the action stolidly.

"How's your survey going?" Robbie asked.

Cook went back on alert. "Hmm?"

"Your survey. How's it going?"

"Fine."

"Who've you talked to besides Mom and Dad?"

"Oh, people in the neighborhood."

"Like who?"

"Oh, Mary across the street. The old guy next door. People in the Loop."

"What do you ask them?"

"Say, is this guy the right batter? Wasn't a woman supposed to bat next?"

Robbie looked at his scorecard. "He's the right one." They watched him ground out to the second baseman. Robbie marked his scorecard and said, "What do you ask them?"

Cook cleared his throat. "Well, first I ask them if they were born and raised in St. Louis. They have to be natives."

"Hunh?" Robbie made a face.

"'Native' means someone who was born and raised in the area." Etymology! Cook thought. A guaranteed conversation killer. "It's from the same Latin word that gives us 'nativity.' We get lots of words from that root. We get—"

"Hey, *I'm* a native. Interview *me.*"

"I will," said Cook.

"Go ahead."

"No, no. I'm saving you."

"But I want to hear what you ask them."

"Okay. Let me think of a good example." Cook knew nothing whatsoever about the St. Louis dialect—not even if there was one. He would have to fall back on general principles. He watched the second batter hit a ground ball to Dan, who threw him out at first. Robbie marked his scorecard. Then he turned and looked at Cook.

"A long time ago," said Cook, "linguists came up with a bunch of words to ask people all over the country. If people say certain words, then a linguist can tell where they're from."

"Like what?"

"Well, how would you call a cow?"

"Hunh?"

"How would you call a cow?"

"I don't know. Dial nine-one-one?"

Cook laughed. "No. I mean in person. If you were standing at a fence, looking at a cow in the field, and you wanted to call her to you, what would you say?"

"I'd say, 'Hey, cow, get your buns over here.'"

"Exactly," Cook said without hesitation. "And that identifies you as a St. Louisan."

"Really?"

"Sure. The use of 'buns' is typical of St. Louisans."

"Dang," Robbie said, fascinated. "Did Mom and Dad say that, too?"

Cook thought for a moment. "They probably would. I haven't asked them yet. Don't warn them. I've got to surprise them with the question."

"What else? This is neat."

"Let me think." Cook wandered far and wide over his mental linguistic atlas, beating the bushes for an example. "What do you call the long thing you sit on in your living room?"

"A 'couch'?"

"Right."

"Or a 'sofa,'" Robbie added quickly.

"Do you say 'sofa'? Do you actually say it?"

Robbie's face went sheepish in a way Cook recognized: bad-informant guilt. "Not really."

"When I was growing up I had an unusual word for a couch. I called it a 'chesterfield.'" Cook said this proudly. It was the only interesting thing in his dialect. But the ball field rang with Robbie's laughter.

"Dang!" he said. "That's so dumb. How come you called it that?"

Cook shrugged. "There's this little area in California where people say 'chesterfield' for couch. If they have it in San Francisco, your dad probably grew up saying it, too."

"You know what? My teacher says 'davenport.' She calls a couch a 'davenport.'"

"Where's she from?"

"Nebraska." Robbie rolled his eyes. "She's always talking about how wonderful Nebraska is."

The bases had become loaded as they talked, and Robbie suddenly dropped linguistics and focused intently on the action on the field. Cook watched, too—watched two runs score while Robbie groaned. But then a woman flied out to the center fielder, who was playing way in, almost at second base, and Dan's team came in to bat.

Cook suddenly realized that although the game before him provided a natural opportunity for sexual or sexist comments, he hadn't heard any from anybody. He had noticed that the outfielders shifted along gender lines, playing in close when women batted, then going back out for men, but he decided that that wasn't sexist—it was simply pragmatic. In fact, the whole game was a study in accommodation, as if everyone on the field had said, "We know the sexes are different, but we can still play ball together, and here's how we do it."

While Dan's team scored some runs, Cook's attention drifted. He looked up at the nearly full moon just clearing the trees in the east. It was dusk, and something in the fading light made him think of Wabash, with its Sunday picnics lasting into the night. But suddenly someone behind Dan's team bench threw a switch on a pole, and the lights high over the diamond came on, spoiling that brief blend of daylight and moonlight. The lights brought flying insects, which brought out the nighthawks—or maybe the nighthawks had been there all along, and he just now noticed them. They made their funny buzzing noises high above, zigzagging in pursuit of dinner on their odd angular wings. He knew these from Indiana, too. Paula had always looked up and laughed when the nighthawks came out.

After a few more innings, just when Cook was wondering when it would be over, it was, and the players were shaking hands. Dan's team had won, judging from Robbie's noises of satisfaction, though no great celebration broke out on the field. It was just men and women shaking hands as if they had finished a day's work in satisfactory fashion.

Cook waited in the bleachers for the crowd to thin out,

but it took a while. As the team gathered their equipment, there was a lot of talk and laughter. Dan was at the center of it, replaying incidents from the game and teasing some of his teammates. They all seemed reluctant to break up, and did so only after Dan eased away, his equipment bag over his shoulder, calling out good-nights to everyone.

They drove home. Beth took a shower while Dan and Cook read the paper and Robbie practiced the piano. Then Dan helped Robbie with his math homework. Cook settled in the recliner in the sun-room and listened to Dan and Robbie talk about "magic numbers"—the name Robbie's teacher had given negative numbers to take the scare out of them. As Cook watched, he kept expecting Robbie to denounce the label as childish, but Robbie seemed to accept it as a natural name.

When they were done and Robbie was packing up his papers, Dan told Robbie he was particularly delighted with the way he had solved one of the problems. Robbie mentioned that his mother had helped him with it, and Dan suddenly became undelighted. Robbie seemed not to notice this. He kissed his father good night, said good night to Cook, and went upstairs to bed. Shortly afterward, Beth came into the sun-room, wearing pajamas and a robe. Dan immediately told her that he wished she wouldn't help Robbie with his math—she could help him with anything else, but in math it was crucial that he know exactly what Robbie knew, in order to challenge him without discouraging him, and if she helped him, then things would get all confused. Beth seemed a little put out, but she just said okay.

They read for a while. Or rather, Dan and Beth read and Cook pretended to. He kept thinking about what had just happened. In the past, Cook had been impressed with the way Dan helped Robbie—with his geography, at the word processor, every chance he got. On the face of it, Dan was more involved in the boy's education than Beth was. But because Beth taught all day herself, it was only natural that tutoring Robbie fell to Dan. Cook had no problem with this. What bothered him was that Dan had shown a bully-ing, superior side just now. He seemed to be saying that Beth was an idiot to think she could help Robbie with his math. Of course, Dan would have denied this; he would have said he was just advocating good pedagogy. But Cook, in Beth's place, would have felt bullied.

"It's still early," Beth said, tossing her magazine aside. "Want to watch a movie tape?"

"Sure," said Dan. "If we don't fight about it."

"We won't," Beth said. She looked at Cook. "Not in front of company." Cook smiled.

Dan went to a green notebook on the TV stand—his di-rectory of videotapes he had recorded. He opened it and read. *"The Third Man?"*

Beth made a face. "Don't you have it practically memo-rized?"

"I like the music," Dan said as he continued to scan the list. *"Local Hero?"*

"Another musical favorite. No. We've seen it too re-cently."

"Zorba the Greek?"

"We have that?" Beth said with interest. "Sure. It's been a lifetime since we saw it." She turned to Cook.

"Great," said Cook, though he recalled, with unease, a certain opposition in the film between scholarliness and sex-ual vitality.

Dan picked out the tape and put it into the VCR. The movie wasn't at the beginning of the tape. He began to search for it, but every time he ran it something other than the movie appeared on the screen.

"Kojak?" Beth said. "Wrong Greek. What's he doing on there?"

"I don't know," Dan muttered.

Cook sensed a tension in the air, and he asked them about it. Hunching over the VCR, Dan said he *was* tense, he *was*. He explained why. Recording movies was his responsibility, because Beth hadn't mastered the timer on the VCR. This meant that Dan bore the blame in case of failure—in case the recording ended before the show did, or as sometimes happened, he taped the wrong show altogether. Dan reported this with interest—with more than interest; with *fervor*— as if he was seeing an unfair pattern of responsibility and recrimination for the first time. Beth made no comment.

A burst of music with opening credits told them that Dan had finally found the movie. He did a Greek dance to the couch and said, "I'm off the hook, Jeremy. Off the meat hook." He settled down and put an arm around Beth. Cook kicked his shoes off and leaned back in the recliner, relieved that he could stop thinking about their marriage for a couple of hours.

Some minutes later, as they were traveling to Crete, the Englishman asked Zorba if he was married, and Zorba said something about being a man, and therefore being stupid, and therefore being married. Dan and Cook chuckled. Zorba went on to say he had a wife, children, and a house, and he labeled this state of affairs "the full catastrophe." Dan and Cook laughed loudly.

Beth's silence drew a glance from both of them. Then they looked back at the movie. But after a moment, Dan abruptly leaned away from Beth and put the movie on "Pause."

"What," he said.

She looked at the screen and said nothing.

"What," Dan said again.

She jerked her head at the TV. "Just play it," she said.

"Come on."

Still looking at the screen, she said, "How can you laugh at that? How can you?"

Dan made a noise. "Lighten up, will you?"

"I'm here, Dan. I'm working on being right here with you. But I guess you don't want that. You want to be on that boat, don't you?"

Dan groaned. "God, it never ends. Look, it's a funny line. Jeremy laughed, too."

"Jeremy? Does he count?" Beth looked at Cook. "He's *on* that boat. His position's clear. But how can you laugh at that—especially now?"

"It's *funny,*" Dan said loudly, almost shouting. Then something occurred to him. He pointed a finger at Beth. "You laughed at it in Santa Cruz. I remember. You did."

Beth scoffed. "How on earth can you remember that?"

"I do. You did. We both did. We laughed and laughed."

Beth gave a toss of her head. "If I did, it was because I was young. I was a slave to your view of things."

"And now I have to be a slave to yours? That's what you want, isn't it?"

Beth said nothing.

Dan sighed. "Look. Can't you just enjoy the line? 'The full catastrophe.' It's classic. It's a classic view of marriage."

"It's not *my* view."

"Okay. Fine. It's the classic *male* view, then. Zorba's speaking for men everywhere. He's saying that men don't want to settle down. You can't blame the two men in the room for laughing."

"Yes I can."

"Blame nature. Blame natural selection. Blame Darwin."

"What?" Beth seemed newly irritated.

"It's not in a man's nature to settle down. Natural selection always favors reproduction, right?"

Beth sat still. She would not cooperate. She would not say "Right."

Dan pressed on. "If men hang on to their freedom and try to fertilize everything in sight, then there'll be more offspring. So natural selection encourages that—it makes men what we are. But there's no point in promiscuity in women —no reproductive point. One fertile guy is all it takes. So settling down is easier for women."

"This doesn't have anything to do with anything," said Beth. "Besides, people don't have to be limited by their animal nature. They can rise above it."

"Sure they can," Dan said. "But you've got to recognize

that my nature is different from yours. Mine makes it hard for me to make a commitment. I'm not saying this because I think it's hopeless or anything. I just want some credit."

Beth rolled her eyes. "Great. Congratulations." She shook her head. "It's just an excuse for not working on the marriage."

"No," Dan said firmly. "It's an explanation for why working on the marriage—Jesus, I hate that phrase—is harder for me than it is for you."

"So why get married then?" Beth asked Dan. He looked overwhelmed by the question, caught off guard, completely blank on the subject. Beth turned to Cook. "Why do men marry? Why do they waste our time?"

Cook roused himself, sitting up a bit in the recliner. "In my experience," he said—though his experience was limited to Chapter One of *The Pillow Manual*—"men marry because it's time for them to marry. Being unmarried has become a disadvantage. They see marriage as a stabilizing thing. They do it so they can concentrate on their careers."

Beth made a funny noise in her throat. At least, Cook thought she did. But when he looked at her she seemed surprised at his attention.

"Women are different," Cook went on. "Women marry in order to have this overwhelming experience, this big, transforming... *thing*. So you've got a built-in conflict: women marry for the sake of a big change, and men marry so that things will stay the same."

"The full catastrophe," Dan said, this time with Zorba's accent. He stared at the TV screen, where Anthony Quinn was stuck in a freeze-frame, his eyes at half-mast and his mouth open as if he were about to spew baklava across the poop deck.

Beth looked at Dan. "Well? Does the shoe fit? Is that why you married me?"

Dan made a funny face. "It was so long ago." Beth seemed about to speak, and he added quickly, "It doesn't matter now. Even if that did play a role—the desire for stability—I would never offer it as a reason to stay married now."

"That was my next question," said Beth. "Are you sure?"

"Yeah. I'm sure."

"Really? Are you really sure?"

"As sure as I *can* be. What is this?"

Beth faltered. "I mean just in a *general* way," she said quickly. Something in her face caught Cook's attention—something like fear.

"You mean, do I value stability in a general way?" Dan asked. He seemed confused.

"Yes," said Beth. Cook watched her. She seemed to be encouraging Dan's confusion.

"Sure," Dan said, shrugging. "Stability's nice. But it's not a good reason to stay in a bad marriage."

Beth nodded, satisfied—though with what Cook couldn't have said. He was sure Beth had just experienced something strong. The evidence was the way her discomfort had affected *him*.

Beth suggested, in a fresh and innocent way, that they go ahead and watch the rest of the movie and try not to talk anymore. Dan pushed a button on his remote control, and the movie started up.

It wasn't like Beth to suggest they try not to talk. Cook thought about why she had done this, and about the fear that had touched her. He thought he had it pretty much figured out by the time the boat carrying the two men reached the end of its voyage.

Fifteen

Cook woke up the next morning hot and sweaty from a night of bedclothes-wrestling. As he sat on the side of his bed and stared through his headache at the floor, he wondered what the point of not drinking was if he could still wake up feeling like this.

After a shower and shave he felt a little better. He went to his desk and unfolded THE HORROR! before him

~~She's a bitch.~~
~~He's a prick.~~
~~Money.~~
He's a failure.

He crossed out the last entry and wrote a new one:

She thinks he's a failure.

There, he thought. That was much better. First of all, a guy could be a failure and still have a decent marriage. Look at Mr. and Mrs. Micawber—he was one of the great duds of literature, but they were a delightfully close couple. Being a failure wouldn't necessarily doom a marriage, but being *perceived* as a failure would.

Second, who said Dan was a failure? When Cook had seen him at the ball game the night before—so happy in the midst of his employees, so obviously popular—he had wanted to scrap that hypothesis altogether, though it was less than an hour old, and he *would* have scrapped it if he had had anything to stick in its place.

Now he did. He felt sure that Beth thought Dan was a failure. The monster she had glimpsed and recoiled from the night before was this: she had been on the verge of accusing Dan of staying with her only because his job was connected with her—an idea that was ugly for a number of reasons, one of which was what it said about Dan as a professional success. Beth had begun to duck and cover when she heard herself start to say it, claiming she meant something general —which told Cook she meant something specific. Her dodge had fooled Dan, had snowed him completely.

Cook summoned up an image of Mrs. Micawber, speaking with hope of her husband's prospects, trying to shield him from the pain of the world and the pain of himself. Cook put Beth next to this image, and he found that, viewed this way, he could easily hate her.

Cook got dressed and went downstairs. Dan and Beth had finished breakfast, and passed him on their way up. Dan gave him a curt greeting. Beth gave him a hello and a hard face. Something was up. Bitch attack, prick attack, some predawn complementary schismogenesis—who could say? Cook figured he would be Pillowing his fanny off all day.

He ate a leisurely breakfast and read a long obituary of a former newspaper employee. He took a cup of coffee upstairs with him. Beth was in the TV room on the second floor. She was wearing a tight black leotard, a gold headband, and gold wristbands as she exercised to music and whoops of encouragement from the TV. He glanced at her face. She looked driven and unhappy.

He went on up the stairs and found Dan back at his patching job on the third-floor landing. This time he was working with a huge sponge, running it back and forth to smooth the plaster after he applied it. He explained to Cook that he had to do the work in stages, letting a layer dry before he put on the next one.

"Looks good," Cook said automatically.

"It *is* good," Dan said, seizing Cook's sentence as if it were a lifeline. "Why doesn't she appreciate me? I do all sorts of things. Why doesn't she appreciate me?" He looked at Cook for an actual, true answer. "Okay. Here's an easier question. I'm talking to her, okay? I'm telling her a story. When I'm done, what does she say? She says, 'And?' What do you make of that?"

" 'And?' "

"Yeah. It pisses me off. What's she saying? That my stories are boring? That they're incomplete? That they don't have a point? What's she saying?"

"Maybe she just wants you to go on talking."

Dan frowned. "Why? What about?"

The phone rang at Dan's side, making him jump. He grabbed it and said hello. His body sagged. "Hi, Rose. . . . Yeah, I'm still home. Home is where the heart is, you know. Lemme get Beth." He looked up at the ceiling, rather than down toward where Beth actually was, and hollered, *"Honey! Your mom!"* He waited.

"I don't think she can hear you over that tape," said Cook. "I'll go tell her."

"What's she doing? Her Jane Fonda tape? Or is it Raquel Welch? Or Clare Boothe Luce?"

Cook went down and gave the message to Beth. She received it with ill-disguised irritation at being interrupted. When Cook returned to the third floor, Dan was holding the receiver at arm's length high over the table. He slowly let it descend toward the cradle, lowering it at a steady rate. Cook watched with excitement. Would Beth pick up the extension before it reached the cradle or not? What if she didn't? But she did, and when her "Hi, Mom" came over the line Dan slammed the receiver down the rest of the way.

"When you hang up loudly," Dan said, "can they tell or does it just feel to you like they can?"

Cook shrugged. "I don't know."

"And?"

Cook laughed.

"See?" said Dan. "Isn't it a bitch? Doesn't it make you feel like you don't talk right? I never do stuff like that with Beth —never make her feel bad with subtle digs. With all the things she does that drive me nuts, or the way she manhandles the car, I could really let her have it. But I never say a word."

"What's she do to the car?"

Dan paused and collected his thoughts. "It's a cold winter morning, okay? The oil's just sitting in the pan, right? Now, does she let the engine run quietly a few seconds so the oil can get pumped up and start doing some good?"

"Something tells me the answer is no."

"Damn right. She just bolts away from the curb. And at the end of the day, watch her pull up in front. Or check out the right wheels on her car. She scrapes them on the curb every time, just beats the shit out of them. I could go on and on. At night, she always turns on the car lights *before* she starts the car. Drives me *nuts.*"

"Could she make a similar complaint about you? Is there some area you're dumb in?"

"Sure. Cooking. So what?"

"You're as dumb about cooking as she is about cars?"

"Yeah, but I don't get in the kitchen and manhandle things. I don't bull my way in there and mess up her equipment."

"But she *has* to drive," Cook said.

"I *knew* you were going to say that," Dan said impatiently. "I *knew* it."

Cook felt himself tense. "You say that to Beth all the time—you *knew* she was going to say this, you *knew* she was going to say that. Sometimes sentences are predictable. So what?"

Dan's face went blank. He had no answer. Finally he muttered, "If she has to drive, she should learn how."

"She did. She just learned it a little bit wrong and it's too hard to change."

"What are you saying? I should just live with it?"

"Why did you marry her? So you could admire her clutch work?"

"What's your point? I can't complain about anything? Why are you being such a hard-ass this morning?"

"Complain about *important* things. Hell, you can even complain about these pressing automotive issues. Once. Maybe twice. But—"

"I did. Once or twice. Then I dropped it. I gave up. Every day I watch her blunder, and swallow my outrage. Wouldn't you call that working on the marriage?"

Cook heard the sound of the phone being hung up in the bedroom—loudly—then Beth's footsteps. He was waiting for her to go back to the den, but she stopped at the bottom of the stairs and bawled, *"Honey! Honey!"*

"What?" Dan yelled.

"Our summer is completely ruined."

Dan made a long-suffering face to signal to Cook that whatever might lie behind this extraordinary claim, he, for one, would not have made this leap so quickly. He looked over the railing of the landing, straight down at Beth. So did Cook. He noticed for the first time that Beth had a small cluster of gray hairs at the very top of her head.

"What is it?" Dan said.

"Robbie's camp is canceled. Will you get *down here?"*

"Shit," Dan said softly. "That *is* bad." He set his sponge in the bucket and went downstairs. Cook trotted after him. Dan stopped at the very bottom of the stairs, and Cook had to stop two steps up, which gave him something of an overview. Beth looked distraught.

"Irene Hendricks's mother told Mom that Art's wife and son were in an accident on their way back from Colorado. They're in the hospital. Art canceled the first session."

Dan's face went blank. "Jesus. Are they hurt badly?"

"I don't know. They're hospitalized. It must be pretty bad."

"Did you talk to Art or one of his kids?"

The question seemed to confuse Beth. "I talked to Mom."

Dan headed for the bedroom. "Let's call the camp and see what's what."

"I don't know which son it was," Beth said as she and Cook followed. "I wonder if it was Robbie's counselor. What was his name? Mike?"

"Yeah," said Dan. "Mike." He pressed his lips together and shook his head. "Let's see what the story is." He bent down and searched in the nightstand. "Where's the phone book?"

"Call information," Beth said.

"That costs money. Where is it? There should be a phone book right here."

"It's downstairs. Just call information."

Dan said, "It'll just take a second," and he headed for the door. Beth made an impatient noise, grabbed the phone, and dialed information herself. Dan slowed, stopped, and returned. He said nothing.

"Hermann, Missouri," Beth said into the phone. "Camp Swallow." She began to look frantically on the nightstand. "Where's the pen?" she said. "There was a pen right here. Did you do something with it?"

Dan began to look around for it. Cook took a pen from his pocket and handed it to her. She scribbled the number on the top of a Kleenex box on the nightstand. Then she punched the button to hang up and dialed the camp number.

"Damn. Busy." She dialed again. "Damn it." She said to Dan, "You try. I'm too upset. I can't stand this." She and Dan switched places.

Cook said, "Beth, could you tell me what you meant

when you asked Dan if he had done something with the pen?"

Beth frowned deeply. Before she could answer, Dan said, "Not now, Jeremy." He squinted at the number Beth had written down, then dialed it. "Busy."

Cook said, "Dan, did you feel Beth was blaming you for the pen's absence?"

Dan ignored Cook. He said to Beth, "What else did your mom say?"

"Nothing. Just that it's canceled. What are we going to do with Robbie for those two weeks? We've got to find another camp. We've just got to."

"Well, it's not gonna be—"

"How about Silver Lake? Don't the Webers send Matt there? I wonder if they have any openings."

"Let's establish what the facts are first," said Dan. "I want to talk to Art and establish the facts."

"Who's Art?" said Cook. "Is he the director of the camp?"

Before dialing again, Dan looked at Cook and said, without any acrimony whatsoever, "Jeremy, I kind of think you're going to have to shut the fuck up right now." He dialed, swore, and hung up. He looked at Beth. "Let me get this straight. How did your mom learn about this? Irene Hendricks told her? But how did *she* find out?"

Beth shook her head. "Her *mother* told her."

"Irene's mother told her that camp was canceled?" Dan said skeptically. "How did *she* find out?"

Beth frowned. "Irene told her. What do you think?"

Dan began to look a little wild. "You're saying Irene told her mother, and then her mother turned around and told Irene? That doesn't make any sense."

Beth said, "I'm going to scream. I swear, I'm going to scream."

"Pronouns and antecedents can be a real problem," Cook said.

They stared at him as if debating who should go first. The phone rang and Dan grabbed it. It was clear to Cook right away that a camp counselor was at the other end, informing Dan that the session was indeed canceled. Dan asked about the condition of the director's wife and son—and was it Mike? Yes, it was, but apparently both of them would be all right. At this point Beth tried to speak to Dan, but he shushed her and asked the counselor to repeat something. A moment later, Beth tried again and got shushed again. Dan said goodbye and hung up.

Beth was livid. "Jesus Christ!" she said. "I wanted you to ask them about other camps. Who was that?"

"Susy?" Dan said, as if not sure.

"Well, they would know. Call her back."

"Calm down, damn it," Dan said. "You call her if I'm such a fuckup."

"It's just going to be busy again." Beth took Dan's place at the phone. "That's why you should have asked her when you had the chance."

Cook said to Dan, "All you have to do in that kind of situation is say 'Excuse me' to the party on the phone, and then you can give a hearing to the person you're with."

Dan laughed—a high, strained laugh. "Christ, Jeremy. You sound like Miss Manners." He looked at Beth. "I hate it when I'm on the phone and I'm being talked at from two directions."

"And *I* hate being ignored. Jeremy's right. All you had to do was say 'Excuse me.' What's the big deal?" She dialed the number. It was busy, and she slammed the phone down.

Dan suddenly looked very tired. "Here," he said in a flat tone. "Let me call. I made the mistake, so I'll do the calling. Okay?"

Beth and Dan switched places again. Beth threw Cook a glance.

Cook said, "Beth, how do you feel when Dan suddenly concedes a point like that?"

"She gets a hard-on," Dan said.

"Stop it," said Beth.

"You know, I don't do things for bizarre reasons," Dan

said as he began to dial the phone number. "I imagined Susy was in a hurry, you know? She's probably got this long list of people to call, and they're all gonna be disappointed as hell, and she's upset about the accident, and I just didn't feel right about pumping her for information. So I had a reason. Hey! It's ringing."

"But we have a right to ask her to recommend an alternative," Beth said. "They owe us that. We've been planning on this since December. They—"

"Hello—Susy?" Dan said into the phone, his eyes pleading with Beth to leave him alone right now. "It's Dan Wilson again. Listen, can you recommend any other camps that run the same time that Swallow was going to run?... Well, yeah, I know you don't know their exact schedules, but... Well, forget their schedules. What camps in the area do you think are good?... None? That's pretty bizarre. Surely you ... Yeah, well, of course we love Camp Swallow. Robbie's crazy about it. But surely you... Well. Okay. Yeah. And I'm sorry. I hope everything works out. Bye."

Beth had begun to agitate as the conversation drew to an end, and now she said, "She wouldn't recommend *any?*"

Dan frowned as he hung up. "They're pretty much sold on themselves."

"Shit," said Beth. "Well, let's make some calls and see what's available. I'll go get the Yellow Pages." She headed for the door.

"God," Dan said with disbelief. "We're reduced to the Yellow Pages to pick a camp."

Beth stopped and turned around at the door. "What else are we going to do? Do you have any ideas?" She spoke as if Dan's words—which Cook had taken as a mere aside— were a personal challenge.

"No," Dan said calmly. "It's just not the best way to go about it."

"I know *that*. I'm not going to close my eyes and stab at the page and pick one that way. I just want to see who has openings. Then we'll make inquiries. Okay?"

"Inquiries?"

"Yes. We'll call people we know and see what they know." Beth said this slowly, as if Dan were being a blockhead.

"Yeah. Well...people are just gonna say what they're doing is right."

Beth had turned to go downstairs, but she turned around again. "What?"

"It's like with schools. No parent is going to say they're sending their kid to a crummy school. People are just gonna praise the camp they've chosen."

"So what are you saying? It's hopeless? We ought to give up? You want to take Robbie with us to Italy?"

"No. That's ridiculous. But that's not the only—"

"It's not ridiculous. He's old enough now. We could. And we will, another time. But this trip is just for us. You and me." She looked at him. "Right?"

"Right."

"What were you going to say?"

"Nothing. Go get the Yellow Pages." Dan watched her leave, turned to Cook with his forefinger raised, and lowered it and pointed it straight at him. "Nothing from you. Nothing."

"What?"

"I want to hear nothing from you. No questions. No fucking helpful hints. Not a word."

"Okay."

"Nothing."

"*Okay.*"

"I guess what I'm saying is I want you to leave."

"Leave?"

"Get out of the room. Leave us alone."

"Can't I watch?"

"No. I don't want you here. The contract said the linguist would not be permitted in the bedroom."

"I've never seen such a contract."

"Well, that's what it said. This is the bedroom. I want you to leave."

"But that clause—if it exists—certainly means only that bedroom *activities* need to be private, not—"

Dan laughed. He pursed his lips and prudishly said "bedroom *activities*" in open mockery of Cook. "You're too much. But maybe you're right about what it means. The thing is, there might be bedroom *activities*. You never know what could develop." Dan looked up at Beth, who came in with the Yellow Pages. "Honey, do you want to fuck our brains out while we make these phone calls?"

"Sure. Why not?"

"See, Jeremy?" said Dan, though in truth he looked as surprised at Beth's response as Cook was. "You've got about ten seconds to clear out."

Cook found himself backing out the door. "I demand a full report," he said with cinematic bravado.

Dan laughed and laughed at that.

Cook took a walk in the neighborhood. He came back and tried to read the paper. He took another walk. When he returned, the house was quiet.

He went upstairs and tiptoed to the bedroom door, which was a few inches ajar. He knocked on it and swung it open. The room was empty. Before entering, he turned and called into the rest of the house, "Dan? Beth?"

The silence had a baleful quality. Cook went into the room. The Yellow Pages lay open on the bed to a page reading "Camps," and a series of check marks showed that Dan and Beth had worked through the entire list. On a yellow legal tablet were names of several of them, but they had been crossed out—all but one, which was circled and starred. Cook couldn't quite read the handwriting. It looked like "Big Muffin Camp," but he didn't think that was right. He looked around the room for more clues. All he saw was the pen he had lent to Beth, lying on the floor. He picked it up and put it in his pocket.

Cook shivered with a sudden chill. The evidence of former industry, combined with that of sudden abandonment, unsettled him. He looked out the window to the street below. Both of their cars were there. He looked into the park and up and down the street. Not a soul was in sight. It was as if the planet had suddenly been unpeopled.

He went to the door of the bedroom and called out:

"Dan? Beth?"

Sixteen

Shortly after Cook's lonely search for them, Dan and Beth returned to the house, separately but within minutes of each other. Dan came back with a little bag from the nearby hardware store. This told Cook where he had been, which was good, because Dan didn't. He made it clear he had nothing to say to anybody. Beth came back empty-handed and tight-lipped.

Whatever had happened in the bedroom—whatever blowup had sent them flying in different directions—they weren't going to talk about it. The darkness of silence was upon the marriage.

Cook wandered around the house, silent himself, waiting for the darkness to lift. When lunchtime came, by unspoken agreement each of them got solo tenancy of the kitchen long enough to make a sandwich and get out of there to eat it in private. Beth took her lunch into the bedroom and closed the door. At this point she spoke, though since she was alone it wasn't a very social act. She yelled, "*Still* no air conditioner in here! God *damn* it!"

Cook heard this clearly from his bed, where he was eating his sandwich, and Dan heard it too, for he had come into Cook's room just at that moment. A look of immense fatigue swept over Dan's face. He waited, apparently for elaboration from Beth, and when none came he calmly asked Cook if he would help him get the ladder back on the van so that he could return it to the rental shop.

Cook asked him if he and Beth had found an alternative camp. Dan made a face and said, "Maybe. We've got to check it out."

They went outside and muscled the ladder onto the van roof, where Dan secured it with rope. Then he failed to invite Cook to go with him. Cook forlornly watched him drive off and went back upstairs. His room was stuffy with the midday heat. He opened the balcony door, hoping for a breeze, and settled on the bed.

He read. Now and then he heard Beth stir in the bedroom below. The phone rang, and Beth talked at length. Her voice carried loudly through the floor, but he couldn't make out any actual words. He listened and began to find it interesting to see what tone detail made it through the plaster and floorboards to his ears. But at the height of his interest in this, she hung up. He went back to his reading, grew bored with it, and stood up. Without intending to he began to pace.

"Do you mind?" Beth yelled. *"Do you mind?"*

Cook tiptoed back to his bed. He felt imprisoned. He opened his novel again but found no relief there, only irritation. If the book had been good, Cook thought angrily, then he wouldn't have grown restless, he wouldn't have paced, and Beth wouldn't have yelled at him. Three times already the author had had his character "snap back to reality." Cook hated that. The hero was forever drifting off into a flashback or a reverie, only to be hauled out of it when some banging door or barking dog or volcanic eruption "snapped him back to reality." The hero also "thought to himself" a lot. As opposed to what? Cook wondered—thinking to someone else?

He kept hoping for the sound of Dan's van. He imagined it pulling up in front to the sound of acorns crunching under the wheels; then the front door opening and closing, sending its gentle thud through the timbers of the house; then talk between Dan and Beth—the plain old everyday music. "Mail here yet?" "You seen my keys?" "Where's the rest of the paper?" That was what he longed to hear.

The phone rang again, and Beth talked and talked. Cook bolted. He hurried into his shoes and fairly ran down the stairs and out the front door. He walked around the neighborhood, following the curving streets until he was good and lost. He enjoyed this state for as long as it lasted—until he saw Dan's van zoom by, going in the opposite direction. Since this told him where home was, he was no longer lost, so he turned around with a sigh and headed back. Evidently Dan hadn't seen him when he drove by.

Dan had the rear hatch of the van open and was wrestling with a huge flat box. He brightened somewhat to see Cook. "I got a Ping-Pong table," he said. "Robbie's always wanted one. It might ease the blow about Camp Swallow a little." He hefted one side of the box. "I'd like to get this put up before he gets home."

Cook grabbed the other side and helped slide the box out of the van. They rested it on the rear bumper as Dan slammed the hatch shut.

Beth came around a corner of the house, carrying a lawn sprinkler and dragging a hose. She looked at them. The corners of her mouth were turned down. They watched her set up the sprinkler and turn on the water. She looked at them again and went back inside.

"Beth never was much of a Ping-Pong player," Dan said cryptically. Then he said, "Damn. Too late." Cook followed Dan's gaze down the sidewalk. Robbie was coming home from school. "Don't say anything about the camp right now."

"Of course not," said Cook.

Robbie walked up to them, his knapsack slung over one shoulder. He read the lettering on the side of the box. Cook watched pure joy fill his face, and he wondered when the last time was that *he* had reacted so happily to something.

"Oh, wow!" Robbie said, running to touch the box.

"They've got Ping-Pong at Camp Swallow. I can practice all weekend and be the champ."

Dan's face fell. He looked at Cook and signaled him to lift it up. They hauled it around to the rear deck. Dan asked Robbie to go down to the basement for his toolbox, and he began to tear the cardboard box apart. He worked in brutish silence. Robbie returned with the toolbox, then began to jump around on the deck, hitting an imaginary ball with the palm of his hand and yelling, "He scores!" Cook wondered if Dan found this as unnerving as he did. Robbie turned to his father and said, "Where are the paddles and stuff?"

Dan's face fell again.

"We'll go get them," Cook said quickly. "Come on, Robbie. By the time we get back, maybe the table'll be ready." He looked at Dan. "Just tell me where to go to get them."

Dan gave Cook a look so grateful that Cook braced himself, expecting to be hugged.

When they returned, the table was ready. Dan was sitting on the deck stairs, staring across the lawn at nothing. When Cook and Robbie appeared he gave them a blank look and said, "Oh." It was as if he barely remembered them.

They put up the net, and Robbie and Dan played. Cook was content to fetch balls from the grass when they bounced off the deck. Dan began to relax a little. He even seemed to enjoy the game. He let Robbie win a share of the rallies without being obvious about it. Then he ran Robbie through some low-key exercises, practicing certain shots over and over—always the teacher, thought Cook. Robbie grinned through it all. When a rally was especially long, Robbie's grin would grow with every shot, until he would burst out laughing and flub the shot and collapse across the table.

Beth appeared at the back door. She watched for a while. Dan seemed about to say something to her a couple of times. Robbie asked her to play; she said no, she had some things to do. But she stayed on and watched, half smiling, even laughing once at a funny shot Dan attempted. A little later she went back into the house. Dan grew distracted at that point, repeatedly glancing through the window to follow Beth's movements. Finally, he told Robbie he had to quit for now. He gave his paddle to Cook and went inside.

Cook was a rabid competitor, not given to the paternal self-effacement Dan had shown. His impulse was to smash the ball every chance he got. He had to create an imaginary context for their play—a secret one, unknown to Robbie— to justify letting Robbie win. After experimenting with a few that occurred to him, he finally settled on the fiction that every rally he won knocked a year off his life, and every rally Robbie won added a year, but if Robbie ever accused him of deliberately throwing a rally, Cook's IQ would decline twenty points.

But Cook too became interested in what was going on indoors. He could see through the sun-room window and through the dining room window beyond it all the way into the living room. Beth was sitting on the couch. Dan was leaning against the dining room doorjamb, his back to Cook. They were talking.

Cook said to Robbie, "Do you have any homework to do?"

Robbie said, "Nope. You want to quit playing, don't you?"

"What makes you say that?"

"Whenever Mom and Dad want me to stop doing whatever I'm doing, they ask me if I have any homework."

"You're pretty observant," Cook said. He laid his paddle on the table.

"I've got a good memory, too," Robbie said. "Remember—a liar's got to have a good memory."

"Right," said Cook, peering through the windows again. He was eager to get to Dan and Beth, where the real action was. He gave Robbie an all-purpose smile and went inside.

• • •

"What's the good word?" Cook said, realizing as he used it that this lame greeting was on his hate list in *The Woof of Words*.

Dan, leaning against the dining room doorjamb with his hands in his pockets, looked rather casual from behind. But his face was bleak. Beth sat on the edge of the couch, her legs pressed tightly together.

"We're in the middle of something," Beth said sharply to Cook.

"I know." Cook sat down across from her. She stared at him.

Dan turned to see where Robbie was. Through the windows they could see him tapping a Ping-Pong ball on the table with a paddle.

"Okay," Dan said to Beth. "You called Camp Meramec, and *they* were full up, too. That's when you said we should call the soccer camp."

"I asked you if you thought we should call them," Beth said evenly.

"No. You said you wanted to call them. That's why I got mad."

Beth shook her head. "I *asked* you about it. That's all. And you flew off the handle."

Dan took a deep breath. "Well, even if you just asked, I still couldn't believe you'd consider a soccer camp. Robbie would *hate* it."

"How do you know? You still haven't made that clear."

"Because only kids who are complete soccer nuts go to soccer camp."

"Are you sure?"

"What do you think—I'd make that up? I know kids who have gone." He gestured to the front window, as if they were right at hand, outside. "They're all soccer nuts. Okay?"

"But you didn't make that clear this morning. You just got mad."

Dan blinked a couple of times. "Didn't I say Robbie wouldn't like soccer camp?"

"But you didn't say why."

"I thought it was obvious why. Because he doesn't like soccer enough."

"But you've got to see why I was suggesting it. Robbie plays soccer. He's always on the school team."

"But that's not the same—"

"He plays soccer out in the park—"

"But at a soccer camp they don't just *play* it. They *live* it."

"Okay! I know that now, but I didn't then. Don't you see? You got mad at me for not knowing something I had no way of knowing."

"I thought it was obvious."

"Well it wasn't."

"I thought it was."

"Well it wasn't."

A pause fell. Cook hoped they were done with this particular subject.

"Okay," said Dan. His hands were in his pockets again, his arms stiff at his sides, as if he were cold.

"That's how it started," said Beth.

"It started before then," said Dan.

"When?"

Dan hesitated, his eyes roaming the corners of the room. "It started with the way you approached the whole thing. The way you yelled up the stairs that our summer was ruined."

"Oh come on." Beth sounded more bored than angry, as if she had heard this kind of thing before. "I was upset. Okay?"

"You said it like it was all suddenly my responsibility—"

"That's ridiculous."

"—like you were saying, 'Our summer is ruined, and it's your job to make it better.'"

"I didn't mean that at all!"

"But it felt like that's what you meant."

"Well I *didn't*, okay? How many times do I have to—"

"Okay okay. Anyway, my point is the way you brought it up got us off to a horrible start."

"How *should* I talk? Can't I say what I feel?"

Dan took a deep breath. "Try not to begin conversations with desperate absolutes. 'Our summer is ruined.' You can't say stuff like that."

"Why not? Why not?"

"You just can't."

Beth looked hard at him. "If I can't say things like that, it's hopeless. There's just no hope for us."

"All right. You can say them."

Cook looked closely at Dan. He wasn't joking.

Beth took a moment to react. "Why this sudden permission? You just said that's why we fought—because the first thing I said was hysterical."

"I didn't say it was hysterical."

"You almost did. That's what you meant."

Dan pressed his lips together. "Okay. I *will* say it. It was hysterical."

"That really pisses me off."

Dan gave a helpless laugh. "Shit. I thought you were giving me permission to say that. Can we take a look at it? Can we do that?" His hands came out of his pockets and he used them to present the sentence. "Here it is: 'Our whole summer is completely ruined.' Right?"

Beth said nothing.

"Now," Dan went on, "let's look at that sentence. Was it true?"

"It *felt* like it was."

"I mean, was it true when you said it that our whole summer was completely ruined?"

"Well, our trip was in danger, and the trip was the main

thing happening this summer, and if we couldn't find a camp for Robbie it was probably off, so, yes, it was true."

"But there are a lot of conditions to that, aren't there? '*If we couldn't find a camp*'—that's a condition. You didn't even know for a fact that Camp Swallow had been canceled."

Beth frowned at Dan. "But it *was.*"

"Yes, but you didn't know that for sure at the time. You just had it secondhand. Or thirdhand. Or—"

"So what? The point is it *was* canceled."

"Don't you see what I'm saying? You yell at me that our summer is ruined, when in fact there's this huge possibility of error. Don't you see?"

"This is ridiculous! *The camp was canceled!*"

"I *know* that. I'm trying to explain why we had a fight. My first thought was Jesus Christ, she's all freaked out and she doesn't even have the facts."

Beth sighed deeply. "Can we get off this point? It isn't what we fought about."

"But it established the tone. It set my teeth on edge."

"Fine. Great. Now can we get off it?"

"Sure," said Dan. "Where were we?"

"Soccer camp," said Cook.

They looked at him.

"Right," said Dan. "We decided not to call the soccer camp. That left Big Muddy Camp."

Beth nodded. "You called them."

Dan turned to Cook. "Beth had been doing the calling, and we'd been striking out. We thought our luck might change if I called."

Cook nodded.

"Not because she was *failing* or anything," Dan added quickly. "It was just superstition—you know, time to try something different to change our luck. All the camps were full, and..." He turned to Beth. "Actually, that's what scared me about the place. They had vacancies when nobody else did."

"That doesn't mean anything," Beth retorted. "All by it-self it doesn't mean anything."

Dan started to speak to this, stopped, and turned back to Cook, preferring to address him at the moment. "We had it all planned," he said, a nasality in his tone protesting the fickleness of the gods. "Robbie's camp was going to overlap exactly with our trip—two weeks, starting Monday. He *loved* Camp Swallow last year, so we weren't worried about being out of the country—you know, in case it was a horri-ble experience or anything. There just wasn't any danger of that. But then poof!—Camp Swallow is out of the picture. Big Muddy is a camp he's never been to, none of his friends go to it, and we've never even heard of it."

"What about Beth's parents?" Cook said. "Couldn't Rob-bie stay with them for the two weeks?"

This question produced an awkward pause. Dan went stiff and looked at Beth—he would let her answer.

Beth shook her head. "No," she said simply.

"It's out of the question," said Dan. "They ignore him. I won't have him be ignored for two weeks."

Cook looked at Beth, expecting her to challenge this or to tone it down. She said nothing.

"So where do things stand?" Cook asked, a little con-fused.

Dan shrugged. "We made a tentative reservation at Big Muddy for Robbie. We're going to drive out there with him tomorrow to check it out. If it looks good, we'll go with it."

Cook said, "It sounds like you agreed on a plan. So what's the problem? Why didn't you speak to each other all day?"

"Beth made a bad suggestion," said Dan, looking at her, "and we had a few words about it."

"Oh, drop dead," she said, but without much feeling.

"What was it?" Cook asked.

"She suggested Robbie stay with her parents for the two weeks." Dan's eyes widened and he gave a funny laugh.

"I mentioned it," Beth said softly. "I didn't pursue it."

Dan became agitated. "That's because I didn't *let* you."

Beth turned to Cook. "He started ranting about how I was too committed to finding a camp for Robbie—"

"I still feel that way. I still do."

"—ranting about Robbie's needs—"

"I was making legitimate points. I wasn't ranting."

"—and about how whenever it came down to Robbie's needs versus my needs, I always thought of myself first—"

"I didn't say that."

"—and you know what?" she said, turning to Dan. "You're right. I wasn't thinking of him first. I was thinking of *us*. Have you ever done that? Thought of *us?*"

Dan hung fire—apparently not sure whether to repeat his denial that he had made this claim, pursue Beth's partial surrender to it, or try to deal with her tricky question. He said nothing.

"Why isn't our marriage as important to you as it is to me?" Beth said. "Can you answer that? There've been a few little signs of hope, but I've been stupid. You don't want to go to Italy with me. You'd rather grab the excuse of Robbie's camp. Even if this new one is just slightly less good than Camp Swallow, you're going to say, 'Nope. No way. Not good enough for *my* son.'"

Dan shook his head. "You have no idea what I was saying upstairs, do you?"

"You can't stand the idea of being alone with me for two weeks, can you?" Beth's face seemed about to collapse. She struggled to hold herself together.

"Not when we fight like this," Dan said.

"We fight because you never want to be with me."

For a time, the only sound was a gentle, rhythmic tapping at the back of the house. Robbie was still playing by himself with the Ping-Pong ball.

"How much do you want me?" Beth asked.

"I don't know," Dan said. "Pretty much, I guess."

"I know how much I want you. I want you so much that I'll leave you if I can't have you."

Dan looked at her. "I know."

"Oh," Beth moaned softly. "You say that so sadly, Dan. So weakly. You won't even fight for me, will you?"

Cook sat alone in the living room, listening to the three voices from the deck. Beth had left Cook and Dan to go talk to Robbie, and Dan, hearing their voices, had roused himself from his position against the doorjamb and gone out and joined them. Cook couldn't hear the words, but he knew by an outcry from Robbie that they had given him the news about Camp Swallow.

Dan came back into the living room. He heaved a big sigh and sat down on the couch across from Cook.

"How's he taking it?" Cook asked.

"Awful." Dan stared straight ahead at nothing. He seemed defeated.

"Maybe it'll be great," said Cook. "Maybe it'll be a great camp." Dan didn't respond. Cook sat awhile longer, then stood up, suddenly miserable and restless.

Dan spoke quickly then, stopping him. "It's funny how people remember things differently."

Cook frowned.

"Take an argument," Dan went on. "A husband and a wife can have two completely different memories of it." Dan looked at Cook as if he should be impressed by this observation. "Wouldn't it be nice if you had a recording of a fight so you could compare what each person actually said with what they *claim* they said?"

"Maybe," Cook said guardedly.

Dan looked disappointed. "You don't seem very excited. It sounds like a great idea to me. Why haven't you done it?"

Cook shrugged. "It's not part of the procedure."

"Are you forbidden from doing it?"

Cook resented this reminder that he lacked autonomy. "Of course not."

"The fight Beth and I had in the bedroom—wouldn't you like to have a tape of that?"

"Maybe. But who's got one?"

"I do."

Cook tried to hide his surprise.

"I've got the whole damn thing," Dan said.

"Where? How?"

"Upstairs. On the answering machine in the bedroom. It's got this 'Memo' button that turns it into a regular tape recorder for anyone speaking in the room, in case you want to leave an oral memo for someone. All you've got to do is punch that button." Dan grinned at Cook. "I punched it." He glanced toward the deck, where Beth and Robbie were still talking. Then he leaned forward and spoke more intensely. "When I was done talking to the guy from Big Muddy, I knew we were going to have a fight. I *knew* it. I was staring at the phone. I was thinking how it's the enemy —how it drags bad news into your life and makes you use it to go get more bad news. And then I thought maybe I could get something good out of it for a change. I knew we were doomed to fight, so I reached over and punched 'Memo.' Beth didn't have a clue."

"Have you listened to it since the fight?"

"No no no. That wouldn't have been fair. After the fight I forgot about it, and then when I remembered, I deliberately stayed away from it. I knew we would end up arguing about it. She always distorts our fights when we fight about them. She says I ranted. I didn't rant. I made solid points. But I'd like to let you be the judge of that. It's what you're here for, really." Dan leaned forward still more, so confidential in his manner that Cook feared he might slip off the edge of the couch. "I'd really like to play it for you."

"Don't you think Beth should hear it, too?"

"Of course! Hell, I intend to include her. That's the whole point."

They heard footsteps on the deck, then the sound of the

side gate opening and closing. Beth came in through the dining room and said, "He's going down to Phillip's house to see what his plans are." She turned to Cook. "Phillip's a friend of his who was going to go to Camp Swallow, too." She looked at Dan. "He's trying to drum up some interest in Big Muddy. Maybe he can get a friend to go. He's coping. He's handling it." She sighed. "I ought to throw something together for dinner."

"You sure the camp has more than one vacancy?" Dan asked.

Beth closed her eyes. Dan seemed to sense an attack was coming and preempted it. "I taped the fight we had in the bedroom. It's on the answering machine. We could go listen to it. What do you think?"

Beth's face went through a number of changes. "Is this your idea, Jeremy?"

"No," Dan said for him. "But he's not opposed."

"But what's the point? It's pathetic, Dan. It's so completely beside the point."

"Come on," Dan said. "It'll be great. You'll see."

"What do you hope to get out of it? Some sort of proof of your position or something?"

"Not at all!" Dan said with extreme good nature.

"What made you tape it?"

"It was just an impulse. I punched the 'Memo' button."

"So the whole time we were talking you knew it was being taped?"

"Yeah. But that didn't change anything. I forgot about it after a while. It was a regular argument. Didn't I say the kind of stuff I normally say in a fight? Don't we always say the same thing, over and over?"

Beth gave him a look of immeasurable weariness. "Have you listened to it yet?"

"Nope."

Beth looked away, across the room, at nothing in particular. "If you want to listen to it, go listen to it. I don't care."

"But we want you to join us," said Dan. He might have

been speaking of an excursion to go play miniature golf.

"It's so pointless. This whole thing is pointless." She stood up. "Come on. Let's get it over with."

Dan stood up. Cook had never seen a face so obviously in the act of not grinning.

Upstairs, Dan bustled to the answering machine and fiddled with it awhile. The tape noisily stopped and started several times. It seemed to run backward, then forward, then backward again. Cook wondered if it was going to work. Dan threw an eager glance at Cook, who had sat down on the large bay window seat. Beth was leaning against the footboard of the bed. She had picked up an emery board and was filing her nails.

"Coming right up," Dan said as he punched a button. "It should start right after I talked to the Big Muddy people. That's when I—"

"*—better stop right now, Dan, because there are some things I could say that really shouldn't be said.*"

Dan scowled at the sentence. He punched another button. "That's at the tail end. But well put, honey," he said acidly. "Well spoken."

Beth pressed her lips together and continued filing her nails.

The tape ran fast, stopped, ran again, and stopped again. Dan punched a button.

"*—better stop right now, Dan, because there are some things I could say that really shouldn't be said.*"

"Damn it," said Dan. He punched the buttons and tried it again.

"*—better stop right now, Dan—*"

Dan punched it off. "Fuck!" he said.

"That's it?" Beth said, looking up with a derisive smile. "You dragged us up here for that?"

"What do you want?" Dan protested. "That's all it picked up, the goddamn thing. See?" He punched the button again.

"*—because there are some things I could say that really shouldn't be said.*"

Dan let the tape run on, and the sound of footsteps and a slamming door could be heard as one of them left the room —Beth, Cook assumed, since she had delivered the exit line. This was followed by an empty hiss from the tape. Dan glared at the machine and hissed back at it angrily. "Fuck it," he said, reaching for it.

"Oh what a bitch!"

This sudden cry from the tape seemed to puzzle Dan and made him hesitate. Then he quickly reached for the machine again.

"Hold it!" Beth said. "Let it play."

Dan froze. Cook looked at him. He seemed curious, as if he himself wasn't sure what the tape might reveal.

"Oh what a bitch! Oh! Oh! Oh! What a bitch of a bitch! You've got her, Dan. You've got her, boy." Dan's voice almost sang the words, as if in jubilation. *"Yessirree. She's all yours. You did it, boy. You've got her. Bitch for breakfast, bitch for lunch, bitch for dinner. Whoa. What's that? The front door? Yep. There she goes. Look out, world. Here comes the bitch. Where's she off to? Who knows? Bitch school, maybe. Look at her bitching her way down the sidewalk. Birds of the neighborhood, shit on her, I command you. Cars, kill her. Earth, swallow her. Oh! Oh! Oh!"* His footsteps could be heard on the tape in nervous, agitated pacing. Then the bedroom door banged and the footsteps grew faint. The tape continued to run, but it was just a hiss.

Dan pushed the button to make it stop. "I'm not going to apologize for that." He looked at Beth. "I'm *not*. What you said was much worse."

"What *I* said?"

"That there are things you could say, only they're so horrible you couldn't say them. That's the worst there is. That's why I blew up like that." His voice caught, and he seemed about to blow up again. *"Jesus,* I wish I had the whole thing on tape. I spelled it all out—all the examples, all the evidence. Your stinking idea about soccer camp. Your idea about farming Robbie out to your parents for two weeks in hell. Your desperation for a camp, *any* camp. You didn't even hear what I was saying. Don't you know what I was saying?"

Beth seemed to lean away slightly, toward the door.

Cook said, "Look, Dan, it's too bad about the tape, but—"

"I was saying you're a rotten mother. That's what I was saying. What's more horrible than that? Tell me. What's more horrible than that?"

Seventeen

"**I**'m dead, Jeremy."

"No you're not."

"I'm a goner."

"No. It'll be all right."

"I'm fucked."

"You'll get through it. She'll get over it."

Dan sat on the edge of the window seat, his face pale and blank. From the kitchen Cook heard the scream of the portable dishwasher being rolled out of the way, followed by the clang of a pot.

"See?" Cook said, gesturing to the door and the sounds beyond it. "Life goes on. We'll get over this hump."

Cook spoke with more hope than he felt. Beth had said nothing to Dan in response to his accusation, but after the first wave of shock and hurt, her face had gone hard—harder than Cook had ever seen it. Then she had turned and left the room.

"I don't know," Dan said vaguely. He sighed and went to the closet. He stared into it for a moment, then began to take out his work clothes. "All a guy can do at a time like this is go dig some postholes."

Cook, struggling to make this transition to the banal with Dan, offered to help, but Dan said no, not now, maybe later.

Cook went up to his room. He took THE HORROR! from his shirt pocket as he sat down at his desk, and he set it before him:

~~She's a bitch.~~
~~He's a prick.~~
~~Money.~~
~~He's a failure.~~
She thinks he's a failure.

He picked up the pen on his desk, crossed out his day-old theory, and wrote down a new one:

He thinks she's a bad mother.

This hypothesis had been his easiest yet. Dan had *spoken* it—no need for risky inductive leaps this time.

Of course, Dan had spoken it in anger, but Cook had a theory about that, going back to his days with Paula. It was one of the things they had constantly disagreed about in their year together. Paula believed that people could become so enraged that they would make claims they didn't believe at all—"outlandish" claims, she said, using a ruralism he hated the first time he heard it from her. She said that if people came to the injured partner later and said, "I didn't mean what I said," they spoke the truth. They *didn't* mean it.

Cook's view was that if it came out of your mouth, it was yours. If you said, "You're selfish!" then you believed the person was selfish—and more important, you had been cultivating that belief for some time. Of course, your view might change later, but such a change did not justify the claim that you did not mean what you said. You *did* mean it—every bit of it.

So Cook believed Dan had meant what he said. But he had other problems with it. *Was* Beth a bad mother? She seemed loving, attentive, and genuinely interested in her son—all the things a mother should be. Cook went back through events since his arrival, looking for Robbie-related combustions. Dan's strong words to Beth about helping Robbie with his math was one—a peculiar one, too. Dan had seemed to *want* Beth to be out of the picture—the very thing he was complaining about now. Cook recalled the disagreement on his first night there over whether Robbie should be told the truth about him. Dan wanted to tell him, Beth didn't. Did this make Dan the better parent? Not necessarily, but Dan might have *thought* it did. There had also been a little pronoun disagreement that night, when Dan and Beth had interpreted "*our* books" differently. For Dan, "our" had meant the whole family. For Beth, it had meant just the two of them. Did this mean Beth was a bad mother for excluding Robbie? Dan probably thought so. But from Beth's point of view, it simply meant she was a good wife. Who could say which one was right?

Cook remembered his excitement that night at being able to relate the problem to the Old English pronoun system. Old English? Good God, he thought. Old English had nothing to do with it. Old English was a dead language spoken by a bunch of ax-wielding, head-cleaving twits. What cold, mechanistic notion of language had sent him flying there for an answer? The answer would be found in the messy give-and-take at Dan and Beth's house, in the sloppy present, not in the rigid grammar of a dead tongue.

Cook stood up from the desk and looked out the window. The taste of moo shu pork and General Tso's chicken was suddenly, surprisingly, on his tongue. He smiled grimly at the memory. Not long after Paula had moved in with him, he had taken her to a Chinese restaurant near Wabash. He had ordered the pork under the assumption that he would eat it all. She had ordered the chicken under the assumption that they would divide their portions in half and share them. When their conflicting intentions became clear, there was laughter. Then there were words.

Cook's words were neutral. They had to do with his habits—he always ordered moo shu pork and ate all of it.

Paula's words were ugly. She talked about his failure to accept her into his life. Cook said she was just talking about *her* habits: she was used to sharing dishes, whereas he wasn't. Just when he expected her to agree, she called him a name. She called him a "splendid isolationist."

Cook called her a few things in response. He called her "clingy," "needy," "demanding," "smothering," and "swallowing." She asked him if he wanted to be alone, and he said yes, in a sense he did. It turned out to be a trick question, because instead of taking his answer in the general, spiritual way he had meant it (we're all alone, basically; I need my independence, you need yours; etc.), she got up and left. He ate *all* the moo shu pork and *all* of General Tso's chicken, and he went home with his brain flying on monosodium glutamate.

Later she recanted her words, saying she hadn't meant them. He recanted his, but with the condition that he *had* meant them. They got over the fight. But they never got over the recantation.

He turned back to his desk. As he picked up THE HORROR! it struck him that he should view the list in a new light—not as a progression from darkness to light but as a whole. Or better, as a rotating set of equally legitimate views, each subject to reinvocation at any moment in this dynamic, horrific cycle.

He went downstairs. Beth was at the sink, scrubbing at something. He could tell from the way her butt shook rapidly that she didn't want anything to do with him. Robbie must have still been at his friend's house, though the dinner hour had come and gone. Through the sun-room windows Cook could see Dan taking measurements along one side of the backyard. It was amazing, Cook thought, how Dan was able to find jobs to do around the house. He usually did them with pleasure, too—with a noisy gusto of singing, whistling, and tool banging. At the moment, though, Dan was swearing loudly at the tape measure wriggling on the ground, and Cook went out to help him. Dan let him do this, but it was clear that there would be no extra talk.

They measured eight-foot intervals and dug postholes. Robbie returned and gave his father a somewhat positive report about his friend's interest. Then he went inside to talk to his mother. He was sad, but he seemed to be coping, as Beth had said. Dan and Cook worked until after dark, digging the final holes by the outdoor spotlights on the deck. It was an unusually cool night, with erratic gusts of wind that made Cook look up into the tree branches several times.

When they finished, they went inside, ate some leftover cold spaghetti, and went upstairs. The master bedroom door was closed. They looked in on Robbie. He was sound asleep in his room, lying fully dressed on his bed under the bright overhead light. Dan took off Robbie's shoes and turned out the light. He whispered to Cook that Robbie often fell asleep like this after a tough day.

Dan said good night to Cook and opened the bedroom door. Cook glimpsed a nightstand light—Beth was still up. But as soon as the door opened, she turned it off, and in the light from the hall Cook could see her gather the blanket over her shoulder and turn her back to Dan.

Dan closed the door behind him. Cook paused a moment at the stairs before going on up, but he heard nothing.

When Cook went down for breakfast, the new day was well under way. Beth was slicing a grapefruit at the table while she talked on the phone, which she wedged against her ear with a cocked shoulder. Dan was hunched over the sports section of the newspaper. Robbie was talking nervously and no one was listening to him.

"Hey," Robbie said, brightening to see Cook, "I'll ask you, Jeremy. You're supposed to know about this stuff. What does 'Missouri' mean?"

"I have no idea," said Cook.

"Really? How about 'Mississippi'?"

Cook shrugged. "Search me. Is there any Malt-O-Meal left?"

Beth jabbed a finger toward the stove while she laughed into the phone.

"You don't know what 'Mississippi' means either?" Robbie frowned and looked around for someone with whom he could share his surprise at Cook's deep ignorance. "Okay," he said. "I'll tell you. 'Mississippi' means 'big river,' and 'Missouri' means 'canoe.'"

"Yeah?" Cook called from the stove.

"They don't mean 'big muddy.' People think one of them means 'big muddy.' But they're *wrong*. Neither one does. It's a mistake. And you've got a whole camp named Big Muddy. The whole name is this huge, big, colossal mistake." He spread his arms to indicate its enormity.

Dan folded his newspaper and said to Cook, "Robbie's a little nervous about Big Muddy this morning."

"Hunh!" said Robbie. Cook took this for a denial, but then Robbie said, "A *little?*"

Beth hung up the phone and said to Robbie, "Nancy and Phillip will be here in about fifteen minutes, honey. They're really excited about it. She says if they like it he'll definitely go."

Robbie rolled his eyes. "Wow," he said without enthusiasm.

"Come on," Beth said. "He's a good friend."

"He's an *okay* friend."

"She's going to call Tommy Freneau's mom, too, to see if they're interested in looking at it."

"Hmph," said Robbie.

"Just try to keep an open mind, okay? We'll give it a good look." She turned to Dan. "And don't you minimize his nervousness. He has a right to be apprehensive."

Dan's eyebrows shot up. "I didn't mean to. I just—"

"Are you coming, Jeremy?" Beth asked as he settled down at the table with a bowl of Malt-O-Meal.

"Where?" said Cook. "To Big Muddy?"

"Do you really think he has to?" Dan asked.

"That's for him to decide," Beth snapped.

"Fine," Dan said in a quick high monotone. He was in a good-boy mode.

Robbie said, "I mean, they've *got* to be stupid to pick a name like that. Does everyone sleep in the mud? Do they paint themselves with mud?"

Cook asked Robbie to pass the brown sugar. Robbie did, and then he leaned back in his chair to look at the clock. "My class'd be starting English now, except it's the last day of school, so they're probably starting on the brownies and ice cream." He gave his parents a look. "Wait!" he said, breaking into a grin. "She was gonna make us go over inter-junctions today, because we messed them up on the test. Ha!"

"Isn't it 'inter*jec*tion'?" Dan said, looking at Cook.

Beth made an obscure scoffing noise.

"Interjunctions, interjections," said Robbie. "Who cares?"

"It *is* a dumb part of speech," Cook agreed.

"They're *all* dumb," said Robbie.

"Well, some are more—"

"They're *stupid!*"

"That's enough, Robbie," Beth said.

Robbie emoted with some body language, just to have the last word. Beth asked Dan for the paper, and he handed it to her.

"Not the sports," she snapped.

"I'm giving you the whole thing," Dan protested. Cook looked at the stack in his hand. The sports section was simply on top.

Beth snatched the stack with a sigh. Cook sensed that Dan was doomed today. If a U.N. observer were to shadow him, the objective report at day's end would probably show no offenses whatsoever. But Beth would be on him all day.

The phone rang. Robbie said, "Probably Big Muddy. Canceled because no one wants to go."

"Canceled on account of a mudslide," Cook said, and Robbie laughed and slapped the table. Beth frowned at Cook as she picked up the phone. She said hello, and as she talked she grew animated.

"Great!" she said. "We'll go as soon as you can get here. Bye." She hung up and said to Robbie, "Tommy and his mother are coming, too. He's already gone to school. She'll come by here and we'll stop at school and pick him up on the way."

"That's great," said Dan.

Beth looked at Dan as if he had spoken entirely out of turn—as if he were a plumber shouting out comments on their table talk from under the sink. She dug into her grapefruit. "Let's see," she said. "That makes seven. The van only holds seven, so I guess that lets you out, Jeremy. We'll be back by dinner."

Cook nodded.

"Hey, Jeremy," Robbie said, holding his orange juice glass up. "Here's *mud* in your eye." Robbie laughed and laughed.

"Honey," Beth said to Robbie, "if you're finished you can clear your place and go brush your teeth."

"Hey, Jeremy," Robbie said as he rose and picked up his dishes. "I'll bet they brush their teeth with mud, hunh? I'll bet they—"

"All right, all right," Beth interrupted. "Go." She watched Robbie leave the room and sighed.

Cook wondered what he would do all day. He decided he should wash his clothes and he asked Beth about it. She gave him instructions about the washing machine and dryer. Dan stood up and took his dishes to the sink. The phone rang and he grabbed it.

"Hello? Oh, hi, Rose. Beth's right here. . . . Hunh? Yeah, I'm still home. It takes a heap o' livin', and all that. Here's— . . . Yeah, we're just about on our way to go check it out. Beth can fill you in." He jerked the phone hard away from his ear and held it at arm's length, as if that were the only way to free himself from it. Cook sensed Dan wanted to do one of his phone routines—some charade, some mimed act of long-suppressed violence—but Beth was watching, ready to condemn any behavior from him more ambitious than metabolism. He simply handed her the phone and went out the swinging door.

Beth talked to her mother in a loud, fast, friendly voice. It made Cook want to get out of there. He took his bowl of cereal and a few sections of the newspaper out onto the deck. He imagined Dan upstairs, gritting his teeth, closing doors against Beth's noisy talk.

A few minutes later, Robbie came out and stood across the table from Cook. Cook looked up and nodded in greeting and went back to his paper, but the way Robbie stood there made him look up again. He was eyeing Cook and swiveling a hand back and forth, in imitation of one playing Ping-Pong. His eyebrows were at their highest.

Cook laughed. "Is this your way of suggesting we play?"

"Hunh?" said Robbie, all innocence. "Ping-Pong? Hey— great idea." He ran inside for the paddles and balls.

When Robbie came back out, Cook said, "Do you think you're going to like the camp?"

"I don't know. You serve." He bounced a ball across the table to Cook.

"I hope you do. And I hope your friends do. I'm rooting for you."

"Well, right now you better root for yourself, sucker, because I'm gonna whip your butt." He slapped the table with the palm of his hand. "Ha! They're studying interjunctions and I'm playing Ping-Pong."

Their game quickly developed into a grammar lesson, however. Cook began to utter interjections upon the completion of every point—a different one every time, positive if he won, negative if he lost. Robbie picked it up and tried to match Cook, though sometimes their play stopped for long stretches while he stared up into the sky and struggled to think of a new one.

Dan wandered out and watched for a while. He asked

Robbie if he was ready to go. Robbie said yes. They continued to play.

A little later, Beth opened the door and said, "Come *on*.
Let's *go*. They're all out in front, waiting."

"All right," Dan said, trying to meet her irritation calmly.

"I sent you out here to get him, not to play Ping-Pong."

"You just said to make sure he's ready. He's ready."

"I want to get a book," said Robbie. "And I've got to go
to the bathroom." He hurried into the house past his
mother.

Beth gave Dan a sharp look. "He's ready? Christ." She
went back into the house.

Before following her, Dan made a small gun out of two
pointed fingers and an upraised thumb, and with it he silently shot himself in the head.

Cook roamed the house, fighting off the dogs of loneliness.
He washed his laundry, fussily separating it into numerous
small piles—more to stretch out the task than to prevent
colors from running, a concept that had always mystified
him. He tried to read the paper, then a book, then a magazine. He couldn't concentrate. He wandered the rooms. He
ended up in Dan and Beth's bedroom, staring out the bay
window. He watched an English sparrow fly from a branch
to the gutter overhead and back to the branch, over and
over—a distance of about ten feet.

The phone rang, giving him a jolt. He grabbed it.

"Jeremy. We don't have time to chat. She's waiting for
you."

"Who might that be, Roy?"

"Your date. She's at Topper's. They serve a nice lunch,
I'm told."

Cook sighed. "My date."

"Yes."

"At Topper's."

"Yes."

"You didn't give me much notice, Roy. I might not have been here."

"Where would you have been?"

"Out with my couple. Who knows?"

"The point is you *are* there. Let's not get bollixed by hypotheticals. She's waiting, so get going. Give me a call afterward. I'm most curious about this. Most curious."

As Cook hung up, he resolved to add this use of "most" to his hate list in future editions of *The Woof of Words*.

"Jesus Christ. Look at that guy ordering his lunch. No, not that one. The table in the corner. Yeah. Him. He's been talking to the waiter for ten minutes. Jesus Christ. You'd think he was giving him confidential instructions about when to cut off his life supports, or something like that. Jesus Christ. I hate that. My view is 'Okay, you're my waiter and your name is John. Now gimme my food and get the fuck out of here.'"

Her name was Rita. Cook listened to her, fascinated. It would be wrong to say he was trying to get a handle on her. Her handles stuck out all over—she thrust them at him and made him grab them. It would be wrong to say he didn't like her, because he did, a lot. But there was something it wouldn't be wrong to say that kept eluding him.

She was short—"compact" was the word Cook thought of—with short auburn hair and a sexily tomboyish face from which Cook couldn't take his eyes. He kept wanting to get near it, to nuzzle against it, to explore it. Luckily, she seemed to think well of him. Her first words when he stepped out of the elevator and saw her sitting there waiting for him were "Jeremy? Hey! You're a good-lookin' guy!"

Their waiter brought them their drinks. When he left, Cook said, "You don't drink?" Rita's order had been the same as his—sparkling water with lime.

"No," she said. "I did. But it was a problem. So I

stopped. Which means I've got a problem, but it's less of a problem than I've got when I drink."

Cook could have spoken the entire thought for her. "Me too," he said.

"Really? When did you quit?"

"It'll be a year in two more weeks."

"Hey! That's great. Two and a half years for me. You miss it?"

"Oh . . . all the time."

Rita nodded. "Like now. Scotch on the rocks."

"Right."

"The smell. Like gasoline. The shock of the first taste. The clink of ice. The dew on the glass. The weak taste at the end, diluted, before you reach for another. Then it hits your system. That first hit—the onset. That's the best part. When I was drunk I used to wish I was sober so I could start all over and feel that first effect." She picked up her sparkling water and emptied it in one long drink.

"So why did you quit?"

"Same reason as you, probably. Why take poison every night?"

"You drank at night?" said Cook. "Alone?" This had been his practice.

"Yeah. If I was gonna get drunk I wanted to be alone so I could concentrate on it. No drinking buddies for me. I never understood that notion—drinking buddy."

"Did you say any of this on your questionnaire?"

Rita scrunched up her face as she thought. "Can't remember. Maybe. The damn thing was so long I might have."

Cook smiled. How had Pillow found her? He had been shocked to learn how far Pillow had gone for her—Laramie, Wyoming, where she had lived all of her life. She said she had received a letter from Pillow early that week with a hundred-dollar bill enclosed and a promise of a large check to come if she filled out the enclosed questionnaire. She did so and returned it by express mail, as instructed. The next day she received a phone call from Pillow proposing this date with Cook, for a payment Rita would not reveal. She said she hated it when people talked about money. In fact, she went on a rampage about the subject, wryly imitating the many subtle ways "true assholes" revealed their salaries. So she simply said Pillow's payment was "so large it would make you sick, it would make you vomit, you would get down on your knees and puke." Rita had no idea what prompted Pillow to contact her to begin with. She had no ties to St. Louis, or any to the Pillow Agency, Dan and Beth, or linguistics. How could she? She was an auto mechanic for a Chrysler dealership in Laramie.

Their salads came. Rita dug into hers. She was as fast an eater as he was. She asked him about his work. He told her about his days at the Wabash Institute. As they talked, Cook noticed a fidgetiness about her. He remembered seeing a TV science show late one night—when he was drunk, probably —about obesity in Pima Indians. It showed a fat Pima who just sat; when he sat, he *really* sat. Then it showed a fidgety Pima, for whom sitting was a kinetic activity. This guy was as lean as a strip of beef jerky. Rita fidgeted the same way.

This made Cook look at himself. He had finished his salad, and his right hand was shredding a book of matches he had evidently begun to play with some time before. His left hand was moving his water glass from square to square on the patterned tablecloth, as in a board game. His feet, crossed at the ankles, twitched like a hummingbird's wings. His anus contracted on a schedule beyond his understanding. He felt as if he were sitting in the midst of a vast industrial complex. And Rita matched him. She was all over the place. Her water glass advanced, retreated, moved from side to side. Soon Cook would jump it with his own and take possession of it.

Rita asked him what he did for the Pillow Agency. When he answered this, she burst out laughing.

"Where do you hang out?" she asked. "Under the bed?"

"No," said Cook. "The bedroom is forbidden." He tried to remember how Pillow had expressed it the day he was hired. "Bedroom activities are better learned about in after-the-fact reports by both parties than by direct observation."

"Oh, balls," Rita said. "That's no fun. You know, it's funny how I've never actually watched. Very few people have, I suppose—I mean watched someone else, in person, doing it. Such an important thing, and we've never watched anyone else. I've done it, many times, and I hope to again this afternoon, but I've never actually watched. How about you?"

Cook's grin was both tense and joyful. He looked at her. She smiled and looked away, suddenly self-conscious. But she filled the conversational void with a nonverbal: her toes began tickling the inside of his thighs under the table, working their way to his crotch. His reaction? A quick survey of the restaurant to see that they were unobserved, followed by a glance at the tablecloth to check its length. His deeper reaction? The brutal truth was that he had always wanted a woman to do this to him, and here she was! When her toes reached their destination, one of the places his blood rushed to was his ears, and he seemed to hear all four Beatles sing out at once, "RITA!"

He undertook part two of his fantasy. Slipping his right foot out of his shoe and congratulating himself for putting on clean socks for the occasion, he began his own under-the-table journey into the unknown. He watched her face. She was still looking off to the side—a modest touch he deeply appreciated. She smiled dreamily. His foot made steady progress, and it arrived along with their entrees, which the waiter set before them. Cook thanked him more loudly than necessary, and they both sat up, reshod themselves, and began to eat.

"Tell me about the couple," Rita said. Cook had always liked that conversational move—"Tell me about"—and he practiced it whenever he got the chance. It was the clearest signal of genuine interest. But you couldn't say "Tell me *all* about." Just "Tell me about."

He started with Beth. He described her as objectively as possible.

"Sounds like a bitch," Rita said.

Cook thought he should present the other side. He told her about Dan, and he had barely finished narrating one incident when she interrupted with a laugh.

"What a prick," she said.

They finished their entrees at exactly the same time. A moment before the waiter removed their plates, Cook observed that Rita was as indifferent to food as he was. The evidence for this was that without either of them noticing, he had mistakenly eaten the chicken she had ordered, and she had wolfed down his beef.

The waiter asked if they would like coffee. Cook looked at Rita. She looked at him. They said no simultaneously. Cook hoped she was in a hurry for the same reason he was.

They walked to Rita's car, which was parked right in front of the building. She snorted at it. "It's a rental. Completely out of tune. It's so easy. Why don't they keep 'em in tune?"

"We can take mine," said Cook. "It's parked up in the next block."

"Nah. Get in. We're in a hurry, aren't we? Important business." She laughed.

As a driver she was like Cook—aggressive, defensive, and harshly judgmental. She made wisecracks about other motorists as they traveled along the edge of Forest Park: "Nice signal," "Turn, dickhead," and "C'mon, Pop, drive it or park it." She also made passing comments on the golfers in the park, slowing down once to watch one old fellow's drive go awry. She laughed cruelly.

But Cook was bothered. Rita didn't seem to care about the mood she was setting with her reckless sarcasms. Her tone implied that she was indifferent to their destination and what they were going to do when they got there. She acted as if they were on their way to a hockey game, or to a tour of a slaughterhouse. In other words, she wasn't being very *romantic*. Cook jerked slightly in his seat with this thought. The word was almost completely unfamiliar to him. He wanted to say to himself, "I didn't know you cared."

But he recognized her behavior well enough. It was a kind of cool disinvestment. She was protecting herself. She didn't want to put too much stock in the upcoming event. If Cook had been driving, he probably would have done the same thing. Simply being in the passenger's seat had given him a fresh perspective.

He decided to step outside himself even further. He touched Rita's shoulder and said, "I'm really looking forward to making love with you."

She looked at him. Her mouth popped open into a smile —a warm smile. "Me too, Jeremy."

Cook was heartened by her response, but not for what it did for their moment together in the car or even for what it might do for their time together afterward. He was heartened because if she could come out from under her protective cover when encouraged to do so, it meant that he could, too.

Eighteen

"There was sex, Roy."

"Ah. I knew there would be. Let's hear about it."

"Which part?"

"Everything. I plan to learn a great deal from this report."

"Let me be sure I understand it first, okay? I'm still reeling. Rita is basically . . . me."

"Yes."

"She's Jeremy Cook with tits."

"Nicely put."

"And yet she can't be a *perfect* equivalent. Surely you can't have found such a person."

"Of course I can. I *did*."

"But—"

"My questionnaire is a most delicate instrument, Jeremy. I hope you're not going to tell me you had a problem with her."

"Well, yes and no. She's great—funny, lively, and lots of other things, and sex was the easiest thing in the world. Hell, it was almost too easy—like being alone. Not alone, exactly, but . . . I don't know. I could barely tell what she was doing from what I was doing, if you know what I mean."

"Mmm."

"But it was great. I was instantly comfortable with her."

"As comfortable as you are with yourself."

This gave Cook pause. "She made me a little *un*comfortable with myself, actually. She made me see something I wasn't too happy with."

"Nonsense."

"I mean it. I liked her, but I didn't want to *be* her."

"What are you talking about?"

"She's not giving enough."

Pillow made a protesting noise. "What could you have possibly wanted from her that she didn't give you?"

"I wanted whatever people mean when they say that."

"What?"

"I'm new at this, Roy. Bear with me. I felt a certain... distance."

"Doggone it, Jeremy. Don't change your tune on me now. Is this the man who slept with sixteen women in five years and found nary a one of them lovable?"

"Well..."

"I matched you two on the basis of how you answered my questions. If you feel differently now, *you're* the one to blame. Don't come crying to me. I won't have it."

"I'm not coming crying to you, Roy. I'm just telling you how I felt about her."

Pillow sighed. "This is a very disappointing report."

Cook was suddenly afraid Pillow was going to hang up on him. "While I've got you, Roy," he said, looking at *The Pillow Manual* open before him, "'Day Four: Missy Pillow.' What the hell?"

Pillow gasped. "Don't tell me you're done Pillowing. Don't tell me that."

"Okay, I won't tell you."

"But you *must* be if you... How can you possibly be done Pillowing?"

"I'm fast, Roy. Okay?"

"Pillowing can go on for weeks. For months!"

"Too late, Roy," said Cook. "I've turned the page."

Pillow made some unhappy noises. "In light of your

breakneck pace, I must say that if this assignment fails, I wash my hands of it. Don't come crying to me if it blows up in your face."

"I won't come crying to you, Roy." This seemed to be Pillow's phrase for the day. "Just tell me what 'Missy Pillow' means."

"Missy Pillow is my daughter, Jeremy. By my first wife. As a child, she loved to visit her grandparents. She just *loved* it. The grandparents are the parents of one spouse, but they are the in-laws of the other spouse." Pillow paused as if momentarily overwhelmed by this realization. "'Missy Pillow' means to visit the in-laws."

"Sounds simple enough."

"So you feel you know what to do?"

"Sure. We visit the in-laws. No problem."

Pillow chuckled. "Got you."

"What?"

"Got you. I get 'em every time." Pillow chuckled some more. "Which in-laws did you think of?"

"Beth's parents. Dan's in-laws. Why?"

"Why didn't you think of the other pair?"

"Well," said Cook, suddenly defensive, "they're not a pair, for one thing. Dan's mother is dead."

"Since when," Pillow said peevishly, "does spousal death make the surviving spouse not an in-law?"

"What's your point, Roy?"

"My point is that in every marriage one pair of in-laws looms large, and one pair looms small. The staff out in the field always picks the pair that looms large—automatically, without even thinking of the pair they're ignoring. It tickles me every time. Now, may I change the subject?"

This was always a dangerous proposition, but Cook said yes.

"This morning," said Pillow, "I discovered a new thinker in my reading—a German fellow. He believes that happiness is to be found not in the mating of true opposites, which we tested with mixed results on your first date—"

"With wretched results."

"—nor does it lie in the mating of mirror images—our most recent experiment. He believes that our original family constellations dictate the harmony of our future pairings. He says that people do best in a marriage that duplicates their sibling relationships. A younger brother of a sister should marry a woman who herself is an older sister to a brother. Each partner will then fall into accustomed roles of nurturer and nurtured. His theory extends even to the friends we have. A man who has an older brother tends to seek out friends who have a younger brother. Are you with me?"

"What about only children?"

"What do you care?" Pillow snapped. "Now, your sister is older than you, correct?"

"Yes."

"My questionnaire tells me that your last date—Rita—is *younger* than her brother."

"So?"

"That's why it didn't work. If she were older than her brother she would have been perfect for you. You would have married her."

Cook laughed. "You sound pretty convinced, Roy."

"Why not? It makes perfect sense."

Cook had never seen Pillow in intellectual action. It was rather frightening. "You just discovered this guy's ideas this morning? I wouldn't go applying them all over the place already. Science doesn't work that way. Take it slow, Roy."

"I should note," Pillow went on, "that the logical extension of this theory is that men should marry their sisters."

"I suppose it is."

There was a pause. Then Pillow said, "Your sister—is she married?"

Cook laughed. "Yes."

"A sound marriage? Not on the rocks at all?"

"Come on, Roy. Get serious."

"We have to be open to new things, Jeremy. They called Ponce de León a madman, too."

"He *was*."

"Oh." Pillow seemed disappointed.

Cook heard the click of Pillow's call-waiting signal. "You want to get that, Roy?"

"No. It's just Mrs. Pillow."

"Go ahead. I'll wait."

"I'm telling you it's just Mrs. Pillow. She's always calling me at the office."

"You say that like it's an annoyance, Roy."

Pillow made an astonished noise. "How dare you Pillow me!"

Cook laughed.

"You think it's funny?" Pillow said angrily.

Cook sobered up. "Sorry, Roy. I thought you were joking. I didn't mean—"

But Pillow had hung up on him.

Cook went downstairs. His family was still not back from Big Muddy, even though it was after dinnertime. He went into the kitchen, sliced an apple, and put a gob of peanut butter on the plate, into which he would dip the apple slices. He had seen Robbie do this and admired the simplicity of the dish. It would be as good a dinner as any. He took the plate into the living room and set it on the coffee table. He stood at the window as he ate, staring out.

In the park across the street, a woman was training her dog on a leash. She would take a few steps and then make a sharp turn without warning; then came another few steps and another sharp turn. The dog was supposed to follow. Cook watched the woman do this for ten minutes solid. He imagined her walking like that without the dog—she would look like an idiot. He decided she looked like an idiot even *with* the dog.

He turned away from the window and sat down on the couch. His plate was empty. He had eaten the apple slices without being conscious of them. He remembered a theory

that Paula had once volunteered: that Cook's oft-proclaimed
boredom with food was really a comment on his feelings
about people. In today's world, she said, food was a vehicle
for social interaction. Rather than frankly say he hated people, Cook said he hated food. This was the theory. Cook, of
course, had immediately objected to it.

He looked around the room. Everything his eye touched
told a story about Dan, Beth, or Robbie, as if he had known
them for years—the bowl on the coffee table, empty of
Hershey Kisses; Dan's decorative maps on the wall; the
record shelf ("This isn't Dittersdorf"); the computer in the
dining room, where Cook had come upon Robbie playing a
game called "Paperboy" and had said, "You know, Robbie,
when I was a boy I really *was* a paperboy," to which Robbie
had said, "Get out of town." Cook's eye fell on the piano.
He had bragged to Robbie that he could play it—a blunder,
because Robbie had been after him ever since to play a duet
with him.

Robbie intrigued him. He faded in and out of childhood
like Wordsworth. Sometimes he seemed almost adult—in
argument, or in laughter. He had a rich belly laugh that
didn't threaten to shatter skulls, as some children's laughter
did. But at other times he was clearly just a boy. He was
certainly all boy at the piano. He had a single style—fast and
loud, legato be damned. Cook had read somewhere that
whenever John Philip Sousa tried to extend his range by
writing a ballad, conductors would direct it at march tempo;
Robbie did the same to whatever came his way. Beth was
patient with him, though. Cook had overheard her giving a
brief lesson to him, and she hadn't commented at all on his
goose-stepping rhythm. She just let him play that way, as if
confident he would outgrow it.

Her own piano style was markedly different. Everything
she played was slow. Beethoven, Schumann, Gershwin—
whatever it was, it was slow. The past four days she had
been working on "The Man I Love." She played part of it
every day, one new measure per session. She had told Cook

that was the only way she could learn Gershwin. She worked hard at it. One night after dinner, she had played the same phrase at least fifty times. Cook, sitting in the living room, had let out a mock scream of one driven over the edge—a *yahhh!* Beth had stopped playing but had not turned around. Dan had looked up at Cook from the couch and shaken his head soberly at him. The message was "Don't ever do that again." When Beth resumed playing, Cook didn't do it again.

As for Dan, he played what Cook thought of as a "sarcastic" piano. He deliberately overplayed grandiose pieces, accompanying them with moans and shouts. He trivialized Chopin's "Polonaise Militaire" with this method. He was sarcastic with light pieces as well. On one occasion, Cook listened to him bark laughter all the way through "The Happy Farmer," and then play it in a minor key, sobbing. This was followed by "The Missouri Waltz"—a lovely arrangement of it, but Dan embellished it by bellowing Trumanisms throughout: "The buck stops here!" "If you can't stand the heat, get out of the kitchen!" During this strange festival, Beth had said to Cook in the kitchen, "You're a new audience for him." Cook doubted this and said that Dan didn't even seem to know he was within earshot. Beth shook her head. "He knows," she said.

Cook took his empty plate into the kitchen and rinsed it. He went back to the window and stared out for a while. The woman and her dog were gone. Perhaps the dog had turned on her and chased her down the street. His gaze fell on Beth's car, parked at the curb. Parked *against* the curb, from the look of it. Even from this distance he could see the damage on her wheels and hubcaps that Dan had complained about. He stared at them for a while. Then he decided to go upstairs and take a shower.

Ten minutes later, even under the stream of water, he could hear Robbie's noisy footsteps on the second floor. He smiled and quickly finished his shower and got dressed.

When he came into the living room he found Beth lying

on the couch, listening to a Mozart flute concerto. Her arm was raised across her eyes, shielding them. Cook slowed as he entered, not sure whether to stay. Beth opened her eyes and looked at him for a moment, then gave him a small finger-waggle of hello with the hand across her eyes.

Cook heard a shout from the deck. Through the windows he could see Dan and Robbie playing Ping-Pong.

Beth sat up and blinked her eyes. She ran a hand through her hair.

"How was it?" Cook asked.

"It was great," she said without emotion. "I'm sorry we're so late. We had dinner on the road. The kids were hungry."

"How's the camp?"

"It's great," she said, again blandly, almost sadly. "Robbie liked it, the people are nice, they seem to have good values. It looks just fine. Can you turn that down?" She pointed to the CD player.

Cook turned the volume down. "So... No problem?"

"No problem. He starts on Sunday. It looks like both his friends are going to go, too."

"You don't sound happy enough."

Beth smiled weakly. "I'm just tired."

"Have you been crying?"

"No." She looked down. "Yes."

"You want to talk?"

She shook her head. "Just the same old thing." She looked up and said in a thinner voice, "Not quite the same old thing. I think it's over."

"No."

She nodded insistently. "I think it is."

They were silent for a moment. Dan came into the room and gave Cook a cheerful hello. Behind him, through the windows, Cook could see Robbie still playing Ping-Pong, now with one of his friends from down the street.

Dan seemed charged with energy. He said to Beth, "You call your mom?"

"No." She seemed to have to struggle to say more. "Why?"

"She's going to be curious about the camp. She's probably going to call any minute. Might as well beat her to it." Dan performed a strange finger-snapping routine involving both hands. He acted as if he might burst into song at any moment. "And they were coming over Sunday, but that's when Big Muddy starts, so we'll have to cancel that."

Cook was about to speak, to say that *he* would like to see some sort of get-together, but Beth roused herself and beat him to it. "I wonder if they could come tomorrow."

"That's kind of soon," said Dan.

"They'll come. I'll call Bruce, too."

Dan made his deep "Bruuuce" noise. "I meant it's kind of soon for us to get ready."

"What's to get ready? We'll grill some fish and hamburgers, I'll make a salad, and you and Robbie can make some peppermint ice cream."

"But we've got to get Robbie ready for camp the next day. If they stay late we'll—"

"They can come for lunch. They'll be gone by late afternoon. What's the big deal?"

Dan turned to Cook. "You got any linguistic activities scheduled that might render this gala event out of the question? I'd be grateful if you did."

Cook shook his head. He was pleased that Missy Pillow had been so easy to arrange—he assumed the in-laws' visiting them was as good as their visiting the in-laws, and if it wasn't, Pillow could go to hell. But he was mainly struck by the shift of agenda. In one breath Beth declares, "It's over," and in the next she plans a little luncheon party?

Dan sighed. He repeated his request that Beth call her mother and said he was going to take a shower. Beth asked him to take it on the third floor because she wanted to take a bath in the second-floor bathroom. Dan said, "Okay by me," and headed up the stairs, singing something Cook didn't recognize.

Cook was torn. He wanted to talk to Beth more, but he had something to say to Dan, too. Beth got up and went to the receiver. The Mozart had ended and she switched to FM. A blast of music made Cook jump, and Beth nodded with satisfaction. Cook hurried after Dan and caught up with him on the second floor, where he was taking a bath towel from the hall closet.

"That was a good move, Dan," he said, "suggesting Beth call her mom. You headed off an aggravation. I know her calls get on your nerves."

Dan peeled off his T-shirt and nodded, full of self-satisfaction. He threw his shirt over his bare shoulder. "You know, Jeremy, if you can just handle little things like this, you can make a marriage work. It's not *big* things that wreck a marriage, but a lot of little things added together." He headed up the stairs to the third floor.

"What happened today?" Cook asked as he followed him. "You're in a different mood. This morning you seemed completely defeated."

"Ah," Dan said triumphantly. "Right you are." When he reached the third-floor landing he turned and faced Cook. He puffed his chest out a little. "I've got some new ideas about marriage, Jeremy. First there's my Parallel Lines Theory of Marriage. Marriage is coexistence, basically. It's two people doing their thing under the same roof. It doesn't have to be anything more than that. But when trouble comes up, someone has to be nice to make the trouble go away. That's my Be Nice Theory of Marriage. Sometimes one partner has to be nicer than the other, maybe two or three times nicer, or *ten* times nicer. When it reaches a multiple of ten, that's my Eat Lots of Shit Theory of Marriage." Dan had started off calmly but had worked himself up a bit. He paused and collected himself.

"I've been nice all day," he went on. "I've been eating shit all day. Rational men everywhere would applaud me." He waved his arm, as if addressing a throng of them. Standing there on the small landing, his shirt thrown across his shoulder, he looked a bit like a Roman senator giving a speech. "Rational men would say, 'Dan is working on his marriage. Dan is saving his marriage.' I feel good. Eating shit makes you feel good. I feel pretty damned civilized right now." He turned away before Cook could answer, and went into the bathroom.

Cook stood there for a while, thinking about Dan's theories. He began to walk slowly down the stairs. When he reached the landing between the third and second floors, the phone rang. He could hear the rings from two phones—the one in the second-floor bedroom and the one on the landing above him. He listened for Beth's footsteps, but apparently the music drowned out the kitchen phone. After four rings, he decided to answer it himself and trotted up to the landing.

Dan bolted out of the bathroom. He was naked except for a towel around his waist. At least he wasn't wet, Cook observed. Dan grabbed the phone and barked a hello, listened a moment, and set the receiver on the table without another word. He leaned over the railing and yelled for Beth. Then he yelled again—a pained, primitive scream. From the phone Cook heard a woman's voice—Beth's mother, he guessed—saying she could call back if this was an inconvenient time, but Dan, hanging over the railing, bellowed again.

The volume on the music suddenly went down. Beth yelled, "Did you say something?"

Dan didn't answer. He had stepped back to the phone and was staring at it.

Beth shouted, "Did you call me?"

Dan still didn't answer. He had the phone fixed in a fiendish gaze. Cook finally yelled down the stairs, "Phone!"

Still staring, Dan said, "Stand clear." Then he undertook a remarkable thing. First, he rotated the towel encircling his waist so that the slit was at the exact rear. This allowed him direct access to the crack between his buttocks—ordinarily not a pressing need in the telephonic arena, but it enabled him to do what he did next, namely, pick up the receiver and insert it through the slit of the towel into the crevice of his buttock cheeks. Cook watched with growing interest. By clenching his cheeks in a way that reminded Cook of marble statuary, Dan was able to hold the phone without using his hands at all. As if to call this to Cook's attention, he raised his hands above his head. At this point, the towel fell from his waist to the floor, and Cook, viewing Dan's profile, was privileged to behold two projections, one of pale flaccid flesh, the other of hard jet-black plastic.

The railing on the landing featured one-inch-square wooden pickets, and Dan now made use of these as a prop in the next act of his drama. He twirled so that the phone, still in its viselike clench, pointed straight at the pickets. He pressed his cheeks with his hands for a secure hold, then squatted and backed into the pickets. On making contact, he proceeded to scrape the phone back and forth along them like a little boy scraping a stick on his way to school. Back and forth he went, his pace quickening, until the phone popped free and clattered to the floor, where it rolled and twisted as if propelled by the puzzled female voices coming out of it.

Dan grabbed the phone and hung it up. He picked up his towel from the floor and returned to the bathroom.

The rest of the night was fairly normal. After his shower, Dan went downstairs to the bedroom and closed the door. Beth continued to listen to music in the living room. Cook went right to THE HORROR! Given Dan's behavior, he just *had* to strike his old hypothesis and enter a new one. He beheld the result:

> ~~She's a bitch.~~
> ~~He's a prick.~~
> ~~Money.~~
> ~~He's a failure.~~
> ~~She thinks he's a failure.~~
> ~~He thinks she's a bad mother.~~
> The in-laws.

Then he lay down on his bed and read, hoping that he didn't get called to the phone.

Some time later, he went downstairs. Robbie was in his room, getting things organized for camp. He handed Cook a sheet titled "Big Muddy Checklist" and asked him to read the items aloud one by one. They worked through the list, with Robbie calling out "Check!" for each item. He sounded like Ike on the eve of D-Day. Just when things were at their messiest—when everything was strewn all over the floor— Robbie suddenly got tired and said he was going to bed. Cook imagined him getting up in the middle of the night to go to the bathroom and stumbling over the mess. When Robbie went to brush his teeth, Cook quietly cleared a little path from the bed to the door.

He went back up to his room. He heard Beth come up and go into the second-floor bathroom, then into the bedroom. She closed the door behind her. He heard their voices through the floor, but just a few sentences—short ones, with long pauses between them. Then there was no sound at all.

Cook read well into the night. He felt on call, like a doctor. But no one beeped him.

The next morning, when Cook went into the bathroom to wash up, he looked out the window to the backyard. Dan was down there mixing concrete in a wheelbarrow.

"Let me get this straight," Cook said to the window glass. "Your in-laws are coming for lunch in a couple of hours. Your son is going to camp for two weeks tomorrow. You're going to Italy for two weeks the day after that. Your marriage is approaching meltdown. And you're putting up fence posts." He watched Dan through the window— watched him pull and push the sloshy mix with the hoe— and he wondered just who Dan was. What made him tick, and what did he want, and what did he fear?

Nineteen

They were playing Meet the Linguist. Cook hated to play Meet the Linguist.

The in-laws had arrived in a bunch, and Beth had herded everyone out onto the deck, where her parents had settled at the glass table, and Cook—again introduced as "an old college friend"—had ended up with brother Bruce near the hors d'oeuvres table. After some chat about Bruce's printing plant, Bruce asked Cook what his line of work was ("General linguistics," said Cook), then what the *point* of it was.

Cook said, simply, that linguistics was "interesting."

Bruce said, "So say something interesting."

Bruce's wife, Doris, walked up to them at that moment and said, "Yes. Say something interesting." She said it in a light way clearly intended to make up for her husband's aggression. She had been with the two of them earlier, but when they had started to talk about the printing business she had drifted down the deck to the table, where Beth was talking with her parents about Robbie's new camp. Now she was back with Cook and her husband. She had a tired look that suited her apparent dissatisfaction with the available conversation.

Cook tried not to disappoint her. First off, he told them

why so many unrelated languages have words sounding like "mama" and "papa" that *mean* "mama" and "papa." Then he told them about the three levels of diction in English, giving them examples of triplets for the same concept, one native English, one borrowed from French, and one borrowed from Latin, increasing in formality in that order: "fear," "terror," "trepidation"; "goodness," "virtue," "probity." Finally, he gave them his killer of an explanation for why some people say "Missouree" and others say "Missouruh."

Doris seemed as fascinated as her energy level allowed her to be. But Bruce was a tough sell. All he had given Cook was a nod, a frown, and a cleared throat. Cook decided it was time to tell him about Thoreau's Indian.

"One more little linguistic story," he said. "Henry Thoreau writes about it in one of his travel books. Thoreau was on a canoe trip with a friend, on some river in Maine, and they picked up an Indian who traveled with them for a few days. One night around the campfire, Thoreau and his friend were discussing some point, gesturing in the normal way. The Indian knew very little English—too little to follow their talk—but at the end of every exchange, he would say, 'He beat,' pointing either to Thoreau or to Thoreau's friend, depending on who he thought had won. The Indian had appointed himself judge of their chat, and he was picking the winner just from their gestures!"

Doris laughed. "Talk about competitive," she said. Cook looked at her husband. Bruce evidently found no personal meaning in the story. He was busy frowning at the remains of the shrimp he had just bitten.

"Beth," Bruce called, "where'd you get these shrimp?"

Beth stopped in midsentence—she had been speaking to her mother—and gave Bruce a blank look. "In the open-air market."

"They tell you they were fresh?"

"No," she said impassively. She turned back to her mother.

"Because they're *not*," her brother said. "They've been

frozen." Getting no further response from Beth, he speared another shrimp with a toothpick, dipped it in some red sauce, and held it out for Cook. Something in Cook rose up in resistance, but he dutifully took it and ate it.

"Well?" said Bruce.

Cook chewed and looked at the sweat glistening on Bruce's forehead.

"Well?"

"Let him taste it, honey," said Doris.

"How long does it take to taste a shrimp?" Bruce said to her, his eyes still on Cook. "Well? Frozen?"

Cook swallowed. "I have no idea," he said.

"If you had to say, what would it be?"

"I couldn't."

"If you *had* to."

Cook laughed. "I *do* have to, what with the way you're going on, and I still can't."

"If your life depended on it."

Cook glanced at Doris.

"He's always like this," she said.

"I'm holding a shotgun to your head," Bruce said. "If you refuse to answer, I shoot. Now, frozen or not?"

"Coming through!" Dan called out as he backed into the screen door from inside. He sounded almost like a happy host. His hands were occupied with a platter, on which lay sprawled a huge raw fish. "Coming through!" Since no one was in his way, and since he easily managed the door by himself, his cries hung in the air, unanswered. He threw a grin out that didn't seem to land on anyone and went down the stairs to the patio.

Cook wanted two things: to avoid being shot by Bruce's shotgun, and to get a closer look at Beth's parents in action —presumably the point of Missy Pillow. Thus far he had gotten the merest impression of them. Beth's father had a remote air, but Cook couldn't tell if this came from arrogance, shyness, the general distractedness of age, or specific confusion about who Cook was. As for Beth's mother,

Cook associated her with Dan's phone antics, and on meeting her he had found it hard to look her square in the face. His only feeling about her, based on a few sentences of hers that had drifted his way, was that she was absolutely conventional.

Cook felt it would have been rude to leave Bruce and Doris and go directly to the table to be with Beth's parents. He hit on a plan. He would excuse himself, ostensibly to help Dan at the grill, and once he had checked in with Dan, he would ease over to the table where Beth sat with her parents. This felt like the typical sort of foolish maneuvering he engaged in at parties to avoid bores—or that he feared others engaged in to avoid *him*. He excused himself and trotted down the stairs. Behind him, a pretend shotgun went off, and he heard Doris say, "Oh *stop* it."

At the patio grill, Dan was staring at the glowing stack of coals. He took no notice of Cook. "Okay," he said unconvincingly. He set the platter on the rock wall, picked up a small dead branch from the ground, and spread the coals out with it. He stared at the result. "Okay," he said.

"Nothing but the best tools, eh, Dan?" said Bruce, suddenly appearing from behind Cook.

Dan frowned. Then he looked at the branch, with its smoldering tip. Cook had the impression that Dan wanted to poke Bruce in the eye with it. But he just dropped it and put the grill over the coals. He picked up the fish platter and eased the fish onto the grill. He looked at the fish. "Okay," he said.

Bruce said, "Don't you have hamburgers or something for the kids?"

"Oh, shit," said Dan, and he turned and hurried to the stairs and into the house. As he went in, Robbie came out with Bruce's two children—a noisy boy somewhat older than Robbie and a docile-looking girl a little younger. They headed for the Ping-Pong table. Beth's father swung his chair around, away from the glass table, to watch the children. He called out to them, but they didn't seem to hear him. Doris was now at the table with the adults, uninvolved in their conversation. Her glance fell on Cook, and they looked at each other for a moment.

Bruce chuckled. "Old Danny boy," he said, shaking his head. He eased the fish over to one side of the grill, where there were no coals underneath. "His heart's just not in it. He hates having the family over—always has. So look what he does. He forgets the burgers and puts the fish on first. Your heart's got to be in a thing or you might as well not do it." He looked at Cook. "Am I right?"

Cook was reluctant to agree with anything coming from Bruce, but he said, "Yes. You're right."

"Get into it or get out of it. That's my philosophy. Take the business. I knew it was there if I wanted it. But did I want it? A son inherits a family business, everyone says big deal, he sat on his ass and it fell in his lap. You have to fight that all your life. Did I want people saying big deal, it fell in his lap?" He grinned. "Hell, yes. Because I *loved* it. I *loved* the print shop. I've loved it since I was a kid. And over the years, it's become mine. It's become mine as much as if I'd built it out of an empty lot. That's because I was into it. That's what it takes."

"Who owns it, exactly?"

Bruce took a moment to answer. He seemed a little disappointed that Cook hadn't responded directly to his self-lionization. "Dad, Beth, and me. He's handing it over to us, year by year. He's no kid." Bruce looked up at the deck. A quarrel over the rules had broken out among the children. Beth's father shouted something to them, and they quieted down and resumed playing.

"Dad's an amazing guy," Bruce said. "Great business instincts. It's tough for him to let go of it. Just think about it." Bruce looked at Cook. "Your own kid taking over everything you've created, and in a year it could be right in the toilet. It must be awful. I'd hate it if I was him."

"He's probably proud," Cook said. "If the business is going well..."

"Sure it is. But you never know."

"But if it's going well, he's probably proud."

"But you never know what'll happen! It's terrifying!"

The screen door banged. They watched Dan come out with a platter of hamburger patties. Bruce frowned in annoyance. "What in the hell is he doing now?"

Dan had set the platter on the broad railing and had gone to the Ping-Pong table, where Robbie was shouting at his older cousin. Dan said that if there was any more arguing he would put the equipment away.

"That's what *I* said," Dan's father-in-law called out.

Dan began to explain the rules to the children, slowly and carefully, demonstrating each one with the ball. Bruce laughed softly as he watched. He was no longer impatient for the hamburgers and even seemed amused by Dan's detailed instructions.

"What about Dan's role in the business?" Cook asked.

Bruce's face became expressionless, save for a quizzical smile at one corner of his mouth. "Why do you ask?"

Cook shrugged. "Just curious."

Bruce looked up to the deck. "Danny boy's a loser. I'll tell you why. He's a vacuum cleaner of information. When he came into the business, he learned everything I knew in less than six months. He drives me nuts. There I was, been in the business since I was a kid, and Danny boy comes along and sucks it all up in six months. And I wasn't the one who taught him all he knows—I can't even get the satisfaction of saying that. He just watched and asked everybody a million questions. They all loved it—the pressmen, the salespeople, all of them. They loved it and spilled their guts. Dad, too. Dan would spend whole evenings with him, pumping him and pumping him."

"All of that makes him a loser?"

"It makes him a loser if he's gonna throw it all away. He's a natural, and he's gonna give it all up."

"What do you mean?"

"He's quitting the business. He wants to teach! Grammar

school! How's that for taking a cut in salary?"

Cook was so surprised he felt panicked. He felt he must have missed key signs. "Are you sure?"

Bruce nodded. "I get the pleasure of being the only one who knows. He's been working up the guts to tell Beth. And Dad. I've known about it officially for about a month, but I saw it coming down the pike a long time ago." He looked at Cook. "You obviously didn't know. And I've gone and told you. That's just too bad, isn't it? The whole thing has me pissed off."

Cook looked to the deck. Dan was still demonstrating the rules, holding on to the ball and thereby holding the children's attention. Cook said, "If he's unhappy there, he's got a right to quit."

Bruce shook his head. "It's a dumb move. He's a loser."   •

"Is that why you're so anxious about the business? Because he's leaving?"

"Hell no," Bruce said sharply. He began to fuss with the grill.

Dan's voice came to them from the deck as he called a parting word to the children: "It's supposed to be fun, okay?" He picked up the platter of hamburgers and walked down the stairs to the patio.

Cook waited uneasily, feeling pummeled by questions. When did Dan plan to quit? How would Beth take his decision? Why hadn't he told her? Cook distractedly watched Bruce's son miss the Ping-Pong ball and run after it. He watched him lift his foot up and deliberately crush it, then pick it up and show it to Robbie with a grin.

Robbie burst into tears. Dan heard or sensed something was wrong, and turned around in time to see Robbie throw down his paddle and run into the house. Beth stood up from the table and went after him. Dan gave Bruce the hamburgers and went back up the stairs and followed Beth into the house.

Bruce saw the crushed ball, but evidently he hadn't seen the precipitating event. As he put the hamburgers on he said,

"What's the big deal? Don't they have another ball? Why would a kid bust out crying like that?"

Cook excused himself—yet again—from Bruce and headed for the house. When he reached the deck, he heard Beth's mother asking her husband what was going on. Doris was at the far end of the deck with her son, asking him the same question. Beth's mother looked at Cook and called out cheerfully, "Lots of excitement!" Cook frowned and went into the house.

He went through the kitchen and paused at the bottom of the stairs. In the upstairs den, Robbie was throwing a fit. Cook had never heard anything like it. Robbie was banging doors, stomping his feet, and screaming in unearthly wails. After one huge bang, Cook heard Dan yell loudly at Robbie to *stop* it, just *stop* it, and then Beth yelled, though whether at Dan or Robbie he couldn't tell. Then the only sound was Robbie crying softly, and Dan and Beth asking him what was the matter, what had happened.

Cook backed away through the swinging door into the kitchen. Listening to this crisis, he felt like more of an intruder than he had felt in all the time he'd been at the house.

Doris came into the kitchen. She looked sad on top of looking tired. "How is he?" she said.

"They're up there with him. I don't know."

"My son's the world's worst loser. It really upsets me."

Cook couldn't think of anything to say to that. He was glad, though, that she had some sense of what had happened.

Doris sighed. "Beth was about to set the table in the dining room. She wants to eat in there instead of outside, because it's getting so hot."

"I'll help," said Cook.

They began to carry the dishes and utensils Beth had set out from the kitchen into the dining room. With each trip Cook glanced through the sun-room windows. Bruce had taken over the chefly duties at the grill. His two children had tracked down another Ping-Pong ball and were playing at the table with it. Beth's parents sat and watched them. Beth's father seemed content, but Beth's mother kept looking impatiently toward the door, as if wondering where everyone was and when they would come back to her. Cook felt a remembered feeling, and he successfully tracked it down to his first night with Beth and Dan, when he had felt guilty for abandoning Beth to go with Dan and Robbie to the library. Now he kept peeking through the windows, masochistically reawakening that guilty feeling with every glimpse of Beth's mother's sour face.

Meanwhile, Doris was playing Meet the Linguist again, but more nicely than her husband played it. She told Cook that she had wanted to major in French in college, but for some reason she hadn't, and Cook didn't quite catch what she did major in. Nor, in his general preoccupation, did he catch what she did for a living, and it was too late to start from scratch and ask her. His end of the conversation rather limped as a result.

Beth came into the kitchen and Doris apologized for her son's behavior. Beth said that Robbie had been keeping some things pent up—that he was apparently more upset about the cancellation of Camp Swallow than she or Dan appreciated, and it had come out all at once. She looked at the dining room table and said, "Hey. Great. Thanks." She looked relieved and pleased, but deeply miserable too, all at the same time. She sighed and went out to gather everyone for lunch.

When they came in, Cook waited until Beth's parents were seated and then pulled out a chair for himself between them. As he sat down, Beth's mother threw a glance at the window air conditioner—a noisy thing that was blasting them with cool air. She wondered aloud when Dan and Beth were going to get central air. She said it in a personally peeved, entitled way that made Cook want to dump his water glass on her head. He looked around for a reaction from Beth's father and Doris, the only others in the room at the moment, but they ignored her. Beth came in from the kitchen with a salad, and Bruce entered bearing the platter of grilled fish and hamburgers. Dan came downstairs, threw Cook an obscure wink, and sat at the far end of the table, opposite his father-in-law. Dan said that Robbie was going to stay upstairs for a while and watch TV, until he felt better. Doris and Bruce's children would eat at the table in the sunroom.

When they were all seated, the conversation opened with a reference to someone's wedding, and for the next half hour the talk never once emerged from the restricted code of local items and family news. Whenever a topic came up that struck Cook as somewhat broader—first a political issue in the city, then a public relations problem a local corporation was having—a personal connection came out: Bruce or his father or mother knew the people in question. Initially, some attempt was made to include Cook in the conversation. Strange names would be explained, characters introduced as they were brought onstage. But after a while, this courtesy was dropped, and the family went about its business in its customary way.

Beth's mother pretty much ran the show. She had a narrow, ruthless conception of what constituted conversation. For one thing, it couldn't dwell for too long on a single topic—that was a sign of failure for her. Her impatience would become palpable, her agitation contagious. If she didn't get a topic shift by innuendo, she would call for it, saying, "Let's talk about something else." In every instance she had her way, though Cook sensed that she went against the general will at least a few times. She also had rigid upper and lower limits on a scale of impersonality. If talk about something became too cold—as it did when Bruce wondered aloud about the point where tax abatement brought diminishing returns—she would shudder and raise her hands in protest. But if talk became too personal—too earthy, too dirty—she didn't like that either. Cook watched, fascinated, as one topic after another came into being, lived a brief, cru-

elly circumscribed life, and then got buried without cere-
mony.

Through all this Beth's father said little. He listened, his
eyes twinkling, and he spoke some, but his speech was slow
compared to his wife's, and she tended to finish things for
him. Dan spoke just enough, like a student who didn't want
his grade brought down for not participating in class. By
this measure Doris flunked. She tuned out in the early going
and was the first to finish eating and begin clearing the table.

When Doris did this, Dan said he was going to make
some ice cream with the children. Bruce said he would help.
Cook and Beth's father, as special guest and patriarch respec-
tively, were ordered to stay seated while the women cleared
the table and took orders for tea and coffee.

Cook asked Beth's father about the business. It was as if
he had flipped a switch on a printer, and it was off on a run
of a hundred thousand copies. Cook just listened for a while.
Then he gently steered the topic toward Bruce's and Dan's
responsibilities. Two things were immediately clear: Beth's
father indeed knew nothing about Dan's plans to quit the
business, and Dan was crucial to its operation. He explained
Dan's and Bruce's roles in terms of a "Mr. Inside" and a
"Mr. Outside." At first Cook felt patronized—he wondered
if Beth's father was going to produce little Play-Doh figures
and have them act out their roles on the table—but then he
realized these were standard terms in the industry.

"Mr. Outside is the guy who handles sales," Beth's father
said, clearing his throat, which tended to be gravelly. "He's
the guy who deals with suppliers, who stays in touch with
manufacturers, all that. Mr. Inside is in charge of operations,
scheduling, and personnel. It takes two people in a shop the
size of ours. It's too much for one man. I know. I did it alone
for forty years."

"Which is which?" Cook asked.

"Dan's Mr. Inside. Bruce is Mr. Outside. They've worked
it out beautifully. Beautifully. They make it easy for each

other." His eyes twinkled under his thick eyebrows. "It wasn't always so easy, let me tell you."

"Is one of those jobs more important than the other?"

"There was a time when it all happened right up here." He tapped his forehead. "I was Mr. Inside *and* Mr. Outside."

"And Mr. Inside-Out," Cook offered.

All he got for his contribution was a frown from Beth's father. "It's gotten too complicated for one man. Too complicated." His voice was extra gravelly now. He cleared it, but with no effect. "Hell, it was too complicated for one man when *I* was doing it." He grinned and shook his head, apparently in amazement at the foolish energy of his younger self. "They're smart, those boys. They know how to make it go without killing themselves."

Cook nodded. "Did you know things would work out this well when Dan decided to—"

"Bah!" Beth's father laughed. "The first day Dan came to work, he says to me, 'Do you ever have to have ideas in this business?' What do you think of that? 'Do you ever have to have ideas?' Christ Almighty. I wanted to throw him out into the street. But he settled down. He learned the ropes. New blood—it pays off. If it doesn't drive you crazy." He laughed again. "Take estimating. I've been a seat-of-the-pants estimator all my life. A customer wanted a job, I'd whip off an estimate just like that." He shook his head. "It's no way to run a business. You can lose customers by being too high, or you can lose money coming in too low, or you can flat confuse 'em by being all over the place with your figures. Dan's got a computer program that does estimating, down to the penny. Took him no time at all to tailor it to our shop. He plugs in the numbers and out it comes, almost as fast as seat-of-the-pants."

"And that's something you wouldn't have done on your own?"

"Me? Bah! Never. Say 'software' to me and I want to punch you in the face."

"Are you threatening the poor man, dear?" Beth's mother had appeared with a tray of cups and saucers. She set it down and began to distribute them around the table.

Beth's father seemed to lose his momentum with this interruption, so Cook said to her, "We're talking about the business. About Dan and Bruce as partners."

"Ah. They're a perfect pair," she said brightly. "I've said so from the beginning. Poor Bruce is a worrier. He wakes up every morning expecting a disaster to happen. But Dan..." She screwed her face up. "As far as I can tell, Dan wakes up grinning. He always expects the best."

"It's a good system," Beth's father said. "Checks and balances—that's what you want. A business needs an optimist and a pessimist. It's tough for one guy to be both. Me? I had to be both. It's tough for one guy to do that...."

With the recapitulation of this theme, Cook had a sudden feeling that he had known the family for years, that he was indeed an old college friend of Dan's and had heard the same stories, heard people presenting themselves in the same light, over and over.

They continued to talk—Beth's father now giving the history of the printers the firm had purchased over the years— as the others drifted in and out of the dining room. Doris came in, sat down, and half listened for a while before she left. Bruce passed through the dining room into the living room, where he sat down and thumbed through a *National Geographic*. The coffee was still brewing and the ice cream wasn't ready yet. There was a certain drift to the proceedings.

Beth's father said, "Of course, with Dan in the picture now, the question of succession is a whole lot simpler."

"It is?" said Cook.

"Sure it is. And succession is tricky stuff, tricky as hell. The original plan was for Beth and Bruce to get equal shares. But if you think about it, you see the problem. Bruce is *in* it, running it. If it took off, shouldn't *he* get the benefit?

Or if it went the other way, if he ran it into the ground, shouldn't *he* be the one to eat it? Beth shouldn't be penalized for that, should she? See the problem?"

"Yes. I see it."

"The solution was to have the business appraised the moment I officially retired, to have a fixed value assigned to it. Bruce could buy Beth out for half that assessed value—no more, no less. If the business took off, good for Bruce, he'd get the benefit of it. But if he ran it into the ground, he'd have to eat it. Her half would be solid, but he'd have to eat it. You follow? You with me?"

"Sure." Cook glanced at Bruce, who was still in the living room. He had tossed his magazine back onto the pile and it had slid off onto the floor. He picked it up and put it on the coffee table, then left the room by the other door, into the entryway.

"But now, with Dan in the picture, we've scrapped all that. I didn't even have the business appraised—a pain in the ass anyway. Dan and Bruce are in it together, fifty-fifty. Whatever comes down the pike, they share it, fifty-fifty. I've had new papers drawn up, if I can just get that son-in-law of mine to come over and sign them."

"So Dan's share is half of the business? But what if something happens? What if, let's say, Dan and Beth got a divorce?"

"Nice talk," said Beth, coming into the room with a tray of small bowls filled with ice cream. A stick of peppermint stood up in each one.

Beth's father said to her, "When can I get that husband of yours to sign these papers?"

Beth shrugged. "Anytime." She distributed the bowls around the table and sat down.

"I'm anxious to do it. It's my way of saying something important to him."

Beth's mother, returning to her chair, said, "Ah. The succession." She gave the word a dramatic pronunciation and rolled her eyes to the ceiling. She looked at Cook to make sure of his attention, and she seemed pleased to have it. "Talking about it makes us feel like such royalty."

Cook smiled minimally. He wondered where Dan was. Bruce and Doris were in the sun-room, talking in low, tense voices. He wondered if something was up with the kids again. Finally, Bruce and Doris joined the others at the table.

"Everything is wonderful," Beth's father growled, looking at his ice cream, addressing no one in particular. Dan came in and sat down.

Bruce took a deep breath. He scooted his chair back and stood up. "I can't eat this." He too was looking at his ice cream. "I've got to get back to the shop. I can't eat this," he said again, "or I might eat *it,* and I don't want to eat *it.*" He looked toward his father, but his eyes seemed to glance off him into midair. Without saying goodbye to anybody, he left the room and went out the front door.

Doris patted her lips with her napkin and went after him. She caught him out on the front porch, where they talked— Cook heard their voices, but indistinctly. He kept waiting for someone at the table to say something. Finally, Beth's mother did.

"Lots of excitement," she said.

Twenty

Cook stood at the living room window and watched Bruce and his wife and children get into their car and drive off. That left Beth, Dan, and Beth's parents on the sidewalk. Beth seemed reluctant to part with them and hung on, chatting. Dan was there just to be a good sport, Cook guessed.

He watched Dan give his father-in-law a final handshake and his mother-in-law a final peck before coming back to the house, leaving Beth with her parents. When Dan came in, he started to walk through the entryway, but he saw Cook at the window and joined him there.

"Is Bruce okay?" Cook asked.

Dan shrugged. "This morning one of the printers acted up, and the client's inflexible, so he's worried. It's just one of those things that can drive you nuts."

"His problem seems to run deeper than that."

"Yeah. It does."

"Nobody seemed surprised by what he said. Nobody seemed upset."

"It happens all the time."

"That's awful."

"You're right. It is. We're just used to it."

Cook saw a tall, striking-looking man pull up in front of the house on a bicycle. Everything he wore was geared for cycling. He could have stepped out of a catalog.

"That's Ron," said Dan. "Mary's husband. The bike nut."

Cook nodded. He wished he could pick the guy up and plunk him down on an inner-city playground, just to see the kids hoot at him for the way he was dressed. He watched Beth's parents take a few steps toward him. Beth's father shook hands with him, evidently renewing an acquaintance.

"Look at that," said Dan. "Money attracts money. Ron's got it and Beth's folks know it." He sighed. "Look at Beth. Jesus, all she wants is a nice warm goodbye, and they're sucking up to Ron."

Cook looked at Dan. He was staring coldly at the scene on the street.

"It's like when they came to see Robbie for the first time," Dan said. "They were in Hawaii when he was born—he was two weeks early—so they didn't see him in the hospital. I picked them up at the airport and brought them here before I took them home. When we got here, I expected Rose to leap out of the car and run to the front door. I thought she'd be dying to see her new grandson. What's she do? She notices the new landscaping job across the street at Ron and Mary's house, and she walks over there for a look-see, because she's thinking of having hers done. I could have killed her."

Ron was pulling off his bike gloves with a great flourish, like a court dandy. Beth stood alone, her arms folded across her chest.

Cook said, "Do you think Beth's upset right now?"

"Yeah. They're bastards. But Beth's not so innocent herself. She's got the money fever too."

Cook was silent for a while. Then he said, "Bruce told me you're quitting the business."

"Fuck," said Dan. He said it angrily, but in a resigned way, too, as if acknowledging that it had to come out sooner or later.

"Is it definite?"

"Fuck," he said again.

"You plan to teach?"

"Don't press me on this. I'm not ready to talk about it. Here comes Beth, anyway. Don't say another word about it."

Outside, Beth had more or less given up on her parents and offered them a final wave as she headed for the house. Dan and Cook moved away from the window. Beth came in and gave them a brief smile—a sad smile, it seemed to Cook—and went into the kitchen. She began to clean up. Dan went in there as well—to comfort her in her time of need, Cook assumed. But he heard the back door slam. Frowning, he went to the window at the rear of the dining room. Dan was in the backyard, hunched over one of the remaining postholes, measuring its depth with a tape measure.

Cook went into the kitchen. Beth was at the sink. "Are you all right?" he asked.

She turned around. "Not really. Oh, Robbie wants to see you. He asked me to send you up. What'd you think of everybody?"

"You're not like any of them," Cook said. He headed for the stairs and heard a faint laugh of surprise from Beth behind him.

He paused at the landing between the first and second floors and sat down on the little bench in the alcove. He took THE HORROR! from his pocket and unfolded it.

~~She's a bitch.~~
~~He's a prick.~~
~~Money.~~
~~He's a failure.~~
~~She thinks he's a failure.~~
~~He thinks she's a bad mother.~~
The in-laws.

In the kitchen, Beth turned off the water. Cook heard something in its place: she was crying. He wanted to go to her, but he couldn't. It would only make things worse, as if *he* knew what to do for her even if Dan didn't. He waited for her crying to subside, and in time it did.

He focused on his list. He crossed out the last line. The in-laws were a horror all right, but the greater horror was Dan's failure to help Beth deal with them—his failure to be with her when she needed him, his failure just to *be* with her. He wrote down the new entry:

Dan.

Then he went up to see Robbie.

The den door was slightly ajar, and it opened wider with his knock. Robbie looked up at him from the floor, scooted to the TV, and turned it off. "A liar must have a good memory," he said. There was a challenge in his voice.

"What?" said Cook.

Robbie stood up and said, "Follow me."

Cook stepped aside to let him pass through the door. Robbie climbed the stairs to the third floor. Cook followed —up to his room and to his desk, where Robbie opened a drawer without apology. He took out *The Pillow Manual* and slammed it on the desk. His hands were shaking—with so many feelings, Cook guessed, that they were beyond counting. For all his confidence, Robbie was not a boy who regularly challenged adults like this. He was angry, but he was also afraid.

"Yes," Cook said. "I'm here to help your parents—to help their marriage."

"You lied."

"Yes."

"You all lied."

"Your parents thought it would worry you if you knew."

"Good thinking! Good thinking!"

Cook didn't know what this meant, exactly. "Look. We were probably wrong to keep it a secret, because it makes things look worse than they are."

Robbie stared at him.

"Just because I'm here doesn't mean your parents are going to get a divorce. They're trying *not* to get a divorce. They're trying to stay married."

"How come they need you?"

"Sometimes people need help. Look. You ever been in the hospital?"

"Nope."

"You ever know anyone who had to go to the hospital?"

"Jason. He had something wrong with his stomach."

"Who's Jason?"

"The prick that stomped on my Ping-Pong ball."

"Oh. Okay. Well, when he went to the hospital, did everyone think he was going to die?"

"He *should* have. I wish he did."

"Okay. Okay. But nobody thought he was going to die just because he went there."

"I wish he did."

"Okay. Okay. The point is I'm like the hospital. Your parents brought their marriage to me so it would get better."

"My grandma died in a hospital. In California."

Cook pressed his lips together. "Yes. Sometimes people do die in hospitals. And sometimes marriages die. But when people work on it, like your mom and dad are doing, there's less chance of that."

Robbie stared at the floor. Cook looked at him and felt an ache. "When you said a liar must have a good memory—"

"Dad's from San Francisco," Robbie said, looking up. "You told me you were interviewing people who were born in St. Louis. So how come you interviewed Dad? You forgot that, didn't you?" He looked hard at Cook. "Are Mom and Dad really going to Italy?"

Cook frowned. "Sure. What did you think?"

"Nothing."

"Come on. What did you think?"

"Nothing."

"Come *on*."

Robbie made an odd face. "I thought they were gonna go somewhere and get a divorce."

"Geez, Robbie. Don't you think they would talk to you about it first? You think they would sneak off and do that?"

"They sneaked *you* in here."

"That's different."

"How?"

"It just *is*."

To Cook's surprise, Robbie seemed satisfied with this juvenile insistence. "How come this is called *The Pillow Manual?*" he asked.

"Because the place I work for is called the Pillow Agency."

Robbie laughed. "That's dumb."

"Yeah. Listen, do you want to talk to your mom and dad about this now?"

"No."

"I think you should. It would make you feel better."

"No. Don't tell them I know."

"What? I *have* to."

"No you don't. I don't want them to know I know."

Cook frowned. "Why?"

Robbie shrugged.

"Do you want revenge because they kept it a secret from you? Do you want them to think they've still got you fooled?"

A huge grin broke out on Robbie's face. "That's a great idea."

"Geez, I didn't mean to suggest it. I just—"

"It's great. It's perfect."

"But I think you need to talk about it with them."

"Nah."

"You sure?"

"*Yeah*. How many times do I—"

"Okay okay. But don't get any crazy theories."

"Okay."

"And stay out of my desk."

"Okay." Robbie's eyes fell on *The Pillow Manual*. "Actually, I was just looking for Hershey Kisses. I've gotta go pack now." He headed for the door but stopped and turned around. "Are you gonna be here when I get back from camp?"

"I don't know. I'll come visit if I'm not, though."

"Okay."

Cook watched him leave. He went to the window and stared out into the park. Life at the Wilsons' was getting more complicated by the minute. A sad woman crying at the kitchen sink, an unhappy man with his head in a posthole, and a worried boy searching through Cook's desk for clues about his family's future. What next?

He went to his desk and opened *The Pillow Manual* to the next pink seal:

DAY FIVE
Roy Pillow, Jr.

He stared at the page for several minutes, collecting himself. Then he went to the landing for the phone and brought it back to his desk and dialed Pillow's number.

"Pillow," barked Pillow.

"Roy," said Cook. " 'Roy Pillow, Jr.' What the hell?"

Pillow mmmed. "Has Missy Pillow been satisfied?"

"She's very happy. Trust me. Now 'Roy Pillow, Jr.' What the hell?"

Pillow chuckled fiendishly. "Roy Pillow, Jr., is my son, Jeremy. By my second wife. He was a little dickens as a boy. Just full of mischief. He loved to put snakes and spiders in the darnedest places—in my shoes, under my pillow, that sort of thing."

"Sounds great, Roy."

"Oh, we had some lively times, let me tell you. That was before his mother packed him up and moved out of my life."

"I'm sorry, Roy."

"No need to be," Pillow said brightly. He seemed upbeat. "I want you to do what Roy Pillow, Jr., did. I want you to track down some snakes and spiders, and I want you to find a good place to plant them to surprise your couple. One snake or spider for each."

"What—"

"I'm speaking figuratively, of course."

Cook relaxed slightly. "Of course."

"A 'snake' or 'spider' in this context is any piece of information that packs a surprise. You've been nosing around awhile, so you must have found a few snakes and spiders. Find some good places to hide them. Sneak them into a conversation in unexpected places, like in a subordinate clause, or—my favorite—a nominative absolute. What you want is any little slimy or crawly thing that'll shock them, Jeremy, shock them right out of their pants until they're standing naked before you—if you'll allow me another metaphor."

"Agh!" bellowed Cook, jerking the phone away from his face. Pillow's words had awakened a lively memory.

"Jeremy? What is it?"

Cook held the receiver gingerly, with two fingers, and spoke into it from a distance. "Roy, I'm talking to you from a phone that was all but up the asshole of our client."

Pillow took some time to absorb this. *"The Pillow Manual* is silent on that subject, Jeremy. Now, if I might move on to something more pleasant, we need to set up your next date. You won't have any grounds for complaint this time. No matter what happens, you can't come crying to me."

"Don't be too sure, Roy. Who's the babe?"

Pillow fell silent. Then he chuckled. "Jeremy, across the river in Illinois there are lots of nice apple farms."

"You want me to date an apple farmer?"

"No, no. Just listen. In the fall, St. Louisans like to drive out there and pick apples."

"I'll remember that, Roy. A hot tip—I appreciate it."

"One of the farms is called U-Pick."

"Cute."

"U-Pick, Jeremy. U-Pick."

"I heard you, Roy."

"I'm saying it to you now. U-Pick."

"Are you telling me I get to pick my own date?"

"Exactly."

Cook laughed. "I've had that freedom all along, Roy. I haven't exactly exercised it lately, but—"

"Of course you've had that freedom. I'm offering you more than freedom. I'm telling you that you may date anyone in the world of your choice. The Pillow Agency is at your disposal."

"*Anyone?*"

"Anyone. I shall make the overtures, provide whatever incentives are necessary, and furnish transportation to St. Louis and lodging for one night. Think about women you've been adoring from afar—women way out of your class, light-years beyond your reach. I'm interested in seeing what happens when your fantasies come true. Take your time with this. Think about movie stars, ballerinas, musicians—one of our staff was nuts for a flautist in the Boston Pops Orchestra—newscasters, wispy poetesses, stockbrokers—one of our boys fell for an investment banker he'd seen on *Wall Street Week*. I'm afraid she pretty much chewed him up and spit him out—you never know how these things will turn out. But the sky's the limit, Jeremy. I'm offering you anybody you want. Take your time, and—"

"You know, Roy, I've been thinking about Elizabeth Taylor a lot."

"Oh? She *is* nice. A tad older than you, but she's every bit as lovely as she once was, now that she's lost all that weight."

"No, no. I've been thinking about her and Richard Burton. She married him twice."

"Yes, but they're divorced, aren't they? In fact, if I'm not mistaken, I do believe he's dead, Jeremy. He should be no obstacle."

"No, Roy. You don't understand. I've just been thinking about people who marry someone twice—people who go back and try again."

"Yes? And?"

"I want to try that."

"I don't follow."

"I want you to find Paula."

"Who?"

"Paula Annette Nouvelles. That's her full name."

"Ah. And a lovely name it is, too. Is she French? One of our staff fell for an Italian actress, and we incurred considerable expense getting her, but, as I promised you—"

"No, Roy. She's not French. She's a Hoosier."

"Come again?"

"She's an old girlfriend of mine from Indiana. I don't know where she is now. You'll have to track her down."

Pillow paused for so long that Cook actually forgot he was on the phone. He sat there with the receiver pressed against his ear, thinking about Paula and wondering how Pillow would find her.

"Don't you like me, Jeremy?" said Pillow, back in his ear. "You thwart me at every turn. You came crying to me about the two previous arrangements I made for you. Here I am offering you anyone you want—anyone!—and you make a mockery of the offer by going back to the dirty-clothes hamper for yesterday's laundry. No one in the history of the Pillow Agency has ever picked an old girlfriend for this assignment."

"It's what I want, Roy. You promised. Now, you got a pen? Listen carefully. I'll tell you everything I know about her. I've got a postcard here. Let me grab it and give you the postmark. You can start there."

When Cook came downstairs, it didn't take him long to realize that Roy Pillow, Jr.—that little bugger—would have to wait for a day, until Robbie was gone. Dan and Beth were focusing their energy on him. Dan had asked Robbie to help him pour the concrete for the remaining postholes, and Cook stayed out of the way so that father and son could work together. Later, Beth helped Robbie pack, using the dining room table as the final staging area. Cook hung around in case anything developed, but nothing did. By dinnertime Robbie was ready to go. This freed up the evening for the family, and Beth and Dan asked Robbie what he wanted to do. Dan said he could have three wishes—three *reasonable* wishes. Robbie grinned, made a few ridiculous suggestions, and finally said, "I want to order a pizza, play a duet with Jeremy, and play Trivial Pursuit with everybody."

The pizza part of the evening was fine. Cook was a little nervous about the duet. He asked Robbie to wait until Dan and Beth were out of the room. When they went upstairs to do some packing of their own, Robbie seized the moment. He suggested "Country Gardens," and Cook agreed—at least he knew the tune. Cook sat down on the bench, cracked his knuckles as a joke, and found himself looking at a bass part with notes as unfamiliar as Kickapoo adverbs. He told Robbie that he used to be a trumpet player and suggested they switch, so that he could play the treble clef. They did, but Robbie took off at an impossibly brisk tempo. Cook tried to keep up, paying a price of at least one error per measure. Robbie encouraged him with shouts of "Good!" and "Hey!" but Cook had to slow it down. Robbie let him do this by stages until the tempo crawled to a complete stop.

They tried it again. Cook hit upon a new strategy that allowed him to keep up: omitting notes. This might have met with more success if he hadn't been responsible for the melody. Robbie allowed this to go on for a while, but then he came to a stop and looked down at the keyboard, shaking his head as if to say there was no hope.

"I've got it," Robbie suddenly said. Then he left. Cook sat alone on the bench, wondering if "it" consisted of abandoning the incompetent at the piano. He stood up as Robbie returned with a tape recorder. Robbie set it on the bench, turned it on, and sat down and raced through the bass part. Then he rewound the tape, pressed "Play," and played the melody over the bass accompaniment, throwing sidelong grins at Cook like a whorehouse ragtimer. Evidently there was no insult intended here, so Cook tried not to feel any.

When they played Trivial Pursuit, they used two editions of the game—the regular one for the adults and a junior one when it was Robbie's turn. Beth won the first game, Dan the second. As for Cook, he would race into the lead, amassing little pies in intimidating succession until he hit the pink category: popular entertainment. He would die there while Dan and Beth passed him. After the first two games, they teamed up, with Cook and Robbie playing against Dan and Beth. Robbie did not suffer from Cook's abnormal ignorance of American culture, and he held his own in the pink category. Together they won the two games they played. Robbie kept insisting on doing foolish things like high-fiving Cook after victories, but Cook was having fun, and he allowed himself to be slapped around.

As they packed the game up, Robbie loudly asked Cook how his survey was going. Cook said fine. Beth threw a nervous glance at Dan and told Robbie to go brush his teeth and get ready for bed. Robbie said just a sec, and he asked Cook how come he hung around the house so much if he was studying the language of all of St. Louis. Cook said that was a good question. Dan said it was time for all good campers to go to bed. Robbie said, "Yeah. It'll be good to hit the old *pillow*. Right, Jeremy? Right?"

Cook said right.

The next morning they took Robbie to camp—or rather, to a West County school parking lot, the pickup spot for the Big Muddy bus. Robbie was so nervous that he barely thought to say goodbye to Cook. He scanned the faces of the other children on the lot, located his two friends from school, and huddled with them. Cook stayed at the car, leaning against it with his arms folded and watching from a distance while Dan and Beth helped Robbie with his bags and talked with other parents.

Eventually the children boarded, and with a honk and a roar the bus sped out of the lot. Dan and Beth ended up on the wrong side of the bus to wave goodbye to Robbie. He was on Cook's side, sitting at a window, and as the bus pulled away, he leaned out and hollered to Cook, "Keep the faith, baby." Cook smiled and waved.

Twenty-one

Cook played with snakes and spiders in the back seat on the way home. Sitting there by himself, with Mom and Dad in front, he felt just like a little Roy Pillow, Jr.

He had gone over THE HORROR! again the night before, and he had taken another look at the first-night questionnaire. As a result, he had a witch's brew of beasts to choose from. He played quietly—a good little boy. Since each partner was to be surprised by one snake or spider, he arranged his creatures in pairs, like Noah.

Dan, Beth thinks you're a failure.

Beth, you've communicated to Dan that he's a failure just enough to make him feel like one.

He liked that pair pretty well. He liked the thematic link provided by "failure," and he liked the what-goes-around-comes-around *pow!* back in Beth's face.

Dan, Beth's not a bad mother.

Beth, Dan's not a failure.

Nicely balanced, that.

Dan, you know exactly when Beth needs you, and you just walk away.

Beth, you've got a perpetual grudge about not getting what is rightfully yours from Dan, but it comes out at the wrong times, making you into a bitch.

That pair was guaranteed to foster discussion.

There were other candidates, but Cook kept them in their cages for the moment. He thought about all he had been through with Dan and Beth. It felt like a lot, but considering how long they had been married, it was no doubt a tiny sample from a rich tradition. This led Cook to one simple question: what possessed two intelligent people of good will who were in pursuit of the same goal to snarl at each other like jackals over a carcass? Didn't they both want the marriage to thrive?

Beth certainly did. She worked as hard on the marriage as Dan did on the house. But Dan must have wanted it, too. Why else would he hang in there through such misery? Why else would he tolerate Cook's nagging omnipresence? But what kind of marriage did Dan want? One where he and Beth coexisted? A marriage of "parallel lines," as he had put it? If so, then he and Beth, though intelligent and good-willed, weren't pursuing the same goal after all. And the answer to Cook's question was that the question was flawed. Dan and Beth snarled at each other like jackals because they wanted different things.

In the front seat, Dan's parallel line swerved a bit toward Beth as he asked, "What time is our flight tomorrow?"

"To New York or to Rome?" she asked, turning to look at him.

"New York."

"Late morning. Around eleven. I'll check when we get home." She paused. "Why?"

"Just wondering."

Beth continued to look at Dan a moment, then turned and faced forward again. Dan exited Highway 40 and zigzagged until he picked up another highway heading north. To the west, the weather was strange. Huge, dark clouds sat heavily in the distance, but closer—so close that Cook felt he could touch them—white puffs brightly lit by the sun were streaking from south to north. The two cloud groups seemed to be from different worlds. Cook felt as if he were gazing into a fantastic diorama.

"How about the New York to Rome flight?" Dan asked.

"It leaves at six-thirty. We have a long layover, but we decided to do it that way instead of taking a risk on missing our connection. Remember?"

"Oh, yeah."

"Why?"

Dan shrugged. "Just curious." He glanced at Beth. "Shall we ask him about house-sitting?"

"Sure." Beth turned toward Cook. "Jeremy, would you like to stay in the house for the two weeks we're gone?"

Cook felt a dumb look play across his face.

"You don't have another place to stay in St. Louis, do you?" she said.

"No."

"Were you going somewhere?"

"No." The fact of the matter was that he had planned nothing at all, and he felt embarrassed to admit this. He also felt a little out of touch with reality. By nature he was a poor advance planner, but this was ridiculous.

"Then stay at the house. You could do the watering and save us some money there, and we could save you rent for two weeks. Besides, we don't like to leave the house empty. You'd be doing us a favor."

"Let me think about it," said Cook. Beth looked at him a moment longer, smiled, and turned back around.

"All I ask," said Dan, looking at Cook in the rearview mirror, "is that if you get any action, change the sheets."

Beth gave Dan a tired but affectionate look. "I knew you were going to say that."

Dan exited the highway and drove through a commercial area Cook recognized from his two adventures at Topper's. But Cook's attention was on himself, not on his surroundings. The only explanation he could think of for his lack of planning was that he had become dependent on Pillow. Insofar as he had thought about his future, he had assumed Pillow would dictate it to him.

Beth sighed and looked out the window. "I'm blue," she said. "I miss Robbie already."

"Yeah," said Dan. "Try to work on imagining him being noisy or messy. That helps."

"I guess."

They rode in silence for a while. Then Dan said, "Did he say anything more to you about what happened yesterday?"

"No," said Beth, turning to Dan with interest. She paused. "Why?"

Dan shrugged. "Just curious."

Cook burst out laughing.

Dan looked at him in the mirror. "You find the memory of Robbie crying funny?"

"No," said Cook. "Sorry."

"What is it?" said Beth.

"Nothing," Cook said. "Sorry." But he promptly burst out laughing again.

"Goddammit," said Dan.

"Sorry," Cook said quickly. "Sorry sorry sorry."

Dan muttered something under his breath and then fell silent. Beth gave Cook a funny frown that was hard to read.

Cook was about to laugh again, but he stopped it by talking. "The reason I'm laughing is that the same thing happened three times in a row."

"What thing?" said Beth.

"You said 'Why?' and Dan shrugged and grunted."

"So what?" said Dan.

Cook said, "Beth wants to talk. You don't. That's what. It's funny to see it like that. It's just so obvious."

"Oh, get a job," Dan muttered.

"I have a job, Dan. How about you?"

Dan flinched. "I've got a job. I've got a helluva lot more of a job than you do."

"Honey," Beth said.

"Not from what I hear," said Cook. He had chosen his first beast.

Dan fell silent.

Beth frowned and looked from Cook to Dan.

Cook let the beast all the way out of its cage. "Beth, you'll be interested to learn that Dan plans to quit the family business and become a schoolteacher."

"Fuck you," Dan snapped over his shoulder.

Beth had given a little laugh of confusion at Cook's words, but now she stared at Dan. "What? What's going on?"

"It's something I'm thinking about," Dan said. "I'm considering it."

"Bruce says it's a certainty," Cook said.

"Shut up!" Dan yelled.

"What are you talking about?" Beth said, now looking panicked.

Dan took a deep breath and said, "I'm thinking of quitting the business."

Beth stared at him. "I don't believe it."

"Believe it," Dan said soberly.

Beth shook her head. "I'm not hearing you right. This isn't happening."

"It's happening," Dan said. He came to a stop at a red light and looked at Beth. "It happens all the time. People change jobs."

"God, you're serious, aren't you? What are you going to do?"

"I want to be a schoolteacher. Like you."

Beth's mouth was wide open. She closed it, swallowed, and opened it again. "I'm going to be sick."

"No you're not. You'll get used to it."

"Oh?" Beth said, her eyes hardening. "Where? In some stinking little house? Do you know what you would make as a teacher compared to what you make now?"

The light changed to green and Dan pulled forward.

"We'll have to make some adjustments," he said calmly. "It can be done."

Beth jerked in her seat with frustration and rage. "It's all decided, isn't it? You're talking like it's all over. Bruce knows about it. Jeremy knows about it. When did you plan to tell me? After you told Robbie?"

"I was going to wait until after the trip."

"Great. So considerate." She shook her head again. "I can't believe this. After all they've done for you."

Dan calmly pulled the car over to the curb, turned off the ignition, and set the emergency brake. He turned to Beth and said, "Will you please think about what you're saying? Will you *please* just listen to your fucking self?"

Beth glared at him.

"You know that I've done as much for the business as it's done for me. You know that."

"They didn't have to take you in."

"Take me in? They gave me the job because they knew I'd be good at it. And I have been. Now I'm ready for something else."

Cook released his second beast. "Beth talks like that, Dan, because deep down she believes you're a failure. I'll be quiet now."

"Get out, Jeremy," Dan said. "Get out of the fucking car."

Cook didn't move.

Beth had whirled on Cook and was giving him a hard, brittle look. "How dare you say that! I don't think any such thing."

Cook sat still. This Roy Pillow, Jr., business was tough. He liked Missy Pillow a lot better.

Dan said to Beth, "I'm miserable in my work. You know that."

"You've never said you wanted to do something else. And *teaching?* You've never said a word about teaching."

"Yes I have. You just haven't heard me."

"You'd be making a fraction of what you make now."

"Yep. A small fraction, too."

Beth's eyes widened. "You're gloating! You're gloating!"

"No I'm not."

"You're punishing me! You're loving this!"

"I am not. Why would I want to punish you?"

Beth took a deep breath. "God, I'm gonna be sick."

Dan stared at Beth. He seemed to be waiting for the outcome of her prediction. "Is Jeremy right? Do you think I'm a failure?"

"Of course not."

"I don't believe you."

"What?"

"You think I'm a failure."

"You're just attacking me because you feel guilty for hurting me."

Dan gave a little laugh. "You said I was gloating and loving it. Now you're saying I feel guilty about it. Which is true? They both can't—"

"Oh fuck you."

There was a pause. Dan cleared his throat and seemed to regroup his thoughts. "Look at your father," he said. "He was tremendously successful. He's this big American hero in your family—the model of what a man should be. Look at Bruce. He's bought that image and he's a slave to it. That's why he's a wreck. You've bought it, too. I'm not a complete man to you."

Beth stared at him. "It's pathetic to hear you talk like this."

"You mean it's unmanly?"

Beth turned to Cook, appealing for help. "He's obsessed with manliness. Have I ever said anything about manliness? Have I?" She looked back at Dan. "It's *your* hangup."

"It's my hangup because it's yours. You've made it mine. You've fucked me up." Dan raised his hands, making two anguished claws in front of him. "When we met and fell in love, I was everything to you. I could do anything. I knew all there was to know about all there is in the world. You thought I was just...wonderful. And then, year by year, we've lost that. We end up here, I end up in the business, you make comparisons, and I shrink. Don't you remember how you saw me? Don't you? That's all I want."

"We're grown up now, Dan. College is over."

Dan's eyes flashed. "That's really—"

"People with ten-year-olds shouldn't be wondering what they're going to do with their lives."

"And wives who love their husbands should give them the freedom to do what they want to. Christ. I tell you I'm miserable in my work and you whine about moving into a stinking little house. Your first reaction is selfish. It's *always* selfish. It's always 'What about me?' Well, I'm saying this is what I'm going to do, and if it means we have to downgrade, we have to downgrade, and if you can't hack it, it's just too bad."

Beth wrestled with the door handle and flung open the car door. She got out and stormed down the sidewalk. Cook looked around, curious now to see where they were. He recognized the library across the street. She wouldn't have far to walk.

Cook said, "I remember your mentioning once that she sometimes gets up and leaves in the middle of an argument."

"Fuck you," Dan said. Evidently he was going to hold a grudge for a while. They watched Beth. She turned a corner and disappeared from view. "Damn it," Dan said. He grabbed his door handle. "You drive home, okay? You know where we are? Take a right at the second light, then take the very next right, and that brings you back to the house. Okay?"

"Where are you going?"

Dan paused, frowning, the door half open. "After Beth, you idiot."

"Why?"

This time Dan turned his frown fully on Cook. "Because she's upset!" He got out and hurried down the sidewalk after her.

Cook drove the car home. He went inside and put Dan's

keys on the kitchen counter. No one was on the first floor. Upstairs, he found the bedroom door closed and heard speech on the other side of it—rapid and insistent speech. He knocked on the door.

"No," Dan said.

"No," said Beth.

Cook stood there a moment, baffled. How could they exclude him at a time like this? Sneaking into the bedroom was a dirty trick.

He went up to his room and lay down on the bed, staring at the ceiling as he listened to the sounds from the room below. He heard no distinct words—just a flow of sounds. It was like listening to a river. After a while he heard their bedroom door open. He jumped to his feet and hurried down the stairs, catching them when they reached the first floor. Beth was in the lead. She went through the swinging door into the kitchen, letting it bang into Dan. Dan went through it and let it bang into Cook.

"It's not a shock," Dan said, as he had been saying all the way down the stairs. "It's not a shock at all. I *knew* you thought I was a failure. In fact saying it is a way of putting it out there for us to look at. We can see how wrong it is."

Beth was behind the open refrigerator door. When she stood up she looked more distressed than Cook had ever seen her. Her eyes went to him, then to Dan. Dan ignored Cook.

"It's like when I called you a bad mother. It's a distortion. You know it's a distortion. You know *I* know it, or you never would have forgiven me."

"Who says I have?" Beth snapped. She set down the diet soda she had taken from the refrigerator and opened a cupboard door. She took a cracker from a metal bin, but then she changed her mind and put it back. She picked up the soda and tried to open it, but she had some trouble with it.

"Want me to help you with that?" Dan said.

She yanked open a drawer, took out a fork, and used it to pry the tab open.

Dan said, "Right now you're probably thinking the marriage is either over, or it's going to go on in a very different way than you ever imagined it." He hesitated. "And you're right." He seemed a little surprised, as if his original intention had been to suggest some third idea.

Beth burst out crying. "It's hopeless," she said.

"No it's not," Dan said, taking a step toward her.

"I can't say anything!" She wiped her eyes. "I know what I should say, and I can't. I know I should say, 'Whatever you want. Wherever you want to work, honey. Whatever makes you happy.' I should say, 'If the business makes you unhappy and you want to teach, I'll back you all the way.' But I can't!"

"You just did," Dan said sadly.

Beth shook her head.

"You said it beautifully."

"Oh God," she said, and she seemed to heave all her anguish out in those two words.

The phone rang. Cook leaped to grab it before anyone else could, jostling Dan aside as he did. He wanted them to keep talking, to stay on track.

It was Beth's mother. As soon as Cook said, "Hi, Rose," Beth signaled with a violent head shake that she didn't want to talk to her and left the kitchen. Dan was right behind her. Cook told Beth's mother no one else was there. He put off her attempts to be sociable with him and hung up. But by the time he reached the second floor the bedroom door was already closed.

He went back up to his room and lay down and listened some more. Then he went to his little yellow desk. He was definitely done with "Roy Pillow, Jr.," the little bastard, and was glad to turn a new leaf of *The Pillow Manual:*

DAY SIX
Mrs. Pillow.

He went to the phone. For the first time in his experience, Roy Pillow was not at the office. Cook let the phone ring and ring. He dialed Pillow's number a dozen times in the next hour, both at the office and at home. He felt disoriented, abandoned, orphaned. Pillow at the office—this was a fact of life he had come to expect. Pillow *not* at the office meant that something was wrong. Unless Pillow was out tracking down Paula? He comforted himself with that thought. But what if something was *horribly* wrong? What if Pillow had dropped dead? That would mean he wasn't on Paula's trail at all. The thought terrified him.

Cook went down to the first floor and out onto the deck. It had rained the night before—the thunder had nearly thrown him out of bed once—but the day was hot now and muggier than ever. He went back inside, turned on the air conditioner in the sun-room, and closed the French doors. He turned on the radio and stretched out in the recliner, waiting for further developments.

Some time later, he heard the thud of the front door. He jumped to his feet and went to the living room window. Beth was getting into her car. He watched her drive off and went upstairs. The bedroom door was still closed. He sighed and returned to the sun-room.

A few minutes later, Dan came into the kitchen and got himself some iced tea. Cook turned off the radio, joined him in the kitchen, and followed him into the living room. They both sat down.

Dan took a long drink and said, "Something has happened."

"What? Where did Beth go?"

"Just to the drugstore, to get some stuff for the trip. I didn't mean that. I meant there's been some give. She appreciates my position. She's still freaked out, but she can see my side now."

"I knew she would. You said she storms out of an argument when she senses you're right. That's why she got out of the car. I knew she suddenly saw it from your side."

Dan smiled slightly. He took a swallow of iced tea.

"You're right about her, Dan. Her views are traditional as hell. Mainstream American."

"Yeah. It's a bitch."

"Money. Manhood. You're completely right."

"Yeah. I always did think I had a legitimate beef."

"She's got to change—"

"Yeah. And I think she will. She's got a helluva lot of character."

"—but you've got to change first."

Dan seemed to trip in his forward progress. "Beth's screwed up, so I've got to change?"

"Let me explain," said Cook.

"No."

"You see, Beth's got this weakness—this major, major weakness. But you've got to be strong enough to let her be weak in that way. You've got to absorb it. Everybody's got a big weakness, okay? And everybody who loves somebody has got to know their big weakness and absorb it." Cook had said all this fast, for fear of being interrupted. But Dan was listening, so he slowed and caught his breath. "Right now, Beth's weakness hits you right where you're already insecure, so you lash out to bring her down, which makes her lash back. Imagine it differently. Imagine her being weak, and instead of getting mad you go to her. You comfort her. You say, 'There, there.' Hell, you did it when you got out of the car and went after her."

"I didn't say, 'There, there.'"

"But you went after her. Unlike yesterday. Remember? We were watching Beth and her parents on the sidewalk, and you said Beth was upset, and what did you do? You went and stuck your head in a posthole. What an asshole!"

"What an asshole!" said Dan—but not in agreement. He seemed to be experimenting with the words, testing them.

"You've got the power to make her feel all better when she's unhappy. You've got the power."

Dan shook his head. "Where do you get this stuff? You sound so *sure*."

"I am. I can see what Beth wants, because she doesn't

want it from me. She wants you to be a man, and that means you've got to stop being a man."

"What is this—Zen counseling?"

"You've got to stop being a man in the sense of being an isolated dumbshit. You've got to be big and strong for her. Like in 'The Man I Love.' She plays it all the time. It's about what she wants: a man who's big and strong. You've got to be big and strong enough to become more womanly with her."

Dan laughed. "Jesus. Did she tell you all this? Is that where you got it?"

"No. No woman would put it this way. They see it as being manly when you become womanly."

Dan snorted. He took a drink of iced tea.

"My advice to you now, Dan, is to chat."

Dan laughed.

"I mean it," said Cook. "Chat. That's how people are people together. They chat."

"I don't *want* to chat. I hate to chat."

"You've probably never tried it."

"What do you mean, anyway? Chat. Does that mean talk about what she wants to talk about?"

"Well, when you're with her, what do you want to talk about?"

"Nothing."

This time Cook laughed. "You're such a man. You're not a prick or a failure. You're just a man."

A wild look of incomprehension swept over Dan's face.

"What do you want?" Cook asked. "To be alone? Is that it?"

"I want peace—peace in the valley. I just want to get on with my life."

"Is Beth included?"

Dan took a sharp breath. "Not like she wants to be. She wants to be . . . She wants me to think of nothing but her."

"What were you going to say?"

Dan hesitated. "I was going to say she wants to be the most important thing in my life."

"Why didn't you say it?"

"You know why." Dan stood up and looked out the window. "She's *supposed* to be the most important thing in my life. You think I don't know that? Hell, that's why I hate talking about this stuff. I know I don't have the feelings I'm supposed to have, and I hate myself for it."

"But you *can* have them."

"God," Dan said, shaking his head, "I'm just like her. I know what I *should* say, but it's so hard."

Cook stood up and joined Dan at the window. "It's hard because the two of you have been enemies. When that changes, everything will change." Through the trees in the park he thought he saw Beth's car. "Is that Beth?"

"Yeah."

Cook watched the car approach the corner of the park. "Someday she'll say stuff that used to hurt you, and you'll be able to hold her and say 'There, there.' And all the other stuff will be a joke, too." He gestured out the window. "There'll come a time when she pulls up to the curb and scrapes the tires, and you'll just say, 'Why, that's Beth! She's home! Isn't it wonderful?'"

They watched her round the corner of the park, slowing without shifting down. When she accelerated out of the turn, they could hear the engine strain and ping. When she came to a stop, they heard the cruel sound of rubber and hubcap scraping on the curb.

Cook looked at Dan. His mouth and eyes were wide open in a frozen look of wild good cheer. Cook wasn't sure if Dan was mocking his prediction or trying to make it come true.

Twenty-two

Wmbhile Dan and Beth packed and talked, Cook put in a lot of one-sided phone time, trying to find out what "Mrs. Pillow" meant. Cook caught snatches of Dan and Beth's noise whenever one of them came out of the bedroom for something. The rest of the time, they were behind that door, going cold turkey without the linguist.

When Cook wasn't trying to reach Pillow, he was in the sun-room, reading and listening to an FM station's pledge drive, interspersed with classical pieces requested by the listeners. After a couple of hours of this, he took Robbie's portable radio out to the front porch and listened to part of a Cardinals baseball game. He had seen St. Louisans doing this on their front porches, and he wanted to see what possible pleasure there could be in it. The old guy from next door came out onto his porch to take stock of things. He spied Cook and waved, but he did not call him Dan. He asked Cook what the score was. Cook had no idea, so he made one up, and the old man swore and went back into his house.

When Cook came back inside, Dan and Beth were in the kitchen, talking. Cook paused at the swinging door, cracked it open slightly, and listened.

"God," said Dan. "They're playing all the most boring ones you can name. The worst ones."

"Yeah," said Beth. "'Bolero.' Give me a break."

"And 'Academic Festival Overture.'"

"Agh. Really?"

"Yeah, while you were out. And that 'Greensleeves' thing."

"No!"

"Shall we call something in? Something tolerable to listen to?"

"Sure. But what?"

"I know," said Dan. "No English composers. That'll be our request. We'll pledge at the hundred-dollar level if they promise to play no English composers for an entire year."

Beth laughed. "Better make it fifty dollars."

"Why?"

"You know why. Got to cut back. Downgrade."

Cook heard noises. Conflict? He listened hard. The noises proved to be scampering footsteps, and he jumped back from the door as Beth shot past and up the stairs, with Dan close behind. Both of them laughed to see him there.

Cook stared at himself in the wall mirror and listened as they predictably romped their way to the bedroom, where the door closed, as he knew it would. What next? Would that horrible nightmare of college life be replayed—hearing your roommate go at it through the walls? He went back to the sun-room, closed the door, and turned the air conditioner fan on high.

About a half hour later, Dan came in and nodded to Cook. He sat down on the couch. Something seemed to be on his mind. Beth came in a moment later and stood next to the couch.

"Shall we tell him?" she said.

"It's no big deal," said Dan.

"I agree, but he should still know about it." Beth turned to Cook. "A few minutes ago, we tried to...Well, what happened was—"

"It was a failed fuck," Dan said bluntly.

"Pardon me?" said Cook. He hoped he hadn't heard right.

Dan shrugged. "It happens."

"I didn't know you had a name for it," Beth said with a little laugh.

Christ, Cook thought. The one subject he had been lucky to avoid so far, and now here it was. "Tell me all about it," he said.

"It just wasn't there," Dan said. "We packed it in."

"We're getting along fine right now," said Beth, looking at Dan. "I can't figure out what went wrong."

"It happens," Dan said with another shrug. "It's like a bad meal somewhere. You move on. You write it off."

There was a long pause. They seemed to expect Cook to say something. "How far did you get?" he asked.

"I was exactly nine minutes from ejaculation," Dan said.

"Get serious," Cook said. "I mean from the other end."

"We don't fool around with that," Dan said sternly.

"Ooh," Beth said.

"There was that one attempt though, wasn't there, honey? In New Orleans?"

Beth laughed. "God, what possessed us?"

"Damn it," said Cook. "You know what I mean. From the beginning. How long had you been at it before you gave up?"

"Quite a while, actually," Beth said.

"What happened at the moment of failure?"

Beth looked at Dan, as if for help with her answer. "You spoke first. You said, 'You're not here.'"

Dan frowned. "No I didn't."

"Yes you did."

"No *way*. I said . . . something else. I'm sure of it. Let me think. I said, 'Where are you?'"

"Okay," said Beth. "It's the same thing."

"No it's not."

"Sure it is. You were complaining that I wasn't into it."

Dan looked as dumb as a two-by-four. Suddenly, understanding seemed to dawn on all parts of his face at once. "No no no. You misunderstood me. I wanted to find out where you were in terms of arousal. I wanted to know what you wanted next."

Beth's face went blank. "Oh," she said, also rather dumbly. "Gee. You don't usually *ask,* you know. I mean, you don't usually *ask.*"

"I figured we should try to communicate more."

She smiled ruefully. "Nice try."

"You thought I was accusing you of not being involved?"

"Not accusing, really. I wouldn't say *accusing.* I don't like that word. *Accusing.*"

"Whatever. You thought it was like an impatient whine or something. 'Where *are* you?' Like, 'Where *are* you, because you're certainly not here.'"

"Yes." Beth nodded swiftly several times. "Yes."

"Why didn't you correct me? You were into it, right?"

"Sure. Couldn't you tell?"

"If I was mistaken, why didn't you correct me?"

"Because I thought you were trying to tell me *you* weren't into it."

"Jesus!" Dan laughed a big, full-throated laugh. "What a pair we are. Come on. Let's go back."

Beth smiled, reached out, and took his hand.

As they left the room together, Cook nodded with satisfaction. That wasn't so bad, he thought.

Fifteen minutes later, Dan came back into the sun-room. Cook sensed something was wrong again. Dan had the downcast look of someone plagued by nagging constipation.

Dan looked forlornly out a window onto the backyard. "Once you get off to a bad start..." His voice died.

Beth came into the room. "Let's face it—we weren't in the mood. It's no problem."

Dan gave Cook a funny look. "Geez. We get along and now we can't screw."

"It's not you," said Cook. "It's the trip. Nobody can make love when they know they're going to fly over the ocean the next day." Eager to discourage any follow-up questions, Cook stood up and offered to take them out to dinner. He had noticed a Jamaican restaurant in the Loop and said he wanted to take them there. Beth said that was nice, but she was worried that they had too much to do. Cook said he would go get some takeout. They said great and gave him their orders.

At dinner, Beth raved about her chicken and asked Dan to try some. She held it out right in front of his mouth. He took it and chewed it. A funny look crossed his face. "I've always hated that," he said. He blinked the rapid eyeblinks of a man with a new insight.

"What," said Beth.

"When you feed me stuff."

Beth tensed. "What are you saying?"

"Don't get nervous. I'm just registering this feeling. It's never occurred to me before. I hate it when you feed me."

"It's not like I do it every five minutes."

"Even if you did it once a year, I would hate it."

"Why?"

"Because I can feed myself."

Cook laughed.

Beth looked at Cook. "You've got this new behavior, Jeremy. This inappropriate laughter. It's really annoying. Knock it off."

"Sorry," Cook said. "It's just another little thing. From your point of view it's a sharing thing—you want to share an experience with Dan. But he sees it as being fed. For you it's romantic, but it makes him feel infantile."

Beth said, "When he gives me a taste of something, I don't feel infantile."

"But you're a woman," Cook said.

"What's that got to do with it?"

"Something," Cook said. It was the best he could do. He looked to Dan for support.

Dan groaned. "God, it never ends."

After dinner, Dan and Beth finished packing. They let Cook into the bedroom at that point, asking him to brainstorm with them about things they might have forgotten. Beth produced an Italian phrase book and slaughtered this daughter of Latin. Cook taught her the values of Italian *c* and *g,* and he introduced her to the foreign joy of pure monophthongs and unaspirated consonants. As for Dan, Cook taught him the rich array of Italian gestures—the forearm jerk, the cheek screw, the eyelid pull, and the chin flick—cautioning him to use them only from a safe distance, from a passing train, say, or a departing jet. He also sat them down and admonished them strongly to keep colorful bits of Italian out of their cards and letters home.

When it was clear that they would finish packing with some time to spare, Dan mysteriously slipped out of the house for about twenty minutes. When he came back he held a videotape in the air.

"*The African Queen,*" he said to Beth. "You said we saw it in the sun-room together, and you had a nice thought about the many films we would watch there, and I had no memory of it at all. I want to start over."

"Aw," said Beth.

So when they were all packed, they watched it. They watched Bogey become transformed by love from the scrappy, independent Mr. Allnut into the cuddly Charlie. The more cuddly Bogey got, the more cuddly Dan and Beth got. Cook finally excused himself with the explanation that he was afraid of leeches and wanted to avoid that scene.

In the morning, the first thing Cook did was try to reach Pillow. There was no answer, either at Pillow's home or at the office. Cook was becoming panicked. He had developed the conviction, and wasn't able to shake it, that Pillow was the only person in the world who could find Paula. If Pillow didn't do it, Cook would never see her again.

Downstairs, Dan and Beth had already eaten breakfast and were getting ready to go. They gave Cook some hurried instructions about the house and loaded up the van.

On the way to the airport, they fell behind a truck with the state of Missouri painted on its back doors. Dan pointed to it and said, "Missouri's got a stupid shape."

"Compared to what?" said Beth.

"Compared to Colorado," said Dan. "Colorado's got a solid shape. Or California. All bumpy on the coast and nice and straight on the east side."

"That's ridiculous," said Beth.

"Minnesota's got a nice shape," Cook offered. He leaned forward from the seat behind them, an elbow on Dan's seat and one on Beth's.

"A *very* nice shape," Dan said warmly.

"And Vermont?" said Cook.

"Very nice."

"Tennessee?"

"Oh! Outstanding. A parallelogram."

"This is ridiculous," said Beth.

"It is," Dan agreed without warning. Cook felt abandoned, all alone with the subject. He leaned back and stared out the window. Dan suddenly laughed. He said to Cook, "When Beth and I travel, I usually drive. That means she's the map reader. Talk about material for conflict." He looked at Beth.

She groaned and turned to Cook. "It's awful. Dan'll say, 'Where's the turnoff to such and such?' and I won't know how to find it. Or he'll say, 'How far to a rest stop?' and I can never figure out which of those stupid little symbols means rest stop."

"And I'll get mad as hell," said Dan. "Mad as hell."

Beth looked at him, then back at Cook. "One time we were driving to California, and we were in Kansas or someplace, near the border, and Dan was asking me to check something, and I wanted to look at the next state, so I turned the page. But the atlas was arranged alphabetically, so the next map was of, I don't know, Louisiana or something—"

"Kentucky," said Dan.

"Kentucky. So I said, 'Where do I look?' and Dan said, 'Just look up the state to the west of Kansas.' Now, I didn't know what state was to the west of Kansas, because I didn't *care* what state was to the west of Kansas. Dan knew I didn't know, but he wouldn't tell me. He got mad. *He* got mad. I should have been the one to get mad."

"What an asshole!" said Dan.

"It makes me mad now just to remember it," Beth said.

"What an asshole!" Dan said again.

At the airport, Cook got out at the curb to help them with their bags. Dan insisted on a promise from Cook that he would be at their airport gate when they got back. He wanted to give Cook an immediate report on their trip. "Every little thing," he said. "Every word, every goddamn preposition, every little thing." Cook promised. There was a pause. On impulse, Cook told them that he had hopes of seeing Paula again, perhaps soon.

"Aw," said Beth. "That's nice."

"Don't fuck it up this time," Dan said. He laughed cruelly. Then he surprised Cook with a hug. Cook got one from Beth too, and he watched them go into the airport, standing there and waving until a security guy told him to get back in the van and move it.

Cook had noticed that in movies whenever people opened the door to a house or an apartment, either someone was there waiting for them or the phone instantly rang. But when he returned from the airport, neither thing happened. He tried Pillow again. There was still no answer. He had a wild urge for a drink and frowned it away. *Then* the phone rang.

It was Pillow. "Jeremy, F. F. Sweet is coming to town."

"Roy! I've been trying to reach you. I . . . What did you say?"

"F. F. Sweet is coming to town. To sign books. It's in the paper." Pillow chuckled. "Read all about it." He chuckled some more.

"Today's paper?"

"F. F. Sweet is coming to town," Pillow said, "and so is F. F. Sweet."

"What?"

"F. F. Sweet and F. F. Sweet are coming to town." Pillow was cackling now. He sounded like a chicken.

"Goddammit, Roy. You know you can't conjoin coreferential nouns. What are you talking about?"

"F. F. Sweet," said Pillow, completely out of control now, "and F. F. Sweet . . ." He cackled and brayed.

"Roy. Snap out of it. 'Day Six: Mrs. Pillow.' What the hell?"

Pillow gave a stifled cry.

"Roy?"

Another stifled cry. A moan.

"Roy? Are you all right?"

After a long silence, Pillow said tonelessly, "There is no Mrs. Pillow."

"What do you mean? There's been a change in procedure?"

"Oh! If only it were as simple as that!"

"What are you talking about?"

"There is no Mrs. Pillow. She's left me!"

"No," Cook said, shocked. "Oh, Roy. I'm sorry."

"She says I'm always at the office. She says I don't care about her—all I care about is my work. She accused me of not paying any attention to her. She says I never help around the house. She cried. She called me a beast. She threw things at me. She threw a candle at me, a wet sponge, and a small double-A battery. She's gone back to her mother, Jeremy. She packed a suitcase and took a bus back to her mother's."

"I'm sorry, Roy." Cook tried to think of something more to say, but he was stupefied by the sheer averageness of the Pillows' spat. It sounded like something out of a comic strip. He wondered if Mrs. Pillow made "boohoo" noises when she cried.

"I'm pretty much ready to pack it in, Jeremy."

"No, Roy. Don't do that. You of all people should know that a marriage has its ups and downs."

"A marriage? I'm not talking about a marriage. My marriage is dead, Jeremy—dead as a beached whale. I'm talking about the Pillow Agency. There's no point to it now."

Cook clenched the phone. His first thought was of Paula. "Roy, you're saving marriages. Don't you realize that?"

"Bah! Can't even save my own."

"You don't know that. You might be able to work it out. But even if you can't—I mean, I don't believe it'll come to that, but just assuming you can't—it still doesn't mean you should give up on all marriages. You're doing good work, Roy."

"You're just worried about your precious Hoosier," Pillow said bitterly.

"That's not fair," Cook said. "I'm concerned about you, and I'm concerned about the Wilsons. What do I do next with them?"

"Who cares? Forget it. They're doomed. They're all doomed. I want to study something new. How about the Bushmen, Jeremy? They seem nice. Ever been to Africa?"

Cook felt short of breath. He felt as if he were dealing with a madman holding a gun to a hostage's head. And the hostage was Paula. "Since you mentioned it, what about my date? Do you still plan to arrange it?"

"Still *plan* to? No."

Cook swallowed. "Oh."

"I don't *plan* to because I already *have* arranged it. She's waiting."

"What? Where?"

"That should be obvious. Don't bother to give me a report, though. I don't care about any of that anymore."

"Where the hell is she?"

"Have fun. Have all the fun you can—until you meet *the horror*. Ha! Then you'll wish you were out on the Kalahari with Roy Pillow—out there transcribing those tricky consonants. Yes indeed." Pillow made some clicking noises with his tongue.

"Roy, wait. You've got to tell me."

"Tell you what? What 'Mrs. Pillow' means? For the record, eh? Such a tidy mind you have, Jeremy. I admire that in a linguist. Certainly I'll tell you. The first Mrs. Pillow left me. The activity is named in her honor. She went away. As it happens, so did the second Mrs. Pillow, the third, and now the fourth. So, what does 'Mrs. Pillow' mean?"

"Roy, I don't want to play any guessing games. You've got to tell me where Paula is."

"What does 'Mrs. Pillow' mean? Come on, Jeremy. For old times' sake."

Cook felt the top of his head blasting off. "Roy, I don't give a flying fuck—"

"Very well. I'll tell you. 'Mrs. Pillow' means 'Go away.'"

"'Go away'?"

"You're done with the Wilsons. Case closed."

Cook felt an instant sadness. The feeling had never hit him so quickly like this.

Pillow said, "Case closed. Agency closed." He began to click with his tongue again.

"But what about Paula?"

Pillow clicked, sucked, and popped his farewell.

Cook screamed into the phone, but Pillow was gone. He tried to call him back, but the line was busy. He made himself calm down, tracked down a phone book, and called Topper's. He described Paula in adoring detail, but she wasn't there. Then he tried Pillow again, but got no response at all—not even a busy signal. Perhaps Pillow had begun to dismantle the Pillow Agency literally, starting by tearing the phone out.

Cook grabbed his keys and headed for the door. Maybe the maître d' was wrong—maybe Paula *was* there, or maybe she was waiting for him outside the elevators on the top floor, not visible from the restaurant, or maybe she was in the lobby of the building. The point was she was *around*, somewhere near, and he had to find her.

Twenty-three

The maître d' who could walk backward recognized Cook and worked hard with him searching for Paula, no doubt curious about what this new regular customer's third date would look like. But she was nowhere in the building.

This left Cook with no plan. It also left him with no car. In his haste and fear that he would miss Paula, he had given up searching for a legal parking place after one circuit of the block and had parked in an alley, off to one side amidst some Dumpsters. His car had been towed as quickly as if it had vaporized. Cook stopped swearing in order to ask some pedestrians in the area where a car might go when it was towed, but all he got was gregarious speculation.

He set out grimly for the Wilsons'—a two-mile walk. He would call the airport and page Paula, or leave a message for her—something like "Leave town and I die." He would find the keys to Dan's car and drive there. Then, if time allowed, he would swing by Pillow's office and rough him up a bit.

He discussed this plan with himself, quite happy with it, as he walked. But he decided he should call the airport as soon as possible. He remembered there were pay phones at the library, which he would pass if he stayed on Delmar.

When he reached the library, he saw a sign in the window announcing quite calmly that F. F. Sweet, author of *A Valen-*

tine for Val, would be on hand to sign copies of his new book, *Another Valentine for Val.* Cook began to snort involuntarily. He read the sign again, finding it hard to concentrate. He compared the date and time of this splendid happening with the present moment, and when he saw that they matched precisely, he felt a smacking sensation, like that of two hands slapping him hard on each cheek at the same time. He peered through the window. There was a line stretching from a table, and all sorts of noisy activity. It was about to get even noisier. He reached for the door handle.

"Don't go in there, Jeremy," someone said. But not just someone. It was Paula.

Her hair was shorter, and she was so tanned that *she* looked like an Indian, but it was Paula, and at the sight of her Cook let out a shout he had never heard from himself before.

He grabbed her, held her, kissed her, pawed her, and then steered her across the street to a frozen custard place, jabbering the whole time. He sat her down at an outdoor table and bought her a cone, demanding extra toppings of Snickers chunks from the guy behind the counter, a stingy ignoramus who knew nothing of matters of the heart. Cook kept looking back at her while his order was being filled. She was wearing a loose, sleeveless white thing on top and khaki shorts with big button-flap pockets. She looked as if she had just returned from a safari.

He gave her the cone and sat down and watched her take a huge bite of the frozen custard. She always bit frozen things —ice cream, Popsicles, ice cubes. His happiness suddenly became clouded by the simple, specific fear that she would leave and he would never see her do this again. Had he made a strategic blunder by showing too much of his joy? He began to rein himself in. He knew how to do this all right.

"What were you doing over there?" Cook asked, looking across the street to the library.

"Looking for you," Paula said cockily.

"But how did you know I would be there?"

"Your funny boss told me. Mr. Pillows." She took another bite of her custard.

Cook frowned. "Pillow. How did *he* know?"

"What's he boss *of*, Jeremy? What kind of outfit is it?"

Cook suddenly realized he couldn't tell her. She would say he was unfit for the job, and they would fight and she would leave. He said nothing.

"I heard about Wabash folding," she went on. "I was so sad. I have such nice memories of the place. You'll have to tell me where everyone ended up. But I've been worried about you. What do you do? You a marriage counselor or something? That's what your boss said." She took another big bite. "Come on. Tell me."

Cook sighed. She was always way ahead of him. It drove him nuts. "I'm afraid to."

"Afraid? Why?"

"You'll laugh."

"So what?"

"We'll fight."

"I hope not."

"You'll leave."

"Why do you say that?"

"You left before."

"You wanted me to."

Cook fell silent.

"You don't deny it," she said.

Cook took a deep breath. "I keep feeling like I'm going to cry."

Paula leaned forward. "Is anything wrong? Has someone died? I mean it. Are you okay?"

"I'm just so full of emotion. Seeing you."

Paula looked at him strangely. At first she must have thought he was joking, because her body tensed. Then she relaxed slightly.

"What are you looking at?" she asked suspiciously.

"You."

"Why? It's not like you."

Cook wanted to say, "Because I love you." And more. He wanted to say he would follow her on his knees wherever she went. And he would start right now—he would drop to his knees and crawl under the table and hug her bare brown legs. That was what he would do.

But instead, he said, "How did my boss get you to come here?"

Paula smirked behind her custard. "I'll tell you in a minute. First tell me what you do."

What the hell, thought Cook, and he told her. Paula did laugh, a lot, but only where Cook wanted her to, and he told her more and more of the kinds of things that made her laugh—he knew how to do this. He found he could do quite a good imitation of Pillow. What a joy it was to share his experience of this man with her! But even as she laughed, Cook could tell she was interested in Dan and Beth's fate.

"So what's going to happen to them?" she asked.

"I think they'll be all right. Dan knows he has to change."

"But can he?"

"Sure. Why not?"

"Men hate to change," she said flatly.

"*Everybody* hates to change. How would *you* like to change?"

"I don't need to."

"But if you had to. Look, what's marriage? It's being close, right? It's *wanting* to be close."

"Sure," she said.

"Who spends more time being close with people before marriage—men or women?"

"Women."

"By a long shot, right?"

"Sure."

"Okay. That's the whole point. Men are untrained for marriage. When they say 'I do' they should immediately add 'But I don't know how!' After the wedding, they're in for years of wondering what's wrong, or maybe years of thinking *nothing's* wrong, and one day the wife turns to the guy and says, 'Something's wrong,' and he's dead from that moment on—it's either change, buddy, or burn in hell for the rest of the marriage. Now, just pretend it's the opposite. Pretend that marriage required all the things men are good at—withdrawal, toughing it out alone, hiding feelings instead of just blurting them out. Could you change into such a person?"

"God, it would be awful. Who would want to?"

"But that's the fix men are in. We've got to change just as much."

"But it's a change for the better."

"I know that. But nobody else does."

Paula smiled. "I think maybe there are one or two other guys out there who know it, too, Jeremy." She studied him. "So you really believe this stuff? You're not just parroting what I used to tell you?"

Cook frowned. "You never told me this."

"But I did. Word for word."

"I don't think so."

Paula laughed and shook her head. When she did this, her short hair shook slightly. It used to flow over her shoulders. He liked it this way. He had managed to touch it when he hugged her, and he liked the feel of it. He grew nervous again. She was already halfway through her cone. When she finished, what reason would she have to stay? But she'd shown up for his date. That meant something, didn't it?

He said, "You were going to tell me how Pillow got you to come here."

Paula winced—an inscrutable wince. "He told me I had to come to St. Louis or someone would sue me."

"Who?"

"F. F. Sweet."

Cook was silent. First, he hated to hear that name on her lovely lips. Second, what the hell did she mean?

Paula said, "The latest issue of *Linguistic Inquiry* has an article about your work on Kickapoo adverbs."

"No kidding," Cook said hotly.

"You've seen it, then. The author is F. F. Sweet."

"You think I didn't see that, too?" Cook glared across the street at the library. The line was beginning to spill out the front door onto the sidewalk. "Did you recognize the name? It's the same twit who wrote about that stupid Indian boy with his bloody valentines. And he's *here.*"

"Actually, someone else wrote the *Linguistic Inquiry* article and used F. F. Sweet's name."

Cook flinched as if wired to a generator.

"Actually," she said, looking at him, "*I* wrote it."

Cook's face was somewhere in his hands. It stayed there a long time. He looked up and said, "Why?"

"Lots of reasons. Your theory was wrong, for one thing. I *told* you it was wrong when we were together, but you just told me to be a good girl and go finish my dissertation— which is pretty funny, because it was my Pottawatomie data that showed me what was wrong with your Kickapoo stuff in the first place. I'd worked out most of my thoughts about it before I went back to M.I.T. to defend, and as soon as I was done with that I went to Oklahoma and worked for a while with some great informants. I've been there ever since, actually. I just got a Kartoffel grant that'll keep me afloat for a year, if I live frugally, which I'm good at." She had lapsed into a leisurely, self-satisfied manner. She must have seen that Cook did not share in her satisfaction, and she became more businesslike.

"Anyway, the point is I was mad at you. Remember the punch line to that old Kickapoo joke?" Paula looked up to the sky and delivered it. Her pronunciation was so good that someone else seemed to have taken possession of her body for a moment. "Remember? It means 'A wronged woman can make a man feel like dung.' I wanted to do that. But I mainly wanted to kill the issue of *your* brains versus *my* brains. So—did it work?"

Cook stared at her, barely comprehending what she was saying.

"Too early to say, I guess," Paula said. "I used F. F.

Sweet's name because his little book is such a nice statement about giving your love to someone and getting it back many times over. I always hated the way you made fun of it. I thought my article would carry a little extra punch with his name on it. How about it?"

Cook felt brainless, like one of those dumb china dolls he'd seen in the backs of cars, with their round heads bobbing endlessly on a spring.

"The editors weren't any trouble at all. They loved the article. They said such a critique was long overdue—oops, sorry. They think I'm some free-lance linguist named F. F. Sweet. But your boss tried to give me trouble. He called and told me the real F. F. Sweet was thinking of suing me for using his name, and I had to come to St. Louis for a deposition or something." Paula laughed. "I thought it was you on the phone, pretending to be a lawyer. I'd heard you were in St. Louis, and I figured you'd found out who wrote the article and were trying to get back at me. I said, 'Come off it, Jeremy.' When I said your name, it must have freaked your boss out, because he broke down and apologized all over the place. He told me the truth. I think I understand it. He offered you a date with any woman in the world, and you picked me?" She grinned.

Cook didn't grin.

"Anyway," she went on, "your boss sort of threw himself at my mercy. He begged me to come to St. Louis. Actually, I was delighted—the Historical Society here has a tremendous Pottawatomie archive, and he was paying my way. He told me to be at this library today at one o'clock. He wanted the two F. F. Sweets on hand, just to make trouble. He said you really liked surprises like that—which surprised *me*, actually. You're just full of changes, aren't you? The only thing I can't figure out is how he learned I wrote the article."

"He's got a hell of a network," Cook said grimly.

"So," Paula said, as if everything were settled now, "your couple is on their way to Europe? Are you done with them?"

"You didn't have to do what you did," Cook said.

"I know. But it was the best way to show you I could wipe out the things you think make you worthy and still love you."

Cook found this too theoretical. Did she still love him? He couldn't understand her sentence.

Paula said, "Tell me what you think this horror in your couple's marriage is. You never said."

Cook's hand went automatically to his shirt pocket. It was still there. He took it out and unfolded it on the table.

> ~~She's a bitch.~~
> ~~He's a prick.~~
> ~~Money.~~
> ~~He's a failure.~~
> ~~She thinks he's a failure.~~
> ~~He thinks she's a bad mother.~~
> ~~The in-laws.~~
> Dan.

Something was wrong with it. Pillow had said there was a horror at the core of every marriage, and it was the very same horror. Dan wasn't in every marriage. Clearly a generalization needed to be made. Cook sighed, took out his pen, crossed out "Dan," and entered his final theory on the subject:

> The man.

"What are you doing?" Paula asked.

Cook stared at the words. He slowly folded the paper and put it back in his pocket.

"What is it?" said Paula.

He couldn't tell her. She would see it as an admission that he was to blame for their breakup. She would beat him over the head with it. She was so damned competitive. That was her weakness. That was what he would have to absorb—if she still wanted him.

"Tell me," she said.

"The horror is failing to believe that the other person can change."

"Really?" She seemed a little disappointed and looked off into the distance. But she was thinking. Her eyes came back to his. "Yeah. I guess that *is* important."

"Listen. I love you and want to stay with you forever."

Paula blinked. "What? You quoting someone? You want me to guess who? We haven't done that in a while, have we? Sure, I'm game. Say it again."

Cook's heart sank. He knew that the restatement of a difficult assertion was always harder than the original statement. He watched her pop the last bit of cone into her mouth and crunch it. He said, "I love you, Paula." He shuddered with a violent chill. This perplexed him. So did the tears springing to his eyes.

Paula sat very still. She looked so hard to reach, so far away.

"Do you love me?" he asked. He now saw that there were tears in her eyes as well.

"Always have," she said.

"Will you stay?" he asked.

"Always will," she said.